The COVERT BUCCANEER

a novel

S. LUCIA KANTER ST. AMOUR

© 2025 S. Lucia Kanter St. Amour

All rights reserved.

No part of this publication may be reproduced, stored or uploaded in a retrieval system—including AI training datasets or large language model databases—or transmitted in any form or by any means, electronic, mechanical, photocopying, recording, or otherwise, without the prior written permission of the publisher.

Cover and book design by Asya Blue Design

Published by Pactum Factum Press
447 Sutter Street, Suite 405
San Francisco, California

Library of Congress Control Number: 2025915920

ISBN 979-8-9927528-0-9 (Hardcover)
ISBN 979-8-9927528-1-6 (Paperback)
ISBN 979-8-9927528-4-7 (Ebook)

To those displaced from their homeland, past and present; the women whose stories are untold; and anyone who doesn't fit neatly into a category.

Also for Lisa, my beloved and intrepid fellow buccaneer.

Also by S. Lucia Kanter St. Amour

For the Forces of Good: The Superpower of Everyday Negotiation

The Money Fairy

Indispensable: Are Feminists Getting Women's Rights Wrong?

Moms Get Mad

For the Forces of Good: Sidekick Journal & Workbook

Author's Preface on Historical Authenticity, Complexity, and the Messiness of the Human Condition

History is neither simple nor sanitized. It is layered, contradictory, and often uncomfortable. It doesn't come to us prepackaged with modern sensibilities, nor does it unfold in ways that align neatly with contemporary values. In *The Covert Buccaneer*, I have sought to capture the realities of two distinct time periods with meticulous attention to primary sources, ensuring that the voices, conflicts, and social norms of each era are depicted with honesty rather than revisionist hindsight.

The diary passages in this novel reflect the actual language and evolving perspectives of a young person growing up in the 1860s — a time when prejudices were deeply ingrained, yet personal experiences had the power to challenge them. Teddy's journey, like that of so many historical figures, is one of transformation. Erasing her initial biases would mean erasing her growth.

Similarly, the modern timeline embraces the duality of human nature — the push and pull between duty and desire, selflessness and exhaustion, idealism and pragmatism. Ellie is a woman riddled with self-doubt and juggling impossible demands; her struggles as a special needs mother and attorney are drawn from real, lived experiences. Her story is not meant to fit a simplistic narrative of martyrdom or effortless strength — it is meant to be real.

This novel is not here to comfort. It's here to provoke, to ignite discussion, and to illuminate untold stories, past and present. The history of women — especially those who defied convention — has often been buried or diluted. I have chosen not to dilute this one.

I ask that you resist the temptation to yield to surface-level "hot takes" that might otherwise misinterpret the book's complexity. Instead, I invite you to step into this world with an open heart and mind, not to judge but to embrace — or at least examine — its contradictions and to allow its characters the space to be flawed, courageous, misguided, incongruous, and transformative — just as real people are.

If you find yourself questioning Teddy and Ellie — at times irked by them, noticing their flaws and inconsistencies (and gossiping about them with friends) — I've done something right.

—S. Lucia Kanter St. Amour

PART ONE

CHAPTER 1
ELLIE

January 10, 2019. San Francisco, California.

A quarter past three, and the fog swaggered in, taunted into a rematch by the Golden Gate's bratty undertow. Although born and raised just outside Chicago, where she had stoically braved real winters, the wet, windy San Francisco fog chilled Ellie down to the bone.

Ellie pulled a pashmina around her shoulders and slid past her clunky desk to shut the drafty window. Turning back, she studied her client, Fernanda Salinas. They had just spent the past two hours in deposition in a conference room down the hall, facing down the attorney for Assurance Underwriters of California. Fernanda, a refugee from western Mexico, had been fired from her hotel housekeeping job after catching her hand in a fire door, which had been pushed open by a frazzled banquet manager.

Instead of filing a workers' compensation report and covering the hospital bill for X-rays, surgery, and physical therapy, the hotel management had sent Fernanda her pink slip, firing her from the job and cutting off her meager income. The result was the eviction of Fernanda and her three children from their small, cockroach-infested apartment, as she'd struggled to pay her medical bills. No rent, no mercy.

When she had come to Elizabeth House, a women's shelter in

Oakland, for help, they had a waitlist for housing women with children, but an outreach worker had put Fernanda in touch with the San Francisco Immigrant Legal Defense Collaborative, where Ellie had started working just two months ago. The offices at 4 Embarcadero Center were a departure from the sleek marbled suites at Hutton & Fetterer, where she'd previously worked; here, the surfaces were firmly chipboard, but she had been buoyed by the work and felt a sense of worth. Now, she saw Fernanda's face, eyes shining, tears trickling down her cheeks.

Moments earlier, the attorney for Assurance had paused the testimony and pulled Ellie aside with an offer. A settlement — today, if her client would sign now. Ellie had known exactly what that meant. They saw the same thing she did in the medical records. The damaged finger wasn't healing well, and there was a real risk of amputation. They wanted to cut their losses and close the case before that certainty.

The case was worth much more. But she also knew Fernanda's situation — no home, no income, no time left to wait.

"How long?" asked Fernanda. "How long for the money?"

"Oh," said Ellie. "Well, there'll be a bit of paperwork, but it'll come through in a couple of weeks. They tend to want to tie these things up and close them off."

Fernanda nodded.

"Yes, yes, I'll sign; can I sign now?" Fernanda clasped her hands on the table, supporting her still-recovering right hand with her left.

Ellie's stomach tightened. Fifteen grand was a fortune to Fernanda — but waiting a few months could mean twice that. Maybe more. Today's offer was a pittance to Assurance; their reputation of denying and delaying claims, wringing people to the point of desperation, was legendary. Ellie had trained in a shark tank. If only Fernanda would let her circle a little longer.

Ellie hesitated. "Yes, we can draw up the paperwork today. But Fernanda ... you're sure? Just a few months more and —"

How could she put it to Fernanda? How could she persuade this woman to wait even a day longer in this horrendous situation?

"*Escucha*, Fernanda. *Podría ser mejor esperar.*"

Ellie used her Spanish skills with most clients who came through the door. It was a requirement of the job, as they assisted a continual flux of refugees like Fernanda who had traversed the Sonoran Desert to California, leaving behind homelands ravaged by drought and famine. But Ellie's fluency was also a way to gain the confidence of her clients.

She explained that if Fernanda could wait just a few months, the Qualified Medical Evaluator's report could double the settlement — if not more.

"Your treatment will be covered and your medical debt wiped clean with a settlement now or later anyway, but the difference of real money in your pocket, if you could wait, could be substantial," she said.

Fernanda shook her head.

"No," she said. "No more waiting. If this money is coming, I can look for an apartment and tell the social worker. I can bring my children home!"

"I get that," said Ellie. "You've waited more than long enough. But I know there's more money to be had. Look, I can squeeze another ten thousand from them, and you can still sign today. With your permission, I'd like to counteroffer at $30,000, let them negotiate me down to twenty-five thousand, and hold firm. Fernanda, this is what I do. They will make that deal. Do you trust me?"

Ellie watched the few seconds it took for her client's fear to dissolve. Then, Fernanda leapt from her seat, rushed toward a startled Ellie, and threw her arms around her.

"I trust you! Yes. *¡Gracias — usted es un ángel!* Thank you so much. You are saving my life!"

Ellie thought an "angel" should do more to level the playing field. Still, she patted Fernanda on the back and held her embrace for a few moments. She couldn't imagine hugging any client at Hutton & Fetterer. There, things were strictly business, and any emotional outburst would have been frowned upon.

On the wall opposite, Ellie glimpsed the small watermark forming on the fiberboard drop-ceiling. Below the watermark, the hands of the dated analog clock ticked her deeper into the danger zone. Her heart thumped an all-too-familiar rhythm of anxiety. It would be touch and go to finish up with Fernanda and get to Nathan's day care pick-up in the Presidio. Their policy of charging a dollar per minute late made every after-work drive a gauntlet of luck and breath-holding with the Columbus Avenue traffic lights. Plus, her older son, Luca, would be dropped off at their door in North Beach by his program bus.

So, Ellie quelled her frustration — not just at Fernanda's gratitude but at the entire situation. At the paltry sum offered by an insurance carrier whose executives took home half a million dollars a year. At the possibility that Fernanda could be permanently disfigured by an accident that wasn't her fault. And worst of all, at the fact that Fernanda's three young children had been taken from her and placed in foster care — not because she was unfit but because she no longer had a home to bring them to. Ellie heard the echo of Fernanda's frightened words, whispered during their first interview, an impression of her terminating employer in stilted English:

"*You're an illegal; you don't have any rights; just be glad we don't report you to ICE.*"

As Ellie detached from Fernanda's embrace, she wanted to say, "I know it's hard. You're going to be okay. Here is chocolate and two million dollars."

Instead she said, "Let's get that deal done and sign the paperwork." She smiled. "And you can call your social worker with the news."

Fernanda wiped her tears and smoothed down her shirt. She straightened up and moved toward the door with a new air of dignity.

Ellie had lost count of how often she wished the deck weren't so stacked against women like Fernanda. Taking a breath, she pulled open the door and guided her client down the corridor. A small battle won.

Ellie peeled out of the parking garage onto Drumm Street. Traffic was the first chance all day for her mind to wander. As she braked her way down the street, she heard the telltale clang of a cable car on California Street just a couple of blocks away.

The Workers' Rights unit of the ILDC was not where Ellie had pictured she would be at this point in her legal career. Up until nine months ago, she'd been a rising star at the prestigious, global law firm Hutton & Fetterer on Market Street. Their multi-floored offices, with pristine marbled lobbies, walls of windows overlooking the bay, and copious staff, were a palace compared to the offices she clocked in and out of each day now.

She had tumbled far from the sleek art-bedecked conference rooms and the *de rigueur* Jura Giga espresso machines producing delicate crema for discerning Fortune 100 clients. Prefer a fresh and frothy matcha latte? An invisible minion would make it so.

She had been the senior associate in her department when Luca — just eighteen months old at the time — was diagnosed with several disabling conditions. She was on family leave after the birth of her younger son, Nathan, when the news came. His diagnoses, while not shocking to Ellie — she had suspected that Luca was not reaching his milestones despite family protestations that he was "just slow to start" and that she was being an overly worried "new mom" — had launched her into an aggressive early intervention regimen.

Within a month, Ellie found herself managing a team of fourteen professionals to assist him, as well as securing him a spot in a sought-after research study at the MIND Institute at the University of California's Davis Medical Center in Sacramento. While she knew she was doing the absolute best for her son, she worried constantly, barely ate, and slept so little that she had begun having hypnagogic hallucinations.

With two children under the age of two at home, Ellie had been forced to request a little extra leave time from the firm to line up reinforced childcare so that she could return to her job properly — knowing things were taken care of domestically. The firm did not take kindly to the request. HR informed her in a cold, formal email that she would receive three days additional leave, but beyond that, it "might be in [her] interest to consider all long-term options." Post two maternity leaves, Ellie read between the lines: if she needed more time off, it meant she couldn't do the job. And there were plenty of other willing, childless employees ready to fill her seat at the table.

Exhausted from her situation, Ellie had been too tired to get angry. She didn't have the strength for a rebuttal — to point out her stellar performance or her enviable and well-regarded client relationships. Nor did she write back to HR to remind them that she'd taken less leave than any other woman at the firm who had had a baby. Not that there were many of them.

Ellie drummed her fingers on the steering wheel, spotting a mom in designer athleisure bounce along the sidewalk, all toned limbs and post-Caribbean glow. *Must be nice.* Ellie couldn't help but wonder how some women made it look so easy.

Bouncy Mom reminded Ellie of the paralegal who had gotten pregnant and never returned to the firm. They had the same swishing blond hair, tied high in a ponytail. Ellie recalled the paralegal's baby shower, held a few weeks after Luca's first birthday, where one of the partners, munching on a slice of pink buttercream-frosted cake, said, "This is the last of the pregnant women, right? There won't be anymore?"

Everyone had laughed. Ellie had forced a tight-lipped smile while she'd felt the color drain from her face. She wasn't sure if it was the hormones now surging through her body (she was only nine weeks pregnant with Nathan) or the dread of revealing her impending news. She hadn't intended to get pregnant again so quickly, but there they were.

Looming motherhood was often a point of chitchat in the office, always with an acerbic edge. Ellie had served on an interview panel with two male partners for a prospective associate — an assured, well-qualified young woman. The candidate had nailed the interview — confident, sharp, exactly what the firm needed. Ellie was about to say so when —

"Did you see that engagement ring?"

"Sure did. So, she'll get married, then get pregnant, then want maternity leave, then come back part time, then get pregnant again …" The two men shrugged.

How illuminating. Who needed a life coach when these oracles could chart your entire life trajectory between the conference room and the elevator?

The woman didn't get the job.

Snapping out of her reverie, Ellie found that she was turning from Lombard Street onto Presidio Parkway. She checked the clock. Nine minutes late. She jumped out of her Odyssey, doing her best to mask her bedraggled state, and met the day care worker at the door, who was holding Nathan's hand.

"Hi there!" Ellie smiled.

The caregiver sighed at Ellie, let go of Nathan's hand, and gently pushed him toward her. Nathan reached up and cheerily cried, "Mama!" as he proudly held out a card of construction paper decorated with glitter.

Oh, it warmed her heart to see her squishy, squeezy little guy! She picked up Nathan and planted two juicy Italian mamma kisses on his sparkled chubby cheek.

"See you tomorrow," she sang to the caregiver, but the door was already closed.

Ellie buckled Nathan into his car seat, ruffled his tousled hair (was that dried glue?), and hopped back into the driver's seat to push out into traffic. By the time she turned onto Greenwich Street, her apartment building — perched at the foot of Coit Tower — came into view. Luca's school bus was already there.

Anika Owens, Ellie's neighbor, best friend, and general guardian angel, had come to Ellie's rescue once again and was holding out her hand for Luca's. Her fiery five-year-old daughter, Leila, wiggled beside her, while her more cautious four-year-old son, Milo, held her other hand. Ellie waved, parked, and freed Nathan from his seat. She smiled with relief as she approached her friend.

"What are you in for this month in late fees?" Anika asked, knowingly.

"Thirty-four bucks," said Ellie.

"Ouch!" said Anika.

Ellie shrugged. "And the year is young!"

They scrambled up the stairs of the five-unit building, where, to Ellie's enormous relief, Anika said she had started dinner and headed straight to her apartment. Ellie exhaled for what felt like the first time in days.

In Anika's apartment, Ellie watched the four children scatter across the play area, marked out by colored mats on the floor. Luca climbed into his favorite spot: a velvet eggplant-colored worn armchair that overlooked the street. He wordlessly settled into his usual position, leaning back to gaze giddily at the ceiling fan.

Leila and Milo unburdened the sofa of its cushions and throw blankets and began constructing a "secret" fort. Nathan, wiped out from day care misadventures, lay on the mat and sleepily steered Milo's *Thomas the Tank Engine* caravan along a wooden track while quietly narrating a conversation between the engines. When his route encountered a blockage in the form of the family's seventy-five-pound black Labrador, Bravo, who was splayed across the tracks, he simply repurposed the dog into a hill that the intrepid engines capably climbed. The gentle hill snored but didn't budge, well accustomed to little hands.

Anika handed Ellie a glass of freshly uncorked Pinot Noir before returning to the kitchen to stir a steaming pot.

"Well, dear, how was your day?" she asked ironically. It was a long-running bit of theater between them, this golden time they'd formed over the years, when Anika would treat Ellie like her returning husband before Anika's real husband, Ben, did come home from work.

Ellie chuckled at her friend's rendering of domestic bliss and felt the cortisol drain from her body as she sat down on a counter stool and took a sip of Anika's favorite red wine, tasting notes of dark cherry with a whisper of vanilla.

"Chaotic!" said Ellie, her voice raised over the din of the playing children.

Toeing her ballet flats off and letting them drop to the floor, Ellie tucked one leg up under the other. This was her favorite part of the day. By far. And since her divorce was finalized just five months ago, it would be the only time she spent with another adult for the rest of the evening.

"So, just another day that ends in *y*, then?" Anika said, pouring milk into a sippy cup while stirring a bubbling puttanesca sauce — Ellie's recipe, actually. Even when Ellie didn't come to Anika's, she always cooked fresh, no matter how tired she was. If she couldn't control much else, at least her boys would grow up with the smell of their mother's sauce marinating in their DNA.

Anika stepped away from the stove and handed Nathan the sippy cup. She knew he'd be tired after his day and the milk would comfort him. Ellie loved how they could mother each other's children and often secretly wished they could set up a combined household where they could raise their kids together.

Through the kitchen window, the tower glowed warmly in the winter's early nightfall, snuggled in a blanket of fog as the last of the day's tourists descended the stone steps. Ellie's eyes fell back to Anika, and she watched as her best friend moved gracefully about the kitchen again, hands reaching out to close cupboard doors, folding a dish towel, and removing plates from a high shelf for dinner.

"What time will Ben be home?" asked Ellie loudly over the white noise of the exhaust fan.

"Oh, your guess is as good as mine," said Anika with an artificial casualness, her back to Ellie. "It used to always be six, like clockwork. But these days it could be seven, eight p.m. Nine, if he goes to the gym."

Ellie frowned. Ben, originally from London, was, in her opinion, a strange match for her deeply spiritual friend. While Anika had a daily morning chanting routine and practiced Buddhism, Ben was self-absorbed and materialistic; he had two favorite subjects: himself and money.

Their apartment had Sashiko-stitched floor cushions, trailing plants, and a candle always burning — out of reach of the children. Ben, however, had little interest in domestic life. A cupboard door still clung on by one hinge in the kitchen (he'd promised Anika he would fix it months ago), and the three-foot-tall weeds in their private garden had become an eyesore. He had much more interest in his Ted Baker suits and BMW

M5 than he had, it seemed to Ellie, in his wife and children.

As a C-suite executive for a robotic toy company based in the city of his birth, he seemed to be finding reasons lately to travel there more and more often. While Anika barely complained, the days were too long with two young children to be alone with her thoughts in the apartment all day. It was unfair, thought Ellie, and she couldn't help but hold it against Ben. As parents, both members of the couple were grieving, but one of those parents had unchecked freedom and seemed to be taking great advantage of that fact.

Anika carried two plates of pasta over to the counter and handed one to Ellie before perching beside her.

"We'll eat and then I'll feed the herd," she said, blowing the steam off her plate. "It's too hot for little mouths anyway."

Ellie tasted the sauce and swallowed a mouthful quickly; the food was piping, but the aroma rising from the plate was too inviting to wait. Ellie loved these cozy evenings spent wrapped up in friendship after a hectic day. She felt, fleetingly, like a teenager again, lolling about and laughing with a school friend, long before the reality of life as a professional and mom had come to bear.

"Anything planned for the weekend?" asked Anika, taking a sip of her own wine.

Ellie shrugged. Typically, she and the kids would climb the steps to Coit Tower, chat with some tourists, wander the rotunda with its floor-to-ceiling New Deal–era murals, where the bustling artwork was their private I-spy game canvas — always noticing some new detail, and Ellie would hoist the boys up to the viewfinders to marvel at the panorama. It checked all the right boxes: no cost, exercise, fresh air, socialization, and entertainment.

"Oh, you know, the classics — laundry, hunting down the smell of decay in the fridge, and rappelling down the Transamerica Pyramid."

"Joe taking the boys this weekend?" asked Anika.

"For a few hours on Saturday," said Ellie flatly.

This was their custody arrangement after long and often difficult conversations. Ellie had come to accept that Joe was unable to cope with

Luca's additional needs, and Nathan was still very much attached to her.

"He'll have them in the evenings, when I start supervising the law students," Ellie continued. "Which reminds me, I've got some prep to do. I guess *that's* how I'll be spending my weekend!"

As part of her new role at the ILDC, Ellie had agreed to periodic after-hours mentoring at their Workers' Rights Clinic, a partnership with the two nearby University of California law schools at San Francisco Civic Center and the Berkeley campus. She would, alongside other lawyers, oversee the free public clinic where law students enrolled for course credit and advised clients seeking help with work-related legal problems.

"You know, you really should get on the apps," urged Anika.

"Oh, the apps," said Ellie, throwing her eyes to the nine-foot ceiling, a coveted feature of old North Beach architecture. "Not this again!"

"Yes, the apps, Captain Fabulous! It's what all the it girls are doing! You're still young and a smoke show, Elle Belle!"

"How do you even know about 'the apps'?" teased Ellie. "You're married!"

"I decline to answer on the grounds it may incriminate me. Don't worry about it. I know things."

Ellie seriously doubted that she was a "smoke show" or that any sane adult would be romantically drawn to a thirty-seven-year-old mother of two kids, one with severe special needs. She suspected it was Anika's way of considering her own options out loud without acting on them.

"I'll do that," agreed Ellie, sarcastically. "I'll squeeze it in, in between let's see ... solving global warming, performing legal miracles, dodging fundraising emails from day care, Luca's neurology appointments, Costco runs, baking apology brownies for Luca's bus driver, and —"

"Leila! Off! Bravo is not a pony!"

Bravo, who had awoken from his slumber, was now staggering under the five-year-old's weight. Leila dismounted and looked sheepish. Ellie was glad for the kind of friendship she and Anika had where they could yell at each other's kids.

"You know what your problem is?" Anika pressed on, undeterred.

"You're undersexed. You need a night — or ten — with a man who knows his way around a woman and will feed you cake while you wear nothing but the shirt he has liberated from his glistening, chiseled torso."

"You're so right, my shameless bestie," Ellie deadpanned. "But honestly? I'd settle for twenty minutes at a day spa and a man with that come-hither look that says, 'Hi there. I'm Nick, and I'll be doing your hot stone foot massage.'"

"*A cent'anni!*"

They clinked glasses and laughed. A golden moment of satisfied silence stretched between them — until a tug-of-war broke out between Nathan and Leila, with Leila on the losing end of a robotic, voice-controlled dinosaur. One perk of Ben's job was the regular stream of prototype toys for the kids to beta test, which kept him looking very slick in their eyes.

Ellie suspected Leila was annoyed at being admonished for fashioning Bravo as her trusty steed and was taking it out on sweet little Nathan.

"He won't give it back, Mom!" cried Leila.

"Just give it to him, Leila!" said Anika firmly. "You can play with it anytime!"

"It's mine!" wailed Leila, with a stomp of her foot.

She yanked the toy from Nathan's hands, twisting his fingers in the process.

He started to shriek.

"Leila!" scolded Anika.

She set her glass down and walked over to the children. She crouched down and held out the dinosaur to Nathan.

"Nathan, you can borrow this from Leila, okay?"

Nathan reached for the toy and nodded, his lower lip trembling.

"Leila," Anika said, placing her hand firmly on her daughter's arm, "we don't pull like that. You hurt Nathan, okay? Now, you choose a different toy, and when Nathan goes home, you can have the dinosaur then."

Leila turned away in a huff, scampered to the armchair beside Luca, and buried her head under a cushion. Luca, ever mute, didn't turn his eyes away from the ceiling fan.

"Not fair!" Leila whined.

It was Anika's turn to throw her eyes upward as she rejoined Ellie at the counter.

"And so, the siege commences," she said.

"Yup," said Ellie. "We ride at dawn."

They managed a few more bites of pasta, and Leila's muffled cries faded as she grew bored with her own foul mood. They watched as she rejoined Milo and plopped down, forcibly frowning, arms folded defiantly on an upturned cushion.

"You could really do with Ben being back before bedtime, right?" nudged Ellie.

Anika looked at her plate listlessly.

"I want him to come home all day. But when he does, he's grumpy and tired and doesn't want to play with the kids and it's just … tense. It's easier for me to do it all myself."

"Because that's fair," deadpanned Ellie.

"Welcome to the glories of motherhood," said Anika with the feigned cheer of a greeter at a family theme park. "I can't believe I'm using the word *adulting*, but here we are."

"I'm worried about you." Ellie dropped her voice, looking directly at her friend now. "It's coming up to a year. I know it's … looming."

Anika's eyes became glassy.

"I just feel worse," she murmured as tears tripped from her lower lids onto her cheeks. "They say it gets easier with time, but I think I actually feel worse."

Ellie nodded. "I know." She placed her hand on Anika's leg, feeling helpless to meaningfully salve her friend's hurting heart. Anika's joggers showed stains of domesticity — splattered oil, a smear of puttanesca sauce, and … something … else from earlier in the day. Her painter's-palette tableau was a far cry from Ben's always crisp and breezy *GQ*-ready appearance.

"I know it's his way of coping," said Anika. She was practiced at explaining and excusing Ben. "Avoidance. I mean, I know *what's* going on. But it's hard to live through it."

As a licensed therapist, Anika understood the complexity of messy emotions better than most, but she had not been able to bring herself to return to her job at the International School just yet — much to Ben's disappointment. While Ellie often thought that she needed to get out of the house more and put her profession to use, she could see why Anika couldn't face going back to tackling other people's problems just yet.

Ellie wanted to shake Ben. Clearly, he was finding more ways to stay away from home. Anika had confided in her a little while ago her suspicions that Ben was seeing another woman in London after she'd found a dinner receipt from a romantic bistro in a jacket pocket. When she noticed the date, she recalled that he had told her he'd ordered takeout to his hotel room that night. She remembered the date so clearly because it was her birthday. Who had been out to an intimate dinner with Ben on his wife's birthday, thousands of miles from home?

Because it was weeks after the fact, she felt she couldn't confront him, but Ellie thought that Anika's suspicions were spot on. It made her dislike the man even more. She could very well imagine him at dinner with a shiny, stylish, stain-free woman, ordering the best wine on the menu, bragging about how he always traveled business class because he couldn't "deal with economy."

From behind the sofa came the buzzing of Ellie's phone in her bag. She ignored it, annoyed. She was used to her phone going off in the evening — no one thought anything of calling her at all hours of every day at Hutton & Fetterer — but she hadn't yet received an after-hours call from the ILDC, and she wasn't keen to start up that trend again.

Dinnertime was sacred, and she hadn't even taken three sips of her wine.

The buzzing stopped momentarily before starting again.

"Darn it." Ellie reluctantly set down her fork.

She pulled her phone from her bag. Dad. Calling from Chicago.

"Dad?" Her father, Stanley Benvenuto, very aware of her busy schedule with either clients or children, usually sent a text first to arrange a phone conversation. Something was up.

"Ellie," said her father, and Ellie could hear the panic in his voice. "I've been trying to reach you! It's *Nonno*. He's taken a turn. The hospital called. Can you get over there?"

"Oh my gosh!" cried Ellie, her cortisol surging again. "Oh, Dad! I didn't see my phone. I was having dinner. I'll go straight there! Is he in pain?"

"I don't know. I think it's worse than that. I think ..."

Ellie heard her father's voice break.

"It's not looking good."

She could hear the tears stuck in his throat.

Ellie stood, staring out the window at the lights illuminating Coit Tower. Tears now filled her eyes too. In the rush home from day care, she hadn't even thought to check her phone. The evenings were such a circus.

Enzo, her grandfather, had, up until last year, shared his home with Ellie's grandmother, Genevieve, where they'd lived in Berkeley for the past fifty-plus years. When Genevieve passed away from cancer, a short, shocking illness in the end, Enzo began to decline. He was lost without his beloved wife, and Ellie had helped her father arrange for a home caregiver, a quiet and capable woman named Thais who was the oldest of eight siblings and had migrated from Brazil. Last week Thais had taken him to the hospital with breathing difficulties. Ellie had just visited him on Sunday, and while he'd been weak, his spirits were good.

Ellie ended the call, threw her phone into her bag, and rushed to put on her shoes.

"Anika. It's my nonno, I have to go. Would you mind?" Ellie waved at the children.

"I've got this," said Anika, resting her own fork on her plate and standing up. "Go!"

"Thank you!" She rushed over to plant a kiss on Luca's and Nathan's heads. "Mommy'll be back soon. You stay here and play. Ani will give you dinner, 'kay?" She pivoted quickly to avoid meeting Nathan's confused

17

little face.

Grabbing her car keys, Ellie rushed out the door and sprinted down the stairs. Her heart drummed in her chest as she jumped into the Odyssey and started the engine.

She turned right onto Stockton Street, calculating the fastest route to the Bay Bridge. She pressed her eyelids hard, forcing back tears. The feeling in her stomach swirled and churned as she drove, and she tried to ignore what her premonition was telling her.

Nonno couldn't be gone already, could he? She couldn't lose him like this — not without a goodbye.

CHAPTER 2
ELLIE

January 11, 2019. Berkeley, California.

Ellie drove past the stately Claremont Hotel, the historic wedding cake sentinel that did double duty as an iconic resort and southeast gateway to the UC Berkeley (referred to as simply "Cal") campus. Lit gloriously against the inky January evening and shadowy foliage, it was a welcoming foray to Piedmont Avenue, which was lined with many elegant (and some tired) sorority and fraternity houses. Campus was quiet, with many students still returning from holidays before the winter school term began. There was little rhyme to the architecture of the mansion houses constructed originally as manor homes for their previous wealthy owners, now housing the brightest and best students from all over the world in shared conclaves.

They passed a student in a Golden Bears Cal hoodie, having just stepped off the AC Transit bus outside the International House at the intersection of Bancroft and Piedmont, her large roller suitcase standing, handle to the sky on the sidewalk. Ellie thought how her whole life was ahead of her and suppressed an impulse to lower the window and shout to her, "Stay free!"

Usually, when Ellie drove these streets, a serenity washed over her, for it was here that she had spent some of her happiest days—without realizing it at the time. She still heard her grandfather's gruff voice in her head, habitually addressing her by her full name—*Georgina Ellis Benvenuto, buck up and show them what you're made of!*

It was on the north side of Berkeley and campus that she had lived with Enzo and Genevieve, and where she and her father Stanley, now beside her in the front passenger seat, had grown up. But today, there was no calm to be had. Today, her stomach swirled in a charcoal pit of sorrow

She'd reached Alta Bates hospital yesterday evening, sped through the green corridors past the nurse's station toward Enzo's room only to feel an urgent, grabbing hand pulling her back.

She'd wriggled, spinning to face the Filipina nurse. "I'm Ellie Benvenuto," she cried. "I need to see my grandfather, Enzo …" Her voice faltered. As she looked at the nurse's face, she already knew. She was too late.

"Ms. Benvenuto," said the nurse quietly.

Ellie dropped her eyes, focusing on the nurse's name tag: *Marisol.*

"I'm sorry, Ms. Benvenuto. He's gone. I can tell you … he went peacefully." Marisol's voice had the compassionate cadence of someone practiced in doling out bad news to loved ones.

Ellie stared blankly at her for a moment, while Marisol took a step back and gently dropped Ellie's arm.

"He's … gone?" said Ellie, her voice a whisper.

Marisol nodded.

"I'm very sorry," she said. "Let me come in with you. He went just a short time ago. We were with him, Ms. Benvenuto. He wasn't alone."

How long was a short time? Ten minutes? Half an hour? Ellie had raced here as fast as she could, cursing the cement truck and closed lane that held her up on the Bay Bridge, swollen with rush-hour traffic.

In shock, Ellie allowed Marisol to bring her into the room where Enzo lay, a white sheet pulled over his head. When the nurse carefully folded it down, it looked as though he were just sleeping. He even seemed to be … smiling. Ellie reached for his hand, but already the warmth had begun to cool. It was then that she broke down.

When she'd recovered somewhat, Marisol left her to sit with Enzo, and Ellie took out her phone to call her father. Three missed calls. Dang it! She hadn't paired her phone with the Honda she'd bought after she and Joe divorced because she wasn't a fan of phone distractions, hands-free or otherwise, while responsible for two young lives in the back seat. Ellie rebuked herself now; if she'd done so, she would have gotten Stanley's earlier calls and made it in time to be there for Enzo, who'd always been there for her. She tapped the icon on her phone to call her father back.

"Dad," choked Ellie, through her tears.

"I know," he said, his voice also cracking. "I know. They called me."

For the next hour, while Ellie sat beside her beloved grandfather's still body, she thought about how she had never quite felt so alone. Now, Enzo and Genevieve were both gone. They'd been so much more than figureheads, as she had spent her formative college years living with them in their small three-bedroom house on Le Conte Avenue. They'd been protective and encouraging, always so proud of her, sizing up her college boyfriends and putting up with her moodiness while studying for the law school entrance exam. When they had needed more care as they grew older, she had been there — closer to them than to her own parents, who lived in Chicago.

Her father, who had been checking flights as they spoke, wouldn't land until the next day, Friday. She'd typed a short, to-the-point email to her brother Leo, who was an environmental engineer working on projects all across sub-Saharan Africa and was notoriously difficult to contact. Joe would be understanding through this and look after the boys when she needed, but that shared intimacy of being there for her was long gone.

She called Anika.

"I'm so sorry," said Anika, while Milo called in the background. "What a blow. My heart hurts for you, Elle. I know what he meant to you."

By the time she got back from the hospital, the children were zonked out on the sofa in Anika's apartment, and together they lifted the boys over to Ellie's and put them straight into bed, peeling off their clothes and finding pajamas without switching the lights on. Ben had been in the shower, and Ellie was relieved she didn't have to make conversation about what had just happened. In her living room, Anika embraced her tightly.

"Thank you," said Ellie. "Thank you for everything."

"Try to get some rest," said Anika. "I put a bowl of puttanesca in your fridge. I know you won't feel like eating, but it's there and it will keep a couple of days."

Ellie smiled. They shared keys to each other's homes. Some days it seemed their shared coming and going was what held everything together.

After a fitful night of sobbing and reliving memories of both her beloved grandparents, Ellie rose for work that morning, eyes red-ringed and puffy. She felt as if she hadn't slept at all. She would go in, sort out some case work, and leave early to allow for Nathan's (punctual) pickup and Stanley's from the airport; his flight was due that evening, according to his early morning text message — always in caps and always signed, *LOVE, DAD* despite her repeated instruction that texts didn't require a sign-off. She was relieved it was Friday, and she would have the weekend to spend with her father while they attended to all too familiar end-of-life affairs, having dealt with the loss of her grandmother less than a year ago.

Stanley was chatty when she picked him up, leaving out no detail about his flight snacks, about friends of his at the Chicago Curling Club, about a plumbing problem at the house, about their dog, a golden retriever named *Dogzilla*, who Stanley complained was "completely irresponsible" for the countless tennis balls he failed to retrieve and who had arthritis. Ellie figured he was filling the space with banality to save them talking about what was really happening. She couldn't bring herself to join in and responded with neutral "*mmm*s" and "*aaah*s." She felt exhausted and emotional and was glad Joe had taken the boys early for the weekend.

At Le Conte Avenue, they pulled up in front of Enzo's two-story brown shingled house, in somewhat disrepair from years of weathering. It pained Ellie to see the house in darkness, knowing Enzo would never come home again. As they walked up the path, the winter overgrowth pushing past the edges of the stepping stones, Ellie watched her step. The door was sticky, and a stagnant smell greeted them — the odor of a house unaired and unlived in — when she pushed it open. Enzo had been in the hospital for only a week, and yet the house already groaned in his absence. Stanley set his suitcase in the front hall and moved through the house, switching on lights. Perhaps he, too, felt the sense of loneliness and lack of light.

Ellie put the kettle on the stove and dug through the kitchen drawer where she remembered Genevieve had kept an assortment of tea that she suspected was still stashed there. Enzo was strictly a coffee man, but Genevieve had loved to drink black tea, and now, even though she normally avoided caffeine, Ellie decided that tonight was different.

Tonight, she needed the boost.

She sat on the saggy sofa while Stanley ran his hands over Enzo's black leather recliner, finally sinking into the throne from which his father had ranted over many a Cal-versus-Stanford football game. They sipped from their steaming cups in silence for some moments.

"Well," said Stanley brightly, "looks like I'm an orphan now!"

"Dad! Not helpful!"

Yet they both chuckled. It was a moment of levity amid their murky grief.

"I feel so sad," said Ellie. "It's like a sharp stone in my gut."

"I know," her father said. "It is sad, but he had a long life. We're all only here temporarily." He seemed comfortable speaking only in platitudes.

"I can't believe I didn't get to say goodbye," said Ellie, finally admitting her guilt. "If I'd just checked my phone earlier … or had it connected with my car like I should have. I should've been there with him in the end, but he died alone … without any of us … in a hospital!" Tears brimmed in her eyes again. They seemed to be hanging there all day, her grief like the sword of Damocles threatening to crush her spirit on repeat.

"You know, Ellie," Stanley shared, "my grandfather died in a hospital bed, and I did make it in time to say goodbye. He was already one foot in the next place and mumbling about camping in Golden Gate Park and Enrico Caruso singing opera. I'm not even sure he knew I was there, and I can tell you this much: it didn't make it any easier. You can't beat yourself up. Look, I wasn't even in the same city, and he was my dad! That's life. Your nonno's looking down on us right now, I betcha, saying, 'Hey, that's my seat! What are you doing drinking tea?'"

They chuckled again. Her father was an upbeat person. It was nice to see him, even if the circumstances were bleak.

"You'll be okay to stay here?" she asked, even though she knew the answer. Stanley would prefer his childhood home to her tumultuous, child-dominated apartment.

"Sure," said her father, "just like old times."

After Genevieve had died, Stanley had stayed with Enzo in the house too. Neither of them had expected he would be back to stay again in a similar circumstance in such a short time.

"We're lucky he wasn't a hoarder!" said Ellie. "I mean, the place is pretty tidy, right?"

"Looks like that lady you hired was doing a good job," said Stanley.

"She wasn't his housekeeper, Dad. But yeah, Thais took good care of him."

She had called Thais to tell her of Enzo's death last night and felt both guilt and relief when the caregiver told her how shocked she was, as she had only been to visit Enzo that morning in the hospital, the last kindly visitor Enzo had whom he'd known just a short time. The tears overwhelmed Ellie, and she let out a sob.

Her sudden outburst made her father flinch.

"Ellie belly!" he said, joining her on the sofa and rubbing her shoulder.

"I'm sorry, Dad," she said. "I know you don't need this. I'm just really upset."

"Aww," offered her father, tenderly. There was nothing more he could say. He let her cry, still patting her back.

When she had composed herself again, pulling a Kleenex from her sleeve just like Genevieve used to do, her father confessed he'd been worrying about her.

"You've had a tough year," he said. "First your nonna, then all the business with Joe …"

Ellie groaned. She did *not* want to talk about her divorce.

"And then, of course, that job of yours and all the trouble with that law firm."

Ellie stiffened. She really didn't want to discuss *that* either.

"Have you done anything about it?" he said gingerly. "You really should, you know; I've been thinking about it a lot. I know you're the lawyer and you know this business, but I was reading a case in the *New York Times* the other day about a woman who was forced out of her job and ..."

"Dad." Ellie stood. "I really don't want to talk about it, okay?" She sniffed loudly and squared her shoulders. "And besides, you're right, this *is* my business. I know what I'm doing."

"I know you do," he said. "But sometimes you can't see the woods for the trees. When it's your own situation ... sometimes things need pointing out —"

"Dad!" Ellie could feel the panicked dropping of her heart into her stomach.

Stanley held his hands up in defeat.

"Okay, okay, Elle. But listen ... maybe think about coming back to Chicago with me for a little break? We could bring the boys to see their grandma. I'll pay for the tickets."

The thought of packing up the boys — Luca, in particular — made Ellie feel even more drained.

"Martin Luther King holiday is next weekend, and my return flight is Friday," Stanley said. "Don't you get an extra day off at that supposedly family-friendly nonprofit that I'm sure underpays you?"

He sighed and Ellie could see how grey and weary he was in the face.

"You look really tired," said Ellie.

"Traveling takes it out of me. I'm beat," he said.

"Why don't you go to bed? I'll come back in the morning and bring breakfast."

"All right, Elle."

Suddenly, Ellie felt desperately weary too. Part of her wanted to go up to her old room, get under the blankets, and close her eyes. She felt that here she would dream of her nonno and nonna. Here she could be close to them. Here, sleeping, it would be as if they were all still under one peaceful roof.

Ellie returned the following morning with fresh bear claw pastries from Nabolom bakery. She knew her dad's weak spot for "a really legitimate bear claw," as he put it — and her mother, Simona's, mission to keep him from such temptations. But now was a time for comfort. For everyone. She and Stanley needed to organize next steps for, most immediately, Enzo's cremation and honoring his additional final wishes. Enzo hadn't mentioned the whereabouts of key documents, such as a last will and testament, bank and investment accounts, and the like, so they had some hunting to do.

Ellie turned on the stove again, this time for the moka pot, and scanned the quaint kitchen with its faded wallpaper of fruit baskets, and speckled beige Formica countertops. Her eyes paused at sentimental objects of her grandparents' life: the blue Spode Italian ceramic serving trays Genevieve had used for holiday dinners; the hand-painted tea set Enzo had brought back to Genevieve from Japan after World War II; the heavy marble mortar and pestle passed down through generations and reputedly originating from Carrara, Italy.

Enzo had few of the modern conveniences she had in her apartment, like the instant hot water tap. Her grandparents had only capitulated to a microwave when she'd brought one home during her first year of college, telling Genevieve it didn't make sense to keep a single plate of dinner warm in the oven for her. She had lobbied for a modern electric coffee maker, but Enzo wouldn't hear of it, a pure devotee of his stovetop moka pot. "All an automatic machine produces is brown water," Enzo had insisted. "Too quick. Not enough contact of water with the coffee grounds." This was, perhaps, understandable from a man who had roasted and ground his own beans.

Finding a spray bottle of cleanser, she wiped down the countertops. When done in the kitchen, she moved into the living room and began to swab the shelves as peachy rays of morning sun sliced through the opening in the drapes. As often happened when she was upset, Ellie found that cleaning soothed her agitated mind. It provided instant gratification of reward to effort. Stanley busied himself rifling through the sideboard and chest of drawers in search of Enzo's personal documents.

Pausing to pick up a photo of Enzo and Genevieve smiling inside a silver-plated frame, Ellie hugged the photo to her chest. It was such a sweet picture of two people who seemed truly in love. They would need an image for the online announcement of Enzo's death. Maybe this would do.

Ellie placed the picture back on the shelf next to the leatherbound, gilt-edged, illustrated two-volume set of Enzo's favorite book, *The Count of Monte Cristo*, which he would ask Ellie to regularly read to him after dinner, as he'd relaxed with a pipe and a glass of homemade limoncello in his great black leather recliner. She smiled again, remembering those cozy moments, and their animated discussion over what Enzo revered as the OG of superhero stories, and noticed a large wooden box protruding from the bottom shelf. She recognized it from the attic when she would help Genevieve haul out Christmas decorations. It was years since she'd seen it, and she'd never even looked inside it. What was it doing here in the living room? Had Enzo lugged it all the way down the retractable attic stairs (she had, after all, pulled her car in front of the house this past year to catch him in the act of shakily ascending a ladder to clean his rain gutters)? He shouldn't have done that! Is that what caused the attack that had landed him in the hospital? Hadn't he asked Thais for help?

Ellie's mind was spiraling again. She squeezed her eyes to avoid another onslaught of stinging tears.

She tossed the dusting rag over her shoulder and eased the box out from its position onto the floor, leaving a rectangular space of pristine mahogany, showing just how much dust had accumulated on the shelves. She took the cloth and wiped around the box space before running her palm over the lid of the box, feeling the smooth curve of the material, almost like satin. Was it rosewood? It was heavy, with the bearing of a treasure chest, as if housing precious and valuable contents. Intrigued, she lifted the lid and, sitting crisscrossed on the rug, saw that it was filled with a potpourri of possessions.

Ellie carefully shuffled through stacks of news clippings, a collection of antique pipes, a small mother-of-pearl-handled magnifying glass, an intact pocket watch with a patina at the edges, and a pouch made of some animal hide. Scattered photographs and letters lay beneath other items she didn't even recognize. She lifted out a large wooden contraption the shape of a pie wedge. It was a splintered, rickety sextant with levers inside a crossbow shape and looked like something Galileo might have used. Beneath the sextant was a large ridged rock, the color of the caramel swirl Fenton's ice cream Genevieve used to serve on Sundays after lunch. As she examined it, Ellie thought it actually resembled some sort of giant … molar? She wondered if it was a fossil.

Where had all this stuff come from? In all the time she'd spent in that house having conversations with her grandparents, she had never been shown these artifacts and family memorabilia.

Underneath the rock was a gauzy swatch of faded fabric with a Native American design (as best she could discern from the textiles she'd seen in Anika's apartment). It was handmade by the looks of it and very, very old. Ellie unraveled it to find a long, skinny, sharp metal rod, almost like a skewer, at the end of which was some sort of carving. She had absolutely no idea what the instrument was used for. A type of letter opener? Miniature campfire poker? Extra-long toothpick?

Sifting through the black-and-white photographs and daguerreotypes, she inspected the faces, imagining she noticed some tawny-complected family resemblances to Nathan and Luca!

A saddle-brown, soft leatherbound notebook caught her eye. She lifted it from the box and ran her hands over the smooth, worn cover. She opened it to find a handwritten inscription, the writing childish, with large loops and curves.

The Diary of Theodora Mary Ellis
Boston, Massachusetts 1867
(Private).

Wait. What?

Theodora Ellis? Ellie knew that name from somewhere. Yes — she'd seen it in the family tree that Stanley had painstakingly scribed some years back. Yet no one had ever mentioned this *Theodora*, as far as Ellie could remember.

Theodora was Ellie's great-great-grandmother.

Ellie's skin prickled. Sitting with her back to the orange-and-brown-tweed couch, she turned the first yellowed page and began to read.

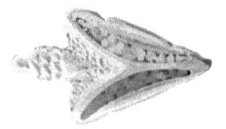

CHAPTER 3
TEDDY

April 4, 1867. Boston, Massachusetts.

I was born, so they tell me, on March 30, 1854, outside a small town on Cape Cod, Massachusetts, called North Sandwich. North Sandwich is about 15 miles from Plymouth and one of my ancestors landed at Plymouth in 1630 from England. He married a woman of the Bourne family who had come over on The Mayflower in 1620 and it was they who settled at North Sandwich and why, I guess, the Ellis family has lived there ever since.

Papa says that we belong to a distinct group of settlers – that we are descended from one of the oldest surviving families in these parts, and that gives us an edge over all the newcomers to this country. And there's a lot of them, these days, he says, all nationalities showing up looking to make their luck, even though we were here first, and should have more rights in that regard.

The Ellis family got the land where our house is built from the Indians. Papa has a land deed on a piece of tree bark signed by the cross of the Indian Chief Quochatecy and it's dated 1668, so that proves everything he says is true. We do deserve respect for our heritage!

The Ellises were adventurers and many of the men over the years went off to be sailors and soldiers and pioneers. Papa says all the folks in our family have a wandering heart.

I don't know what sort of heart I have.

Still, the old household is there, although none of us live there at the moment, which is a great shame and the first time, Papa said, in over two hundred years, that the Ellises have absented themselves from North Sandwich.

My full name is Theodora Mary Ellis and we moved to Boston last year for no good reason that I could see. Here, I go to the primary school and it is here that I bring my diary to write in because school half bores me to death.

I like to write and I like to read, but I hate schoolwork, which is boring and of no consequence I feel to anyone. I sneak my notebook in that Papa got me for my 13th birthday and now it is the 4th April 1867 and I write, in secret, because the teacher, Miss Elmes, has her back to the class. She is not an attentive teacher. Even if she had her front to the class, I suspect she would not see me, or notice.

My diary is a pretty notebook with a cover of calf skin. I have other gifts of calf skin, like my dainty gloves, a hair slide which holds my hair from my face and a leather satchel that I keep drawings in, as Papa is in the livestock business and it's easy for him to come upon these things.

We only moved to Boston last year and it has been hard to grow used to. I miss the countryside and running in the fields and spending time down by the water, fishing and carving things from branches with my penknife.

Stepmother says I should have been a boy.

Maybe she's right.

Stepmother is my stepmother because my real mother died when I was five. I don't have many memories of her, only that there was a lot of wailing in the house followed by a lot of quietness and praying and Papa was all white in the face. And then Papa was around all the time except when he had to go to work driving cattle and Josephine my older sister was in charge of the house then and she liked to use the wooden spoon to whack you on the arm or behind if she didn't like your manners.

Folks always said I was the perfect image of my father, which I found very strange considering he has a big dark bushy beard. I used to stare at him when I was younger and try to picture my hair on him and him in a dress and that made me giggle and then Josephine would wave the wooden spoon at me.

There were four children in our family that Mama left behind when she went to heaven.

Josephine is the oldest and the wickedest. She was eleven when Mama died and so she took on the family to mind us. I don't think she really wanted to do this, because I have only ever known her to be sour and maybe that is why.

Victor came next, and he was nine when Mama died and I never really paid much heed to him for he didn't want a little sister trailing after him and so, over time, I stopped running after him but I think that maybe I should have kept on trailing him for when he was eleven, he drowned in the lily pond after borrowing a boat and losing his oar and finding himself tipped over and not able to breathe at all.

I was afraid of the lily pond because we had often seen snakes in there and if there's one thing I'm fearful of in this world, it's snakes.

I expect that's what Victor was thinking about when he got tipped in. That and the water closing in over his head.

Josephine was very upset and cried for a long time afterwards. Papa cried too and I hadn't seen him cry even when Mama died, so I knew this was a very hard thing for us all. I did not cry for I felt that someone needed to be strong for the family, but I felt enormous guilt over not being with him as his little sister.

Perhaps I could have saved him or at least gone to get help.

That left me the second oldest then, and after me came Beatrice, three years younger, a sweet little thing who we call Trixie, although she does trail me around sometimes, which I don't like, as I prefer to be on my own.

I have one lithograph of my mother. She looks cold and sad I think, and I can see how I don't look like her at all. Josephine does, about the eyes, and maybe Trixie too. But it's hard to see because the picture is so small and it's grey and black and not color like in real life at all. I have never had my photograph taken, but Papa says we will get one done this year, the whole family, in Boston, for he knows just the man to do it on Washington Street.

In North Sandwich we didn't have any help in the household as there wasn't much money around and we had to do everything ourselves.

There was a half-witted man around the village named Leone. Some said he had been disappointed in love, or his sweetheart died, and it threw his mind out of balance. He was perfectly harmless and was supposed to live in a cave somewhere back in the woods. He would disappear for a week or two at a time, no one knowing where he went. He was a kind of utility man around the village. A woman would see him and say, "Leone, take this umbrella to Mrs. Burgess and tell her I am coming to call on her this afternoon." Another might say, "Leone, go up to the store and get me a peak of potatoes."

But his specialty was cutting wood, and all of us kids were fascinated by the big old axe he carried, most everywhere. That axe was the sharpest axe in the world it was said. It could slice an apple thinly the same as a big piece of wood.

Leone never knocked but just came straight into the kitchen and I wasn't scared of him, not really, not if Josephine was around.

One day Josephine had him at work chopping wood in our yard, and I was close by watching him, wood chips flying everywhere and you had to be careful and shield your eyes in case a splinter went right in there and got stuck.

Josephine had been sweeping, and she came to the door and said, "Leone, bring me an armful of wood," and Leone left his big shiny axe in a log, half cut and went off into the house.

Now, the axe, being a thing of talk among all the boys of the neighborhood, was right in front of me. I knew just about every boy and some girls probably, wanted a go of it. And here it was, just me and the log half cut and the big old axe.

The temptation was too much.

I took up the axe, raised it and brought it down, whack! on the log. Well, that first blow brought Leone running. He dropped the armful of wood in the middle of the kitchen floor, right at Josephine's feet and came flying out the door after me.

I turned and ran. I ran like a hare being chased by a whippet and when I looked behind, I saw Leone was after me with the axe and Josephine was after him with the broom.

"Don't you touch a hair on her head, Leone!" screeched Josephine.

I jumped into a field and hid in the undergrowth of a butternut tree, one of the best hiding spots I knew and lucky I was able to get to it but I had to lie there for some hours till it was safe to come out and Leone was gone.

The incident caused a coolness between Leone and me and so I cut his acquaintance. If I saw him coming, I would cross the road. We didn't see eye-to-eye properly after that but all the boys and girls in North Sandwich knew I was the girl who had swung the axe and I think many were rightly jealous and also in awe of me too maybe over that.

Boston, where we live now, is just all right. Here in the city, it's houses and houses and houses and parklands ain't the same as the fields I know in North Sandwich. They just ain't.

Stepmother says I shouldn't say "ain't" and that I need deportment and refinement lessons because I've been running half wild ever since my mother died. This makes Josephine mad, because everyone knows Josephine did her best, even if she was mostly cross all the time, and so Stepmother and her don't see eye-to-eye, the same way as me and Leone didn't.

In fact, when I think about it, I suppose I don't quite see eye-to-eye with Stepmother either but Josephine said that's always the way with stepmothers and she seems to know about these things, her about to turn nineteen and all.

Before we left for Boston, I did patch things up with Leone in a way for he came into the yard one day, just after I'd borrowed two doughnuts that Josephine had left on the kitchen table to cool. Thinking that I'd maybe hurt his feelings over the axe incident, I said, "Hello Leone, don't you want a doughnut?"

I held them out and he took both!

As I walked out the yard, I realized how foolish I'd been. One would have done just as well as two!

"You old pig!" I said as he walked away and couldn't quite hear me. "I hope they choke yer!"

Sometimes I see a look in Josephine eyes, like she wants to choke Stepmother.

Stepmother is a very prim and proper lady and has never really taken to Josephine or Trixie or me. We are the original women of Papa's household. I suppose it's hard for a woman to come into an already-made family to take over from a mother who is long dead and from a daughter who has her own way of doing things and a grumpy cross look on her face.

I find the best way to deal with Stepmother is to keep out of her way. The less she sees of me, the better. That's hard here in Boston, because mostly folks stay inside their houses, only going out for visits or for shopping excursions, neither of which I have much time for.

Stepmother says I'm getting to an age now where I need to be learning how to be a lady and if I want any kind of future at all, I have to get my education and refine myself.

I'm not sure how I'm supposed to refine myself but I feel fine being unrefined, thank you very much.

The thing I've been thinking is that boys really do have it best. They can wear trousers, or short pants, allowing them to jump and climb and even ride a horse with ease.

Last year, when we first came here, Stepmother had two new dresses made for me for school and she said when I was fourteen, I had to start wearing a corset and she would let me off till then. She threatens to drag me shopping to Jordan Marsh nearly every week and I always have to find an excuse as to why I can't go. I suppose I can see that my body is changing and as much as I try to hide it, it always damn pokes through and I feel that corset creeping up on me, closer and closer, tighter and tighter, squeezing my chest into my very throat.

I know once I put that thing on, I won't be able to bend and even sitting will be uncomfortable. I don't want to wear a bustle dress and I don't want to have to put my hair up, neither. Josephine says I have no choice about the corset and I'm lucky that I won't have a whole household to run by myself and children to look after while wearing one.

"You're not old before your time," she says, "like me."

I have no idea what she means by that. But she has been doing a lot of shopping lately herself with brown paper packages arriving to the house at all hours. And she's been taking a great interest in her appearance, I've noticed, piling her hair high and wearing pearl drop earrings and scent.

Sometimes I hear her humming and singing to herself, which is not like Josephine at all.

April 16, 1867

I write in this diary most days in school but yesterday I very nearly got caught by Mrs. Elmes, mostly, I'd say, because I was too quiet, which she noticed.

It's rare I'm too quiet. She says I'm a fidgeter.

Now, I'm writing in my bedroom which I share with Josephine and Trixie and I suppose I will pass the time, for there really is not much to do when I'm at home. Perhaps I will describe the house where I live, here in Beacon Hill.

The house is red brick with black shutters, a glossy black door with a big brass knocker and black gas lanterns set in the walls outside. The streets are cobbled which are noisy if ever a cart or cab passes by.

In this house we have a lot of modern appliances some of which Stepmother ordered from the catalogs she likes to read. We have a stove here which we didn't have in North Sandwich.

There, Josephine did all the cooking on the big fire in our fireplace, which was five or six feet wide with a crane on one side that could be swung out over the fire to hold the kettles for boiling. On top of the mantelpiece, we kept a vase to hold lamplighters and the oil we burned was whale oil. In that house, we had a good bedroom and a good parlor, which we never used unless we had company.

All the best things were in the parlor. The best carpet and furniture, our souvenir shells, glass ornaments, paper flowers and the family Bible. Here in Boston, Stepmother has folks over to her parlor all the time and I suppose it's nice to use the room, but then, I think, well, it just doesn't feel special no more.

I miss our big brick oven in North Sandwich. Every Wednesday and Saturday, Josephine had a fire built in it and when it was hot and the fire had burned out and the ashes were raked, she had her pies, cakes, brown bread and beans all ready and she put them in the oven with a long-handled iron shovel. The items that required the longest time were put in the back part to bake and the beans were left in overnight. I don't think the food tastes the same here in Boston. The air doesn't smell the same and neither does the bread.

Papa's business is good now but for a long time in North Sandwich, it wasn't. I guess that's why we're able to have the extra help now in the house with a house girl who comes in to clean and the cook who prepares food, but she doesn't spend all day here and we share her with another house.

Daddy's job is to drive hogs and cattle and bring them into Boston to sell and he has to be away for long spells on the road, going as far out as Ohio and sometimes Chicago and back. We have an uncle in Chicago but I've never met him, for he was one of the wanderers who left North Sandwich when he was young.

I've begged Papa to take me with him on the road but he says he doubts I'd have the stamina to ride out so long. I've told him it would be not a bother, for I was always good with horses and I'd dress in trousers and overalls and a wide felt hat like him and no one would even have to know I was a girl and sometimes I can see that he's considering it but he knows it won't please Stepmother and so far, he hasn't brought me with him.

Often, I think if Victor were here, he'd have been long out helping Papa on the road and that sometimes he'd like to bring me for family company, only because I'm a girl, I'm not allowed.

If I was a boy he wouldn't think twice about it.

Sometimes I wonder what would have happened if Stepmother had never come along at all. I think we'd still be in North Sandwich for one thing, because it was Stepmother who comes from Boston and who wanted to move back here.

The first we knew about Stepmother was when a letter arrived from Papa from Boston, saying he was again "embarking on the sea of matrimony." Trixie wanted to know what "matrimony" was because we called her a "Mother's Moany" when she was cribbin' and she thought it was something to do with her, but Josephine reassured her it had resolutely nothing to do with her and all to do with Papa's "lust and greed."

"Your father has made a fool of himself and married a widow with three children and he with three of his own!"

After she said that she went quiet and said we weren't to repeat her words and she was sorry for saying them and Trixie asked her what "lust" meant and Josephine said if Trixie ever uttered the word out loud again, she'd take the stick to her behind. Josephine wasn't afraid to use the stick. Mostly she used the spoon or hairbrush, but the stick was the worst.

Josephine went about the house, banging and clattering, pulling out all the cupboards and embarking on a big cleaning spree after that. We had a turkey killed for the welcoming dinner and it was hard to be useful while also keeping out of Josephine's way for no matter what we did, she was liable to shriek at us at any moment.

Two days later, the new family arrived, Stepmother in the biggest bonnet I'd ever seen, with tiny ornamental cherries and oranges all piled up on top. I don't know how they didn't topple right off her head. She brought with her Henrietta, a young lady about the same age as Victor, had he lived, and Willie, who was a year older than me. Henry, her youngest son, was two years older than Trixie. We all sat in the kitchen, Trixie and me on one side of the fireplace, Willie and Henry on the other, staring. Josephine sat at the table with Papa, looking on at the new stepmother and Henrietta.

I wondered why you'd call your daughter Henrietta and your son Henry and thought how Stepmother must like that name very much indeed.

Stepmother had a smile on her face but you could see it was hard for her to keep it, as she kept looking about the kitchen, her eyes darting all over the place, on the surfaces, on the cupboards and on the soot that hung on the spiderwebs in the corner, missed by Josephine's big flapping broom. She was sizing everything up, taking account of all before her. And it was clear to me, and Josephine too, likely, that she didn't care much for what she saw.

The next morning, Willie and I went out to get acquainted. He was evidently homesick. He did not like the house, he said. He did not like the smell in the air and I sniffed but all I could smell were farmer bonfires, which always burned at that time of year. It wasn't a bad smell, I thought. We were used to the burning smell of fires out here.

I offered to run him a race down Schoolhouse Hill.

He said boys did not run races in Boston.

I asked him if he could jump over the fence with two rails in it.

He said boys did not jump fences in Boston.

I said, "I think you are some pumpkins up in Boston. I think I can lick yer!" and I put my fist right up in his face and he backed off and away from me.

"No one talks of fighting in Boston," he said, "except the Irish boys."

I said, "Oh, yeah, well, I wish you were an Irish boy then, instead of a stupid Bostonian!"

He said that Boston had everything! And I said, "Oh yeah, like what?"

"The museum." He scrunched his nose at me. "It's got everything in the whole world in it. Boston Common, the biggest common in the world! And we got the Bunker Hill Monument and it has two hundred and ninety-four steps to the top!"

I didn't care much for any monument. I thought Willie was the biggest sissy I ever met.

I didn't know then that Stepmother was not to be messed with. That Stepmother never had any plans to settle in North Sandwich probably and it was city life or no life for her.

She went and persuaded Papa that with his livestock business, he'd be better off in Boston anyway and it didn't take long for him to have us all pack up and take our house in Beacon Hill and move away from the homestead that had been in our family for two hundred years.

Trixie took to moaning again every night for a week after the move until Stepmother brought her into Jordan Marsh's where she picked out a soft doll and that was the end of the moaning.

But I was too old for dolls.

If I go out, Stepmother wants to know where I'm going. She has a tail on me all the time, the freedom I used to have left behind, floating in the sky, somewhere over North Sandwich.

There's only one thing for it in my eyes and that's to convince Papa that he's got to take me on the road. If he did that, I'd be days away from here. There'd be no talk of dresses or corsets, of deportment and posture. I'd have the road ahead and adventure in my grasp!

Yessir, there's only one thing for it and that's to convince Papa.

Dear diary, I will do it, if it's the last thing I do.

I'm an Ellis and the Ellises were built to explore!

(Even if I am only an Ellis girl.)

CHAPTER 4
ELLIE

January 18–21, 2019. Chicago, Illinois.

The weekend in Chicago got off to a frazzled start when Luca—rattled by the airport and the disruption of routine—had a drawn-out meltdown just before takeoff from San Francisco International. Ellie had braced for it. She'd deployed her usual arsenal of defense gear: compression vest, chewy toy, noise-canceling headphones. But it was still too much, especially past his bedtime.

As days went, this one had been a high-wire act worthy of a Vegas residency—just without the comp'd drinks—all while humming "Elmo's World" under her breath.

That morning, after dropping off Nathan, she'd driven Luca to his weekly appointment at the UC Davis MIND Institute in Sacramento—a ninety-mile haul each way. Of course, traffic had been brutal. But she never skipped those sessions. Not when they were so vital to his progress. Not even if she was clinging to her last nerve. Not in a hundred lifetimes.

Luca was now used to the doctors and speech, physical, and occupational therapists. They knew just how to handle him, and the visits there and back were familiar to him by now. His language still hadn't developed, but he was making new sounds and had gained some motor skills, like finally holding his own sippy cup. Ellie was proud of these triumphs, not just of Luca but of herself for finding him what must have been the best care in the world. Still, he was usually tired after the appointments, and there was no rest for the weary, as they'd booked a red-eye flight for Friday night. It was the only way Ellie could make it work, and she figured they would all sleep on the plane. Stanley had changed his own flight to accompany them and paid for theirs in the process.

Ellie knew that neither the trip nor the weekend would be easy; it was so tricky to take Luca out of his home environment. But with Enzo's death, and the shock she was feeling, she'd agreed to her father's idea. Now was the time to be with family. It would be challenging but worth it, she hoped.

Simona collected their groggy group from O'Hare International arrivals at dawn, pulling up in her Volkswagen Jetta SportWagen and pursing her lips as she handed out coats and hats for the children that, along with little snow boots, she'd borrowed from a neighbor. Ellie had thought to bring the classic camel coat her parents had given her from Marshall Field's her last Christmas at home before leaving for college and that they swore would last her a lifetime.

They all put on their extra layers, Stanley helping Ellie secure the boys in two rented child safety seats while Simona placed their bags in the hatchback. Stanley was attached to the boys now, having spent a whole week seeing them at either Enzo's house or Ellie's apartment. He remained bright and cheerful, at odds with Simona's stoic manner. Ellie knew her mother wasn't a morning person and probably resented the early morning collection, but still, here they all were, together at last.

"You look tired, Ellie," Simona said as she checked her rearview mirror and pulled out of the parking space.

"Thanks, Mom," said Ellie, scoffing a little. "News flash: I am!"

Ellie and her mother had a somewhat arm's-length relationship. Simona was successful in her field as an epidemiologist. She was cool, levelheaded, intelligent, and unflappable in many ways. But she hadn't been a cuddly, homemade-sauce-making mother. Stanley's warmth had more than made up for it; Ellie had always felt loved, but now, as a mother herself, she could see how their relationship was strained. They just weren't particularly close.

"Snow!" shouted Nathan and he pointed excitedly at the grey-white mounds that had been plowed onto the sides of the road, forming snowbanks.

"Yes, snow!" said Ellie wearily.

She had been looking forward to the boys' reaction to the Chicago weather she considered inclement and didn't miss. Now, admittedly, something about the crisp air that had bitten her ears and nose as they'd stood waiting for Simona's car calmed her. Later, she would let them stumble through the snow in her parents' yard — maybe even build a snowman.

Stanley and Simona had purchased the once rundown gable-front farmhouse when they could scarcely rub two nickels together as young parents, then spent years remodeling. Now, entering the house through the expansive front porch, Ellie breathed the familiar smell of her childhood home. Yet it smelled mustier, older perhaps. For the first time — as it was such a long time since she'd been there, having been dealing with childbirth and the travails of motherhood, among other things — she realized that her parents were aging.

As Dogzilla greeted the whole crew with face licks all around, Ellie noticed the decor looked saggy and tired, with newspapers and books scattered about. Standards had slipped. Were her parents unable to keep up with housework anymore, or had they simply taken a more relaxed approach?

Nathan just could not wait to get into the snow.

"Outside!" he cried after they got the bags in. As Simona began preparing a breakfast of eggs over the stove, he ran to the glass doors and repeated, "Outside!"

"We will, Glitter-Bug," Ellie said, crossing to her youngest and wrapping her arms around him. "But let's put something in your tummy first!"

Despite his fatigue, Stanley took the two boys on a house tour. They had been there before but only as babies, with no recollection of it.

"So," said Simona, as she moved the spatula around the pan.
"So," said Ellie.
"A long week."
"Not for you," said Ellie. "Total freedom with Dad gone!"
"Ha!" said Simona. "Yeah, lots of peace and quiet."
Ellie wasn't quite sure what to say to Simona, not feeling totally at ease in her presence, especially when they hadn't seen each other in so long. Ellie felt pressure to always impress her mother. To tell her of achievements, of goals she'd conquered that Simona had envisioned for her. Simona had always been an advocate for women's rights and rallied against societal norms imposed by "The Patriarchy." She had urged Ellie to pursue a less female-dominated field, as she had done herself, and had successfully steered her away from her original plan to parlay her facility with languages into a career as a diplomatic interpreter — a decision Ellie felt was, perhaps, the original sin. She should have followed her heart. She may not have been able to make day-care pick-up on time, but she could correctly combine the past conditional with the imperfect subjunctive in multiple languages. So hey, she had that going for her.

As it turned out, Ellie had perforce taken on "The Patriarchy" in her jobs and had regularly run rings around her male counterparts, intellectually. She had gone toe to toe with the men who told her to sit in a corner and take notes, and up against misogynistic comments, snickers, and juvenile sexist nose-thumbing.

And look where that had gotten her.

"How's the new job going?" asked Simona, as if reading her mind.

"Good, Mom," replied Ellie, as her eyes fell on a dusty shelf where a pink Depression glass pitcher from Simona's own mother's farmhouse had sat for as long as she could remember.

"The case load is a lot, and we're dealing with tough problems, you know, with what some of these clients have been through! But it feels like worthy work. Like I'm making a difference."

"That's good," said her mom, "that you feel that way."

Ellie went silent. She had suspected that Simona was disappointed that she had bowed out of Hutton & Fetterer in the end. She wasn't sure if her mom felt annoyed that she'd caved rather than going another round in the ring, or pure anger at how she had been treated. A wave of guilt, so familiar to her now, heaved in her stomach. The feeling that she should have toughed it out. That she shouldn't have accepted defeat so easily. That she should have stood her ground.

"Hey, Mom," said Ellie, abruptly changing the subject as the thought struck her, "what do you know about Enzo's side of the family — the Ellises? I found a diary in a box in his house, from Theodora Ellis. Dad doesn't seem to know much, says he can only vaguely remember her being mentioned. Do you remember anything? You know what Dad is like when it comes to detail."

"*Theodora?*" Simona frowned as she spooned eggs onto two warmed plates.

"Well, I guess she went by *Teddy*," said Ellie.

"That rings a bell." Simona paused. "Wasn't she a suffragist or something?"

"Was she? I don't know," said Ellie, her interest piqued. "I've started reading her diary. Her stories are fascinating! She's only thirteen. She sounds like a character!"

"You know Genevieve gave me a box before she died. Letters and things for safekeeping. I think she knew in a way that she was ... you know. That she wouldn't be around for much longer."

"That's sad," said Ellie.

"A woman's intuition," said her mother.

"Maybe we could have a look later?"

"Tomorrow maybe," said Simona. "We're meeting Martha this afternoon, remember?"

Ellie climbed the paisley-patterned carpeted stairs and grasped the brass railing as her eyes drew upward. The ceiling in the lobby of The Palmer House hotel, situated on East Monroe Street, was breathtaking. It reminded Ellie of cathedral interiors she'd seen in Italy on family trips. It was filled with color and gilt, with smooth-cornered shapes and patterns spread out in an ornate mosaic. Three large panels depicted three Greek gods, the names of which Simona had drummed into Ellie when she was young. Aphrodite, the goddess of love; Apollo, the god of sun; and Plutus, the god of wealth.

It was natural for Martha to suggest meeting here, as it was her regular haunt. Nestled under a section of the blue line of the elevated train, called "The El" by Chicagoans, it was only a few minutes from Water Tower Place, where Simona and Ellie had just spent two carefree hours browsing the shops and which was just a block from where Martha worked as a head buyer for Saks Fifth Avenue.

Ellie had released herself into the break. They had dropped Stanley, Luca, and Nathan at the historic Shedd Aquarium on the way, Ellie surrendering to two little boys with ants in their pants and their grandfather who would not be left home to nap. Stanley, seeming a kid again himself, had even offered to take the boys sledding the following day. Despite her initial reservations that Luca couldn't support himself, Stanley assured her he would stay on the sled with him.

Then she felt guilty again. She should be the one to sled with Luca. She was so used to doing everything herself, it was taking time to accept help. But she could feel the built-up tension beginning to leave her body. It was such a liberating feeling, though not one she trusted would last.

Ellie couldn't wait to see what her mother's oldest friend would be wearing today. One of the reasons Ellie maintained a keen sense of style herself, even on her worst days, was due to the art and daily habit of putting herself together that she'd learned from Martha.

Martha was already at their table in the Lockwood restaurant when Ellie and Simona glided in, and she slid out from the semicircle booth to kiss them both on the cheek, giving Ellie a chance to take in her midnight-blue St. John's knit suit, embossed with bright gold buttons along the jacket's placket, matched with a taupe and grey Schiaparelli scarf and suede Dior ankle boots.

"Mmmmm. What's your fragrance, Martha?" asked Ellie, as she tucked in beside her. "It's divine."

"Bond No. 9 New York, Gold Coast," replied Martha. "New. I'll send it to you."

A perk of a family friend who worked in haute fashion meant intermittent boxes arrived at her apartment in San Francisco, filled with Martha's cast-offs. Sometimes the clothes were brand-new, labels still attached; other times they were vintage items that Martha had finally parted with in another of her wardrobe purges. She would include jewelry, scarves, and on one occasion, a Bottega handbag. And she usually included perfume, always wanting to try a new scent for herself.

Sometimes Ellie felt, as she unpacked the box, the items wrapped carefully in tissue paper, that she was the surrogate daughter Martha had never had. She'd been married three times but bore no children. Whether by choice, Ellie never knew and didn't dare ask, but she had a hunch. Martha was a woman who valued, above all, her independence and freedom.

When Ellie was very young, she could remember her mother shushing her while on a phone interview for a new job. Afterward she'd scolded her, "Mommy's new job doesn't know she's a mommy. You almost gave the game away, Els!"

Ellie didn't know what the game was or that she'd even been playing it.

Martha and Simona had met in the early seventies, during the second wave of feminism, when they'd both worked as shopgirls at Saks. While Simona eventually left to pursue her master's degree and a career in public health, Martha continued to rise in the Saks ranks. To Ellie she was always a sophisticated, glamorous woman, permanently flawlessly assembled.

Ellie marveled at Martha's thick, glossy hair — how did she keep it that way? She absently tugged at her own dull, dry strands, aware she hadn't set foot in a salon in months. Meanwhile, social media droned on about "self-care" as if it were a universal right. Did scraping mashed banana from a booster chair count as a skin treatment? Martha, catching her gaze, reached into her Hermès flap bag, her David Yurman bracelets sliding effortlessly down an impeccably moisturized wrist.

"I brought something," she teased and placed a well-worn deck of cards on the table.

Ellie broke into a grin.

"Oh, Martha, never change," she said.

Martha was known for her card-reading prowess, and when Ellie was a student at Adlai E. Stevenson High School just outside of Chicago and trying to figure out her life plan at age sixteen, Martha had read Ellie's tarot cards, which had directly influenced her to apply to UC Berkeley for college and then law school. It had been an unusual choice for a girl in her small Midwest town, and she was the only one in her high school to do so, but with Simona's influence and Martha's card reading, the stars had aligned.

She studied the set Martha had brought. But these weren't tarot. These were different from the cards she'd used in the past; they were round, for one thing. Ellie didn't recognize the images either.

Interrupted by a tall, dapper waiter, the women quickly gave their orders, Ellie opting for Caesar salad and flatbread, Martha ordering a crisp bottle of sparkling rosé to share.

"Please draw three cards, Ellie," Martha said solemnly once the waiter had left.

Ellie paused over the cards, letting her fingers choose where they wanted to go, as if a magnet was drawing her to just the right circles.

Martha turned them over one by one, and like the three gods that Ellie used to rhyme off when they passed through the lobby when she was a child, Martha named the three cards that Ellie had chosen with proclaim: "Entangled Lovers! Sword and Shield! Ah, the Enchanted Valley, I've never drawn that card for anyone before!"

Simona and Ellie leaned in as Martha studied the three cards, the first, a glowing image that reminded Ellie of a Gustav Klimt painting or Himalayan salt rock, such was its light. The third card, the Enchanted Valley, depicted a unicorn set in a gold-and-green forest against a lavender-and-coral sunset.

"Ellie, my dear, there are places on this beautiful planet where the veil between the physical and mystical realm is porous. These places are called portals, vortexes, or spirit gateways. In mythology, they are revered as venues where things beyond ordinary reality can unfold. The Enchanted Valley is one such place and divulged only to the few who have the vision and heart to be open to them."

Simona regarded Ellie, as if something she'd always known had been confirmed.

"The sacred landscape wants you to know that profound transformation is afoot, Ellie," continued Martha. "Wondrous events are unfurling. Meaningful revelations and inner illuminations are close at hand. It is now much easier to manifest your dreams. This is an excellent time to step into your visions for your future. Your actions in the coming year will generate big results. Gateways are opening to show you the places where the veil is especially thin, which you can access with your power, love, and integrity. Wonders are blossoming in your life, including great love. Watch for them. Open your heart to hallowed, magical energy. The more you become aware of the small marvels in your life, the more they will magnify."

Ellie actually gulped at the reading. Great love! Ha! There wasn't even the sniff of a man in her life right now! Who on earth would be interested in a divorced mom in her situation? And "easy" now to "manifest her dreams"?

"Oh, Martha," said Ellie. "That all seems so … far-fetched right now. Is it some kind of celestial joke?" She dabbed at her uninvited tears.

"Yet your eyes tell a different story," purred Martha. "And, as we all know, the eyes are the window to the soul. The cards have been right before for you."

"Where's that wine?" called Ellie, keen to break the attention of her mom and Martha who were now peering at her too meaningfully. "Sorry, but I am not falling into the marriage trap again. Nope, no siree. Not. A. Chance."

"Who said anything about marriage?" Simona said, her eyes also slightly shiny. It seemed the reading had affected her too. "Great love doesn't necessarily mean marriage."

As the waiter approached their table to uncork the bottle, Ellie couldn't help but ponder the meaning behind her mother's words. Did Simona have another great love? Was she reading more into the cards than Ellie? Or did Martha know something about them all that even they had yet to put into words?

CHAPTER 5
TEDDY

June 4, 1867. Boston, Massachusetts.

School is the worst thing in my life by far. I have to get up early, and in North Sandwich, that never bothered me much, but here in Boston it bothers me very much, because I have to get washed and dressed and my hair must be pulled back and I have to be "clean and presentable," according to Stepmother and when I used to get up early in North Sandwich it was to watch the sun break over the trees. Not to go to school in a tight dress. What a bother.

Back in North Sandwich, there were always jobs that needed doing, like collecting eggs or going for milk or tackling some weeds or helping Josephine with the laundry, but here in Boston, we don't have any chickens and Stepmother sends our laundry out.

There's no front garden; our front door steps right onto the cobbled street.

I don't have these jobs anymore because Stepmother warns I'm going to behave like a lady, and ladies don't go round in overalls whacking at weeds.

Miss Elmes, our teacher, is forever admonishing me. She says I have the brains but I don't "apply myself."

Well, truth be told, I don't think she applies herself to teaching. She's terribly boring. And that's why I hate school and all its rules and rhyming, rhyming, rhyming by rote.

The thing is, I do like books. Whenever Papa went on the road, he used to bring me home some penny paperbacks and as I got better at reading and started moving on to more difficult texts, he said I was well ahead of my age. He said I was better read than him and even better with figures too! To be a man in business you need to know your figures, so this was really saying something!

My favorite books so far are *Oliver Twist* by Charles Dickens and *Crime and Punishment* by Dostoyevsky, which is a very long book but I got through it alright 'cause it's all about what it means to be good or wicked. Last week Papa came back from Chicago with a book so long it's two books. It's by Alexandre Dumas — something about a count. I have yet to start it but I'm not sure if I'm going to like it as it's set in France and I'm not sure how I feel about the French. Miss Elmes is always drumming French grammar into us and it very much puts me off.

When we lived in North Sandwich, Papa used to sit us down around the fire in evenings and tell us his own stories.

He had a great many stories about my great grandfather on my mother's side. He was a justice of the peace and the only magistrate in the district and was known as the Squire. He lived in North Sandwich from around the year 1690 to 1750, which is a very long time for a man and he had accumulated considerable cash money. As there were no bonds, mortgages or stocks back then, he wasn't quite sure what to do with it all.

He decided he would like to invest it and would lend it out to folks with interest. If he heard of anyone who was building a new house or a vessel he would walk twenty or thirty miles to see if he could lend them some money. What he could not lend, he kept in the house in an oak chest.

At that time, they were having a lot of trouble with witches, all over New England and some of the other colonies too. The test was to throw suspected persons, who were almost always women, into a pond. If they could swim, they were witches for sure and left in deep water to fatigue and drown. If they could not swim, they hauled them out and I suppose apologized.

I often wondered if I could be a witch, for I am a very good swimmer.

There were different charms to keep the witches away as it was widely known that witches were money mad and would fly away with all of it, if they could get a hold of it. Every Christmas the squire would kill a hog and while it was warm, hang it up on a beam and drop all his money down through the hog, one piece at a time.

This was supposed to keep it witch-proof for a year. Witches were never known to fly away with money that had been treated in that way.

One way to know if a witch had been in a house was if the brine spoiled in a barrel of pork. It would go all rancid and frothy and that is what happened to the squire's wife one day when she visited the cellar to look in the barrel. They knew then that a witch had been in the house and was after their money, so the squire took all their money from the oak chest, put it in a canvas bag and carried it out to the woods along the track road, where they hauled their kindling from, and buried it.

When he came back, he said he'd buried the money three feet deep where the witches could not find it. For a long time, their minds were easy in regard to the money. When the squire died, he died very suddenly and he'd never told anyone where the money was buried.

To this day in North Sandwich, folks dig holes along that road in search of the treasure. We call them "money holes."

Papa says that in our family, we have a habit of earning lots of money and losing it again. It happened to him too after Mama died. He'd been doing very well in business and then things took a turn and went down and that's why we had to let go of our help and things in the house began to get worse and Josephine got all agitated.

Now Papa's luck is on the rise again for we have a fine house here in Boston and Stepmother seems to have plenty of money to spend in Jordan Marsh's. I hope our luck stays and we don't lose it again.

The squire was known to be very lucky in business at times and could strike it rich, even when the odds were against him. Papa told us that he once agreed to insure a man who had two vessels that had not returned home from the West Indies. It was presumed that they'd been wrecked or captured by pirates. The man said if the squire insured him, he could have the second vessel should it appear back and this is indeed what happened.

But the squire, being only a farmer with no nautical experience did not know what to do with the ship. He asked his friends and some would advise one thing, some another. The night before he went to Boston to see to the ship, he met an old sailor in our local country store and on hearing of his inexperience, as a joke, the old sailor told him to "load her with warming pans."

The squire did not realize this was a joke, for he was not to know the West Indies was so warm they had resolutely no need for warming pans in their beds. The long-handled pans were filled with ashes and coals from the fire and placed between the sheets on cold winter nights, something regularly used in North Sandwich and Boston.

And so, the squire purchased as many warming pans as he could find and loaded them on the ship, to the great amusement of the sailors and merchants who delivered them to the dock.

When the planters came aboard the vessel in the West Indies to see what was for sale, they were quite taken with the warming pans.

"What fine things they would be to dip our molasses with and fill the barrels!"

And they bought every warming pan on board and so the squire made a tidy profit. Papa called it the "Squire's luck."

Now, here in Boston, Papa doesn't seem to have much time to tell us stories. In fact, I'm not at all sure if he's even sat us down once since we've been here.

I suppose that's why he brings me the books.

He is always too busy it seems with Stepmother organizing grand dinners for him. They eat dinner alone each evening at the dining table, while we are fed our suppers early and told to go to bed.

Josephine does not stand for this, for she is not a child, and she is often out herself to supper. I miss our nights around the fire though, just the four of us.

My last story of Papa's that I will tell here, for I do not know what I will do with this diary, or even if I will keep these pages that I have written (for my thoughts change all the time and I do not wish Stepmother to find it and read it), is about the Declaration of Independence, a story that Papa swears is true.

He told us that when Thomas Jefferson was in the declaration writing business, he received a hurry up order to have the declaration written for the printer at four o'clock.

Jefferson duly wrote it out and gave it to his clerk to copy and then went to lunch. The original document read "all men are knot created equal," and when the clerk who was copying it out came to the word "knot," he said out loud, "I don't think 'not' is spelled with a 'k.'"

Now as this was before Noah Webster's time, and he had no dictionary to refer to, there proceeded a conversation in the office.

"N-o-t, not," said the other clerk. "But knot, k-n-o-t, that is spelled with a k."

They got into an argument, which descended into a heated exchange where the two men squared up to each other. Right at that moment, Jefferson returned, came into the office and roared, "Cut it out! And get to work on that declaration, the printer must have it by four o'clock!"

The clerk, not used to hearing such slang from Mr. Jefferson, took him at his word and thought he meant "cut out" the word and so he did and the declaration forever more read, "All men are created equal."

Papa said that if Mr. Jefferson meant to say, "all men are created with equal rights," then he agreed with him, but he had a poor way of saying it.

I am not quite sure how I feel about folks being born equal. Two people can be of the same parents and yet have very different minds and outlooks. How can everyone be equal?

Right now, I am looking forward to summer and the end of the school term.

I am so tired of these inside walls.

The best day of the summer is the 4th of July, it is all Willie's friends talk about now, even in April.

We will need all our pocket money to buy firecrackers, pinwheels, Roman candles and skyrockets. Willie says one yellow cracker is worth two red ones and this gives me a notion to try my hand at some trading business even if I'm perhaps a little too old for firecrackers.

June 17, 1867

Oh, I have found myself in some trouble! It is of my own doing.

However, the involvement of Stepmother caused much of the ruckus, in my opinion, and I have truly turned against her now.

It turns out I will miss the 4th of July in Boston. I will have to give all my fireworks to Willie before I leave. This has me a little annoyed, truth be told, but as Papa is still so angry with me, I have to swallow it.

There were two incidents that led to this situation, only one of which I am quite ashamed of.

The first, and the most shameful, was an incident with the cobbler, Mr. Pratt. My shoe needed mending and I went to his shop to leave it to be fixed.

Papa had given me ten cents to pay for it and I'd laid the money on the stairs for some reason and forgot where I left it. Stepmother found it and gave it back to my father, unbeknownst to me.

I told Mr. Pratt that I would pay him when I returned for the shoe and went home in search of the coin. That evening, Papa asked me if I had paid Mr. Pratt and not wanting to admit my carelessness, I said "Yes, sir."

Papa said, "*Did* you pay him? I gave you ten cents and yet your mother found that on the stairs?" (Papa has a habit of calling Stepmother "mother" which only Trixie tolerates).

I said, "Maybe you had two coins and dropped one on the stairs?"

"I think you are telling a fib, but before giving you a whipping, I shall go and ask Mr. Pratt if you paid him, like you said."

I went up to my room and sat on my bed to study some way out of the difficulty. I had no money. Neither Willie nor Henry had any that I could borrow. Josephine was away visiting the Hartfords, where she seemed to spend a lot of time lately.

I looked through my trunk to see if I had anything I could sell for ten cents, but there was nothing. Mr. Pratt had to be paid before nine o'clock the next morning, if I was to escape a thrashing.

All that night, I couldn't sleep, thinking over the problem, but as dawn broke an idea came to me. I would do as many debtors had done and resort to paying a high interest for an extension of time! I had learned from the squire! Interest on a loan was the way to go! I would go to Mr. Pratt and tell him that when my father called, he was to say I'd paid the ten cents and to let it run until next week when I would surely figure out a way to make some money. I would pay him fifteen cents instead of ten for his trouble.

Well, Papa did call in and when Mr. Pratt said the bill had been paid, Papa was flummoxed for the coin that he had given to me had a small scratch on it and he knew that I had certainly lost the original coin.

He knew that I was fibbing in some way and this greatly displeased him. He didn't like to think he'd been outsmarted.

That evening, I was called to the parlor, where Stepmother sat with her arms folded, and Papa stood in front of the fireplace with his arms behind his back.

How, they wanted to know, had I paid the money to Mr. Pratt?

Unable to get myself out of the bind, I repeated that I had paid it with Father's coin.

Papa produced the coin and said he knew that I was lying.

And still, I would not admit the truth.

Papa said lying to one's parents was the greatest offense there was for if there was no trust within the family, then my ethics and morals did not stand up to scrutiny at all.

These words greatly saddened me and I longed to tell the truth. I wanted Papa to have the utmost trust in me, but I did not know how to get myself out of the fix.

They dismissed me and said they would think on a punishment appropriate for the crime.

The very next day my examination results arrived from the schoolhouse. It turned out that I had failed French (how I hate that language!) and Latin (an utter waste of time).

Miss Elmes remarked that I had not put the effort in.

The truth was I could have done better. I did understand more than I let on and perhaps, in a sort of protest, I had not put any effort in, for I felt Miss Elmes, in her weak attempt at teaching, made everything boring and inane and half the class was asleep most of the time. Why let her think she was a good tutor?

Stepmother left the results envelope on the high mantelpiece in the parlor. And again, for a second night in a row, I was called to stand in front of them in shame.

"I know you are better than this," Papa declared. "I know you have brains, Teddy. Why do you not use them?"

Papa said it appeared that I was lazy. That ever since coming to Boston I was languishing and they could stand it no longer.

I wanted to say that ever since we'd come to Boston, I had barely seen Father and perhaps it was him who was languishing, but I knew if I said that I would get a whipping right there and then and so I kept my mouth closed.

Stepmother said I had become "insolent." She said I was no longer a child and could not be treated as one. She would no longer stand for my "cheek."

"I am not cheeky!" I cried, but Papa raised his voice and said this was an exact example of what Stepmother meant.

"I will not have an insolent daughter," he said and they dismissed me again and ordered me to stay in my bedroom.

I knew then that they were discussing something very serious about me.

Two days later, I was called for a third time to the parlor.

By now, I had become used to being reprimanded.

Papa looked solemn. Stepmother looked smug.

"Teddy," said my father, "we have found your behavior this week to be truly reprehensible. It is simply not acceptable. We do not care for your demeanor, nor the change we see in you."

I thought that I hadn't changed that much. I still felt like me, the same

Teddy that I was in North Sandwich. It was Stepmother who had changed Father.

"We have telegrammed your uncle in Chicago and he has agreed to take you for the summer. This will give you plenty of time to think upon your actions. A summer of hard manual work will show you just how important it is to apply yourself to your education, if you want to do any better for yourself."

Chicago? On my uncle's farm?

If this was meant as a punishment, it must be Stepmother's doing (and the best punishment I could have been given).

I knew that my uncle had two sons, but I could not really remember my cousins. Nor could I remember my uncle and his wife for that matter.

But a farm! A whole summer spent out of the city.

I nodded my head solemnly, accepting my punishment.

I thought wickedly how Stepmother wasn't playing the game well. What an adventure!

"We will travel on Thursday," said Papa. "For I will be driving cattle back from Chicago and it will suit then."

Traveling with Papa! Finally, my hopes had come true!

"I understand," I said, bowing my head and looking very forlorn. "I apologize for the trouble I have caused."

When Josephine heard she said Stepmother wouldn't be happy till she'd packed all of us off.

But I thought that maybe lying and doing poorly in exams was not a bad way to get what you wanted.

Who says the truth wins?

'Huge disaster': Deadly Kerala floods displace over 800,000
Reporting by Al Jazeera, 19 August 2018

More than 800,000 people have been displaced in Kerala, as the death toll from the worst flooding to hit the southern Indian state jumped to at least 370, with losses to infrastructure pegged at almost $3bn.

As the rains subsided on Sunday, relief efforts focused on rescuing those marooned in isolated places for days and airdropping supplies to others, police and officials said.

Kerala has been lashed by torrential monsoon rains since the end of May, triggering landslides and flash floods that have swept away entire villages. Incessant downpours since August 8 have killed more than 190 people and left thousands more stranded.

"In a matter of three to four days, we have been able to move nearly 850,000 people to shelters," TM Thomas Isaac, Kerala's finance minister, told Al Jazeera.

"I think the total number of displaced persons, including those who have been moved to relatives' or friends' houses, would be well over 1.5 million," he added in a phone interview from Alappuzha, Kerala.

On Sunday alone, 22,000 people were evacuated from their homes, but a large number of people continue to voluntarily live in flooded houses.

"We saw many people whose ground floors of their homes were knee and waist-deep in the water," said Al Jazeera's Andrew Thomas, reporting from Andoor.

"They are living upstairs because they want to stay where they are," he said.

"So, the overall figure of people whose homes have been flooded and have been affected by this disaster is in the millions," Thomas added. "It really is a huge disaster in this part of India."

CHAPTER 6
ELLIE

January 22, 2019. San Francisco and Berkeley, California.

Ellie knew she shouldn't stop at Boudin Bakery in Four Embarcadero Center for her usual coffee and sourdough English muffin — she had only fifteen minutes before her first client appointment. But she needed the jump start and ducked in anyway.

She took out her phone, scanning her emails, in an attempt to get a head start. This morning had been a Greek tragedy with Nathan, who normally went into day care happily, clinging to her like a bridesmaid's shapewear, and she'd had to peel his little hands from her shoulders while he'd cried, "No Mama! No!"

She had heard his wails as she walked back to her car. Glancing back, she caught a final glimpse of his little crumpled face before the day-care worker closed the door. She'd sat in the Odyssey and had to take two slow deep breaths before she could start the engine.

The special trip and extended time together in Chicago seemed to have made it harder for Nathan now to detach. They had enjoyed the family time so much; she'd realized how important it was for them all to be together, and she felt guilt at not having visited her parents since the children were born. Strange how it had taken a death to unite them once again.

This morning, she was meeting a new client who was an immigrant from India, and as Ellie raced out the door of Boudin, past the stay-at-home moms and nannies who came to the center's plaza, directly across from the Ferry Building, to enjoy the water features and art displays, she managed to pull up the client's intake file and start reading as the escalator carried her to the second floor of the ILDC.

As she reached the office, she saw that two women dressed in saris, their dark hair in contrast to the beautiful pinks and greens of the silk, were already seated in the waiting room, among a number of other clients and babbling children. They were used to clients bringing their children, as many of the clientele had no childcare or support whatsoever. Books in simple Spanish and donated toys and games had been added over time and were regularly scattered across the waiting room's threadbare carpeted floor.

A set of crutches lay beside the client in the deep-pink sari, and Ellie expected that was Hansa. She had come from Kerala, in India, after the terrible flooding there the previous year, which had left the entire district underwater and caused devastating landslides.

"Half an hour early," whispered the receptionist to Ellie, who sped past, raising her eyebrows in apology. Ellie didn't like to appear flustered and generally didn't. But some mornings, like today with a tragic Nathan and an exhausting weekend behind her, were more difficult than others.

Ellie sat at her desk and took a moment to compose herself, sipping her coffee and nibbling her muffin, before returning to the waiting room to call, "Hansa Nambootiri."

Warily, Hansa stood with her crutches. The woman beside her also rose. Ellie pointed the way and let Hansa set the pace, hopping toward the office, her crutches making a *tap, tap, tap* on the laminate flooring.

Inside her office, Ellie shook hands with a listless Hansa, who barely met her gaze. The younger woman, Hansa's sister, Rashila, she informed Ellie, in contrast, shook her hand firmly and looked her dead in the eye. It was easy to see who the more dominant sister was. Hansa clasped a set of papers to her chest as she sat stiffly in her chair.

"Tell me what happened that brought you here today, in your own words, Hansa," said Ellie, gently as she leaned toward the two women, pen in hand. Ellie preferred not to have a keyboard and computer screen between her and her clients, especially in a first meeting.

Rashila didn't give Hansa a chance to speak. "My sister has a very good case. She was treated very badly, and look how she has been left! She cannot walk properly and can't afford the hospital fees! What can she do?"

Hansa did not look up.

"I can help," said Ellie. "Hansa, if you, in your own words, could tell me what happened?"

"They left oil on the floor!" Rashila cried. "Olive oil! What did they expect would happen? That back room was a death trap! And rats too! Customers buying those things and rats running all around. They should be shut down!"

Ellie inhaled. This wasn't uncommon. The injured worker who would come in had been so beaten down by their situation, often leading to depression and a lack of confidence that meant they could barely speak for themselves. They often brought a more outspoken family member. But Ellie needed to hear from Hansa herself.

"Rashila, I appreciate you coming with your sister today. I can see how much you care about her. Now, if you could let Hansa speak, as I need to hear it from her?"

Rebuke heeded, Rashila reluctantly sat back in her chair.

"I was taking in a delivery," murmured Hansa, after a pause. "We always got most of our deliveries on a Tuesday. You had to unpack the boxes, check the invoices, put them into the system, and get them out onto the shop floor. You had to make room, and you had to try and find somewhere to store the new stock. It was always the busiest day."

"Yes," said Ellie, glad that she was finally getting some detail. Hansa's voice was mouselike, wobbling as she spoke. Rashila squirmed.

"Roberto brought the boxes in from the truck; he opened them up for me, you know, because they came on these pallets. And that day, a big pallet had fallen, and all these little bottles of olive oil had rolled out and smashed, and he was very annoyed and said he wasn't cleaning it up as it wasn't his fault. But I did not think it was my job to clean it up, as I only took in the stock for the shelves, and I also had a shop full of customers."

Ellie nodded intently while taking notes. She sensed Rashila settling down now. The words rushed more urgently from Hansa.

"So, I went back to the shop floor because the atmosphere was very bad, and Roberto was kicking boxes and everything, and I came back later, maybe an hour later, as the shop was busy, but I knew I had to get this stock in or our boss would be very angry, and I walked out, and the oil had leaked all across the floor, and still Roberto had not cleaned it up. And I slipped, right up into the air, and landed on a box of cookies, you know, all packaged up. It was hard, rock hard, and I came down on my knee on the corner, and I felt a pop and, oh the pain! It had gone out of place. I couldn't get up, and I called for Roberto, but he wasn't there, and I lay there for a long time because he never came back, and there was only Fadila in the shop, and she found me because she was going on her lunch, but she couldn't get me off the floor, as I couldn't move. And so they called the ambulance. I was crying. It was terrible."

She finally took a breath, and Ellie could tell she was right back in that moment, reliving the trauma.

Ellie spread out the photos of the stockroom of the discount dollar store in Fremont where Hansa worked. Rashila had included them in the initial intake inquiry, in an envelope of paperwork including a mess of Hansa's medical bills, their travel and visa documents, a flyer they'd found on workers' rights, and screenshot printouts of menacing, passive-aggressive texts from her employer.

The stockroom was a disaster zone.

Exposed wiring hung from the ceiling, looping over patchy holes in the drywall, revealing yards of pink fiberglass that any employee in there would be breathing. Hansa had taken a picture of a hole in the wall, which she said Roberto had punched, to demonstrate the rage issues she'd faced with him, and some close-ups of rodent droppings.

Through the text printouts, Ellie could see that the sisters had been in regular contact about the conditions at the store, and the texts and photographs were good evidence. Hansa had not returned to the store or any other job since her accident.

In her quiet, faltering voice, Hansa explained to Ellie what it had been like to work at the discount dollar store. As well as the endless tasks of unpacking, stocking, stacking shelves, and serving customers (the stock job, she realized, the more Hansa spoke, was certainly part of Roberto's job, which he was shirking), she had been given late-night shifts, week after week, despite requesting that she be scheduled for the shifts she was told she'd be working when she'd first taken the job.

This meant manning and closing the store late at night on her own, next to a convenience mart known to be a hot spot for drug dealers. Shoplifting was rife at the dollar store, something the manager had told Hansa was her fault when it happened and even threatened to deduct from her wages.

"And what have the doctors said about your injury?" asked Ellie kindly. "Going forward."

Hansa met Ellie's gaze for the first time.

"Total knee replacement."

The three women let the silence sit for a moment.

"Well, Hansa," said Ellie, leaning even farther forward to show compassion. "As far as I can see, we have a 'Serious & Willful Misconduct' claim here, alongside the standard underlying Workers' Compensation injury claim. I've read through the text correspondence from your employer, and it's unconscionable. If you would like to me proceed, I can start the paperwork to file with the Workers' Compensation Appeals Board. This will start disability payments for you and keep your treatment going. As for your medical bills, try to put them out of your mind, as we'll be holding the insurance carrier responsible for those — past and future. These cases do tend to take some time — longer than you'd like. But it's the mechanism we have for this sort of claim, and we're here to make sure you receive all of the compensation and benefits available."

"Yes," said Rashila. "That would be very good, thank you."

Ellie nodded. She sensed she hadn't heard the full story, that there was more to this. But it was enough for a first meeting that had been difficult for Hansa.

"If you find anything else in the meantime, correspondence, photographs, or think of anything else you need to add, just send it straight to me."

Ellie took a business card from a holder on her desk and handed it across. Rashila leaned forward to take it so that Hansa didn't have to move. She seemed to anticipate how every movement was now painful for her sister.

"You know, this is my job; I see cases like this every day, and I will do everything in my power to help you, Hansa. You came to the right place."

Hansa did not lift her head but nodded slightly.

Rashila pursed her lips.

"Thank you, Ms. Benvenuto," she said.

Rashila didn't add any more platitudes, but Ellie could tell by her slumped shoulders as she left the office that she finally felt some sense of relief and that they might, just might, be finding the help they needed in their desperate situation.

"You're very welcome, Rashila," she said, as they all made their way, slowly, carefully out to the lobby.

Hansa was terrified to fall again, Ellie realized, as she watched her crutch past reception. She knew how much life could change in an instant, with one small slip.

One moment could change everything forever.

"How was Chicago? Good trip?" asked Joe as Ellie shuffled Nathan and Luca through the door of his spacious townhouse, and stayed on the doorstep as they toddled in, Nathan heading straight for the toys their father kept in a big wooden chest; Luca, for the old beanbag Joe had taken with him after the divorce.

"Yes, good," said Ellie, wanting to be polite, but really, really needing to be down those steps and back in her car.

It was early evening as she dropped the kids off, and she felt guilty again about all the shuttling around that day; they had only flown in from Chicago the previous evening, and after Nathan's unraveling at day care that morning, she'd had to pick him up after work, rush home to meet Luca off his bus, and fold everyone back into the car to drop them off at Joe's so that she could get to UC Berkeley Law School where she was supervising at the Workers' Rights Clinic that evening.

And another awe-inspiring Tuesday of acrobatic, suspenseful, time-space-defying mothering would be commemorated by ... no one.

The clinic was a partnership between the school's Civil Rights Clinic and the ILDC and offered a double whammy of interesting employment law lectures from expert guest speakers for law school clinic students for the first hour, followed by two more hours of practicum, where the students interviewed and advised workers on their rights and whether they might be able to take legal action. The workers who came to the clinic got the advice for free, but it had to be supervised by licensed lawyers, which is where Ellie came in, taking turns with other ILDC attorneys on a rotation.

"It was nice to see Mom and Dad and spend the time, you know," said Ellie as she turned for the steps. "The boys loved the snow!"

"I'll bet," said Joe.

Joe had offered to come to Ellie's apartment for convenience, but Ellie didn't really want her ex-husband spending hours in what was now her own personal and private space. Neither could they stay the night, with Joe's early work hours and Luca's bus set to arrive at her apartment in the morning. This did mean she'd be getting the boys to bed late on clinic supervision nights like this. Perhaps that was selfish, but she couldn't keep piling on more reasons to feel guilty.

"And how are you feeling ... you know, after ...?"

Enzo. Joe meant Enzo.

"Fine!" said Ellie, brightly. Too brightly. "Well, I mean, you know."

She turned away again. This was awkward. But he was trying with her — to be a friend.

"I've been reading this diary," she said, turning back again and now realizing something. "I found it in Enzo's house, in his things; it's the diary of my great-great-grandmother, Theodora — *Teddy*."

"No way," said Joe.

"I was reading it on the plane home, I'm nearly finished with it, and I was thinking of our family and Enzo and all about this young woman that would have been his grandmother, and all the time I was reading, I felt ..."

Her voice trailed off.

"I dunno. It felt comforting. Not sad."

Ellie checked her watch. She hesitated for a half-second, the weight of the diary still lingering in her thoughts.

"I really gotta run!" she said and, taking the steps two at a time, hopped back into her car.

One of the perks of working at the ILDC that, in fact, did "underpay" her, as was not lost on her father, was a parking space at Four Embarcadero Center, which was right at a BART station, the San Francisco Bay Area's commuter rail system. Ellie parked her car to take BART to the downtown Berkeley station to avoid rush-hour traffic across the Bay Bridge. It was an easy walk to the UC Berkeley campus from there. It was also an opportunity to keep reading Teddy's diary. She found herself thinking about the diary and longing to pick it up again whenever she had a few spare minutes. Every time she'd read it, she felt sucked back in time, like she was *right there*. She thought of nothing else while she read, and her heart sank that she was nearing the end of it now. She savored the pages, one by one, lost to her relation, now long gone.

She eked out the last few pages, not wanting her connection to Teddy to end — like a fine wine, she savored each line, sip by sip. As long as she was reading that diary, she was connected to Enzo and Genevieve. It was hard to explain, but that was how she felt. Grief could be funny like that. Better to dance with it than to wrestle.

The one regret she had about her weekend in Chicago was not getting round to finding Genevieve's things down in the basement. Her mother hadn't seemed interested, and they'd been busy, so Ellie hadn't pushed it.

She felt drained before she even made her way to the small lecture room. Professor Eleanor Hayes already stood before the new class of law clinic students, her presence no-nonsense.

The walls, lined with legal tomes that bore witness to decades of jurisprudential evolution, seemed to lean in, as if eager to contribute to the wisdom she was about to impart — although the reality was that most of the books were rarely taken from their shelves, modern digital research methods having taken over.

"Good evening, everyone," Professor Hayes began. "Tonight, we delve into the fundamentals of employment discrimination law, an active and constantly evolving field that tests both our legal acumen and our commitment to equality."

She paced slowly in front of the whiteboard, clicking her laser pointer to life and illuminating a slide titled "The Anatomy of an Employment Discrimination Case."

"First, let's understand the foundation and establishing what we call a *prima facie* case," she continued, pointing to the first bullet point. "Discrimination in the workplace occurs when an employee is treated unfavorably — not just for any reason but because of a *protected category* such as race, color, religion, sex, sexual orientation, pregnancy or related condition, national origin, age, disability, to name a few. These protected categories are cataloged in federal and state legislation and, in turn, interpreted by the courts. The words 'discrimination' and 'harassment' often get bandied about casually, but they are legal terms of art with specific elements that must be satisfied. Just because something is unfair doesn't mean it's illegal or actionable. To proceed, a discrimination or harassment case must have a legal 'hook' — a connection to a protected category."

Ellie smiled, memories washing over her. Years ago, she had sat where these students now sat — fresh-faced, eager, unaware of how much the real world would test their ideals. Now, she was working in the exact field being outlined by Hayes. Almost all of the cases she handled at the ILDC came back to a prejudice from the employer, not always apparent at first. The students, a mix of earnest alongside apprehensive and mostly young faces, typed notes into their laptops as Hayes transitioned from point to point.

"Identifying a potential claim involves not just recognizing these biases but understanding how they manifest in hiring, promotions, job assignments, and terminations, in other words, actionable *adverse actions*. It's about the subtleties, the patterns, and, most crucially, the impacts."

Hayes clicked to a new slide featuring a case study involving a qualified female employee overlooked for a promotion in favor of a less qualified male colleague.

"Let's dissect this," she said, her tone now more interactive. "What aspects of this situation suggest discrimination? How do we approach analyzing the viability of this scenario as a colorable claim?"

A hand shot up before Hayes had even finished her question. She nodded to a young woman in the second row.

"If the promotion criteria were supposedly based on performance metrics, but we can demonstrate that those metrics were applied inconsistently, would that suffice for a prima facie case?" the earnest student asked, her voice tinged with both curiosity and uncertainty.

Hayes's eyes lit up with approval. "Inconsistency in the application of supposedly objective criteria, for example, height and weight requirements that used to be in place for flight attendants and firefighters, can indeed suggest bias. This is what we would call a *disparate impact* case. The other typical manifestation of discrimination is called a *disparate treatment* case. Establishing a prima facie case doesn't require absolute proof of discrimination initially. In fact, most evidence is circumstantial. It's about showing that an unlawful motive could plausibly be at play and then a nexus between that motive and the actions that were taken and whether those qualify as actionable adverse actions."

She walked back to the podium, tapping the screen to bring up a flowchart of the legal process in such cases, from first exhausting internal complaint procedures within the workplace to filing a complaint with the Equal Employment Opportunity Commission (EEOC) to the potential for litigation.

"As future defenders of justice, you'll often start here, at the EEOC. It's crucial to understand their procedures, the importance of timely filing, and how mediation can often resolve issues. Eighty-five percent of employment discrimination cases are settled short of trial."

Professor Hayes spent the rest of her lecture diving deeper: gathering evidence, the importance of meticulous documentation, and the ethical considerations that must guide their actions. Each point was punctuated with real cases, the nuances illustrating the harsh realities of the legal landscape.

As the lecture neared its end, Hayes looked over her class, a sense of solemnity settling over the room.

"Remember," she concluded, "this field isn't just about legal victories; it's about people. It's about fairness, dignity, and making our society a little more just with every case. For the next two hours, you will be taking in information from workers waiting in the library who may or may not have a valid claim, then debriefing with your mentoring attorneys here in this room before returning to the worker with legal advice that you explain to them in an understandable way."

When Hayes dismissed the students, Ellie rose from her seat and quickly made her way to the professor, who was collapsing her laptop and rolling up the charger.

"Professor Hayes," said Ellie, reaching out her hand to shake the seasoned veteran's. "Ellie Benvenuto, I'm one of the supervising attorneys tonight — ILDC? I just wanted to say your lecture resonated with me. I'm new to this area of law, and it's been a challenge. But I appreciate how you summed it up. 'Making our society a little more just with every case you handle.'"

Professor Hayes thrust her laptop into Ellie's chest.

"Carry this to my car, will you? I have arthritis and there was no one here to help me earlier."

Taken aback, Ellie blinked.

"Oh. Sure," she said and watched as the prickly professor packed up the rest of her things.

Sheesh, thought Ellie as she followed Hayes out of the now-empty lecture hall, toward the parking lot. *So much for "It's about people."* She made a mental note should she ever have the pleasure of addressing her own students. "Kindness and empathy go a long way," she would tell them. "These qualities are not a 'nice to have.' They're an *imperative*..."

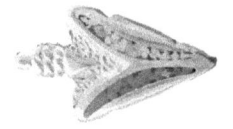

CHAPTER 7

TEDDY

June 30, 1867. Evanston, Illinois, near Chicago.

All the meat for New York and Boston is shipped in alive, and New York, by all accounts, is a dirty, crowded place, with a great appetite for hogs and cows and bull calves, but Papa, knowing the Boston market best, liked to drive his animals there, mostly.

It takes a long time to fetch the animals, drive them to the stockyard, fatten them up in the feedlots so they'll pack all the muscle on, get them onto the railcars and unload and feed them and reload them again at Suspension Bridge and again at Albany before carting them right into the city, to the slaughterhouses, to feed the hungry mouths of the good people of the city.

I don't have much of a taste for meat, but Stepmother was forever creating dishes with the cook which she thought were "French" and once they made a raw beef dish, with the meat served pink as my tongue all mixed up with onions and capers and I refused to eat it, because I thought it was something a savage might eat on the plains.

The Indians were well known to take the meat of the buffalo and eat it right there and then, all warm with blood squirting down their chins. And here we were, doing the same only with onions and capers.

Savages.

I told Stepmother I'd stick to my beans. She said I had no class. I thought to myself she had no taste in that sour mouth of hers.

Papa made some stops on our train journey to Chicago to make arrangements for his return when he would be driving the cattle. Something I noticed about Papa is how he always smiles at everyone he meets, how he looks at the men in the stockyards and coach houses real hard and pumps their hands up and down and says, "Good to see you, sir!"

They always smiled back. He had a joke for everyone, a pinch of tobacco or snuff if they wanted it, but he always offered it whether they did or not and it was easy to see how he had made a success in his line of the cattle business.

Papa has a charm about him, I reckon. People like him. He could get anything he wanted from anyone, I thought, as we traveled the thousand miles toward Chicago, past Albany, past the cool, misty, magical Niagara Falls, that Papa said were always his favorite part of the journey, on to Cleveland before making our way to Chicago.

I want to be just like Papa.

My uncle's farm is located twelve miles outside the city and for the final part of the journey Papa hired two horses. I liked climbing up on the mare and feeling her big thick back under me, solid. They insisted I used a saddle, and I didn't want to as that was never the way I rode a horse in North Sandwich, but Papa said I had to and so I had to sit on that uncomfortable thing making my back sore, the whole way along. Papa laughed and said I was like a Comanche Indian, the way I rode a horse, and I didn't like that one bit.

It was a lot of time to be spending together, the most I could remember and even though he ribbed me a bit, Papa always had a fondness for me, I got to thinking. Maybe it was that Stepmother clouded it a bit. I wanted to ask him about Mama, for I found that my memories of her were fading but I was too timid and worried that he would scold me for it.

"Papa," I said, as we made our way down the road, the rhythm of the horses' hooves *clip-clop*ping ever so gentle, because I'd got to thinking how we'd be separated soon, and I'd be left with Uncle and his family who I didn't have much acquaintance with. "You know when it's time for me to come back, at the end of the summer?"

"Yes," Papa said, all wary.

"Well, I was thinking, instead of me catching the train, why don't we arrange it so that I can come with you with the herd, driving? I'd have all that farming experience with Uncle and all by then."

Papa burst out laughing.

"Teddy, you should have been born a boy!"

"Yessir," I said. "More's the pity."

"What would Stepmother think of you driving cattle with the boys?"

I didn't care what she thought, truth be told.

"I could do it, I swear!"

"Ladies don't swear."

He laughed then because he could see that I meant what I said and I suppose, spending all that time with me, he realized that I didn't very much like the rules of being a girl and I guess he felt sorry for me a little.

"We'll see," he said and then I had hope.

Maybe I could have an adventure on the way back, just Papa and me and the other herders, making our own way across all that land, past those rivers, stopping right by the grand Niagara Falls. I just have to get through the summer first. Learn to be a farmer. Do my chores. Which I know I can do rightly. Didn't we keep fowl and a horse and a cow ourselves back in North Sandwich? There'd be nothing to it, I reckoned.

Nothing to it at all.

July 7, 1867

Well, turns out, I know nothing. Not a damn thing.

What I thought we had in North Sandwich turns out to be barely a farm at all. What a yak I was when I imagined this farm in my head.

Uncle's farm is fifty acres and a fine farm it is too, all laid out in ten-acre fields, fenced in. In one he raises corn, in another wheat, and one he keeps for hay. There are acres for pastures, for clover, for the seed and fodder, and for sorghum (for molasses).

One of the best parts of the farm is the two-acre orchard and the same size again for the garden that supplies the house with vegetables and flowers. Uncle had been out to California and made money mining and so he'd been able to buy up this whole farm himself. I was a bit envious when I realized how Uncle and his wife and my two cousins lived.

They had everything they ever wanted on this farm.

Aunty is nothing like Stepmother. She laughs and bakes and sews and smiles all the time at Uncle and the children. I didn't know women who ran houses could be like that.

My cousins are younger than me and see me as quite the curiosity and I quite like their little heads bobbing along trailing after me on the farm.

At first, I was put to work in the house with Aunty, but after a time, they could see that I longed to be outside and as I kept offering to do heavy work in the yard, in the outhouses, and in the orchard and fields, Uncle said I could give a hand because Papa had already told him that I had the strength of any young man and wasn't afraid of hard work. Papa didn't say that to *me*, of course, but Uncle said it as I forked hay high up onto a hayrick.

"Well, your father said you weren't afraid of hard work, and I guess there it is? Have you any experience with horses, Teddy?"

"Yessir," I said, and this was true for I had ridden the horse we had at home bareback all over North Sandwich and tried out most of the neighbors' mares and geldings too.

What I didn't know was Uncle wasn't just talking about trotting around the farm but the breaking in of horses! Uncle had a yearling stallion called Devil and it was wild as a mad March hare, bucking and jumping and yelling in the paddock. Uncle started off by putting heavy sacks of grain on his back to get him used to the weight and then he climbed up and leaned on him, which the stallion hated and bucked and jumped and tried to throw him off again and again, but Uncle persisted.

He did this every evening for a week, until finally he progressed to putting his whole body weight on the horse and then sitting on him over and over again and even though the stallion threw him many times, Uncle seemed to be able to just roll away. He'd go right back over to that fierce beast and start again. In two weeks, Uncle had that horse cantering round the paddock, his head high in the bridle and under total control.

"Easy does it," Uncle said.

I think he is one brave man.

I am still half afraid of Devil, because Devil by name, Devil by nature, and I keep out of his way whenever I have to cross into the paddock.

No point taking any chances when it comes to nature, I think.

July 29, 1867

And now I have some news to report.

I don't suppose I'm proud of it and actually, I feel quite foolish, and I begged Uncle not to send word home about it all, but he said, under the circumstances, he just had to and so he sent a letter to Papa and Stepmother so we're waiting on their return response.

I just hope they don't call on me to go home. I would surely hate that. Things had been going very well here on the farm, even though I've not been here long. I'd come along a lot with the livestock Uncle keeps and the planting and growing of crops, for I enjoyed so much being out in the fields, doing all the work there was to be done.

Uncle got some trust in me and showed me much of the runnings of the farm. He taught me how to store the feed properly, how to spread it out and manage it so all the animals had enough. He showed me the books for the farm where he wrote down all his costings and seeds purchased and manure and the calendar where he wrote what harvests were due when and how many workers they would need to hire and for when, depending on weather changes.

Maybe it was because I was blood, or maybe it was because Uncle had no daughters of his own, but he took quite the shine to me and he got me out into the fields to help with all manner of jobs on the farm, which I liked because I'd discovered that being out in the open, with the sun beating down and the breeze sailing by, with butterflies and insects buzzing, made a girl probably the happiest she could be in her whole life.

Well, four days ago, because everyone's been counting the time since, I was out with Uncle in the field, and he was harrowing the wheat field because we're to plant it up for the August harvest. Uncle was driving the harrow with a pair of mules who he said were only half broken in, when Aunty came all the way up to the field and said she wasn't happy with my youngest cousin's fever, who she'd been looking after all night and the previous day.

"I think he needs a doctor," she told Uncle, and I could see the worry in his eyes.

Uncle looked to the harrow and back to Aunty and then at me and that's when I got the bravery and idea because I had been helping him drive the harrow and Uncle had showed me the full technique of how to make sure you lined it all up and didn't miss a spot at all.

"I can do this!" I said, trying to be as much help as possible while also trying not to let my voice sound all squeaky like a child. I knew I was growing up on this farm, was nearly grown now completely and I wanted the responsibility.

"I don't know," Uncle said, shaking his head. "These mules are only half broken in. I think I'll bring them in, and we'll go again tomorrow."

But it was a nice fine day for harrowing and leaving till tomorrow ran the risk of the rain coming in and making the ground muddy and heavy and too wet for the task and I could see that Uncle was torn.

"I can do it!" I said again, firmly.

"If we leave now, we'll catch the doctor in his surgery," said Aunty.

"I can drive them, Uncle," I said again.

And so, Uncle left me in charge, going off with my worried aunty and cousin toward town and oh, how big I felt in the field with those two beasts under my control and that metal harrow, sailing along the top of the soil like a boat on water, sending up stones and old straw and my concentration on nothing but the land in front of me, up and down, forward and back, tilling that soil for the food that we would grow and eat.

I felt at one with the world, a part of nature itself, and I felt that I had learned a new skill, and that perhaps, like my forebears before me, I could turn my hand to anything, farming now, mining maybe in the future, for it was certain I had a way with these things.

Proudly I looked back to where I had harrowed all by myself and I suppose the Lord does say that pride comes before a fall, for on that very turn, the buckle on the lines got caught and I had to stop the mules and reach over to clear the line, but, with my hand reaching out, the damn animal got spooked and he bucked and took off, fast. I tried to grab the lines, but the mule went at such a speed that it lifted the harrow right up into the air and as I fell forward and under it, it came right back down, the last long metal tooth on the right striking me deep into my back.

The tooth went in and came right back out again, meaning I wasn't impaled, but the wound was very deep for that tooth was many inches long and I could feel where it had gone down, deep, as though to my very bowels at the front. I lay there, shocked, as the two stupid mules ran on, and wondered what on earth I should do, all alone in that field and with the blood trickling from my back, thinking that surely, surely, I was punctured the whole way through inside.

I got up and managed to stumble back to the house, the energy coming from somewhere, because by the time I got in the door I near collapsed in the kitchen. There was no one else there only my older cousin, who'd been left behind to wait for Uncle and Aunt's return.

"Call Charlie," I told him, for I knew that Charlie, one of Uncle's farmhands, was in the orchard and I could not think of who else might be around to assist.

When Charlie came he went all white in the face and he said, "All right, Miss, you'll be all right," but I knew by his demeanor that this wasn't what he really thought at all and I must have passed out then because when I awoke I heard the hooves of a horse leaving the yard and when I awoke again, I was in bed, having been put there by someone and there was a big wad on my back and the doctor, the very doctor Uncle and Aunty had gone to see, was now leaning over me with his tobacco breath. As my eyes cleared, I could see that Uncle and Aunty were in the bedroom too, looking very worried.

"You have a very deep wound," said the doctor firmly. "You must stay in bed, lay just like we have you now, no movement if you can help it and no rolling backwards. Tummy forward, alright?"

There was such a throbbing in my back that I thought there was no way I'd be able to roll back onto it anyway, but at the same time, there was an edge about my head, a blurriness or a cloud, as if the pain was being kept back, even though it was all still there. The doctor told me he'd given me something for the pain and dressed the wound.

"You're a very lucky young lady," he said. "Five minutes before you die you won't be any nearer death than you were when that tooth struck you. It went in less than an eighth of an inch of your spinal column!"

I suppose the spinal column is important.

I could see Aunty's face then and she looked as though she might cry, but being quite a brave woman, she held it all together. It was later that Uncle told me he would have to inform my father and I begged him not to send the letter for surely they would all agree that it turned out I was not suitable for farm work at all and I would be better off at home in Boston sewing hankies all day.

"I'm sorry, Uncle," I said, battling tears that kept damn appearing round my eyes. I was thinking how the field remained unharrowed and the rain was closing in. "I'm ever so sorry."

"Accidents happen," he said. "I just wish I'd never left you with those untamed animals. But I guess we know one thing now."

I looked up at him from the bed, feeling all that pain weaving and waving in my back.

"Nothing keeps a good Ellis down!"

The good Ellis was me!

I sure was happy at him saying that. I had never really heard compliments like that before, but here on this farm, Uncle and Aunt are quick with the kind words. It was a very nice feeling. I could grow used to it alright. And so I hope against hope, that I will not be summoned home now over all this fuss.

I'm ever so sorry for making such a stupid mistake. I told Uncle I'd never do anything like it again.

"Teddy," he said, "we all make mistakes, but likely you won't make this one again!"

I told him I would definitely be keeping away from harrow spikes from now on. Definitely.

And for some reason, that made him laugh.

August 8, 1867

Papa's letter came! He did not say I had to go home!

Instead, he said he was very sorry to hear of my accident but that he knew I was a strong young woman and that, all going well, the best thing was to recuperate here on the farm, for putting me on a train when I was so badly injured would not be a good idea.

I was ever so relieved. No more wondering and waiting.

Last night, when Aunty thought I was asleep, for I've been sleeping ever so much since my wounding, I heard her whisper to Uncle about the letter, that more likely it was Stepmother who didn't care to look after me and that was the real reason my father had suggested I stay on the farm.

That stung a little, to think that perhaps Papa would prefer to leave me 1,000 miles from home than have me back in Boston to look after me, but at the same time it was what I wanted, to be left here near Chicago for the summer, to get back to what I wanted to be doing, not lying in bed all day, eating up the snacks Aunty brought.

Alright then, I quite like the snack eating part.

I've been reading the *New York Ledger*, which Uncle has collected for years, and the back numbers are all packed in a box in order, so I don't have to wait a whole week to find out what happened to the heroine who was left on the verge of a precipice, one foot already slipped over, the other sliding; I can just reach for the next issue and continue my exciting reading!

Always it is the woman who needs saving. Never is it the man who is saved by the woman, but surely that happens sometimes? I wonder if there will ever be any stories about thirteen-year-old girls who get injured and manage to drag themselves to safety, without any help at all!

Perhaps I'll have to write them myself!

I like the pirate stories for they remind me of Boston on the coast but what surprises me is how much I've been enjoying the Indian stories and tales of the pioneers saddling up and going "out west," coming across many different tribes along the way, some who are peaceful, but most who are bloodthirsty scalp hunters and you have to keep out of their way at all costs.

I'm nearly at the end of the box now. I reckon I will finish the last magazine by tomorrow and it's good timing because Doc comes tomorrow, and Uncle says he might give me the all clear.

August 13, 1867

I finished all the *New York Ledger*s! And ... I got the all clear! My back still hurts something awful, but the doctor says I have healed exceptionally fast, which he puts down to my health and age, and I've already returned to my duties on the farm.

Aunty says I need to take it slowly, but with the medicine she gives me, I'm certainly on the mend. Uncle says it's good to have me back.

August 18, 1867

Well, today was a day!

Seen as I've been mostly back to myself, Aunty and Uncle decided to take me to Chicago City, where Uncle had business and Aunty said she and I could visit some stores to buy household items and maybe treat ourselves to a cream tea.

Whenever Stepmother suggested these outings, I felt squirmy, but with Aunty it was different, for she's kindly and witty and we have talk of all sorts and I never think she's looking down her nose at me.

The streets were so wide in Chicago, and it felt good to be among all those buildings and people again. Though I love the farm, the city is familiar now, too.

Aunty told me today as we made our way around Field & Leiter dry goods shop, that she and Uncle have enjoyed having me on the farm and that I'm welcome back next year too, should I like it!

The unfortunate reality is that in just a few short weeks, the harvest will be over and it'll be time for me to make my way eastwards again, for school will be starting up again and I have to go, whether I like it or not. Stepmother was very adamant about that in her last letter.

Aunty bought me a new pair of leather boots and two dresses off the hanger, which I don't mind at all as the cotton is soft and the necklines dainty without being fussy, as I don't like much fuss. She let me choose three new hair ribbons and a set of handkerchiefs and I was rather pleased with my purchases packaged and tied up with string. I didn't feel bad about Aunty buying them either as she said it was payment for all the work I've been doing!

We went to a store called P. B. Weare & Co. where we were to meet Uncle and when we walked in, Uncle waved us in and introduced us to Mr. Portus Weare himself. I thought he was a very noble looking man, bald headed, the remainder of what hair he'd left all neatly trimmed and tidy. I saw him shake Aunty's hand and he seemed to appreciate her plain good looks for Aunty was as hearty as any woman I'd seen in the countryside.

"This is my niece, Teddy," said Uncle and I reached for P. B. Weare's hand too and shook it. His hand was soft, with no calluses, not like Uncle's or even my hands after all the hard work this summer.

"This one's bright as a button!" Uncle smiled and then he told Mr. Weare all about my accident, which I thought was a little embarrassing when you heard it spoken out loud.

"Wow, siree." Mr. Weare whistled. "A strong 'un!"

"Not a fly on her," said Uncle.

I felt bashful at such words, but my cheeks did not glow red which I was most grateful for. They had a terrible habit of doing that lately, the blood rushing to them with the heat of a furnace on a steam train.

As we made our goodbyes, I opened the door of the store with my head turned and walked slap bang into a man coming right in, the smell of his body odor going up my nose, my face slamming into his chest.

"Oh my!" I said, jumping back. "Beggin' your pardon, mister!"

The man looked down and I saw that he had the brownest eyes I'd ever seen with bronze flecks, and his skin was bronzed too.

He put his hand out and touched my elbow to ensure I was steady.

"Sincere apologies," he said and he smiled.

And there it was. That damn furnace. Burning my cheeks like the flaming fires of hell.

"George!" said Mr. Weare. "Do you mind watching where you're going?"

I figured George wanted to say that the incident had not been his fault, that it was in fact MY fault that the collision had occurred in the first place. But George just laughed, his teeth white against his skin, his mouth wide and friendly. He stepped aside and half bowed.

"I will Mr. Weare," he said and he winked at me. "I will."

When we got out of the shop, Uncle leading us to where he'd parked the phaeton, I touched my face and found that my cheeks were still glowing red. I'm not sure if it was the fumble or the feeling of the man's chest against my nose, but either way, I felt butterflies all up in my tummy and realized that it wasn't something I'd felt before.

Hot and curious and embarrassed and excited all rolled into one.

Something was happening to me, I thought, although if you asked me to bet money on what, I wouldn't have been able to tell you.

I will be returning to Boston a different person, I expect. Theodora Ellis, calloused, canny, more worldly wise.

Battle scarred.

Tough.

Ready to take on whatever else life heaves at me!

CHAPTER 8
ELLIE

February 7, 2019. Sacramento and San Francisco, California.

Ellie strapped Nathan tightly into his car seat, feeling the heavy mist of the Bay's morning marine layer dripping on her back and hair. When she had both boys buckled in and the engine started, she caught a glimpse of herself in the rearview mirror. The minimal makeup she'd quickly applied had already melted. And her hair. So much for the swishy, shiny look. It was just going to be one of those bad hair days!

As she drove through the morning traffic approaching the Presidio, Ellie glanced at Nathan's little face peering out the window and felt her heart ache at his quietness. He'd been withdrawn ever since they'd come back from Chicago. It was as though he'd gotten a taste of what it was like to spend all day with her, and he was resisting returning to day care. He wasn't getting as much of her attention as he deserved, she knew. It was Luca, with all his extra needs, that took up most of her spare time, for in the evenings she worked with him on word recognition and picture cards and charted his notes and progression in the reports the MIND Institute had asked her to fill out. As Nathan was doing just fine, he was often left to amuse himself. No matter how thinly she spread herself, it seemed impossible to balance everyone's needs, and she woke up each new day prepared to fail all over again.

A pileup on Highway 80-East to Sacramento deposited Ellie and Luca ten minutes late for their appointment. Luca could always sense her stress levels when they were high and could act out, so she took deep breaths as she rushed into reception, apologizing.

She seemed to be doing a lot of that lately — rushing and apologizing.

Five minutes later, with Luca handed off for his appointment, she was seated at the café, mascara still smudged, hair frizzing and unruly, her vintage jacket giving off an odor as it dried (dry-clean only, thank you San Francisco fog), with Teddy's diary in her hand.

Finally, her adrenaline began to slow. Finally, she could relax into this moment, over her hot chai latte, a treat she permitted herself on these Sacramento trips. Today, she had also indulged in a *pain au chocolat* and, as she bit into it, the flakes fluttered all over the diary. She went to blow them away, just as a man in green scrubs approached and asked, "Is this seat taken?"

The doctor's timing was mortifying, if not comical. Ellie blew the flakes right into his space, across his hands, some landing and sticking to his groin area.

"Oh my God!" exclaimed Ellie. "I am so sorry!"

He laughed.

Ellie looked up to see a doctor she recognized but had never spoken to. He was tall and robust, carrying himself effortlessly, his posture graceful and poised.

"Don't worry." He smiled again.

Ellie stood quickly, took her napkin and began flapping it toward his scrubs to dust off her pastry shower. When she realized what she was doing — she was very close to his groin — she sat back down again abruptly and shook her head in disbelief at her actions.

The doctor looked a little bemused at her strange napkin dance.

"I really am sorry," she said, and she felt a blush rise in her face. "I'm … I … I don't know."

The doctor sat down in the chair and put his tray on the table.

"You're fine," he said. "Honestly, as long as you don't mind that I sit here?"

Ellie looked around. The café had completely filled up with staff on breaks joining other parents and guardians who had taken their charges to the institute that day. Normally she preferred her own space for these precious quiet moments to herself, but sometimes it happened that the tables at the small café had to be shared.

She glanced at the doctor and nodded, before turning back to Teddy's diary. He looked like Hansa, and she presumed he was of Indian origin. His speech was accented too.

Finding it hard to concentrate on the writing in front of her, she glanced up again to notice the doctor studying the diary.

"Is that yours?" he asked. "The diary?"

"Not mine," said Ellie. "Unless you think I look like I was born in 1854."

The doctor broke into a grin. "It's a well-guarded medical secret that a steady diet of flaky pastries reverses the aging process, so you could be very well preserved."

Ellie giggled — actually giggled. In her troll-like state, it must have made her look like the Mad Hatter's first cousin. "I'll be sure to increase my dosage starting tomorrow. And don't worry, your secret is safe with me."

The doctor nodded with a satisfied smile. "But wow, is it that old?"

"Yep." Ellie smiled. "It's my great-great-grandmother's. I found it recently and have been reading it … whenever I get a chance. Which is not often."

"Where was she from?" asked the doctor.

"Born near Boston, and so far she's been to Chicago, but I don't know where she goes next. Actually, I don't know anything about her, really."

"So, an adventure story?"

"Kinda. She has to have somehow met my great-great-grandfather, right? And I'm pretty sure he lived most of this life in San Francisco."

"Well, our family house near Chennai is two hundred years old, and all the grandfathers have their paintings on the wall."

Chennai. So, he was from the southeast of India. Hansa, from Kerala, had come from the most southern end of the country.

"But none of the women," said Ellie. "On the wall?"

"No. You're right; none of the women are on the wall. I don't know much about my great-great-grandmother either."

"I'll bet," said Ellie.

She noticed the doctor's name tag. *Dr. Samarjit Varma*. She tried to go back to her reading, but as she listened to his scrapings on the bowl, she couldn't help but look back up.

"Will you have long to wait?" he asked kindly.

"It depends," said Ellie. "I'm waiting for my son. Today he's having an eye-tracking test, and if that doesn't work out, they might try it again later or wait till next week."

"I understand how these things can go. I work in neurology. So, you visit regularly?"

"Yep," said Ellie. "Usually Thursday, though depends on the clinic and my schedule and what they need to get done."

Dr. Varma had the kindest eyes, Ellie noticed. Dark, thoughtful, and deep. My, he was handsome. It was rude to stare, but she didn't want to look away. Why of all days had she met this lovely-looking doctor when she was looking the worst she had looked … possibly ever?

The doctor drained his juice. Break over.

"Well, I hope the adventure continues," he said, pointing to the diary. "I'm Samarjit Varma. People call me *Sam*."

"Ellie Benvenuto."

She didn't reach out her hand for Sam to shake, but she wanted to. Somehow, it felt too formal — too businesslike — for the easy warmth between them.

"Nice to meet you, Ellie," he said. "See you around, I'm sure."

"Bye." Ellie smiled, consciously smoothing down her rebel hair.

Phew, she thought as Sam walked away; she noticed he moved as though he'd been trained, like a dancer or gymnast or in some other exacting athletic discipline.

Pressure off. Time to try to relax again. Back to Teddy's diary ... only ... there was her phone!

"Ms. Benvenuto," said the receptionist at Luca's clinic — Ellie recognized the voice immediately; she always called when it was time to collect Luca. "Luca's ready for you now. The test didn't go as planned unfortunately, so we're going to try again this afternoon. His next appointment will be in forty-five minutes, if you could come pick him up now?"

Ellie sighed and slid Teddy's diary back into her bag.

There went the break.

Still, as she left the café, meeting Sam had felt unexpectedly inspiring.

The workers' rights clinic that evening was held at UC Hastings College of Law, at San Francisco's Civic Center, an easier journey for Ellie than out to Berkeley, but still, the class falling on the same day as Luca's MIND Institute appointment was a marathon. The workers' rights clinic operated at both the Berkeley and San Francisco law school campuses, to accommodate the guest lecturers and meet the needs of the client population that came to the clinics.

Tonight's lecturer was the one and only Ruby Martinez, who was not only the founding director of the Center for WorkLife Law at the law school, but, in Ellie's considered opinion, a living legend.

Just home from one of her stints testifying before Congress, Ellie wouldn't have been surprised to witness Ruby's arrival via helicopter landing on the roof. Regularly sought out by the media and juggling a zillion speaking invitations, Ruby was a wiry, indefatigable, no-nonsense legal scholar and activist. Ellie was excited to meet her that night and saw it as a mark of her character that she would make time to mentor students when she had so many demands on her schedule.

Ellie, as the day played out, had no time to go home to make herself more presentable than a mom on day three of "dry shampoo will fix it." She'd just about managed to drop the boys off with Joe before landing at the law school's main building, five minutes ahead of Ruby's arrival.

Aware that she was, again, not putting her best foot forward, Ellie grumbled to herself as she scanned the lecture room, but when she turned and spied Ruby, she realized she need not have worried.

Ruby's auburn hair was closely cropped, and she was dressed in khakis and Allbirds, devoid of jewelry or other frivolities. She looked ready to march on Washington at a moment's notice with spare bottles of water and trail mix stashed in her knapsack rather than tutor a class of law students. Ellie immediately felt at ease and warmly shook Ruby's hand, who smiled back. *Some departure from Professor Hayes, huh?* There was no time to chat, as Ellie was immediately called away by a student needing assistance accessing the adjoining room.

When Ruby called the class to order five minutes later, a particular hush descended that, to Ellie, signaled the understanding of the talent that stood before them. Ruby began to speak, addressing the students with the intensity of low rolling thunder.

"Let's get started, everyone. By now, you understand the basics of a workplace discrimination cause of action: prima facie case, protected category, adverse action. Now, it's time to get more nuanced. Not everything fits neatly into a category. Just as a client may believe they have a strong case when they don't, the reverse can also be true: a skilled attorney learns to identify legally actionable situations that a client may not see, or recognize how biases can exist adjacent to a protected category even if not explicitly covered by established law. This is a constantly evolving, fast-paced area of legal specialty, and if you choose it, expect no self-driving cars; you can't fall asleep at the wheel."

The students chuckled. Ruby used the remote clicker to bring up her first slide.

"One example of adjacent bias is caregiver discrimination. It's something that we are actively working on at the Center for WorkLife Law. Although caregiver status is not a protected category, women disproportionately perform caregiving work and thus, it acts as a *de facto* form of gender-based discrimination in the workplace."

Ellie sat up straighter to listen, as Ruby, just limbering up, pressed on.

"Caregiving work is what makes all other work possible. Think about it."

Ruby waited, arms crossed with her direct gaze moving from student to student, letting them ponder her words. After a protracted pause, she advanced to the next slide, depicting a graph, and began to rattle off facts and statistics.

"Failing to shore up the childcare industry means holding back nearly every sector of the economy. Seventy-five percent of care work worldwide is performed by women and girls, is unpaid or low-wage, and is heavily weighted to groups that are traditionally marginalized. It has a profound impact on gender inequality and deepens poverty. In all regions of the world, mothers experience a wage penalty of about 7 percent per child. In the US, it's about 4 percent. Childbearing is seen as an instability and indicator that women are less committed to their careers, all the while they are held to higher performance standards than non-mothers. Top-income earners have less of a penalty than low-income earners, so those who can least afford it pay the most penalty."

Ellie sat glued to her chair, Ruby's words ping-ponging at speed around her mind. *Penalty. Per child. Higher performance standards. Less committed to their careers.* That was exactly how she'd been made to feel at Hutton & Fetterer.

Ruby momentarily relented her rapid-fire oration and looked out again among the students to add, "This gap by women is never … regained … over … time. In fact, at the current rate, it will take more than 250 years to close the gender pay gap."

Ruby advanced to the next slide and continued at a heightened volume and pace. "Inversely, there's a bonus for fatherhood. It's seen as strength, stability, and admirable commitment to work. Fathers see an *increase* with each child of about 6 percent. Do the math. That's a gap of 10 percent in wages between mothers and fathers for the first child, which widens for each child born."

Ellie felt herself tense, almost wincing. She thought of the handshaking and back slaps the men had given each other at work when they'd returned a day or two after their wives had given birth, how they'd gone for drinks at lunch to "wet the baby's head." How the jokes had all been about diapers and late nights and the end of a sex life, and in the week that followed, she'd notice how those same men had often stayed longer in the evenings, and she'd realized they were actively avoiding going home. No wonder they got bonuses and climbed the career ladder when staying late wasn't just easy and rewarded — but the perfect smokescreen for actively avoiding family responsibilities.

Ellie surveyed the room. The students were enraptured. No hands were raised with questions; there was just the *clickety-clack* of fingers flying on keyboards as most feverishly typed notes in an effort to keep up with Ruby.

"The kicker is that these lower wages don't favor the bottom line of companies either. Workplaces in the US are losing $35 billion per year by not tracking caregiver status of their employees, yet organizations and the economy cannot afford to lose women. Why? Mothers are drivers of the economy and the primary shoppers in their households. Seventy percent of US mothers are working and contribute an average of 40 percent to household income. In the poorest families, that number increases to 86 percent."

A brave student's hand shot into the air to interrupt Ruby's flow.

"But this isn't new, is it, Professor Martinez? It's the glass ceiling dilemma, right?" The young woman who asked had short bobbed hair and looked as earnest and as fresh as they came. Ellie sensed the determination from her.

Ruby didn't blink.

"We associate the so-called glass ceiling cases with women barred from top rungs of elite professions, but here we're talking about every occupation from surgeons to law enforcement to grocery clerks. To be clear, caregiving work isn't just about childcare: it's about care for the elderly and disabled as well, all of which disproportionately falls upon women who end up either forfeiting a paid livelihood, voluntarily or otherwise, or maneuvering caregiving work with a 'real' job, unable to meet expectations."

Ellie felt short of breath. Her mind was racing and her heart pumping. A charged silence hung over the room, as if the atmosphere had been sucked out of it and they all sat, motionless, in a vacuum.

"As you gather information and listen to clients' stories, listen carefully. Listen to them like they've never been listened to before. Listen for clues that, although they might not conveniently conform to a category, may still be actionable — and imperative to spot if we are to evolve public policy in this area," concluded Ruby.

Her talk was met with rapturous applause. Ellie jumped up, oversaw the students out toward the dining hall, where clinic clients awaited, and rushed toward Ruby, who had her knapsack already packed.

"We didn't get a chance to speak earlier," said Ellie. "I so enjoyed your talk. It was disturbingly illuminating!"

"Ellie Benvenuto," said Ruby, warmly. "I know who you are. I've heard about the incredible work you're doing. You're such an asset. It's crucial that we have attorneys like you who lean into the work, and your reputation precedes you."

Ellie was taken aback. Ruby Martinez knew who she was and ... had an opinion of her?

"Oh. *My* reputation?" She laughed nervously. "I had no idea. You know your talk really hit close to home with me. There were so many things that ... um ..."

Her voice trailed off, and she shifted from one foot to the other, as Ruby regarded her thoughtfully.

"That you could relate to?"

Ellie nodded, her eyes darting.

Ruby tilted her head. "What's on your mind, Ellie?"

"Well, it's just that ... I was listening and, it got me thinking about ... how I was ... was ..."

"Yes?"

"Well," said Ellie, taking a deep breath. "I was actually fired from my previous law firm after I gave birth to my second child when my first child was diagnosed with disabilities. I was the most senior person in the group, and they wouldn't even have a discussion with me. They just cut me off cold, and while that was quite a shock, there was some other stuff going on as well leading up to that, and ..."

Again, Ellie's voice trailed off. What a torrent! This was a mistake. She suddenly wished for a San Francisco earthquake that would swallow her into a sinkhole. She was stumbling over her words, couldn't organize her thoughts, and didn't want to take up this renowned and brilliant woman's time.

"Let's sit, Ellie. I'd like to hear more. My center is doggedly lobbying right now for caregiver status to be included as a legally protected category in the workplace. We're preparing to present a roster of cases to the EEOC to issue official guidelines as a pathway to legislation, and it's hard to get people to come forward and actually bring lawsuits. Your situation is more important than you may think."

But an overwhelming sense of fear and embarrassment washed over Ellie. She wilted, barely able to summon another word.

"I'd like to," said Ellie. "I would, but I have to see to the students now. Maybe we could talk again?"

"Sure," said Ruby, "whenever you need."

She took a business card from her knapsack, jotted down another number on it, and handed it over to Ellie.

"Just remember that we can help you. Don't let them get away with this. We have connections with attorneys who are ready, willing, and able to take a case like yours."

A case like hers. So, she did have a case then? The thought of it all was too big. She was bone tired. And her evening wasn't near over, not by a long shot.

"Call or text me anytime. That's my personal number there," said Ruby as she walked up the steps from the lecture room toward the exit. "Any time, Ellie."

Ellie sighed, pushed a hand through her tousled hair, and thought about the long shower waiting for her once the kids were asleep — all still some hours away. The caregiving load.

Well, if there was one thing she knew about, it was certainly *that*.

"Kill every buffalo you can! Every buffalo dead is an Indian gone."

—**Colonel Richard Dodge, 1867, Black Hills**

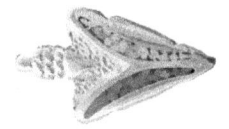

CHAPTER 9
TEDDY

September 29, 1867. Evanston, Illinois.

Papa did not want me to travel on my own back to Boston and there were letters back and forth all through August as to my journey homeward. I don't think it suited Papa to travel westwards for me and as it happened in the end, it was arranged that I would travel as far as Toledo with Uncle and his business associate, Mr. P. B. Weare, because they were going to look at stock for Mr. Weare's store anyway and I would meet Papa there, who would bring me back on the train.

Uncle and P. B. Weare were not taking the train to Toledo but going by horseback and this was the cause of some of the letters, as Papa insisted it was too long of a journey for me, but Uncle wrote back to say there wasn't one bother with my riding skills and I was hardy as they came.

He said I could have taken Devil the stallion if I wanted, but I politely declined!

It was decided that I would wear chaps, a cape and a wide hat so as to blend in on the road. This suited me fine; it was much more comfortable like that on a horse anyway. And besides, as Aunty said, I was still only a "young 'un" and what did it matter how I dressed?

Half of September had gone by when it came time to part. Aunty had fat tears running down her cheeks and I had to bite my lip — for it was all quivering — and wipe my own waterworks with the back of my hand.

"I'll miss you," she said and squeezed me tight.

I wasn't used to affection like it.

I felt all hot in my heart. I couldn't say a thing. No words would come out at all.

My two cousins had made me little presents to keep, a sandbag bunny rabbit, which Aunty had crocheted and they had filled, and some painted pebbles, three in number, which they said were like us, one, two, three.

I don't suppose my own siblings missed me so much back at home. Josephine had only sent one letter all summer and that was to tell me she was engaged now to Master Augustus Hartford. She wrote in big loopy handwriting and sprayed the letter with perfume.

It stank.

I could just imagine her goofy smile now that she officially had a beau, and I reckon her countenance had improved. I didn't know what to think of Augustus Hartford because I had only met him once and he seemed like a dull drip of a fellow, but I supposed there'd be a fuss with the wedding now and then she'd be gone and it would only be me and Trixie left to fend off Stepmother.

I had a strange feeling in my stomach as I rode out of Uncle and Aunty's farm, like I was leaving home, even though I'd only lived there some weeks. It was probably the happiest place I'd ever been. The happiest I'd felt in my whole life.

We met P. B. on the road and he had with him a horse packed with goods for the journey. I was surprised to see another man with him on horseback and when I saw his face under the hat, I realized it was the man I'd crashed into in the shop that day.

George.

He smiled when he saw me and I remembered how kind he'd been about the collision I had caused. I felt my cheeks burn red as we approached, for I had not expected to see this man and, all of a sudden, I was conscious of myself.

Those cursed infernal cheeks. I'd love to know how to stop the fire brigade.

P. B. and Uncle rode on up ahead as they always seemed to have some business to talk about and George and I trotted along behind. He said at first he'd thought Uncle had brought a boy along, but when I came near he knew it was me.

"Can't hide that smile, ma'am," he said.

Ma'am.

Now, I wasn't sure I liked that form of address one bit.

George asked me all manner of questions about myself, about what I thought of this and that, and I wasn't quite sure how to take all this interest, for never before had anyone seemed so concerned as to what *I* thought. After every question, he'd wait till I answered, staring at me intensely, as if my answer mattered most in the world. It was most disconcerting!

George had come from Sicily but moved with his parents as a child and so his accent was not that strong. That explained his bronzed complexion.

After some time, we stopped at a river to let the horses drink and Uncle lit a fire and we made dark coffee and ate bread and beans. I felt satisfied indeed with my stomach full and the coffee buzzing round my head like a honeybee. P. B. said the coffee would keep us going another twenty miles likely, for that's the kind of "good stuff" it was. P. B. knew all about groceries, for he was one of the top merchants in Chicago. He said George was one of his best salesmen and I could see by the way George smiled that he liked the compliment.

I hadn't thought too much about where we were to spend the night, but Aunty had mentioned that we would find a boarding house along the way. This had caused some chat between her and Uncle, for he said I was at risk in a boarding house, though at risk of what I don't know.

Aunty said anything could happen on the road either, that we could be robbed or attacked.

Papa had often talked about the dangers of driving cattle, for rustling was common and those Indian folks were clever at it. They'd steal horses and food if they got it, so you had to keep your wits about you and keep watch all day and all night. It was best if you struck first, to show your firepower and your mettle. I was a bit afraid of meeting Indians along the way, truth be told, but I kept that to myself, for I didn't want to seem like a chicken.

Or worse, a girl.

After another few hours in the saddle, when I didn't want to admit it, but found my buttocks and legs were terribly sore, P. B. put up his hand and brought us all to a halt. He peered off to the side of the trail, down a valley where, between black cherry trees rose the smoke of an encampment.

To my horror I saw they were Indians! I knew by their headgear and horses, which were not rigged up in saddles or bridles like ours, but a mix of skewbald and piebald and all wild looking. P. B. looked on, then dismounted his horse and walked slowly to the top of the ridge. He called down to the Indians and I nearly fainted.

What was he doing?! Why did he alert them to us?

Waiting for the sound of a spear whizzing through the air, like I'd read in the *New York Ledger*s, I watched as P. B. smiled, then turned back to us and gestured. He wanted us to go and meet the Indians!

"Uncle!" I said, helplessly, my fear betraying me now.

"It's alright," said Uncle and I watched as he too disappeared over the edge after P. B.

George looked at me and smiled, steady and reassuring.

"P. B. has a way with the Indians. These are Ojibwe," he said. "Don't you worry."

I had to strain all the way back, as my horse made its way down the hill, and I could feel the coolness of the air in the shelter of the valley. I felt like I was dropping to my death.

There were four Ojibwe at the camp, small in stature, their skin that deep dark color they always wrote about in the magazines, though it wasn't red like it always said. Really it was brown, almost like George's. They sat around a smoking campfire and were all working on a buffalo robe. One was chopping up roots on a flat stone and throwing them into a boiling pot on the fire.

They had all stood up by the time I reached them, and I got off my horse and stood close to her, for I wanted the shelter of her body and felt vulnerable sitting atop.

P. B. offered them a gift straightaway of coffee and biscuits and they took it readily and placed it with their own belongings. They began to examine his bags and, as he walked around his horse with them, I realized they were conversing and would probably make a trade. P. B. smiled and gestured a lot, and he seemed to know some of their language, for they could communicate and seemed to trust him.

I stood well back. I did not trust these Indians.

How did we know they wouldn't turn and scalp us at any second? That's what Indians did, given half the chance with the white man! (Or woman.)

One of the Indians gestured to Uncle and George to sit and they did, letting their horses go toward the river for a drink. My horse was itching with thirst, but I didn't sit down with the others and instead led her to the water by her bridle. I hoped P. B. would do his trade and then we could be on our way as it was getting near dusk now and the nearest town still looked to be at least an hour's ride away. We might have to light lamps should darkness come in quickly.

But there was no moving P. B. After his trading was done — and I could see that he was a businessman, for he drove a hard bargain with those Indians, taking many more items off them than he seemed to be giving away — P. B. announced that the men had asked us to make camp with them.

I shook my head in terror.

No, no.

No, no, no.

I looked to Uncle, thinking he'd be shaking his head like me, but instead he nodded and looked at me to confirm.

"Teddy, tie up your horse over there and give her a good brushing. Then help us with supper."

Supper?

We were going to eat with the savages? The very savages who were known to attack and scalp our own? I knew going on the road was going to be an adventure, but not this kind. Not where we chose to walk into the mouth of danger and dine there.

I brushed down my mare and tried to calm my breathing, but I felt as tense as a catapult pulled all the way back.

When we had looked after the horses, we got to preparing the food and warily I did as I was asked by Uncle without looking up to catch those dangerous Indian eyes. Instead, I glanced at their ponies, noting the decorations they had all in their manes and even paint, it seemed, on their rumps.

The Indians seemed glad of the company and made conversation with Uncle and George and then I realized they were talking about me and asking who was my father? Uncle looked around and laughed and said he didn't know the Ojibwe word for niece, and so he said that he was my father, because it was simply easier.

This made P. B. and George laugh.

One of the Indians pointed at George and then to me and gestured with his hand.

Together?

He was asking if we were together.

George laughed out loud and nodded.

"Not yet," he said. "Not wife yet."

This made everyone laugh then except me and I did not appreciate that they were talking like this about me, no sir, as if I couldn't hear or wasn't there and I turned away and thought about burning the fried beans on purpose, just to show them.

When the food was ready and we ate it out of our tin cans, I was ordered to do the washing up and I was still hot and bothered over this situation we got ourselves in. George said he'd help me because he could see, I think, that I had gone in on myself, and as we gathered the crockery down to the stream to rinse it all over before washing it in water boiled from the pot, George was kindly and told me he hoped I realized he was only joking earlier.

Well, it might have been a joke to him, but I knew those Indians thought that I might be getting on to be his wife, for everyone knew that Indians took their wives young. I stayed quiet, not giving George the satisfaction of going along with their jesting.

"Sure, didn't mean to insult you, Miss Teddy," he said. "I would hate to think I hurt your feelings or somethin'."

I thought on it for a few moments and told him it was alright for he was kindly I knew, and I was feeling all out of sorts there and then.

"I don't understand it," I said, as I watched beans fall from the plates and float away on the stream. "All I ever heard about is how dangerous the Indians are. How they attack us and steal from us and that's why the frontier posts were all set up to protect the white folks."

"Well," said George, "some of that's true. There are tribes who attack. But you know, Miss, the Indians have a lot more to be fearful in white folks than the other way round."

"They're savages," I said, scraping at some buttery grease with my fingers.

"Now, I wouldn't say that," George said, frowning. "I don't think that's a nice word. Would savages sit around the campfire and offer us their food? Would they joke and laugh with us, like you saw?"

I shook my head. I didn't know. All I knew was about what I read. What I'd heard from Papa and his road stories, which, truth be told, I sometimes wondered might have been a bit exaggerated.

"P. B. was engaged to a maiden from the Odawa tribe once," said George. "His family interfered and there was a stop put to it. That's why he loves this camping out, being with the Indian people. He feels connected to them, you see. They have a deep connection with the land and wildlife. P. B. reveres that about them."

I looked back to where P. B. was smoking some sort of elaborate pipe with the Indians now. They were all laughing. It was hard to match up this hard-nosed businessman with these folks in their feathers and moccasins.

"His family gave him the money to buy the store. When he broke off the engagement."

I looked at George. He was letting me in on a secret. I was sure P. B., and Uncle for that matter, would not like me to be knowing this personal business of his.

So P. B. had traded an Indian wife for a business life.

George helped me carry the dishes back up to camp and I got to thinking that maybe these folks weren't so bad if P. B. was so keen on them.

When darkness fell, we rolled out our sleeping mats and blankets and I lay on my back wondering how many snakes were all around us in the nearby undergrowth.

I watched as one of the Ojibwe undressed, peeling off his jacket and changing into a softer wrap-around type of blanket. I noticed how every muscle stood out on his naked torso, lean and square, like a hard slab of flat, square butter. I couldn't turn my eyes away.

He caught me looking and I averted my gaze.

Never before had I been exposed to such men. I didn't know what to think or how to feel. I wrapped myself up tight in my blanket, willing sleep to come so that morning would be here and we would be on our way.

P. B. struck up some sort of chanting with the Indians then and their voices rang out, soulful, creating vibrations that seemed to hang in the air and chase all the spirits away.

Or perhaps they were inviting them in. I didn't know.

Before we drifted off to sleep, I heard P. B. talking with the Ojibwe about a murder that had happened in Arizona where twenty-three Indians had been killed by County Rangers in the Aquarius Mountains. They killed the men, women and children. P. B. said it happened too often. One of the Ojibwe said the white men were shooting buffalo, bang, bang, bang, thousands dropping for no good reason at all. It was a waste. Another said the white men had been chasing the game away. First, they came for the beavers. Now the buffalo were next. Soon they would be gone. Already birds and animals abundant had all but disappeared in places. To say nothing of felling trees for lumber.

"They want us to be farmers," said one of the men. "But it is not our way of life."

"They tell us to move to cities, there, jobs. But there are no jobs. Always, lies," I heard another say.

I was almost asleep when I was taken from my slumber by an almighty scream and we all sat up to find George, biting at his hand and plunging it into the embers of the fire.

We rushed upon him, and he told us, while he held his hand deep in the embers and ash, that a snake had bitten him on the palm. It had crawled into his boots and when he'd lifted them to move them, it had stuck its head out and snapped him, quick as a flash. The word alone sent ice through my veins. I felt my stomach tighten like a fist. A snake. That wretched, slithering devil had been coiled in wait — in his boots, Lord help me! — lying in ambush, biding its time.

I stepped back, my limbs prickling cold despite the sweat on my skin. I knew the bite was done, knew the danger was past, and yet — I could not shake the horror of it. Of something unseen, something silent, lying in wait beneath the surface of the ordinary, ready to punish a person just for reaching where they had every right to reach.

The Ojibwe wanted to know what sort of snake it was, but it was Uncle who said it was most likely a cottonmouth and that George had done the right thing by sucking the poison out and sealing the wound. Still, there was the chance that there was some still in there and as George didn't seem to be feeling pain from his burn, he was running the risk of losing his whole hand, arm or worse.

George was not to go to sleep but to walk it off and we would need to stay up with him to make sure he didn't go into a delirium. Well, I knew there'd be no sleep for me then anyway, for how could I sleep now knowing the worst had happened and that a snake really had come into our camp and done its worst?!

For the rest of the night, we took it in turns keeping George awake and as the hours passed and we listened to the cry of coyotes and owls, the exhaustion overcame me till I begged to be let sleep just for an hour and I lay down on my mat and passed out, snakes be damned.

In the morning, a weary George, now in terrible pain with his burned snakebite hand, was grey in the face but alive. I was glad of that, for I liked George.

I blamed P. B. for setting up this damn camp with the Indians. I bet, had we stopped at a boardinghouse, there wouldn't have been no cottonmouth in our boots!

It was a forlorn party who set off the next morning, except for P. B., who grinned from ear to ear and said he always felt refreshed with the energy of a sprite after a night spent under the stars.

I didn't know what to think. I suppose I had changed my opinion somewhat on the Indians.

But definitely not on snakes. Snakes are still the worst thing God ever invented. Why did he have to set them on the same earth as he invented butterflies and blueberries?

It's one of life's great mysteries, I suppose.

The Ohio Gazette
March 22, 1857

Legislature Declines Protection for Passenger Pigeons

In a session last week, the Ohio State Legislature rejected proposed legislation aimed at protecting the passenger pigeon population. The bill, which sought to impose restrictions on the hunting of this blue-grey fowl — sometimes called *doves* in casual parlance — was struck down following a report from the Committee on Wildlife. According to the committee, the passenger pigeon, famed for its vast flocks that darken the skies, "requires no protection, as its numbers are too great to be diminished by any ordinary means of destruction."

Despite the committee's recommendation to pass the bill, arguing that the pigeons played a crucial role in maintaining forest ecosystems by aiding in seed dispersal and forest regeneration, the Legislature remained unmoved. "The pigeon is here today and gone tomorrow, following its migratory course across this great land. Our citizens need not fear the disappearance of these birds, for their presence is assured as long as our forests stand," continued the report.

Local hunters and trappers hailed the decision, citing the pigeon as an abundant source of food and trade, while some concerned naturalists voiced dissent, warning that unchecked hunting could lead to unforeseen consequences for both the environment and future food supplies. The Legislature, however, opted to safeguard the freedoms of those who rely on the pigeon for their livelihoods.

No further proposals are expected this session, and the debate on the matter appears to be settled, at least for now.

CHAPTER 10
ELLIE

February 23, 2019. Marin County, California.

Saturday dawned unusually warm and sunny. As Ellie parted the curtains and saw the first clusters of tourists already trickling up the hill toward Coit Tower, she had an overwhelming feeling of claustrophobia. She needed space. She needed to feel the air on her skin and a breeze through her hair, sweeping away her thoughts and pent-up pressure. She needed to get away from concrete buildings, from people and all their contrivances of progress. She needed to get out of the city.

Last night in bed, she had turned the last page of Teddy's diary. The childish, inky writing had run out, just like that, halfway down a page. Anxiously, Ellie had leafed through the rest of the notebook, but she already knew by the pit in her stomach that the writing had finished.

There was no more! Her connection to Teddy was over, and Ellie missed her already.

Feeling angsty, she texted Anika, knowing that Ben would have already left for the golf he played early every Saturday morning at the Olympic Club, leaving Anika solo with the children for more hours on her own. He would likely lunch at the club and stay on for drinks — "the 19th hole," as he called it. It drove Ellie crazy that Ben thought it was all right, but Anika always shrugged it off and said it was important for Ben to have his own space.

But what about Anika's space? Still, it did mean she would likely be free this morning.

Hey, Ani, let's ditch this sourdough starter. How about a drive? Ellie texted.

I'm In. Give me half an hour, replied Anika. *Where to?*

Where could they go? They could easily scoot over to Crissy Field or Baker Beach just outside the Presidio, take the ferry to Angel Island, or try Sausalito just on the other side of Golden Gate Bridge. But those spots were magnets for hordes of people on weekends. Ellie longed for some secluded hideaway.

An hour later, Ellie, Anika, and their four combined children were packed into the Odyssey, picnic basket, blankets, bubble wands, and Bravo the black Labrador in the back. As Ellie drove through the familiar streets, toward the Golden Gate and Highway 101-North, she began to feel a release. This was a good idea.

She also marveled at the eight-seater Odyssey, now finally doing the job she had bought it for after the divorce. She had imagined this exact moment: she and Anika traveling around, kids in the back, singing, picnic packed. Well, okay, the children weren't singing yet, but they had a drive ahead!

"What about Olompali in Novato?" suggested Ellie.

The state park had been on her mind ever since she'd read Teddy's entry on camping with Indians.

"Jeez, I haven't been there since I was a kid!" said Anika.

"Last time I went was this community day, when we helped rebuild the … what are they called, like huts? *Kotcha*!" said Ellie, as she drove.

"Gotcha," joked Anika.

Ellie smiled. "How far?"

"About thirty minutes," said Anika.

"Done."

Ellie remembered the park as a huge wide-open space. She remembered lots of people smiling, sharing their picnics, children braiding tule reed, members of the local heritage group and descendants of the

California Coast Miwok tribe being there on the day. But all that must have been fifteen years ago. At least.

The kids were getting a little squirrely by the time they arrived, despite Ellie's cajoles of "Itsy Bitsy Spider" and a few Italian nursery rhymes, passed down by Enzo and Genevieve, that made Leila roll her eyes at the seasoned age of five but were a hit with the three boys. Luca had been stimming from the moment they got in the car, and it was with relief that they drove down the long winding road into Olompali parking lot and let everybody pile out.

It was already hot — especially for February in Northern California. The parking lot looked overgrown, with weeds poking out of curbs and a general air of neglect settled into the faded signage pointing to overgrown paths. Ellie examined the parking machine, which wouldn't accept her card.

"It's asking me to download an app, but I can't get a signal," shouted Ellie from the machine to Anika, who was busy unloading kids and picnic items. Anika looked around at the completely empty parking lot.

"I think we'll be okay." She shrugged.

Reluctantly, Ellie returned to the car, feeling uncomfortable shirking the parking fee — because that wasn't the tragically bland villain origin story she was angling for.

Arms loaded, they made their way down the narrow paths, past gophers nestling in the undergrowth, sending Bravo into a tizzy. Anika kept him on leash, fearing once he was let off, he might disappear for the hills.

"Sheesh, I don't remember it like this," said Ellie as they passed into an unkept forest area. She'd wanted quiet, but this felt a bit desolate.

"Me neither," said Anika. "It's been let go, right?"

The kids didn't seem to mind. They ran ahead, past the closed visitor center, round the path toward the Burdell buildings, an ancient brown shingle barn and tiny prairie porch cottages.

"Which way?" asked Anika, stopping to examine the signs at the path that forked.

"I think it's this way?" said Ellie, hearing the wind rustle through the trees. Already, she could feel her senses calming, tapping into the sounds of nature all around. The sky was azure. The air was warm, filled with the combined scents of early spring flowers and fresh grasses.

"Oh my gosh!" called Anika to the children. "Look!"

A wild black turkey, his fantail displayed, pointedly picked his way through the long grass. He emerged onto the path and turned with his back to the group, completely unfazed.

"Birdy!" said Nathan.

Anika laughed. "Turkey!"

The bird continued on the path before sidestepping into the grass. As Ellie watched, she saw a second bird, its mate, appear. Together they disappeared into the long grass, happily enjoying the sun.

Ellie smiled. "Nature's just on her doorstep, huh?"

"Who needs Whole Foods Market for Thanksgiving?" said Anika.

Ellie belly laughed.

"Right? See, you just saved fifty dollars!"

They got busy spreading out Anika's colorful blankets and unpacking a feast that seemed excessive for just six people and a dog: sandwiches, fresh fruit salad, a risotto Ellie had learned from Genevieve, an assortment of juices, and leftover salted Nutella brownies — her go-to guilt offering for the many people who helped with Luca, despite Anika's finger waggling about palm oil destroying the planet.

Not too shabby for a last-minute trip, Ellie thought. For two women barely holding it all together, they were faking it well.

Leila, Milo, and Nathan were already off in their world of adventure, chasing each other around the towering oaks, Leila challenging Milo to a duel with a fallen branch, and Nathan trying his best to tag along with the older kids, their laughter mingling with the sound of rustling leaves. Luca had already made his way to the recreated Miwok kotcha — a small hut like a teepee, made of braided tule reed — and was happily cocooned inside. Bravo was the uncontested leader of their little pack, his tail wagging furiously as he darted among the children, adding to their excitement, happy to frolic outdoors, and now off leash.

Anika called out, her voice threading through the trees.

"Kids, come on! The food's ready!"

Her announcement was met with an immediate change in direction, as if she were remote controlling a drone, as three of the four children beelined toward the picnic spot, their faces already grubby with dirt and alight with exhilaration.

Ellie made a plate for Luca and brought it to him inside the kotcha, where she understood he felt most comfortable. As she settled with the others around the blanket, Ellie took a moment to appreciate their surroundings.

"Isn't this just perfect?" she said, squinting into the radiant sun and gesturing at the panoramic beauty that the park offered.

Anika nodded.

"Take that, Instagram. Score one for real life — no filters, no hashtags. Mic drop."

Ellie thought how Anika needed this respite just as much as she did. For all the stresses that Ellie faced in her life, juggling her new post-divorce landscape with working, mentoring, and looking after her children, one of course, who had special needs, she wasn't facing the same obstacles and heartbreak as Anika.

She didn't have an absent, possibly philandering husband. And she wasn't clipped into a grief so steep and unrelenting that it felt like she was white-knuckling the zip-line harness, too afraid to let go — or worse, too numb to even feel the drop. Sometimes Ellie wondered if Anika was coping a little *too* well.

Sandwiches were devoured, juice was spilled and quickly cleaned up, and Bravo, ever the opportunist, managed to sneak a few bites himself, much to the children's delight. Ellie and Anika took turns sharing stories of "when we were your age," which, according to Leila, may as well have been the Mesozoic Era — without any internet. They were occasionally interrupted by the children's excited voices sharing discoveries from their earlier explorations, eager to fill their bellies and gallop back to the little creek that seemed to giggle along with them.

After the meal, Leila proposed a game of hide-and-seek, and Anika and Ellie, feeling youthful, joined in. The park, with its myriad hiding spots among the trees, rocks, and small hills, proved the perfect setting for their game. Bravo, confused but thrilled at this new activity, ran around, inadvertently giving away hiding spots with his enthusiastic barking.

When they were spent, Ellie strolled along the herb garden, planted in a ring around the kotcha area. Overgrown plants held up faded signs naming the various types of vegetation that was growing.

> **Coast Live Oak**, Bodega Miwok: *sáata*, Marin Miwok: *sáata*. Acorns, dried, peeled ground into a fine meal, and leached to remove tannin, then boiled for mush or made into bread. Harvest Season: Fall

> **Mugwort Sage**, Bodega Miwok: *po'-to-po'-to*, Marin Miwok: *kísin*. Leaves made into tea to reduce fever and as a remedy for stomachache. Smoked, drunk, and burnt for rituals; leaves rubbed on body to keep bad spirits away. Harvest Season: Spring – Fall

Ellie imagined the native Coast Miwok moving about here, as they had done for some eight thousand years before the whites came. She imagined the women gathering — collecting, pounding, whittling, boiling, drying — their knowledge of food and plants possibly lost forever.

She was glad some of that knowledge had been preserved and took out her phone to snap the various signs about the plants. Perhaps she would be able to add something to her own cooking or home remedies? Perhaps she could connect in some way?

The afternoon waned, the falling temperature foreshadowing a dramatic curtain-drop of fog, the sun projecting long shadows through the trees, painting the scene with chiaroscuro plays of light off shadows. They let nature act as babysitter while they packed up — taking their time.

"The clinic I was supervising on Thursday," Ellie said, "the guest speaker was Ruby Martinez. She was so incredible. You've seen her, right?

She's often a guest on NPR and CNN. Anyway, she really got me thinking. I mentioned to her about Hutton & Fetterer. She said ... well, she thinks I have a case. An important one, she even said."

Anika fixed Ellie with a flat, unblinking stare.

"Well, you of all people should know that, Miss Attorney Action Figure."

"I know," said Ellie, putting her hand up. "I know, I guess. Well, it's just when somebody like Ruby Martinez says it ..."

"And all the times I've said it, they don't count?" said Anika pointedly, and Ellie could see that her hackles were raised. "Just because I'm not a lawyer doesn't mean I can't see when wrong has been done, and your absolute dismissal of my opinion ... well, it kinda blows, Ellie."

Ellie was taken aback.

"Oh for ... come on, Ani. Don't be that way. I don't have problems like the *real* problems my clients have. The stories I hear on a daily basis are heartbreaking. These people — mostly women — have been forced to flee dire situations that mean life or death, or families torn apart. I lost a job. Was it wrong? Yes. It happens. I got another one. My children are safe — just look at them."

She gestured to three small figures zigzagging among the shadows.

"Who are you trying to convince?" asked Anika. "Me or yourself? You fiercely advocate for all these other women getting the stuffing kicked out of their lives but then let a bunch of ivory-towered thugs steamroll you, and you've done nothing about it."

Ellie stopped folding the food-smeared blanket, holding it between the two of them like an iron curtain.

"Is that so?" she said, her temper flaring now. "You're one to preach self-advocacy! What about how you allow your jet-setting husband to treat you? Where is he today, huh? Oh, that's right: off drinking with the 'guys' while you're here, flying solo per usual, with the kids! You're a doormat, Anika, yet you're all fired up to push *me* into battle? And besides, I don't have time for my own lawsuit. No time, no energy. I don't have the luxury to chant for ninety minutes each morning like some people."

Ellie's words hung dense as fog, refusing to clear.

Anika's shocked face froze for a moment before she grimaced, grabbed the soiled blanket from Ellie, and tossed it in a heap on the picnic table.

"Just because you blew up your own marriage doesn't mean I have to detonate mine. I'm not going to be a divorced person. No way. It's too sad."

Ellie, temper boiling, avoiding eye contact with Anika, closed and stacked food containers into a cooler tote, and called for the kids. Her voice had a sharpness that they understood meant business, and they scuttled toward her for home.

She pushed ahead down the path, her arms full, Nathan toddling after her.

"Luca!" called Ellie, her heart pounding, her voice the harshest tone both her kids had ever heard escape from her mouth. "Come. Now!"

The two women packed the car, silently, the children and Bravo climbing in, seemingly aware of the new mood.

After a few minutes of driving into the sun that had dipped along the flat coastal horizon, a seething Anika said in a low voice, "So, I just whittle away my time chanting like a deranged lunatic? That's what you think of me?" Her voice warbled.

"No! I'm sorry," said Ellie, her voice subdued. "I got mad. I shouldn't have said that. Do you really think I'm just some sad, pathetic divorced patsy?"

The molten anger had cooled, and in its place crept the ever-present strangle of guilt, only this time, she had brought it all on herself. How could she have spoken to Anika like that? She was beginning to feel truly loathsome.

"You should be sorry," said Anika, and she folded her arms protectively across her chest.

"I just … I … hate to see you so … lost."

"And what other way should I be, Ellie, huh? I'm messy. Grief is messy. It lurks past its 'best by' shelf date. It hunts and haunts you. This is what it looks like!"

"I know," said Ellie, quietly. "I just think Ben should step up. It pains me that he's so absent —"

"Keep Ben out of this," shot Anika. "My marriage really is none of your business."

Ellie frowned and fell mute. They didn't say another word to each other for the rest of the journey, and by the time they drove up the hill toward their homes, the sour mood had seeped into the back seats, with Leila bickering with Milo and Nathan complaining that his tummy hurt. Some of that mugwort sage would have been handy.

So much for an escape valve outside the city. As Ellie unloaded the car and dropped Anika's belongings at her door, not daring to go in, she felt worse than ever. That was the first time she'd ever fallen out with her best friend, and it made her sick.

She had to make it right. Somehow, she had to fix things. Was there a Miwok herbal remedy for that?

At the door of her apartment sat a large cardboard box, the handwritten postage label stamped *Chicago*. *Oh wow*, thought Ellie, Martha had obviously been prompted to send her another box of goodies after their recent lunch. But strangely, the label didn't quite look like Martha's writing.

With Nathan cranky and Luca stimming, something he tended to do when very tired, she set about bath and bedtime, trying to push the distressing argument with Anika from her mind. Yet the gnawing in the pit of her stomach wouldn't budge. Despite being a lawyer, confrontation made her cringe.

It took another two hours to get the boys settled and the apartment into a state that didn't scream, "There appears to have been a struggle." By the time she finally flopped onto the couch with a glass of wine in hand and a mindless rom-com on TV, she'd nearly forgotten about the package.

"The box!" She hopped up suddenly and went to the kitchen junk drawer to find the box cutter. When she peeled back the packing tape and peered inside, excited to see what labels Martha had grown bored with this time, she was taken aback to see not a single piece of fabric.

Instead, she found a perfume box, a set of brown notebooks piled high, and an envelope on top. She opened the envelope to read a handwritten card from her mother.

Ellie, I found that box of Genevieve's things. There are a few knickknacks and photographs, but I thought you might be interested in these diaries? More of Teddy's like the one you have? I haven't looked through, but perhaps there's something in them if Genevieve kept them. Anyway, just thought I'd send them on to you. Mom.

P.S. The perfume is from Martha. The one you said you liked at lunch.

Ellie felt her heart quicken as she lifted the notebooks one by one and flipped through them. In front of her was something she hadn't even realized she'd been hoping for, but somehow they felt like everything she'd ever been looking for.

There, in neat, careful writing, page after inked page, appeared to be the rest of Teddy's life.

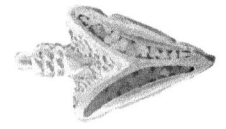

CHAPTER 11
TEDDY

September 2, 1871. Chicago, Illinois.

I think I'm getting better at bookkeeping.

At the start, I thought, heck, this bookkeeping lark sure ain't for me, but that may have been my nerves talking, because Mr. Weare says he reckons I was born to it! Says I'm mighty good at it and I'm the best woman bookkeeper he's ever had. (The only one of course, for I'm the first that we know of!)

I'd like to go back and show that old schoolteacher of mine just how well I'm doing in Mr. Weare's booming store and all the cash coming, my responsibility! And bonds too. I deal with all the paper.

There are a few others I'd like to show too, Stepmother for instance and my poor dead mother. Not that I believe in ghosts. But if she'd like to come back just for a minute to see how fast I can count up a pile of small bills, well, she'd be mighty proud I reckon.

When I look back, I can see how far along I've come, because I really did find it difficult at first, but I suppose with Mr. Weare himself showing me his techniques when it comes to dealing with cash and the big, large banknotes, it all helped. He says I am a fast learner.

But I knew that anyways.

Yesterday three boys were staring in the window, pointing and drawing a crowd. I looked around to see was there a bird or something flown into the store, but I couldn't see anything and a customer came in and said the boys were staring at me, as the first woman bookkeeper they ever saw!

Well, yes, it sure is unusual for a young woman like me to be working a job like this and I don't know of any other women around who work in an office like I do, but I suppose I was always a bit unusual. So Papa said all these years.

I got a letter from Boston yesterday to report that poor Papa hasn't been doing so well lately and has moved back to the old homestead in North Sandwich for the good air. He caught a cold two months ago and it's sat right on his chest and his breathing is getting worse and worse and he hasn't energy even to get out of bed.

Stepmother wrote that it was her idea to send Papa, but I'm not sure if she sent him or if he sent himself as I can't imagine it must have been much fun having Stepmother fussing and being trapped between the sheets all day. Heck, it'd be worth dying just to get away from her!

But I shouldn't think like that.

I worry for Papa.

Uncle came by the store the other day and said he'd also heard that Papa was under the weather and for a big strapping man like Papa, well I guess he was worried too. Aunty was asking after me. She likes that I'm nearby in the city now, though I rarely see her, just the odd time when she comes to town for tea and Mr. Weare says it's alright for me to go off for a half hour and then we get to catching up. She says I'm getting to be a fine young woman, though my manners still leave a little to be desired and she says I could very much improve how I talk, as I sound more like a cattleman, than a refined young office lady!

Office lady. I sure do like the sound of that.

Mr. Weare pays me well, but I don't rightly know what to do with the money, for I have everything a young woman requires. Last year, I bought a second dress, which I wear while my other is laundered, and in consequence, I don't really have much need for anything else — seeing as my bed and board are already covered by Mr. Weare, who pays my landlady.

A few months back, thinking on this large sum I'd saved up, I decided to invest some into George's potato merchanting. Not that he asked for it, but it was obvious to me that it was good business, for he was buying in a large load of potatoes and when I asked him what he could make were he to double the load, it turned out, he could triple his profit, for the costs were in the transport anyway.

So, I gave him enough to double the load and rightly so, it was a great success, and I got back triple what I'd lent. He says I'm a very clever young woman.

But business is mighty easy sometimes, I reckon.

And people sure do love potatoes. Especially those Irish and Polish immigrants who seem to make great stews with them or just boil them up straight. A customer told me that in some parts of Ireland, the diet is only potatoes, nothing else at all, and with so many Irish in the city, the potatoes always sell.

George likes to buy round Jackson white potatoes, as they're considered premium, as the Calicoes often have a streak of red or blue in them or come long in shape, but the Irish still buy them anyways. George has gone out for a fresh load and is due back next week with the new haul in which I've invested again.

I've missed him while he's away. More than I'd like to admit. He's a good friend. He knows me very well. Though I've set him straight on any nonsense.

Men sure do like to put it on sometimes.

What a palaver this week has been.

I feel sick to my stomach over it all. One of the worst few days I've had since I've come to Chicago to work for Mr. Weare.

It all started with this lady, a widow, a very refined woman, southerner, pretty with blond curls around her face, by the name of Mrs. Joubert.

It was no secret that Mr. Weare had taken a shine to her and her five-year-old little girl. He'd been in the store the first day she came in and had ended up serving her himself, for he still likes to work the floor from time to time to keep an eye on things and converse with the customers and they love him for it too.

Well, she came in that day and of course, Mr. Weare, always having an eye for a pretty lady, fussed and fawned over her and that very week he took her to tea and the next week too. We started calling her Juliet, (for Mr. Weare was Romeo!) and Mr. Weare was going around with a big smile on his face like a soft puppy. We could all tell, the way things were going, that if the lady stuck round, it wouldn't be long before Mr. Weare would be fixing to ask for her hand as he'd already told George that she was the type of woman you wanted to be pouring your coffee in the morning.

On Monday, I was covering lunch hour, which I do most days and I don't mind, for it takes me out of the office, which doesn't have a window and can get hot and stuffy and who came in, only Mrs. Southern Belle herself. She was buying up quite a basket of goods; Chinese tea, pounds of sugar, bars of the expensive chocolate imported from Paris.

When I added it all up, she handed me a five-dollar bill and as soon as it landed in my palm, I knew that it was a counterfeit. I held it up to the light and pronounced my assessment, barely thinking who was in front of me, for I know a counterfeit when I see one and the words came tumbling out.

"I beg your pardon," said Mrs. Joubert, her voice all high-pitched and indignant.

I ran my hand over the note and took a real good look at it again, for I wanted to be sure that I wasn't mistaken, but, in the same way as you know you own signature, that if someone else wrote it in handwriting just like your own, you could tell as soon as you saw it that it wasn't yours. For the capital letters might look like yours and the small letters might look like yours but taken together, by the general appearance of the whole, you'd just know that you never wrote it.

Mrs. Joubert, which I always thought was far too fancy a name for her, took the note back and said she had been given it as change in the large dry goods store up the street and I told her she should return it for she had surely been swindled, albeit, I suspected, by accident.

Duly, Mrs. Joubert left the store, her basket of goods sitting on the counter.

When Mr. Weare heard the story, he was very angry with me and said that I had embarrassed the lady. He said that even if the note was counterfeit — which, he assured me it wasn't as Mrs. Joubert had given him the note when they'd met for their tea later that day and he had declared it to be solid — he said I should have let her take the goods and he would have dealt with it afterwards, for Mrs. Joubert was a fine lady and I had made her to feel like a criminal.

I blushed crimson as he berated me in the office and went about my day afterwards feeling sick to my stomach. Never before had I gotten in such trouble.

Well, of course I have gotten in trouble before with Papa but nothing felt as bad as this. I felt I had let Mr. Weare down terribly and made a fool of myself, all the while wondering what else I could have done, for I thought had I taken in a false note it would have been a blow to the business.

How could I have made such a mistake? I was sure the note was counterfeit.

Over the next few days as I was doing the books, I did in fact find some counterfeit notes, two twenty-dollar bills. I spoke with the cashiers who remembered that they'd come from a man, who had come in twice that week to buy something very small only for 50 cents, and each time declared he only had a large note, and they duly took it and gave him change of a ten dollar and five dollar note and the rest in coins.

I didn't bring the issue to Mr. Weare while I tried to decide what was to be done, but warned the cashiers to call me immediately, should the man come in again. I had a plan that I would detain him long enough for the police to be called so that he could be arrested. I just wasn't sure that he would come back again, seeing as he'd been brave (or stupid enough) to come in two times already!

When I got a knock to my office the next day and was called to come out by Albert, who is the only one with half a brain I sometimes think behind those counters, I was sure the man had come back, but instead, I found two detectives who informed me they had arrested the man for counterfeiting and wanted to know had we had any issues with counterfeit money in the store!

I was only too glad to tell them we'd been shortchanged to the tune of forty dollars! And when I told them I had also been handed a five dollar note, which I had my suspicions about, they were very eager to know by whom.

My nerves rattled as I told them about the southern widow, as though Mr. Weare was standing behind me hearing every word I said, but I knew it was the right thing to do, especially as they had asked me directly if we'd had any other counterfeiting attempts.

Their eyes widened when I told them of Mrs. Joubert. They thanked me profusely for my troubles, and left with Mrs. Joubert's address, for I knew where she lived on account of Mr. Weare sending a red rose to her house every Monday. (After their Sunday jaunt, which he enjoyed ever so much!)

I felt terrible, like a spy and I wondered just how in the world I was going to tell Mr. Weare of all the goings-on and my betrayal but as it turned out, in the end, I didn't need to, for it was he who came to me to tell me the most dramatic news, that Mrs. Joubert had been arrested fleeing the city, her bags packed to the hilt with goods she'd been buying all over town!

For Mrs. Joubert was in on the whole ruse, and she wasn't called Mrs. Joubert at all, but Mrs. Ruiz, and she was married to the Mexican man that had passed off the twenty-dollar bills, a known counterfeiter and criminal who had just been let out of jail!

Thanks to the address I'd given, they were able to search the house and found piles of ash in the sheet-iron stove, with some scraps left, showing they'd been burning counterfeit cash, and providing enough evidence to charge Mrs. Joubert, I mean, Mrs. Ruiz, herself.

Well, I never.

The southern belle, a cold, hard criminal. And married! And not a widow at all!

I did think the child she had was rather dark looking.

And me, my nose as keen as a bloodhound, sniffing out trouble, although no one could see it at the time.

Mr. Weare was heartsore and sorry and had a basket of fruit sent to my room as an apology. I didn't need an apology though. What I needed was to earn Mr. Weare's trust again, his goodwill and his knowledge that I would never, ever do anything to harm the store or him. I love working at P. B. Weare's. And I love being a bookkeeper.

As happy as I felt outdoors in coveralls working Uncle and Aunty's farm, I'd say I'm the happiest now in my whole long seventeen years.

I hope nothing as bad as that episode happens again!

October 1, 1871. Chicago.

George back with the potatoes. A good load considering the time of season. He's stored them in a large warehouse that he rents and will be moving them out in bushels over the coming days.

He tried to kiss me on his return, but I told him I was tired of that and he was to try no more. He looked like a kicked kitten, but I have to be firm. I don't have those feelings and I can't make them appear. I might have taken a shine to him when I was only a naive young woman with no world experience. But now that I'm older, I've decided I'll never get married.

How do I make him see this?

He says he wants to marry me before any other man runs away with me. I always laugh but I know he is serious.

Mr. Weare is still heartbroken. Says he thought it was true love. Funny how true love can seem when there's money involved.

October 8, 1871. Chicago.

Fire! Fire everywhere!

Good Lord, pray for us. Pray that we survive!

I hereby leave all my worldly goods, should any remain, to my sister Beatrice Ellis in Boston, which are:

- my spare (cotton and velvet) dress
- my small vanity case, including silver and enamel mirror
- my books, which remain in my holdall
- my diaries
- sum of cash (the amount which I'd prefer not to write down, but which will also be in my holdall).

My older sister Josephine Hartford is already cared for by her husband. Send word to my father, Silas Ellis, in North Sandwich to let him know of my demise should that be the Lord's wish.

(Do not let my stepmother near my remains.)

Theodora Mary Ellis

October 13, 1871. Chicago.

It is as a broken woman that I write now.

Oh, how the world can turn in an instant. How everything that you know and take for granted can be turned on its head. Was it really only a week ago that I lived in the lap of luxury? With a bathroom near my room, with sheets on my bed, with a hot meal on the table with fresh bread each evening?

This past week has been the worst anyone has ever known, worse than anyone could have imagined. Hundreds dead, but no real way of knowing as the flames were so hot they burned everything past ash. I cannot get the roar of the fire out of my ears. Or the smell of smoke from my nose.

This page is full of smudges. For everything burned black.

I was in my room reading before bed when I first heard the commotion. My landlady knocked on my door and we both went out onto the street, she in her dressing gown, where we could see the great plume of fire and smoke.

Never did we think it would reach us. Never did we think it could spread so far, so fast.

They say it was started in a barn, by an Irish woman, Mrs. O'Leary, an immigrant of course; her cow kicked over the oil lamp when she was milking and whoosh, up the barn went. I don't know what the true story is but there sure is a lot of hatred toward that Irish woman now. I suspect there is more to it, for there were other fires in the days before this great fire and the firefighters were exhausted.

And why would she have been milking so late? It makes no sense to me.

Oh my, how quickly the flames spread out from that barn and took their neighbors', house by house, with speed. It was the wood of course, for most of the buildings here are made of timber.

WERE made of timber.

The houses, the paths, the great hoarding advertising, all the fancy adornments, painted wood. We could hear bells ringing and commotion and then a great big fire engine sped past us, but it was too late by then, I think. Not a drop of rain have we had since July.

A tinder box!

My landlady went inside for she has a bad chest, and I could not help myself but move further down the street to see. A crowd had gathered to watch.

"Surely it will not come this way," said one woman and we all nodded in agreement.

Surely it could not?

But surely it could. Oh, how thick and choking the smoke was.

When the glow of the flames crept further, we saw, in horror, that the fire had advanced to just a block away! It was then I realized we would have to leave. We had to get out, for if we were to live, we had to run.

My landlady at first refused. This had been her home, she insisted, for thirty years. She said she would burn there if she had to. But she did not really mean it and she changed and packed a small holdall, the same as I, and we fled, joining with all the others, streaming from their houses, running at times as the crowd surged forward away from the flames.

What a sorry sight we were. Children crying, women yelping, men shouting in panic.

Behind us the flames ate their way, building to building, despite the firemen and their hoses and those who ran to assist. I thought of George, who lived across the river and was surely safe, the flames could not jump across water? And so we made our way toward the bridge. He would not mind my landlady either for she was a quiet dour woman and would not make a fuss.

But the flames did jump the river.

Then they reached the gasworks.

And then we knew that Chicago was lost.

I am so tired as I write. I have lost pounds. Smoke is a rotten smell, it permeates everything, destroys all that is left. Which is not much. Some brick buildings stand like fingers. It's impossible to even know where you are for all the landmarks are gone. They say a hundred thousand people have lost their homes.

We have been sheltering in Lincoln Park and we were lucky that the rain did come for it dampened things down, but by then the fire had burned itself out. The whole city is destroyed. They say four miles have been burned, but when you look out across the city, it feels like more.

The beautiful Palmer House Hotel, barely opened a week, gone. All that fine silk and gold brocade, chandeliers and the freshly painted rooms.

And all our houses.

George found me in Lincoln Park to say P. B. Weare's store burned to the ground. The warehouse too where George had his stock, gone. Field & Leiter where Aunty took me after my accident — also destroyed.

George said Mr. Marshall Field and Levi Leiter set up a temporary shop just today on State Street, between 20th and 22nd Streets, in a section of the city not devoured by fire.

Nobody knows what will happen, what all these poor, wretched homeless will do now. Everything will be difficult. All documents burned. So many separated. Each day, more notes appear, pinned to the board at the Red Cross tent as people travel in from afar in search of their loved ones. We all wear our black smudges, on our faces and on our hands. Our fingers charcoal, our nails filthy.

I volunteered with the Red Cross and was assigned the letter tent, where I sit and write letters all day for people who need it until my hand aches. It is hard now for me even to write this, but I suppose I must record what has been happening. Most of the letters I write are just a few short lines, declaring the safety of various members of the family, but there are some terribly sad ones, from mothers declaring the presumed death of missing children, fathers, sons.

So many have been lost.

I am so utterly exhausted. I've never felt anything like it before.

I sent a letter to Aunty and Uncle, included in the post bag of the letters I write. And a short note to Boston. But it's hard to think beyond here.

All I have now is what I carry in my holdall. I returned with my landlady to see the burnt pile of her home. She shed not a tear, which surprised me, considering she's lost everything.

We must do what we can to assist. It is our duty to help others.

Why God has chosen to visit this terror upon us is a hard prayer to answer. But answer it we must. We will rebuild and we will return, to the city we once were. The will of the Chicago people is strong.

November 11, 1871. Chicago.

George wishes to leave.

I don't agree and have told him so.

Mr. Weare will have the store reopened soon. But George says we can't recover here, not with the stock we've lost. I remind him that I've lost money too. He says it's different for a woman, that it's much harder for a man to have his entire fortune erased. He had everything tied up in it, whereas I kept back part of my savings.

He was foolish to invest every dime he had. Any good bookkeeper will tell you that, to save some for a rainy day! Or, as the case was here, for the day that everything burns!

He is quite depressed.

I don't think Mr. Weare will need a bookkeeper for the moment as he will be operating on minimal staffing and doing it himself likely. We are all very worried.

Winter has come. We are lucky to have found rooms, but they are nothing like the house I lived in with my landlady.

So many remain homeless and destitute. A crisis, they're calling it.

December 23, 1871. Chicago.

Everyone is afraid to light candles and oil lamps. The fire is put out early each evening with sand. The rooms we huddle in are freezing, despite all the bodies in them.

Perhaps George and I have been spending too much time together, but we don't have the luxury that we once had of our own private space, in our own rooms. Sometimes I have to reprimand him, for he speaks to me as though I am his wife. That is one of the reasons I fear traveling with him. It is what everyone will think. That we are married.

My landlady left for New York, where she has a sister. She cried when the train pulled into the station to take her away. It was the first time I saw her tears. She said she thought she would end her days in Chicago, but now she knows it will be New York.

George has a contact called Bugbee who has invited him out to work an unopened claim in a new town they are building called Elizabethtown in New Mexico. He says they're digging a ditch to bring water in from ten miles distant and spending a lot of money on it for they have great faith in the mine. They're building quite a town and his contact thinks it would suit George just rightly.

I don't know why George thinks he'll make a good miner, but he believes he has the skill set for it. I'm not sure that man has ever dug up anything in his whole life, but he sure is keen to start now.

January 14, 1872. Chicago.

Winter is so cold! We long for spring!

New Mexico beginning to sound inviting. George says the air is cleaner, the water unpolluted and that our fortune awaits.

Hands too cold to write more.

March 15, 1872. Chicago.

We leave for Kansas on Tuesday by train. Last stop, Sheridan.

Mr. Weare has lent George money for our transport and supplies and a small fund so that George can set himself up in the mine at New Mexico, which we will pay back once we are earning again properly.

George wants me to wear a wedding ring, for he says the road is dangerous for a young woman and, in some places, the Indians or bandit thieves will take a woman and sell her like a prize cow.

I've told him I'll not wear a wedding ring.

For I have a better idea.

Chicago Tribune
October 19, 1871

The Cow that Kicked Over the Lamp

A reporter of *The Tribune* called upon Mrs. O'Leary, of No. 137 DeKoven Street, in whose barn originated the fire which destroyed the city of Chicago on last Sunday night and Monday morning. It was the intention to "interview" her regarding the cause of the fire and ascertain all about the cow which kicked over the lamp.

She stated that this story was false: she did not go into the barn with a kerosene lamp; she did not milk at night; and she did not know how the fire started. She was asleep when the alarm was given, and was awakened by a neighbor, who rapped on the door and told her that the stable was on fire.

When asked how her house, which is not even scorched, was saved, she replied that there was a hydrant on each side of it, and a hundred of her friends filled buckets with water and threw it on the sides and roof of the building.

CHAPTER 12
ELLIE

March 1, 2019. San Francisco, California.

Ellie placed two Tupperware containers at Anika's door and knocked twice before darting down the stairwell with the boys. The food was both a gift and a practical solution to the day's needs: a cream cheese sandwich and baby carrot sticks for Nathan, whom Anika was picking up that evening, and homemade brownies — *sans* Nutella and evil palm oil — as a treat.

It was a huge relief to be back on speaking terms with Anika. That week, after their trip to Olompali, where they didn't knock on doors, didn't text, didn't even cross paths on the stairwell, was the worst, up there with the early divorce weeks when she and Joe were at a standoff. There was something so shattering about falling out with a female friend — as if she had been rejected by a higher power and nothing would feel right again.

Neither had given in, but after days of unbearable silence, Ellie ached for Anika so much that she'd taken a dish of roasted rosemary potatoes one evening to leave at Anika's door with a soft knock and a simple note:

I'm sorry. Can we make up before my emotional support potatoes get cold?

Half an hour later, Anika had returned the knock on her door and walked right in.

"I don't want to revisit it," said Anika solemnly, holding up her palm. "It's done. I'm sorry that we had such a horrible spat. But we're adults and, you know, and we both miss each other. Besides, your hot buttery carbs get you diplomatic immunity. Well played."

Ellie had nodded, tears filling her eyes.

"I don't know how it got so heated. But I don't ever want that to happen again," she said quietly. They had embraced and Ellie felt such a surge of relief that she couldn't help but let the tears fall.

"It's genetic," Ellie had murmured into her friend's shoulder. "Growing up surrounded by hotheads yelling half in Italian, half in English, half in some medieval expletive-laden tongue … sometimes we just … blow!"

Anika had laughed. "Right. An angry Italian woman is no trifling matter."

Ellie wiped her tears, as she peeled herself from Anika's gauzy linen tunic.

"Want to know the good thing about having a fiery Italian friend?"

Anika shrugged.

Ellie walked straight to the kitchen and grabbed the half bottle of Lambrusco next to the breadbox.

"Italian wine!"

They had both laughed as Ellie poured. They'd sat at the countertop and caught up on the few days they'd missed in each other's lives: how Nathan had shoved a dried bean up his nose at day care, and Ellie had to drop everything to drive over and extract it with tweezers because of some policy that would smite the day care staff from doing it; and how Leila thought Anika must be joking when she told her she was older than Google.

The argument had changed them, Ellie suspected. But perhaps as so often happened in the aftermath of an explosion, it would bring them closer. They both could see how easy it was for everything to fall away and in that short time apart, it was clear how much they needed each other.

Ellie simply wouldn't bring up Ben again, nor would she share her true feelings toward him. Anika just didn't want to hear it. For her part, she suspected Anika wasn't going to push on anything career related. They were at a truce. From now on, no straying into wobbly, painful territory uninvited. They would have to find a new way to let off steam.

No true friendship could survive too much truth, at least not too often. But for the moment, they were back on friendly terms. They needed each other, as they both struggled with their separate demons.

Ellie certainly had hers.

And Anika? Well, Ellie wondered, would Anika ever really be able to face up to hers? She didn't know. And she wasn't qualified to know.

After all, she wasn't a grief counselor.

As Ellie merged onto I-80 East, she double-checked the clock, 9:30 a.m., and saw the dashboard light up with the incoming call from Brad Foley. Finally, she had managed to get her phone paired to the Odyssey, and it was a relief to be able to talk business in the privacy of the car. Luca was almost always quiet in the car, calmed by the rhythm of the road.

Something about her new client's case irked Ellie. She sensed that Hansa Nambootiri might not be sharing something with her, but quite what, she didn't know. The woman seemed reluctant and scared. The more she'd thought about meeting the two sisters afterward, the more she'd realized it was quite unusual for two unmarried women from India to leave their village and come to the US the way they had done, albeit together and under such dire circumstances.

Still, she had gotten the ball rolling in the most essential and obvious vein, which was to file an application for benefits with the Workers' Compensation Appeals Board and to contact opposing counsel for a list of insurance network treating physicians to keep Hansa's medical care moving without her worrying about more out-of-pocket expenses. She had checked the box on Hansa's application for an expanded "Serious & Willful" claim, following up with an additional motion to the Board and a discovery demand. It had been only five weeks since Ellie had filed Hansa's case with the Board, along with an exhaustive demand for discovery evidence. Opposing counsel had already requested a meet and confer by phone.

Brad Foley was an experienced, apathetic attorney — the epitome of a company man — known for his tough negotiations on behalf of insurance companies, this time Labor Guardian for the dollar discount store.

"Well, points for punctuality," muttered Ellie before she pressed to answer, donning her imaginary saber, mask, and foil.

"Hi, Ellie," Brad said. "Thanks for making yourself available."

"Hi, Brad," Ellie replied. "I'm on the road but can chat briefly." *En garde,* she thought.

Brad got right to it.

"Look, you've filed an aggressive claim and discovery demand. I've taken a look at the file and the initial medical treatment records. While I sympathize with your client's situation, we'll need to examine all of her medical records from India. How do we know the extent of her injuries is solely attributable to her slip-and-fall at the insured's job site? I understand she did agricultural labor in her country."

That was true. Hansa had shared with Ellie that in her rural region of Kerala, the women and girls were the primary farmers and food providers for the family and community, with nature also serving as their pharmacy. When extreme climate conditions like drought or monsoon rains made their jobs harder, the all-too-common economic option was a descent into sex trafficking, along with the rise of illness and ebb of education. Hansa's parents couldn't bear to let that happen to Hansa and Rashila. Even if they survived, it was near impossible to regain the opportunity to pursue the cultural status of marriage. Their economic infrastructure was fragile, but the culture had endured intact for thousands of years.

Ellie lunged.

"Brad, first of all, she has a name: *Hansa Nambootiri*. Second, can we get serious? Medical records from India? She'd never been to a doctor in her life before her time in the US. Using that as a scapegoat to wear her down is just bad faith. Ms. Nambootiri has provided photos of the back room, showing not just multiple tripping hazards but exposed electrical wires and insulation among the clutter, not to mention rodent droppings. This isn't just about a spill; it's about a consistently unsafe environment that management failed to address. If you're thinking this is your garden-variety workers' compensation injury, you'll need to step up your game to defend against the S&W claim. Under the circumstances, I'm confident a judge will grant our discovery request for the insured's occupational safety protocols and training records, surveillance camera footage, and correspondence of the store manager."

Brad parried.

"Your client's — erm, Ms. Nam-biti's — photos and allegations are concerning, Ellie, but they don't justify your extensive fishing expedition for corporate records, which also contain proprietary information you aren't entitled to know."

"It's *NAM-BOO-TI-RI*. And I think what you don't want me to know is that, at a minimum, the safety records and protocols don't even exist — which is its own violation. But you know what? No need to respond to that. We have a hearing date set on the discovery issues, and we're comfortable moving forward with it."

Ellie listened to Brad's pause. "Ellie, the extent of discovery you're seeking, along with the natural pacing of a claim like this can leave your client without resolution for another year or more. Does that serve her? What does she really need? Help me help you help her."

Ellie rolled her eyes at Brad's disingenuous magnanimity and responded with a disrobement. "We're staring down the barrel of a total knee replacement, Brad, and you know it. And you also know that your client will be held responsible for additional damages on the S&W claim. Threatening us with delay won't change that. We can wait."

There was another moment of silence, which Ellie let linger before Brad sighed.

"Look, while we dispute the extent of liability, we're open to discussing a reasonable settlement figure along with a nondisclosure agreement and global release of any other employment-related claims."

Ellie, surprised at Brad's change of engagement, pressed: "Feel free to make an offer that reflects the gravity of the situation, your client's oversight, and the impact on Ms. Nambootiri's life, Brad, which I will convey to her. In the meantime, we're keeping the discovery hearing on calendar."

"I'll get back to you, Ellie."

The call ended. They were already broaching settlement? And a *global* settlement? Ellie's Spidey senses were tingling. That wasn't typical in an administrative injury claim.

"Mama thinks Brad tipped his hand, Honey Bear," Ellie announced into the rearview mirror, glancing back at Luca. What were they afraid of? Despite his decoy threats of delay, Ellie now had the feeling it was Brad's client who was in a hurry to make this go away. Since the start of Hansa's case, Ellie sensed she was missing something but just hadn't been able to pin it down.

Yet.

She was determined to get to the bottom of it before allowing Labor Guardian to scurry away with a discount dollar buyout.

It had been folded and tucked into the back cover of the diary, almost completely hidden. Now, Ellie gingerly handled the brittle page, covered in dashes, dots, stars, moons, and other symbols — alongside numbers and nonsensical letters.

On her lap was one of Teddy's journals sent by her mother; she dared not put it on the table in case it picked up a spill or a crumb. These pages were so precious to her, she felt as though she should be using archival gloves.

Feeling a shadow hover above her, she looked up to see who had closed in on her space and caught her breath.

Dr. Sam Varma — smiling at her.

"Is this seat taken?" he asked.

Clearly, it wasn't.

Ellie waved her hand in a *be-my-guest* gesture and felt a surge of adrenaline wash through her. She'd taken extra care today — hair blown dry with her big round brush, minimal makeup perfectly in place, and her favorite formfitting cream cashmere mock turtleneck hugging her just right.

Had she expected to see Sam today? Nope.

Had she hoped to? Yes. And … right on cue, she was blushing like a boy-band groupie at a meet-and-greet.

"No diary today?" asked Sam, still smiling.

Ellie lifted the journal from her lap into view.

"I just got a fresh batch! These seem to be from the 1870s onward. I have a stack. My mother found them in her basement."

"You're kidding," he said. "Someone's whole life in your very hands."

His teeth gleamed, suspiciously flawless, like they had a Hollywood agent. His modesty was not lost on Ellie: as a neurosurgeon, he held life in his hands on a regular basis.

"That's how it feels," Ellie said. "And I've just found this!"

Sam examined the yellowed piece of paper in her hands, eyes narrowing slightly.

"A code?"

"Yes!" Ellie was doubly excited now to share her discovery. "It looks like the cipher might be one letter shifted back, numbers replacing vowels, and symbols for names. It's actually pretty simple once you spot the pattern."

Sam grinned. "Aren't you clever."

More blushing.

"And? Don't leave me hanging. What does it say?"

Ellie *tut*ted, clutching the page to her chest. "Oh, that's top secret. Between me and Teddy."

Sam's grin widened, and he shook his head. "A scholar and a spy. Should've known."

Ellie beamed. She rather liked that.

"You've been keeping well?" he asked, his tone softening.

Was it a question or something else?

"Very well, thank you," Ellie said, matching his pristine manners.

Very well, if *very well* meant being crippled with mom guilt and facing the pressing reality that she couldn't do any of her jobs to the best of her ability — not as a parent, not as a lawyer, not as a mentor, not even as a friend. Treading water was more like it. But why let too much truth kill the buzz?

"Your son's session going better today?" he asked.

Luca.

"So far," said Ellie. "No calls yet."
"Do you live nearby?"
"No, we live in San Francisco."
"Oh, so a drive."
"Yup."

Okay, so ... small talk. *Who are you?* she wanted to ask. *Who are you inside, and why can I scarcely form sentences around you?* Was it an aura? Did he emit some airborne pheromonic potion? She longed to lean in and sniff his neck, his body, feel his stubble against her skin. There had been no one since Joe, and for a long time even married to Joe they had not been intimate.

But now ... well, now ...

"What are you —"

"Do you have —"

They both stopped and laughed.

"You go first," he said kindly, waving his hand over his coffee.

"No, you," said Ellie.

She wanted to climb inside this intoxicating man's head — for starters.

"I was just wondering," said Sam, "do you have a picture? Of this woman whose life you're reading? I mean ... does she look like you?"

Ellie shook her head. "No. I haven't seen one. But I do wonder all the time, what does she look like? Is there a family resemblance, you know?"

"It would be interesting to see," said Sam as he lifted the cup to his lips, "where the beauty came from?" He looked directly into her face.

Ellie blinked, buffering.

Did he just say *beauty*? Maybe she'd mainlined too much hospital-grade espresso and slipped into an alternate universe where devastatingly handsome neurosurgeons casually seduced exhausted moms — because there was no other way this was happening outside a reality TV series.

"I —" Ellie gulped.

And then she giggled. Like a teenager. *Darn it! Grow up, Ellie!*

"I don't normally do this, but I only have a few minutes, and I've been looking out for you, actually, and I'm not scheduled to work the next few Thursdays, so I might miss you."

Ellie's face remained blank as she tried to decode Sam's words.

"I would love to talk to you more, outside of here. About this diary, about your family. About you."

"Oh," said Ellie quietly, totally and utterly thrown.

"Would you be interested in that? Meeting up? Maybe a proper coffee? Or a drink? I don't drink, but you know, somewhere nice. Somewhere not," he waved his hands around him, "a hospital environment!"

Would she? *Hell yes!*

"Sure," she said as nonchalantly as she could. "That would be nice."

"Great," he said and reached into his pocket for his cell phone. "Give me your number, and I'll text you. You'll have my number then, and we can go from there?"

Ellie called out the digits while something surged through her like the dopamine rush of a viral TikTok (or so she'd heard). Lust? Exaltation? Joy?

Sam tapped in her number, and she felt her cell vibrate in her bag against her hip.

"Lucky your son isn't my patient," he said as he got up to leave. "Otherwise, this would not be allowed!"

Lucky indeed.

Ellie waved goodbye and watched Sam walk away, caressing the soft cover of the diary in her lap.

A date. She had a date.

Now … how to fit that into her life too?

Ellie was in a terrific mood as she pulled out of UC Medical Center. Luca was tired and she watched his eyes droop in the rearview mirror. Soon he would drift off to sleep. When her phone rang loudly just a few minutes later, she answered it straightaway and double-checked Luca in the back.

Still asleep.

Sheesh.

"Ellie Benvenuto," Ellie whispered toward the car console, hoping her voice was still loud enough to sound professional.

"Ellie!" said a bright voice, louder than her own.

Ellie winced. "Ruby?"

Ruby Martinez! Plot twist!

"You've been on my mind. Your office gave me your cell number; I hope you don't mind the unscheduled call."

"Not at all," Ellie said, raising her voice enough so that she didn't sound like a budget meditation app narrator.

"I can't get our recent conversation out of my mind," said Ruby. "What you were telling me about your former employer. I feel there's a lot there under the surface. Just waiting to be scratched. I told you we're about to present a roster of cases to the EEOC and you know, something tells me that maybe your case, what happened to you, well, it needs to be included."

Ellie sucked in a breath.

"And before you worry about giving anything away, I know who your former employer was. Let me tell you, Ellie, it's not the first time Hutton & Fetterer has come to my attention."

The name sent a cold wave of dread through Ellie. Even the mere mention of the firm could bring on palpations. It was maddening — that they still had such a hold over her. Of course, thought Ellie, the name of her former employer was on her LinkedIn profile. It wasn't exactly difficult information to sleuth out.

"I understand your hesitation in going up against such a formidable foe, but from what I know of you and your character, with your experience and from what you told me, you have a case on your hands here."

"Ruby," said Ellie firmly, taking another deep breath, summoning the power to discuss this issue that made her stomach sick. "I worked in litigation. It's not just the belly of the beast, it's the lower intestines. It upends lives. I can't have that kind of destabilization with everything I've got on my plate … with what I've already been through this past year. I just don't think I'm in a position to —"

"I get it," said Ruby. "Lawsuits are the worst possible vehicle for social change. Except for nothing, and that's where we are right now. It took more than a decade to pass the Family and Medical Leave Act, and it's very limited. So, when people say, 'Well, the lawsuits are limited achievements,' I say, 'Well, compared to what? We're not in Europe. In the US today, working parents receive supports and benefits that in much of the developed world would be considered scandalously ungenerous.'"

Ellie marveled at Ruby's dauntless determination and wished for a healthy chunk of her mettle. This woman was a weather front, her gale wind leaving nowhere for the faint of mind to seek shelter. But a familiar dread slithered up Ellie's spine. She'd seen exactly how these battles played out — protracted, brutal, designed to grind plaintiffs into dust before they ever saw a courtroom. Hutton & Fetterer had bottomless resources. They didn't just fight lawsuits — they buried people. It wouldn't just be a case. It would be a war, with her sanity, career, and financial stability as collateral.

"I hear you, Ruby. But … is it also possible that they were … right about me? I mean, maybe I just wasn't going to be able to do the job anymore?"

Silence.

"Ruby? Are you there?"

"I'm here," said Ruby, her voice grave now. "It just pains me to hear a woman like you driven to make a statement like that. Truly. You are exactly the right person at the right time to make a difference. You must believe me on that one. Why don't we meet?"

"Sure, okay," agreed Ellie, knowing this would buy her some time to think.

"I know you'll do the right thing," said Ruby. "We'll help you every step of the way."

Huh. Sounded like Ruby was really counting on Ellie. But she wasn't quite on board.

After Ruby hung up, Ellie drove along, her mind a whirr, the highway eating up all her thoughts. What a day. A date *and* a meeting with one of her all-time legal heroes?

Things might be looking up.

CHAPTER 13
TEDDY

March 28, 1872. Sheridan, Kansas.

The plains around Kansas City are covered with sagebrush and not so fertile and attractive as the prairies of Illinois. We saw small bands of buffalo and antelope grazing in the distance as the train passed along.

The grass was getting to green and some wildflowers were in bloom. When the engine stopped to take water at a water tank, we spotted a big rattlesnake on the side of the track! He was shaking and rattling and someone got out to try and kill him, but not a stone or stick was to be found.

A man with two .44 Colt revolvers attached to his belt pulled one of them and shot the snake! Then a man who had pulled up a sagebrush beat it and finished it off. We all looked at it with much curiosity and I saw George cover his hand and the scar from that snake he encountered all those years ago.

I think his hand still pains him sometimes, especially when it gets cold. Lord have mercy, how I hate snakes.

The man who shot the rattler took considerable interest in us and I sat quiet beside George, for this surely was our first test. He did not look at me funny or keep his eyes on me thinking something was strange as far as I could see anyway. The man told us his name was Harry Brooks.

George told him we were on our way to New Mexico, where he had a friend at a place where gold had recently been discovered and we were to make an arrangement with a freighting outfit bound to Santa Fe. We got to talking about whiskey and George said he'd never had one when Harry pointed to me to ask me if I'd ever had a whiskey and I shook my head and said, "No, sir," in the deepest voice I could muster, and he laughed but he didn't look at me like I was a girl.

When the train stopped at a station later, Harry got out, and George looked at me, a grin on his face for I had passed the test. He thought it all very amusing, but truth be told, I feel terribly nervous about the situation, even though, so far, I've been doing alright.

Harry returned to tell us that General Custer had a car on the end of our train if we cared to see him! We went out and saw the general standing in the front platform of his car with a kind of caboose partly used for sleeping quarters. He had blue eyes and heavy golden hair reaching to his shoulders and I thought him quite striking, looking every inch a soldier.

We have seen many soldiers so far. The US Army is all around.

What attracted my attention as much as General Custer did was an Indian sitting on the rear steps of the car. He had his hair braided and it hung down on each side of his face and there were several white eagle feathers sticking in it. He had on fancy buckskin leggings, moccasins on his feet and a bright colored blanket wrapped around his shoulders. Harry Brooks told us the Indian was Custer's favorite scout and bodyguard and went by the name of Bloody Knife!

Before we went back to our car Harry said, "Let me give you boys a little advice."

(Yes, he called me a boy!)

He said he didn't think we were "green" but of life on the frontier, we had not seen so much. He told us Sheridan was a very tough place and called it the "border of civilization." He said when young men come to the frontier and away from the restraining influences they have been accustomed to, their concealed natures will rise to the surface.

"When an educated man falls, he falls the hardest and sinks the deepest," he said. "If a man is a gentleman once, he is a gentleman always. If he is masquerading as a gentleman under certain temptations or misfortunes, the veneering gets knocked off. I would advise you to find some quiet room to lodge in while you look up your freighting outfit and get out of town as soon as possible. If you've got any money, don't show it. Keep only a few dollars in your pockets."

He told us to stay at the Sheridan Lodge as it was the quietest place he knew and told us to look him up if we ran into any trouble.

I guess George was thinking about what trouble we might run into, but all I could think was that my disguise had worked. Harry Brooks thought I was a young man! My hat, my trousers, my jacket and my hair all shorn off, well, I had passed as a boy.

Better than any wedding ring.

We got off the train, and I felt as happy as any young fella could be!

At the Sheridan Lodge, the landlady said she had a double bed unoccupied. It was in a room with another bed occupied by one man. George looked at me and I nodded, and we engaged it. I thought how if I wasn't disguised as a young man, this would certainly have been a problem for us.

When I told George that I would go with him on the road, but only dressed as a man, he had balked. But when he saw that I wasn't for turning he eventually agreed and went and spoke with P. B. Weare to organize the loan.

He did not tell Mr. Weare the nature of my plan. I informed him he didn't need to tell anyone, for it was my idea and my guarantee of safety and he said I sure was a mystifying young woman, and warned me not to let ANYONE know of my real self on the road, for it could mean real trouble for me should a man somewhere take umbrage to my disguise, but if it meant I would go to Elizabethtown with him, then he would accept it.

He only asked that when we got there, I would go back to being a young woman and so I packed my corset and skirt right at the bottom of my carpet bag. I cursed them for taking up so much room.

The landlady told us of a bull train leaving for New Mexico if we wanted to go seek out the boss. She also warned us not to go to the saloon next door, for she expected there to be trouble there that night.

"Last night there was a brutal murder committed at that place," she told us. "It's a saloon with a dance hall out the back and one of the girls was sitting talking to a man to whom she was engaged for the next dance, when one of the toughs of the town came in and asked her to dance with *him*. She said she was engaged, but he insisted, and the two men began quarreling. Well, the girl pulled the man away and as they walked across the dance floor that tough pulled out his gun and shot that man in the back, stone dead! This morning the shooter was found hanging to the railroad bridge just below town. The vigilantes got him. There's a committee, you see, to make the town a safer place and there's a rule that if a shooting occurs in any saloon, the saloon must remain closed for a week. This morning the proprietor tore down that notice and opened the saloon anyway, so I'm expecting trouble!"

George and I tried not to appear shocked at such a story. Such lawlessness. Imagine getting shot in the back like that! And a vigilante committee, no less!

We went and found the boss of the bull train and he told us he knew of the mines which were eighteen miles up in the mountains near Maxwell's Ranch and that he would take us and our trunk to Maxwell for $25 but would not be responsible for the trunk if the Indians took us in.

We asked if there was danger from Indians and he said he thought not, but he put that clause in all his bills of travel. We paid him the money and were told to be there at twelve o'clock the next day.

Later that evening, we returned to the guesthouse passing the saloon next door. The front doors were wide open, and there was dancing in the dance hall but it didn't look busy, as if people were keeping away. We sat around in the guesthouse till about nine o'clock and were just thinking of going to bed when all at once we heard a commotion and ran to the window.

Marching down the street were ten men, two abreast, armed, with the new Winchester repeating rifles. The vigilante committee!

I stood with my mouth open, waiting to see what just might happen. A proper shoot-out and we weren't even in Sheridan a full day!

There was an alley between the hotel and the saloon, and the men and women were climbing out the back windows like rats fleeing a ship.

The committee began firing, one shot each, after the other, bang, bang, bang, over the heads of the occupants of the place! Ten shots in all! We'd never seen anything like it. There was much screaming, but no one hurt in the end. The committee closed up the doors of the saloon and put their notice back up for a week.

The proprietor would lose his week's business. But better that than his head, I thought. We went to bed but could barely sleep for the worrying. The man in our room came in drunk, took off his boots and climbed into bed in his clothes and began snoring like a great big elk.

"This is the quietest place that Harry Brooks knows, huh?" said George in the dark.

I couldn't help but giggle but then covered my mouth, realizing I sounded just like a girl. I am going to have to get used to being a boy.

And bedtime, not to mention my monthly when it comes on, is a dangerous time. I can't use a chamber pot, only the john. And neither can I change in front of anyone else. I suppose when we get to Elizabethtown, I can go back to being a girl.

But truth be told, I quite like being a young man. Ain't it fortunate that *Teddy* works for a boy too! One would almost think I had planned it!

March 29, 1872. Leaving Sheridan, Kansas.

Our bull train is composed of four teams. Each team consists of five yoke of oxen (ten animals) and a large, covered wagon called a prairie schooner, which has oak bows over it so the canvas can be drawn tightly at each end to protect it from rain and snow.

We are hoping for fine weather though.

Behind our hindmost wagon is a small wagon attached with the provisions to be used on the trip, as well as the cooking outfit which has a bunk in it where the night herder sleeps in the daytime. The night herder looks after the camp when we sleep, watching the oxen to make sure they don't stray, and calling the cook at daylight. His horse and another one for general use are hitched behind the cook wagon when we're on the road. We walk alongside the wagons.

Our cook is a silent black man and at suppertime he gets his outfit from the wagon and spreads it on the ground, building a fire with wood he has brought along to prepare our meal. Last night we ate beefsteak and potatoes, bread he bought in a bakery and had tea in pint tin cups. We were ravenous after all the walking and fresh air.

The prairie, far as the eye can see, is level as a floor and covered with grass, wildflowers and sagebrush. The air is pure, fresh and invigorating. It is a joy after the polluted air in Chicago. We all wonder if our lungs are perhaps damaged.

After supper we sat around the fire and listened to the rest of the folk talk until it was time for bed. All the men had brought tick beds with them filled with straw, but our boss, seeing George and I had none, gave us two spare.

When I asked about snakes, the boss man took pity on me and said there was room for us in the cook wagon if we squashed up tight after I showed him the scar on George's hand. It is not something he likes people noticing, but I would take a safe bed over George's embarrassment any day.

In the wagon, just before we went to sleep, George wrapped his arm around me and tried to kiss me. I knocked him in the groin area, hard as I could, and he yelped and pulled his arm back and I told him if he tried any funny business again, next time, I'd do more damage.

He says I've become hard only a few days on the road. I told him Teddy, the young man, is fierce and he'd best not forget it. I think he would have laughed except for the pain of the kick to the groin.

April 20, 1872. Santa Fe Trail.

While no one was paying any mind, I've turned eighteen. A real woman (well, in disguise) on the open plains where real Indians roam! Who would have thought?

We have grown used to the pace of life on the bull train. Almost three weeks have gone by. There is something about this journey, the air, this vast, unaltered land all around us. It has introduced a calmness to both of us, I guess.

I've noticed a big change in George, like a weight has been lifted from his shoulders. The fire in Chicago left him in such a melancholic state. Now, he smiles. He's more like the George I first met.

Some days we take the horses and ride ahead of the train. George carries an Allen revolver with four barrels. The men on the train make much sport of this gun, for they are notoriously unreliable. The gun is charged with powder carried in a flask known as a powder horn. Then you add paper and the bullet, rammed in on top of the powder. It explodes when the hammer strikes a percussion cap. George says it's a very strong shooting revolver, but the men say the most dangerous place to be is behind it!

When we first rode out, leaving us quite exposed, George told me not to worry, that if anything happened, he'd protect us with the gun. I told him that if he could give me a minute's notice before he detonated his hand grenade so I could get as far away as possible, I'd be much obliged!

Yesterday we saw three men coming towards us in the distance when we were riding the horses and the fright came upon us! We took them for Indians and we could see them stopping to look at us with a pair of field glasses. They moved off and did not come near us, much to our relief, though George got the gun ready, just in case.

When the bull train caught up with us, they thought it was a hoot, for the three men had passed them on the way, and it was none other than

Buffalo Bill and two companions! He was on his way to escort General Custer at Sheridan.

The boss told George that he must have moved on when he spotted the Allen revolver through his field glasses!

"He did what any good man would do. He ran!"

All the men laughed and I thought it funny too, but George was a bit humorless about it all. He can be like that sometimes.

Takes things to heart.

April 25, 1872. Santa Fe Trail.

Today we saw some real wild Indians!

One of the men on the train spotted one lying on his stomach scoping us out, right on top of a bank of the arroyo, the dry riverbed, we were camped at.

We all chased him and I saw him weaving in and out, his hair in two braids down his shoulders, naked save for a breech-clout, leggings and moccasins. One of the men tried to shoot at him and the boss man reprimanded him and said the Indian had done nothing to us and probably meant no harm, otherwise he would not be alone and unarmed.

The man responded saying all Indians mean harm and would kill us on spot given half the chance and he should have taken the shot anyway.

After dark we saw them sending up signals and the boss said we had to keep watch all night then in case they came back as he reckoned the Indian was likely sent out as a scout for a hunting party. I was fascinated by the signals, flaming arrows shot into the air. One would curve to the right, the next straight up and the next to the left.

"They are probably making signals to some other party," said the boss man. "They may not intend to attack us, but we better be on watch. If they do attack, it will not be until daylight. I've never known Indians to make an attack in the night, they come just before dark or just after daylight. They take their victims by surprise, never attacking unless they are vastly superior in numbers."

I found it hard to believe that the Indians I'd read about in my *New York Ledger*s were now so close by, sending up arrows, possibly getting ready to come and slaughter us all!

I'm still not sure which frightens me more: snakes or Indians.

I took my turn on the watch and surprised myself by managing to fall asleep, straight after, exhausted. We made it through the night. But I hope we don't come across any more wild Indians before we reach Elizabethtown.

April 30, 1872. Fort Lyon, Colorado Territory.

Fort Lyon, where our cook traded and we had a meal of antelope steak, boiled potatoes, hot cornbread, fried eggs and a big pitcher of milk. What a treat to have fresh eggs and milk! First time eating antelope steak and it was quite tasty.

When we took the horses out last week, we saw buffalo being hunted by a group of Mexicans. They rode their horses into the riverbed where the banks in most places were higher than their heads. George said the wind has to be in the right direction to hunt buffalo.

They went slowly and got right up close, when a bull gave the alarm and the animals started to run and we all after them. A buffalo has short legs, its greatest weight being across the shoulders. They can run quite fast, but a horse can easily out-distance them.

One of the Mexicans selected a young bull and threw his rope and caught him around the horns. The poor thing was brought to such a sudden stop that it fell to its knees. Another Mexican rode up behind and threw the loop of his rope under the buffalo so that the first step it took, it would have to step inside the loop. The Mexican jerked the rope quickly and caught the animal around a hind leg and in the next step threw it on its side.

It took two attempts to cut the young bull's throat with a knife. After skinning the buffalo, they cut the skin into three pieces. They cut off hunks of meat mostly from the hump and hindquarters, placed the meat in the pieces of skin and brought the skin together over the meat, like a parcel almost.

As we had been following and watching in wonder, they cut two strips of meat for George and me. That night was the first meat we'd eaten in a week as we'd been eating bacon straight three times a day until then.

I think I prefer buffalo over antelope. But I can't get the picture of that poor young bull and his big curly head taking that fall. Still, I wasn't complaining when that meat was in my mouth. Food tastes better outside I reckon.

In a few days we reach Bent's Fort and then we will not be too far from our final stop. George is anxious to get to Elizabethtown and is itching to leave the bull train which he claims is the slowest form of transport ever invented. He's probably not wrong.

He hasn't tried anything funny again. I do feel a little bad about the whack I gave him, but that's Buck for you. Shouldn't be crossed and strong as a young buffalo!

May 3, 1872.

As we're near the mountains, the scenery has changed. We have left the plains with their flowers, sagebrush and alkali behind.

Two snowcapped peaks stand just above us, some six thousand feet high and others much higher in the distance. The trail across the mountains covers the Raton Pass, and the land belongs to Dick Wooton, an old hunter and trapper and former friend of Kit Carson, a great frontier man. Papa once gave me a book on Kit Carson.

How strange now to be stomping round the same ground he did.

Papa is on my mind. I have sent two notes to North Sandwich and one to Boston so far. I worry for Papa that he may not recover, and I am all the way out here on the move. George tells me not to worry, that it is the cycle of life. He says I will have my own family one day to worry about. I know he thinks he will be the father of these children, but the thought makes me squirm.

We have to pass through Wooton's toll gate, come down to level country again and then we reach Maxwell's Ranch, where we will head for Elizabethtown. I will miss the boss man and even perhaps those slow, loping bulls, with their enormous horns and plodding hooves. I have enjoyed our journey mostly.

George insists we are on the verge of our fortune.

Bugbee will leave a letter for us in Elizabethtown giving the exact instructions to get to his mine. He, George and, I suppose, me too, will spend the next few weeks digging out the ditch and getting it in working order to sluice out the rock, down to the seam where they think there is gold.

George talks to everyone about mining. I don't find it interesting one bit. As for making our fortune, I'm not so sure.

Somehow, I don't really feel our luck is in.

Five Surprising Facts about William "Buffalo Bill" Cody

His nickname came from a job with the Kansas Pacific Railroad

He supplied twelve bison a day to the hungry workers (killing more than four thousand bison in an eight-month period). This overhunting by him and others contributed to the near extinction of buffalo.

He probably wasn't a rider for the Pony Express

Although he did carry messages on horseback, when the Pony Express existed, Cody was in school in Leavenworth, Kansas, and couldn't have been riding back and forth across Wyoming at the same time.

He supported women's rights and suffrage

He spent time in the presence of women like Annie Oakley and Calamity Jane and supported women's rights, which was revolutionary at the time. In an 1898 *Milwaukee Journal* interview, he is quoted as saying, "Set that down in great big black type that Buffalo Bill favors woman's suffrage… These fellows who prate about the women taking their places make me laugh… If a woman can do the same work that a man can do and do it just as well, she should have the same pay."

He supported civil liberties for Native Americans

"In his writing it's very clear there was tremendous respect for American Indians," says historian Jeremy Johnston. "He would tell his readers that [Native Americans] had every right to resist what was happening to them, and to fight back."

He was a conservationist

He was involved in one of the first federal water development projects and, despite his history of killing bison, he supported their conservation by speaking out against hide-hunting and by pushing for a hunting season.

(Smithsonianmag.com, January 10, 2017)

CHAPTER 14
ELLIE

March 21, 2019. Sacramento, California.

The hotel had looked okay online. Three stars. Understated modern. Not a contender for an HGTV "big reveal" montage—but they weren't in it for the aesthetic.

It had been a last-minute thing, after the clinic had called to say the waitlist had moved in Luca's favor and could he come to the MIND Institute for an overnight EEG in three days' time? Ellie had said yes without hesitation. For Luca, she would make it work.

That left her at a loose end for a whole night in Sacramento. A whole night in the same town as Sam, with whom so far, she'd miraculously squeezed in a tingling coffee date — and he had graciously met her in Berkeley — and a tantalizing two-hour phone conversation after she'd put the boys to bed one night.

She'd texted Sam to set it up, not quite brave enough to call, and at the same time, exhilarated. Sam had offered to host at his place, but Ellie wasn't sure she was ready for that step. What if it all spiraled—awkward pauses punctuated by mismatched kisses—and then she was trapped in his minimalist kitchen for twelve hours, with nowhere to hide but behind the Nespresso machine until it was time to pick up Luca?

She'd spent the afternoon buzzing with anticipation, checking her reflection too many times, spritzing just the right amount of Martha-sponsored Bond No. 9 Gold Coast. But as she pulled into the parking lot and took in the dimly lit exterior—the flickering neon sign missing two letters—that giddy energy evaporated. *Oh no.*

The parking lot was half empty, the wind shuffling garbage along the curb. The hotel was wedged beside a row of shops long past their prime. The scene whispered *Fixer Upper* before-the-reno—with no Chip or Jo in sight. Decidedly unromantic.

Inside, the picture didn't get much better, causing Ellie to wonder how long ago the website photos had been taken. The "modern" décor looked cheap in person, and the receptionist barely spoke as he handed over her key card. She shot Sam a quick text with the room number, then stepped over the worn carpet in the corridor, noticing burn marks, fraying, and a distinct smell of something ... wet dog? Ellie wrinkled her nose. She had arrived an hour early so she could properly prepare for Sam's arrival. Now, her enthusiasm waned—replaced by that particular flavor of misgiving reserved for good intentions gone sideways.

Reaching her room, a young woman overtook her in the corridor, led by a much older man, three times her girth. Ellie watched as the girl passed in a miniskirt and bralette, the man's grip firm, possessive — like she was a prize. Ellie had seen her in the shabby lobby earlier, looking lost. Thai, to Ellie's learned eye. The whole situation was off.

Ellie slipped into her own room, closing the door firmly behind her. She peeled the cheap polyester comforter off the bed and shoved it into a chipped cupboard. She had planned on ordering up champagne to chill, but now she wasn't so sure. In her bag, she'd brought strawberries, chocolate, and new lingerie. She had wanted this to be memorable, but it was shaping up to be memorable for the wrong reasons.

Somewhere in the distance, a vacuum whirred. Outside the window, their room looked onto the highway, and the glass rattled slightly every time a big rig passed. A sharp knock at the door made Ellie catch her breath. Who was that? She peered out to see Sam.

"Sam!" she cried. "You're early!"

So much for being draped in a beguiling pose across the bed in black lace. So far, nothing had gone as planned.

"My last patient canceled. Never happens! Crazy, huh?"

He held out both hands in closed fists in front of her. "Pick a hand."

"That one," said Ellie, pointing to his left.

Sam opened it to reveal a small glass vial. "Breathe in," he said. "Vetiver. Smells like home." Ellie uncapped the vial and took a slow inhale. The scent was deep and earthy, like sun-warmed wood after rain. Ancient. Steady. It settled low in her ribs, like something remembered. She exhaled, a little dizzy — not just from the scent but from the intimacy of it, the way it felt like he was offering her a piece of himself.

"Okay, pick a hand," he said again, holding out only his right.

Ellie laughed and tapped his suspended hand, which opened to reveal a set of dice.

"One roll. High number, I kiss you first. Low number, you kiss me first."

It seemed to Ellie she'd win either way. She blew the dice and let them tumble to the ground. Before she even glanced at the outcome, Sam pulled her in, his hands firm at her waist.

"Hello you," he murmured.

"Hello you."

The moment stretched between them, heat simmering just beneath the surface — until Ellie's self-consciousness caught up with her. She stepped back, raking her fingers through her hair.

"Get out of the doorway already. Come in; make yourself comfortable; I was thinking of ordering up champagne or —"

"Okay, if you like. I don't drink, but don't let that stop you."

Of course. He had told her that before. How could she have forgotten? But Ellie had probably been thinking of herself. Or her own nerves.

The vacuuming stopped. Sam sat on the bed. Ellie sat beside him.

"This isn't as nice as I was expecting," she admitted sheepishly.

"It's fine," he reassured her, tucking a loose section of hair behind her ear.

Ellie got a whiff of wet dog again — a far cry from the vetiver. Where was it coming from?

"I'm not sure I want to order anything up from room service."

"Do they even have room service?" Sam chuckled.

"Oh, God," said Ellie and she gripped his thigh.

Sam leaned in and nuzzled her.

"It's horrible," she said, covering her face with her hands. She had really fumbled this.

"Well, the offer stands to go to my place if you like," he said, pulling her up with both her hands in his. "It's no Palace Hotel, but it has its charms."

Ellie stared into his eyes, wondering if she was crazy to be moving so fast. They'd both been under restraints, always pressed for time to properly get to know each other.

And yet ... she couldn't wait for his hands on her.

Nearby, the sound of a man grunting filled their ears. Ellie cringed, her mind flashing to the ample man she'd seen lumbering down the corridor with the girl in the miniskirt. She caught Sam's eye, and the shared understanding between them cracked into laughter.

She grabbed her unpacked bag. "I've seen all I need to see here."

Ellie wasn't quite sure what to expect from Sam's home, but it was much more stylish and cozy than she'd imagined. It was warm and unpretentious, a perfect reflection of the man himself — thoughtful, tasteful, quietly inviting.

It was spacious and airy, with a plush L-shaped sofa, a gas fireplace, family pictures on the walls, and colorful throws and rugs. A pretty balcony overlooked a stretch of leafy greenbelt, where a winding bike path cut through the trees. Two green potted plants stood like sentries at the railing. He even had candles set in black glass. As Sam moved through the space, he paused to light one, and warm, smoky notes of sandalwood and leather unfurled into the air. The place was spotlessly clean and uncluttered.

"I have a cleaning lady," said Sam with a shrug as he welcomed her in. "I'm so glad she came yesterday!"

"And there was me thinking you lived like this all the time," said Ellie.

"I do, actually!"

"Well, it's a damn sight nicer than that sketchy hotel," said Ellie. "I'm so sorry about that."

"No apologies allowed. You don't need to try, Ellie. Just be," said Sam, a glint in his eye, and they lingered on each other for a moment, Ellie wondering what exactly that thought was. Was it the thought of each other, skin to skin? The thought of pressing together in bed, breathy and sweaty? Or the thought that she was, as Anika had put it, "undersexed" and had only one thing on her mind?

"What would you like to drink?" offered Sam. "Sparkling water? Or I do a mean mocktail?"

"Oooh. Flex your mocktail mixology skills, Dr.!"

While Sam went to the open-plan kitchen, Ellie wandered his living room, studying the photographs. Sam hit a remote control and the sound of Charlie Parker's "A Night in Tunisia" filled the space in surround sound. Ellie stared at a family portrait on the wall. There was Sam, younger, what seemed to be his father and mother and three other women in the photograph.

"Are they your sisters?" she asked.

"Uh-huh," said Sam.

"You were the family favorite, I take it?"

"More like a highly managed experiment."

"That sounds either adorable or insufferable. Which was it?"

"Well, I have a mother who adores me and three sisters who carried me around like a doll. I know women."

"You don't say," said Ellie, her heart skipping to be the subject of his deep knowledge of women.

Another photo showed a young Sam dressed in a long, pleated cloth wrapped around his waist and legs, a fitted shirt, and another long cloth draped over one shoulder. The outfit, with its elegant lines and simple jewelry, reminded Ellie of something dignified for some ceremonial event.

"Look at you. What a cutie."

"That cutie is a dance champion," said Sam as he squeezed a fresh lime into two tall glasses. "Bharatanatyam. One of the oldest classical dance forms in India, with roots tracing back to Tamil Nadu. Traditionally performed by women. I was the only boy."

"Oh my!" Was it getting hot in here? She needed that drink to cool her down.

He was a classical dancer. Well, that explained the posture. And the … everything.

"Tell me what it's like in Chennai," said Ellie, taking a seat and waiting for her drink.

"Very different from here," said Sam as he pressed the glass rims into crushed rock salt. Ellie couldn't help but be impressed with his efforts. "It's quite a big national city; you get people coming from all over India to stay there, as it has really good medical centers and hospitals. That's where I trained. I miss the food. Isn't that what all immigrants say? But truly, I do. The food is very good there."

"Do you ever regret leaving?"

It was such a direct question. Ellie hadn't meant it to sound so probing.

"Sorry, I didn't mean —"

"No," Sam said, shaking his head. "It's totally fine. No, I don't. I wanted some adventure, you know. Something different and exciting. My parents, of course, my mom especially, had mixed feelings when I left. But I just had this calling. To go, see the world. And I always wanted to see America. I loved Michael Jackson growing up. As a dancer, I thought, *wow, I want what he has,* even though it was totally different from what I knew; I was just so attracted to all that. And of course, I always liked beautiful American women too."

He winked at Ellie.

She laughed, slow and syrupy, letting it settle between them.

He made her feel irresistible. What was it with this man who seemed to look through every part of her, her intelligence and burning curiosity? She felt as though she could lay bare her fortitude — her opposing, vulnerable, and jagged parts that she had to hide from the outside world. She felt like Dr. Sam wanted and needed those, that he could epoxy those parts together. She had never felt like this with anyone. Not even with Joe.

"American Italian!" she said.

"I love that. I would love to visit Italy. Chennai is a coastal city, so when the position came up here and I could see it wasn't too far from the coast, I knew I'd be happy here. I like getting to San Francisco when I can."

Sam presented her with the iced, rock-salted tumbler, and Ellie reached up for it, wondering if his comment about San Francisco was a request to visit her. To see her home turf. Ellie thought about hosting the poised doctor in her apartment, showing him her beloved Coit Tower with its twenty-seven murals — full of secret messages, if you knew how to find them. Would he love it too? Would he fit there? It was hard to picture him in her world when she was so enjoying being in his.

They sat over drinks for an hour — delicious, tart, electrifying Ellie from the inside out. They talked about their families (and Teddy), their friends and careers; about music, world events, and a show Ellie had watched about the pink dolphins of the Amazon River.

"They really are pink — and they get even pinker when they're excited!" She was gushing, turning pink herself with forgotten giddiness. And all the while, Sam never took his eyes off her, as if he couldn't get enough.

It was she who made the move. She who could no longer hold his gaze, needing him — to feel him, to touch him, to taste him. He jumped when she lunged at him, grinning before leaning in to meet her, wrapping his arms around her. For the hundredth time since she'd crossed Sam Varma's threshold, Ellie thanked her lucky stars they'd left that tacky hotel behind.

Here was much better. Here, for their first time, in Sam's stylish, welcoming, masculine-smelling condo, was perfect.

They tumbled out of bed later that evening, ravenous.

Ellie suggested takeout but Sam waggled his finger, insisting on cooking.

"I want to give you a taste from home."

"Well, I think I already got a little of that," she said, and his smile deepened, binding itself to the deepest part of her.

Her delicate new lingerie having been hungrily peeled off; she now lounged in Sam's shirt with the sleeves rolled — it smelled of him and swallowed her body — while a now shirtless Sam got to work in the kitchen. She loved to watch his capable hands. And oh, how capable she now knew they were.

Over the past two hours, Ellie had felt as though Sam glimpsed the flame behind her eyes, a yearning for release — and managed to wholly embrace all her incongruous parts. She felt safe and worshipped, reckless and untamed — a part of her unleashed after being caged for so long. He had been confidently kind, patient, and masculine — intoxicatingly intricate and strong.

And she had loved every second of him. His presence was a force field, pulling her in, until surrender felt as inevitable as gravity itself. With him, she had crossed into something uncharted — a world carved out just for her. Here, she wasn't expected to lead, strategize, or decide; she could simply be — held, guided, undone. The anticipation of his control was a whispered vow, humming through her like a slow current, suffusing every nerve, quieting the part of her that was always on.

For once, she could let go. She could come home to herself.

She lay back on the sofa, listening contentedly to the sounds of Sam chopping (fast like a chef), the refrigerator and cupboards opening and closing as he toiled in the kitchen. She closed her eyes to Nina Simone's woeful "Ne Me Quitte Pas" flowing from the speakers, and opened them again to find Sam presenting her with another mocktail, delivered with a full kiss to the mouth.

Ellie placed her free hand on Sam's chest. "This song just wrecks me. Do you know what she's saying?"

"I don't, actually. I don't speak French."

"Well, I do. She's begging her lover not to leave her. It's heartbreaking."

"Then I guess he'd better stick around. Problem solved," Sam said, and he placed another gentle kiss on her lips.

She floated in a hazy reverie, awareness ebbing and surging like warm surf lapping at the shore. Every sensation sharpened, her body entirely hers. Alive. Aching. Sated.

After they ate dinner—a riot of flavors and aromas so vivid and layered it was as if Sam had steamed a rainbow and served it with jasmine rice—he took a cool, moist cake from the fridge.

"I have a sweet tooth," he said, owning his sins.

He told her to close her eyes, then fed her pieces of cake with his fingers, his voice low, thrumming, threading through the moment. Between bites, he murmured to her, teasing, soothing — until, finally:

"Look at me, Ellie."

A command.

His fingers traced along her mouth, his thumb lingering at her bottom lip, testing its softness, its fullness — before leaning in, his own mouth delicately claiming the frosting caught at its corner.

Her eyes implored him, pleading for more — for plunder.

But he held off. Made her wait. Made her suffer for him.

He cradled her face in one graceful sweep of his sinewy hands and kissed her like it was the first time, the last time, the only time.

He owned her in that moment because she let him. She was his — his *my* — and they both understood the power of it. She was the wily cub to his lion as he played with her, teased her — because he could. Escape was irrelevant. There was no need to flee. Anything that threatened her wholeness, her peace, would have to get through Sam first. And he would simply not allow it.

"I've got you, my Ellie," he whispered.

As he finally moved into her, she breathed him in and felt his amperage course through her — kindling something deep and primal.

"Victorious in war." That's what the name *Samarjit* meant in Hindu. Ellie had Googled his name after their first date, wanting to learn more, to understand this man, to know and feel and love everything about him. *Varma*, derived from Sanskrit, meant "shield, protection." The Varmas now tended to work in the fields of medicine, engineering, science, and philanthropy.

As Sam kissed her breasts, taking both in his powerful, precise, surgical hands, the words of Grand Master Oogway of *Kung Fu Panda*, which Nathan watched obsessively, echoed in Ellie's head: "*There are no accidents in this world.*"

She was ready to be shielded. Ready to be consumed completely by Samarjit Varma — victorious, his conquered prize in war. Ready to be set free in the way that truly mattered.

"Take me," she pleaded in a molten whisper.

And to her pleasure, Sam obligingly, immediately, did.

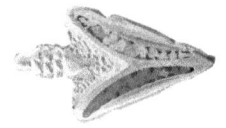

CHAPTER 15
TEDDY

May 28, 1873. Elizabethtown, New Mexico.

George grows more despondent day by day. The slow dawning of our situation eats at him like a worm in a rotten apple. The core is gone. Soon that fat worm will poke its way right out of George's eye socket. We are done for here. I know it, he knows it, Bugbee knows it.

I always felt it in the pit of my stomach that it would not work out for us here at this mine. The question now is what to do. I've had a letter from Mr. Weare, a personal note, which I was not expecting. He writes to George often, but this one was addressed to me. He says he is in need of a bookkeeper again and the position is mine should I like it.

It's very tempting for I know how the job suits me, and I do miss Chicago. He says the city has been rebuilding quickly.

George is sour all day long.

He says we had the fortune in our grasp, but circumstances tore it away from us. I'm not so sure about that. It was unfortunate that the water got turned off just as we nearly finished building that ditch. "Almost at bedrock." He repeats it over and over. "Almost at bedrock."

If the water was still running, I would perhaps be able to take on laundry or something else to earn our keep. George has asked about in town, but no one wants a woman bookkeeper. I can't help but think that if I'd stuck to my plan (and my trousers) maybe we wouldn't be in this predicament. I should never have put that skirt back on and George cannot say anything on the days when I do leave it across my chair, for it can be so muddy up here and it is such a hindrance, especially when you have discovered what it is like not to be bound by it.

But if the water was still running then I guess George and Bugbee would be getting to that bedrock, of course, and perhaps there would be no need for doing laundry anyway.

Elizabethtown bores me half to death.

Yesterday I thought I saw a bear and even though I know bears can climb trees, I shimmied up a great Scots pine for I thought if I'm up here he may pass by me and not see me. Thank goodness I was not wearing my skirt!

Well, that black bear passed me by and guess what, it wasn't a bear at all, but a great big black hog!

Scared me to hell.

This morning, we went to town and when I was in the store an Indian man came in to trade a bow and three arrows. I could not keep my eyes off him. He was tall, taller than you expect most Indians to be, and he smelled of fire smoke and mint all up close. He had the most beautiful woven blanket around him.

He wanted five dollars for the bow and arrows and wouldn't accept anything less. Mr. Moroney offered to trade him for a large glass of whiskey as often Indians will take that instead of money and then fall around drunk because they're not made to handle liquor the way white folk are.

But the Indian said no.

I looked at the bow and arrows and saw that they were quite beautifully made and thinking of that old black bear and me up the tree and how I could have shot him from the tree perhaps, I offered him the five dollars.

It was a stupid thing to do with us having very little money. But I could not help myself. I did not think of George and his sour puss, but that smooth bent bow and that stoic Indian, looking at me, his eyes, dark and brooding almost. I cannot quite describe it, and I would hate if anyone ever read these words that I now write, but a feeling came over me, somewhat like that feeling I had when I first met George, only this was different.

This feeling shot through to my core. It was as though I'd met him before, but not in this life, but in another. Isn't that something? Something queer?

The Indian pushed the bow and arrow over to me and I took the money out of my purse and I gave it to him. He walked out of the store, his stride, big, loping, and then he was gone.

I picked up the bow and Mr. Moroney laughed at me, saying I could have bought the thing for little more than a glass of whiskey, but I knew that Indian man would not have traded. I could tell that he was not one of those Indians to fall around drunk.

The bow was solid in my hand and as we rode back to our cabin, I ran my hands over it, thinking how that Indian must have run his hands over it a thousand times. He must have made it himself, tapering that cherrywood over and over, tying the sinew up tight. I noticed a simple carving at one end, a zigzag pattern with a crescent moon.

I could not hide the bow from George but neither could I tell him how much I'd paid for it and so I fibbed and said I had parted with only a dollar for it.

He said I was a foolish woman, and he was growing tired of me up in these mountains. He was silent then for a long time and I felt quite sorry about my situation and was getting to thinking how maybe I *should* take P. B. up on his offer of Chicago when George announced that a group of miners were leaving Elizabethtown for Virginia City in two days' time and he was going to talk to Bugbee about it, for if we didn't leave soon we would run out of money completely.

Virginia City. I don't know much about that place. But it would mean traveling back over the plains. Maybe I am a foolish woman. But somehow, I feel readier, like a warrior, carrying a piece of that Indian man with me, wherever I go. I suppose I don't mind if we do go to Virginia City. I'm tired of these unforgiving mountains too. I had a bad feeling about this place.

And I guess I was right, wasn't I?

June 16, 1873. Pueblo, Near New Mexico.

It is good to be back on the road and George's spirits have lifted now that adventure is afoot again.

He said not a word when I put on my trousers and appeared with my hair all shorn up again, just made that face he always makes when he sees something he doesn't like. Wrinkles his nose right up and frowns.

Bugbee chuckled to himself but I sat up on my horse, my bow and arrow on my back.

"Did you pack your razor?" Bugbee asked and nearly fell off his mount, laughing so much. I trotted down the side of the mountain thinking it was all very well for Bugbee to find it funny, but he, like George, had lived his whole life in pants and knew nothing of the hardship or the vulnerability of being a young woman on the road.

I knew George was thinking that he knew better than me, but from the talk I'd heard this was no longer the 1848 California Gold Rush and you couldn't get away with things like this now with new laws and hauling people to court for dressing outside your sex.

But the plains were another law onto themselves. I would be fine on the plains. Better than fine.

We packed what we could of our tools and traded the bigger items in town.

I was mighty surprised to see that Indian I bought the bow and arrow off had turned up as a guide, for we were traveling with members of the US Army to a small town called Denver, then on to Cheyenne where we would take the Union Pacific west. He didn't take any notice of me, and I guess didn't recognize me in my garb. I did see him eyeing the bow though.

In the mornings, George and I like to take our horses out over the plains for a gallop, for our horses are very fine saddle horses and enjoy the speed over the plains. I will be sorry to say goodbye to my mare at Cheyenne.

We have to be careful when we gallop due to the prairie dog holes which are all around. The holes are inhabited by a type of ground gopher and they live in large numbers like regular villages under the ground. The entrances to their holes are quite big and a horse can step in one, stumble and fall. I saw a rattlesnake at the entrance to one and our Indian guide — they call him Momo — told us that the rattlesnake, prairie dog and owl live together in the same hole and they help warn each other of danger. Later I did see a little brown owl fly up and flap his wings as we passed, making the most peculiar sound. Imagine having to live in a hole with a rattlesnake!

Momo travels with his wife Helki. She is quite beautiful with sallow skin and her shiny hair plaited down her back. I would like to ask them many questions but I know George would not like it, and, likely, neither would the army.

I know he is a married man (do Indians marry? Surely not properly, like us?) but I find the Indian ever so striking. Last night when I was settling down for the night I caught sight of him, washing before bed, and he lifted his overshirt and I was transfixed. I have grown used to George's torso and Bugbee's too, for they worked shirtless in the summer on the ditch. But this was different. It recalled to me a passage from reading Ann Radcliffe — "There is something in the eloquence of silence that charms the imagination more than words." My imagination felt suddenly like 4th of July firecrackers.

I wanted to run right up to him and embrace him, to lay my head against him, to sniff and smell and feel him, for the muscles on his stomach were hard, like pats of butter from the icebox.

Oh, such words. It is just as well that George is not very literate and would never think to read my scribblings. Thank goodness!

I hope I dream tonight of the Indian. It would not be the first time I've dreamt of Momo.

Something terrible has happened! We are still quite in shock! The road is an unforgiving place. Take it at your peril!

It all started at bedtime two nights ago, when Bugbee got to drinking some whiskey with the army soldiers. George was not too happy about this, for he said Bugbee could not hold his liquor. And indeed, I have seen in our time in Elizabethtown, when he would take to the saloon, like a man with a fire inside him, a fire that could only be quenched by liquor!

When we awoke this morning Bugbee's horse was gone, as was he. The soldiers had not seen him but said that he had been weaving all about last night, a man in a terrible state. Momo held up his tin cup at breakfast and tapped it at the halfway mark and told us that Bugbee had filled his cup with whiskey up to there and drank it! George and I knew that if Bugbee had drank all that, he would have been quite legless!

We saddled up to go and look for him, George and I in one direction, Momo and a somewhat guilty-looking soldier in another. We met on top of a ridge a mile from camp and from the ridge, we spotted Bugbee's horse grazing, but no sign of Bugbee. We spread out again and it was George who found him lying on his back in the middle of a big bunch of cacti.

We tried to get him up, but we could not arouse him. His buck-skinned gloves and his clothes were full of cactus thorns. He was breathing heavily like a man snoring, though he didn't seem in restful sleep. He was quite unconscious.

The men got him across his horse and we led him back to camp. Momo said his horse probably stepped in a prairie dog hole, stumbled and had thrown him a complete somersault down the ridge which was why he was lying on his back. (He didn't say somersault of course but this is what we devised from his gestures; Momo's English is sparse, but he speaks Spanish well, which I've been taking up readily myself.)

There was nothing for it but to put him on the wagon. We arrived at Denver at about five o'clock, which is a small town, much smaller than Pueblo, with only one street running through it, and perhaps fifty small adobe houses on both sides.

A doctor was fetched but he said we needed to prepare ourselves — for Bugbee's neck was broken. Oh, how wretched we all felt. Poor Bugbee. Poor stupid *drunken* Bugbee!

The doctor allowed us to stay in his surgery, for he said it would not be long — the traveling and putting him over the horse having done his broken neck no favors whatsoever. He did not seem in pain but remained altogether unconscious. George asked me to say my prayers over him for I feel they must have brought him some comfort, distraught was he at this tragedy to strike us.

I held poor Bugbee's hand as he passed, George by my side, white as an apparition. He did not shed a tear, but he was very shaken for he and Bugbee (and I too naturally) spent much time together on that mountain outside Elizabethtown.

"He never did find his gold," George choked after Bugbee had breathed his last and I wondered did it make George now more determined than ever to succeed.

For Bugbee.

Momo (who was waiting outside, for he is very loyal like that) and I took our horses back towards camp for George wanted to sit alone with Bugbee for a time, which we understood.

We were to return the next day to dig a grave in Denver, his final resting place.

Something happened, which I quite fear writing down and so I will write it in the private cipher I devised in Chicago — so that no prying eyes may make sense of it.

[CODED]

I write now in code to protect my dear George who I do care for so and who I know would be utterly dejected were he to discover these truths about me. However, I must write them down, as I fear, if I don't I shall simply burst!

It is of course all to do with my dear Momo! For the tension has been building for quite some time between us and as he steadied my horse for me to get astride in Denver, his hand fell to the bow that I keep tied there and he ran his hands over it looking somewhat quizzical and asked if he could see it, to which I agreed and he unpinned it and examined it and declared, "Mine," and he pointed at himself and said, "Molimo." I suppose that is his full name.

I nodded and took off my hat and shook out the hair that I have left. And on his face, there was a dawning, and he said "Elizabethtown," and I nodded again and then, all at once, it was as though he saw me for the first time! I was no longer a young, threadbare man on this journey across the plains, but that forward young woman he'd met that day at the store! The thoughtful woman who understood that such a bow and arrows were worth more than a damned glass of whiskey!

I am still grappling with what happened next but what tragedy and joy can happen in one day!

As Momo looked into my face in that dark Denver Street, it seems that I, not he, approached, for there and then, we embraced and kissed passionately and his lips were all over my face and mine all over his!

I felt as if I could devour him there and then!

We secured our horses and rushed behind an adobe wall, kissing, again and again and again.

"Your wife," I said, and he seemed quite confused. "What about your wife?" I asked again.

"No wife!" he said.

Then I said, "Helki?" and he laughed and laughed and laughed.

"Sister!" he said, then it was my turn to laugh!

I was so terribly fearful that George would come out then and find our horses tethered and wonder what on earth we were up to and so I did not want to delay longer and we rode back to camp.

Momo said he was very happy to be reunited with his bow and arrows and the reason he had sold them in the first place was to send money back to his tribe, who have been facing famine.

I presumed that his tribe were from nearby, but he explained that his tribe was from California, on the coast, and he and Helki had travelled a long way as his job as an army scout can take him anywhere. He said his people were scattered now, and that scouting was not his choice — not truly. He longed to return home.

I felt for this resolute native man, so far from home.

I went to sleep that night and later felt George bed down beside me and felt quite guilty at the night's events. They say shock can make you do strange things.

But this strange thing that happened — I could do it again and again and again forever!

George must not find out anything whatsoever.

Momo and I must keep our delicious secret to ourselves.

No one will suspect him of kissing the young man on this trail so passionately. No one suspects young men of much at all.

It is the women they always watch. And I have cleverly taken all eyes off me.

Yesterday Helki's horse stumbled into a prairie dog hole and she was thrown quite badly. We are experiencing some terrible luck on this journey.

She damaged her wrist and leg as she landed awkwardly on her left side. We put her in the wagon, like we had done Bugbee, and she asked me to fetch her skin bag she carries, in which she revealed many dried herbs and powders, some lumpy, peppered with bark and berries.

I made her a tea under her instructions which she took for pain relief. She told me her wrist and ankle are broken.

The army sergeant said when they get to Cheyenne they will have it looked at but I felt he could quite easily have forgotten the native woman as much as fetch her a doctor. Native women are not seen the same as white women. She is but a burden now, as her purpose with us was as a medicine woman.

Momo is terribly worried. If she can't ride, it's impossible for her to travel on with the army, for they simply will not cart her around in a wagon unable to do her job.

Soon we will all be parted.

[CODED]

As we will reach Cheyenne soon, I let my emotions come over me and I have given him my all. I do not regret it. Not one bit.

I felt delirious afterwards. I am secretly a true, full woman now.

How can I now be separated from such a man? How cruel life is. How wretched I feel thinking about it.

But I must hide my tears from George. He would never understand. And even if he did, I'm not sure my good companion would care.

We have reached Cheyenne. Our train leaves tomorrow, west.

A doctor confirmed the fracture in Helki's wrist and ankle and splinted her wrist and wrapped her leg. He is worried the ankle has dislocated and that infection could set in. She is taking her herb medicine to prevent infection. I told her if she bottled it, she could sell it as she is getting great relief and does not complain.

They are in quite the bind now, for Momo is still contracted for another six months! It is a pity she cannot travel with us. I have grown close to her in the past few days. She has a beautiful, settled spirit. Quite dignified.

Goodness, George surprises me when I least expect it. It was *he* who suggested Helki travel with us to Virginia City. I am questioning whether Bugbee's death has softened him!

Helki will take the railcar with us, for she really is not fit for horse or wagon. Momo will meet her in Virginia City when his contract ceases and they are happy with this arrangement for they are getting nearer and nearer to the coast, where their people are.

It is quite sad what Helki told me about their Miwok tribe; there is only a handful left! She explained that even before the gold rush, settlers took Miwok lands and killed many of the tribe. I could not imagine it. Such barbarism. Since last century, the missionaries arrived to convert them and others, but her family resisted for it was well known that the missions brought great diseases that could not be cured. She said it's the reason she and Momo left for the trails, as at least they could be free.

George says that now that we have ended our journey on the plains, I should return to dressing like a young woman for it is too dangerous to tempt fate any longer but I have argued that we should see how Virginia City pans out first. He does not want me to be taken for a common prostitute! I told him with my soft face and body that I can pass for a young man very well and he need not worry.

Tomorrow Helki will say goodbye to Momo.

I expect she will be very sorrowful!

July 1873. Granger, Wyoming.

George does not understand what saddens me so.

How can one endure such heartache?

September 1873. Virginia City, Nevada.

Oh, how we have grappled these past months to make our life here.

Virginia City has not been as lucrative as we expected. George has bought many stocks, and even traded some, but the times when he made a sum for himself, ended up lost again, through bad trades or useless mines.

I have refused to go back to my dress, much to George's dismay and taken jobs working mines to support us.

The work is harder than I could ever have imagined. The shaft I work currently goes 2,000 feet into the ground and each day. I am lowered down like a rat in a bucket, straight into the mouth of the furnace. The heat is unbearable. The men work in overalls and nothing else, but I of course cannot take off my shirt. They rib me and say I have something to hide. They have large tanks of ice water in the lower levels and we are obliged to stop and throw the water over us, regular, and each time I am terrified they will see my bindings underneath and so I only wear dark clothes.

We are saving to buy more stocks. We must try to pull ourselves up. George always believed he would dig his own lucrative mine, not work someone else's.

Helki's wrist has mended and she has set up a small laundry and is out the door with both laundry and medicine work. Last week when we counted up our wages, we discovered that she earned more than George!

He was most despondent. And yet he is very fond of Helki. I am feeling most tired. Ever since we've got to Virginia City I've had to haul myself out of bed, in a manner I have never experienced. My body aches. My head is weary. Helki gives me teas. They help, but sleep is only a moment and then it is time to rise again.

October 1873. Virginia City, Nevada.

George wishes me to leave the mine and run the laundry with Helki so we can increase our loads. We fear the water is bad here in the city and is making me sick and tired. George has come to work in the mine with me; his stocks have failed again and the mine he was working turned out to be redundant. I preferred it when I was alone down there, for I feel he is watching me closely all day long.

November 1873. Virginia City, Nevada.

My tiredness is gone. I have a renewed vigor, I feel bright and look forward to the future, despite the hardships here. Our seam has proved valuable, and we have finally drawn down some, I always felt this mine would pay off.

Helki has expanded her laundry business though her hands are raw, and her wrist continues to be a bother. I'm not sure if she can continue at such a pace much longer.

George has lost much weight and yet I have gained some! We joked that he has sent it right on over to me!

I think George has set his cap for Helki. They laugh and whisper together and she makes him a soothing tea each evening before bed. There has been no word from Momo. I dream about him. Sometimes, on the breeze, I feel that he is with me. His spirit, guiding me.

George tells me he thinks I'm half-Indian.

I take it as a compliment.

December 1873. Virginia City, Nevada.

Oh wretched day. Oh cursed, wretched day.

I am at sea — lost to the Gods! I will not recover from this! All is lost. Foolish woman. Foolish, foolish, woman.

George is making arrangements for us to leave immediately. I await his beating. It is what I deserve. How we shall come back from this.

We are leaving Virginia City. It is the only way.

Oh, wretched, wretched day.

VIRGINIA CITY BUGLE
December 13, 1873

WOMAN DISCOVERED DOWN MINE

A most shocking event occurred in the O'Reilly shaft on Thursday last after the discovery of a young woman, disguised as a man, caused consternation among the miners. The young woman, who donned a hat and overshirt, despite the raging heat, is thought to have been working in the mine for some four months now, never revealing her identity, and thoroughly fooling all that made her acquaintance.

The shocking discovery was made at 2,000 feet below ground, after a minor accident which shunted two buckets together, injuring the young woman in question. When the miners came to her assistance and insisted on examining for injuries, the shocking discovery was made. Reports also suggest that the young woman may be with child.

One worker told this reporter that the miners are resentful of being fooled so and ran the young woman out of the mine. It's believed the woman's husband was also working the mine and that both, along with a native woman they employ, have fled town. The owner of the mine did not respond to requests for commentary on this shocking and quite unprecedented turn of events.

CHAPTER 16
ELLIE

April 3, 2019. San Francisco, California.

"Please, Ellie!"

"Anika!" Ellie groaned. "No!" She laughed. "You go, it'll be good for you, a night out just the two of you! I'll babysit!"

"First of all, it's not a night out but a corporate mandate, and secondly, my mom is already babysitting, and she will watch your two, so you have no excuse!"

Ellie paused, rapidly searching her brain for another reason to bow out of the Robo Top/Fuji gala dinner scheduled for Saturday night, an event that Anika had been begging her to attend since the weekend. The last thing Ellie needed was a swanky gala and all the performative pomp that came with it: dress, hair, makeup, shoes, golf talk, the economy, and next year's presidential election a constant chatter around the table. The event was in only a few days' time, and she had been looking forward to a quiet weekend of doing mostly nothing. Work, childcare, and the student clinic, not to mention her new romance, were running her ragged. She wanted a break. Not a black-tie Pinterest endurance test.

The gala was a celebration of the recent hush-hush merger of one of Silicon Valley's giants and Ben's robotic company, a deal, Anika claimed, was the reason he'd been so tense and had needed to take so many work trips to his London base. Knowing how moody he had been lately (even though Anika still covered for him and rarely brought him up in conversation since their fallout), Ellie didn't want to appear to endorse her best friend's toxic husband. Surely attending his work event would seem as though she were. But how to say that to Anika without chafing her?

She knew her friend needed the support and was likely nervous about attending the dinner without backup. Everyone was bringing their wives or partners, and Anika felt she had no choice.

Ellie tried again. "I know I'm being super lazy, but I need a break, Ani. Besides, I wouldn't know anyone."

"Super lazy? Is that like regular lazy, but you wear a cape while eating peanut butter from the jar? And you'd know *me*! Come on!" said Anika. "Besides, you're like the homecoming queen at these corporate shindigs. I'm the band geek with my tuba, sitting at the jock table. One of Ben's colleagues had to run off to Singapore on another deal, so we have an extra seat at our table."

Ellie laughed at Anika's self-deprecation. She realized, suddenly, that this would be Anika's first night out since everything. Her friend really did need her. The guilt trip was settling in, and resistance was futile. She had plenty of dresses in her wardrobe care of Martha, anyway. A little *zhuzh-ing*, and she'd be perfectly presentable for a night of forced small talk and excessive wine. She found herself unable to proffer more protests.

Ellie mustered a smile, conceding to Anika's victory. She would go to the Palace Hotel on Saturday night, smile, drink, eat, and make all the small talk in the world. What else were friends for?

"I guess I'm going," said Ellie, to which Anika punched the air and whooped.

"Yay," she said. "Thank you so much, my friend! You won't regret it!"

Ellie's eyes drifted upward, toward the domed glass ceiling, cascading evening light into the sprawling atrium of the Palace Hotel. All around were finely dressed people, and yet Ellie couldn't stop looking at the ceiling. The room was breathtaking. She'd forgotten how stunning the wide atrium was, with its huge gold-and-crystal chandeliers overhanging ionic older marbled columns fit for a Roman palace itself. It had been quite some time since she had been there. No events or meetings had taken her into the historic, luxurious building since she'd left her last role, and she felt excited to be there now. And a part of her did enjoy being dressed up, polished and all set for dinner and drinks now that she was actually there.

It had been a major rush to get ready after work, but she'd managed to fit in a blowout on her lunch break, and as she looked around at the dewy, K-glossed women in sculpted dresses and stealth-wealth stilettos dotting the room, she was glad. She wondered how many had time for a 6 a.m. Peloton session to appease an accountability coach named Ashley—instead of the daily cage match otherwise known as brushing their kids' teeth.

Anika had bought a dress and done her own hair: she said she could never find a hairdresser who understood her curls and, being totally out of her natural habitat, needed extra reassurance that she looked the part. Seeing Anika dressed up but still not quite looking the corporate doll, Ellie realized that tonight was probably much easier for her than for her best friend. Anika belonged more naturally on a yoga mat than strung up in a shiny dress. But she'd been right about one thing: Ellie fit right in.

Ben looked dapper enough in his sharply tailored tux and artful bow tie—an ensemble that whispered refined charm while concealing a human hand grenade, the pin inching closer to release with every jaunty swallow of expensive liquor.

As a tray of champagne glasses floated by, carried by a demure waitress, Ellie swiped two for her and Anika. Ben had immediately dumped them on arrival to glad-hand colleagues, while Anika had looked at her with *thank-God-you're-here* eyes as they watched Ben unabashedly kiss a brunette female colleague on the cheek and pump his male colleagues' hands up and down.

"That's the London team, I think," said Anika as they heard clipped British accents over the din. *Nice of Ben to introduce them*, thought Ellie.

The newly created division was being launched as "Fuji Fun," and roll-up banners featuring the new logo and branding had been placed about the atrium, although to Ellie they looked a little lost in the vast room.

As her eyes scanned the denizens of the regenerative, self-congratulating corporate ecosystem, she lingered on a person she thought she recognized—an attorney she'd once been acquainted with from another firm. The lawyer had been part of its corporate division and had been a hard driver, of the Brad Foley ilk. She'd recently noticed on his LinkedIn that he'd moved to Hutton & Fetterer, and she remembered thinking it was a good catch for them, as he was a real pit bull in negotiations. He was speaking to a woman who ... wait ... was that ...?

Ellie felt a familiar dread taking hold, a mix of nausea and racing heart, blood flushing her cheeks, and the overwhelming urge to flee.

"Jesus, Anika, did Hutton & Fetterer handle the merger?" she whispered.

"Huh?" asked Anika, holding up her glass to watch the light sparkle through it. "No idea, Elle Belle; how would I know something like that?"

Ellie's eyes bounced from lawyer to lawyer as she counted up the faces she knew. The cold dawning that she was now standing among a whole cohort of her ex-colleagues ripped through her. She felt the panic crescendo. She was being confronted with all that she'd left behind, with people she'd hoped never to see again, and she watched them laughing as if taunting her. She was trapped. And what could she do? She couldn't leave Anika now, with the whole night ahead!

"I'm not sure I can stay," she murmured to Anika, turning her whole body around as if to cast off the sight in front of her. "I can't face —"

Alarmed, Anika grabbed her by the arm and squeezed it.

"Ellie," she said, "if I can stay, so can you. Hold your head high. Do you think I'm comfortable either? Do you think I've been looking forward to everyone's sympathetic glances, watching them wonder whether they should talk to me or seeing them turn the other way to avoid me?"

Ellie stared at her friend, their pupils wide and matching, like a pair of cornered animals.

She felt deflated. And then resolved. She could not cower. She simply would not. She straightened her spine as tall as her petite physical stature would allow, held up her chin audaciously, and plastered a smile-cum-grimace on her face.

"Let's grab a drink," she said with a veneer of confidence as she hooked arms with Anika, and they headed to the bar. "A real drink!"

At the bar, Ellie ordered two whiskey sours, and they downed them like a timed exam at a frat party.

"No more of these," said Anika as she set her glass on the bar. "You know I can't handle liquor."

But Ellie needed a little top-shelf liquid courage to survive this dumpster fire of an evening. They moved back to the atrium where Anika made conversation with some colleagues of Ben's she recognized, Ellie holding her breath to see if anybody would bring up the elephant that Anika dreaded most.

Realizing she was hungry, Ellie grabbed a canapé off another floating tray carried by an immaculate waitress and was just putting it in her mouth when she spied "Dan the Man," a raucous partner at Hutton & Fetterer, striding toward her. "Dan the Man" was the nickname given to him by the "bros" at the firm (their creativity knew no bounds). He was one of a posse of men who often went for drinks together in the evenings, and Ellie had detested him.

She shouldn't have left her utility belt at home, she thought fiercely; she could have used it to rappel herself up and out of the glass ceiling of the atrium at this very moment. In desperation, she turned her back, suddenly fascinated with a potted fern, contemplating a future in botanical curation.

But it was too late to avoid Dan's advance. Embodying the hallmark casual arrogance of his compadres, Dan placed both calloused golfing hands on her shoulders with a slight massaging action, in the way men of his kind took license to touch women in "friendly" little ways. Ellie pirouetted on her pointy-toed heels to face him.

"Ellie Benvenuto," he roared, his face too near hers. "What a blast from the past! How's mommy life treating you? Must be pretty sweet to stroll in the park all day, huh?"

He guffawed into her face. Ellie felt her insides shrivel. Dan was a real *enfant terrible* at the firm, though, admittedly, there were so many of them, he was hardly remarkable. The condescension was palpable, igniting a silent rage within her.

Struggling to stay poised in the den of the Minotaur, she channeled her inner Medusa, imagining Dan caught in her laser-loaded gaze and zapping him into a stone memorial: *Here once stood a pasty white dude whose greatest contribution to humanity was halitosis and leveraged buyouts.*

She flashed him a silent, cutting smile, nodded at Anika, and excused herself, saying she was just on her way to the ladies' room. As she marched toward the pristine and delicately perfumed restrooms, she could still feel the weight of Dan's sweaty palms on her shoulders and his skeezy stare. She shuddered.

Ellie's mind whirred like a disco ball. This evening was already turning out way worse than she had expected. How she wished she was at home right now, or even better, wrapped up by Sam, somewhere, anywhere but here.

She pushed open the door of the restroom, opened a toilet stall door, put the lid down, locked the door, and sat and breathed. She would take a few moments of refuge before making her way back to the snake pit.

"Pull yourself together, Ellie," she whispered.

And then, almost involuntarily, she heard it—Enzo's voice, deep and deliberate in her memory: *Georgina Ellis Benvenuto, you hold your nerve.*

She closed her eyes. Just a few more hours and she'd be home. She could do this.

The evening wore on, as welcome drinks moved on to dinner, where wine flowed and the courses seemed to take forever, leaving nothing much else to do but down the booze. But then, this crowd could do that like Olympians.

The seats were arranged so that Ben was between Ellie and Anika, and he held court at the table, cracking jokes and telling long-winded anecdotes at which his British colleagues laughed in commiseration.

The woman he'd kissed on the cheek was sitting directly across from Ben, and Ellie couldn't help but notice how the two kept catching each other's eye. The woman was much younger than them all — Ellie guessed early twenties. She was quiet and standoffish, and Ellie had not spoken a word to her all night, but as she watched, she noticed that her focus was completely and utterly on Ben.

Ellie turned her attention to Anika, to see if she, too, had caught the starry-eyed nymph, but Anika seemed lost in her own world. She barely looked around at all, instead concentrating on her plate, taking gulps from her drink, and generally looking like she'd excused herself mentally from the whole evening. Ellie eyed the bottle of wine on the table and realized that Anika had downed quite a lot of alcohol, far more that she herself had. *Oh crap.* Now that she looked closely, Ellie could see by the glassy look of Anika's eyes that her friend was, in fact, completely wasted.

When dinner finally ended, after a long flurry of droning, predictable speeches, some die-hards rose from their tables and headed for the bar, while others gathered in little clusters to mingle once more. Ellie surveyed the huddles and could identify the sets within the room: tech, management, HR, admin, basking in their latest conquest of the robotic toy world and other life-saving feats.

From the stage, a live band kicked into action, and the atmosphere lifted, as some women rushed the dance floor to whoops of delight. Ben excused himself to the bar, asking Ellie and Anika what they wanted to drink. Anika wanted another wine, and Ben had scurried away before Ellie could even protest that maybe he should get her a sparkling water instead? It was as if he didn't even see his wife, or perhaps he himself was too lubricated by libation to notice Anika's vulnerable state. Ellie glared at Ben's back as he bolted to the bar at warp speed, while his pretty little dark-haired pony — not inconspicuously, Ellie thought — trotted after him. They leaned in toward each other, and Ellie saw Ben give her a quick squeeze.

This evening was too much.

"Want to go to the ladies' room?" Ellie asked Anika, but her oversauced friend waved her away.

"No, thanks."

Ellie lingered a moment before once more making her way to the sanctuary of the gilded restroom, allowing time for the post-dinner crowds to filter out. The marble floors echoed her steps, a stark contrast to the din of the gala outside. She washed her hands first and checked her makeup, enjoying the rush of the warm water against her palms. The makeup she'd applied earlier that afternoon hadn't budged. *Go, Ellie!*

Upon hearing the door open and the sound of two women approaching with the force of minor tempests, she dashed to a stall, still clutching a monogrammed towel in her hands, and shut the door. Oh, how she longed to be alone at home in her pajamas — or swaddled in Sam's shirt, melting into him. She sighed and leaned her head against the side of the stall. She took out her phone and sent Sam a quick kissy-face emoji. They were in daily contact, and Ellie felt a little flutter every time she saw his name pop up on her phone.

Poor Anika. She would have a raging hangover tomorrow, and looking after small children while your head ached was no picnic!

The toilets flushed beside her, and she heard the gather of the two women at the sinks, clucking, admiring each other's dresses while simultaneously running down their own appearance.

"Megan! Ohmagod this merger has been hell. I'm soooo glad it's over. But, oh, I just love that color on you; you should wear it more often."

"Oh, thanks, Olivia. I know, right? What a pressure cooker. And I'm literally obsessed with your highlights; they're new, right? I noticed them the other day when I was at the photocopier."

Megan.

Olivia.

Ellie had worked with Megan and Olivia at Hutton & Fetterer. Megan was an executive assistant for Dan the Man. Olivia was an associate attorney, four years Ellie's junior before her unceremonious departure. Ellie eavesdropped as the two women tittered at the sinks, preening. She dared not emerge from hiding now.

"Did you see who was here?" asked Megan, her voice conspiratorial.

"Who?" asked Olivia, her words muffled by her hand, reapplying either lipstick or lipliner.

"That attorney who used to work in our group — what was her name? I can't think of it. She left — the one with the special needs kid?"

"Who?" asked Olivia again, her voice raising an octave, curiosity piqued.

Ellie heard one of the women — Olivia? — teeter toward the plush peacock-blue tufted bench and plop herself down.

"I swear these Louboutins are plotting to kill me!"

She kicked off a spiky red-bottomed heel—it skittered just under Ellie's stall like a matador's flag waved at the wrong bull. Oh, if only haute footwear were her greatest adversary tonight. Ellie stared at the shoe, contemplating its potential as a makeshift weapon or an instrument of escape.

"I can't remember her name," Megan continued. "but I saw her here! A senior associate —a *pick me* type — a few years ahead of you."

"Not Ellie Benvenuto?" said Olivia.

"Yes!" said Megan. "That's her!"

"You're kidding," said Olivia. "I wondered where she'd gone! She started in litigation, then moved to our corporate group, but then disappeared. Yeah, total *try-hard*. What is she even doing here? Does she even have a job?"

"You'd think she'd be at home wiping bottoms and scarfing string cheese," said Megan.

"She should be!"

There was a lull in the conversation while Ellie tried to normalize her heart rate. She was torn between the instinct to flee and a morbid curiosity to hear every single word. Her experience in handling dozens of depositions told her that when the witness babbles, let the words flow freely.

"Dan said she was, like, the worst," said Megan. "Didn't she totally lose it over some timesheet drama? Tried to snitch on everyone?"

Timesheet-gate. Back when she was pregnant with Nathan, Martin—her then-supervisor—had told her to (illegally) falsify her hours away from work for OB appointments. She'd refused.

"Probably," said Olivia. "Zero chill. Now that I think of it, Roger said she was cringe — good riddance, I guess."

"Yeah," Megan hiccuped, "He said as much to Dan and Warren in an email just before they cut her loose. That she wouldn't be able to toe the line anymore anyway, with her kid's whole deal and all."

Roger.

And Warren.

Oh, Ellie remembered them, all right. She remembered Roger's crowded pink-frosted bottom teeth as he chuckled at the "Is this the last of the pregnant women?" wisecrack by that little toad Warren.

Megan dropped her voice to impersonate a man in a silly voice.

"'Not the good soldier we thought after everything we did for her career.' And 'All these women who think they can do our jobs and come and go as they please popping out babies — like, pick a lane already!'"

Both women burst into a fit of giggles.

"He thinks I don't see his emails," Megan said. "Please. I have access to everything. And yeah, no shocker — zero farewell party for her."

"Not worth the time away from billable hours!" added Olivia, haughtily.

The hairs stood on the back of Ellie's neck as she heard Mean Girl 1 and Mean Girl 2 cackle, drunk on trickle-down toxicity and a cloud of Tom Ford Lost Cherry. Without thinking any further, she stood up, flung open the stall door, picked up Olivia's shoe, and strode to the sinks.

Olivia and Megan dropped their jaws in shock, and Olivia's hand froze from massaging her sore foot.

"Olivia," said Ellie, tucking the shoe under her arm as a hostage and turning on the faucet. "Megan."

Savoring the absolute horror on the women's faces, Ellie unhurriedly took another monogrammed towel, dried her hands, then calmly approached Olivia at the bench.

"I believe this is yours," said Ellie, and set the shoe in her satin lap.

"El — Ellie ..." said Olivia, but Ellie was already retreating, her posture high, head straight, denying the gossiping geese one word of remorse.

In the corridor ahead, she thought she glimpsed Ben disappearing around a corner. She made her way back to the table to check on Anika only to find her weeping, head in her hands.

A chic woman with bobbed sideswept hair, looking helplessly bewildered, sat beside her.

"I ... I don't know what I said," said the woman, who was dressed in a smart and unusual tuxedo-style dress.

"Anika?" asked Ellie gently, rubbing her arm. "What's wrong? Ani?"

Anika shook her head, unable to speak. Suddenly, she stood up.

"I want to go home," she said. "Now."

"That's fine," said Ellie soothingly. "That's fine; let's go find Ben and tell him."

Folding her arms, Anika staggered forward.

"What happened?" Ellie asked the other woman as she stood to follow Anika.

"I've no idea!" said the lady, looking totally confused. "We were talking about our children. I told her mine were driving me mad, that I'd die if I got pregnant again, that I'd rather ... It was a joke! It seemed to upset her!"

"For God's sake," said Ellie. "Her little boy died last year."

"Oh, good Lord," said the woman, mortified, covering her mouth with her hand. "How utterly awful. I'm so sorry — I had no idea!"

Ellie rushed after Anika, who bounced off each table she passed like a steel ball in a pachinko machine, rattling toward its exit.

"Wait!" Ellie cried.

Anika was stupid drunk. In the corridor, she gripped the wall as if she were about to collapse. Ellie had never seen her so far gone.

"He blames me," she slurred. "And he's right. Ben wanted to take Hugo to Stanford hospital, but I thought the transfer from UCSF was too risky. It's my fault ..."

Ellie steadied her friend. "Wait here!" she said, maneuvering Anika onto a low sofa farther up the corridor. "Just wait here a second. I'll go find Ben and call us a car, okay? Please don't move from here, all right?"

Anika nodded, like a child herself, barely able to function.

When Ellie rounded the corner in search of Ben, she found him tucked up tight in a secluded chair with the raven-haired woman, their legs crossed over each other. They had found a quiet corner to escape to, their body language far too intimate and compromising.

"Ben!" Ellie barked, dispensing with decorum.

He looked up, saw her, and leaped from the chair, ejecting the young woman from his knee.

"Ellie!" he blubbered.

Ellie walked right up to him and narrowed her eyes. She looked straight at the young pixie — then back to Ben, branding them both with her knowing exactly what the score was.

"Have you met Vanessa," he said, trying to recover, "from the London team?"

"We were at the same dinner table, Ben," shot back Ellie, adding icily, "but we didn't get acquainted."

What. A. Douchebag.

"Anika needs to go home," said Ellie, shunning the dainty paw Vanessa proffered for shaking. "She's not feeling well. She's had too much to drink."

Ben rolled his eyes contemptuously.

"She can't drink!" he said. "She always gets like this!"

Anika did not always get like this. She rarely, if ever, drank more than a single glass of wine. Tonight, she had drunk because she was desperately uncomfortable, sad, and now, Ellie realized, confronted with the cold stark reality that her husband was having an affair.

"I can't really leave," said Ben. "There're still so many people I need to speak with. Why don't you take her home?"

So, there it was. She was being ordered home by the husband of the year, himself. If he needed to speak to so many people, Ellie thought bitterly, then why was he wasting his precious time with this young British tart draped over him?

"Fine," said Ellie, defeated. "Order us a car. We'll wait in the lobby."

"Great." Ben smiled with the hollow gratitude of a spoiled child who'd expected a pony for his birthday all along. Vanessa stepped back and folded her arms protectively. *Good instinct*, thought Ellie.

Ben now had the whole evening to spend with whomever he wanted, Ellie realized as she walked back to Anika and helped her up off the low sofa. Such freedom with no repercussions. Honestly, at this point, Anika would have been better off settling down with a very wealthy dog — one that wouldn't gaslight her or openly flirt with interns.

"I know," said Anika as they drove through the streets of the financial district, the Transamerica Pyramid tinkling like an ornament and the Bank of America building towering over California Street.

"What, honey?" asked Ellie, squeezing her hand.

They grasped palms in the back seat of the car like two small children on a school tour.

Anika was staring out the window as the car made its way along Kearny Street toward North Beach.

"Everyone thinks I don't know. But I know."

Her voice was low and labored. "I found a receipt. After he came back from London, months ago …"

Anika turned her glassy eyes to Ellie. Ellie just listened, though she already knew this story.

"I remember cuz it was my birthday. And Ben said, 'I had takeout, chicken chow mein,' but I found the receipt."

She was reliving it.

"He went out for dinner after that call. Dinner for two. Wine. All of it. He lied to me. And so, I know. I've known for months."

She turned her head back to the window and rolled it down just enough to let in some fresh air. In her state, Anika forgot she'd mentioned the dinner receipt to Ellie months ago but then wouldn't talk about it anymore. Ellie didn't know how to respond.

"I'm really sorry, Anika," she whispered.

Anika shrugged drunkenly. And then added defiantly, "I will not be divorced."

Ellie, bristling, didn't challenge her. Anika was in no fit state. Even if it did rankle her that her best friend looked down upon her own personal situation. Instead, she squeezed Anika's hand and turned to look out the window.

Under the shadow of Coit Tower, Anika exited the car, steadying herself at the wall while Ellie rummaged for keys. She managed to wobble up the stairs, leaning on the banister for support. Ellie removed her friend's clicky heels and brought her right into the quiet apartment where Bravo met them at the door, tail swishing but, fortunately, not barking; he was intuitive like that.

"Good dog," whispered Ellie, shuffling Anika into her bedroom. Ellie helped her off with her dress and got her, in her underwear, into bed. She fetched a big glass of water and two Tylenol and returned to the bedroom.

"Ani, honey, take these and drink this." Ellie lifted her friend and held the cup to her mouth as she drank, barely conscious, before flopping back onto her pillow. Bravo climbed onto the bed and wedged himself against Anika, sensing she wasn't well. Ellie gave him a couple of pats.

"*Buona notte*, Bravo," she whispered.

She tiptoed to the living room and, one by one, carefully lifted Luca and Nathan, who were "camping" in a tent in the living room with Leila and Milo, who didn't stir. She carried them, in two trips, to their own beds and left the apartment silently, deeming her covert op of getting Anika safely to bed and extracting her kids—without waking Anika's sleeping mother—a successful mission. *Agent Ellie. Woman, myth, legend. She takes her smoothies like she takes her intel: immersion-blended with extra collagen peptides.*

Afterward, she sat, holstering her last nerve like a seasoned operative who knew revenge was best served on legal letterhead, feeling…not tired, like she'd expect, but filled with purpose. How dare Ben treat Anika like that — publicly! What a total unmitigated wanker that he'd risk their family and bring more unhappiness upon them — after the loss of their precious little Hugo.

She rose from the sofa and paced the living room, fire building in her belly. How rigged the world was for weak men — shielding them at all costs. Anika, she knew, would excuse Ben's behavior as "grief." She seemed wholly disinclined to hold him accountable, to expose his selfish, callous actions.

Ellie took a facial wipe and attacked her makeup in the living room mirror. She needed a cold cleanse to get to the dark mascara, but as she stared at her reflection, a thought descended on her.

She looked different. Wilder. Determined.

Angry!

There staring back at her was not a woman defeated by her past but ignited with a resolve to confront it.

Makeup still half smeared, she walked to the dining room table and opened her laptop, her painted nails *click-clack*ing on the keys. She scrolled her inbox and blinked. She was more sober than Anika for sure, but she'd had plenty of alcohol that night. Was it really the best idea to email now?

Yes. Yes, it was, she thought. *All I truly have is right now!*

"Hi, Ruby," she typed with unrepentant fury. "Can you put me in touch with that attorney who you said was eager to take my case? I'm going forward with my lawsuit against H&F."

She hit *send* before she could deliberate it any longer.

The *whoosh* of the email sending shot a thrill of electricity through her. The foggy night air outside seemed to hum with the promise of retribution, the reassuring beacon of her Coit Tower illuminating a resolute course, and she closed her laptop with a decisive snap.

Fuji Fun, indeed.

These fellas wanted to play?

Let's play.

PART TWO

The Brisbane Courier
Wed 1 September 1875

"The Biggest Hotel in the World"
(By our San Francisco Correspondent)

The Palace Hotel will be ready for guests on or about 1st September. San Francisco has not hitherto been without its beautiful hotels and the Lick House, Occidental Grand and Cosmopolitan, all belonging to the first rank, have been the admiration and the resort of travellers from all parts of the world.

The growing importance of this city, however, with its attractions as a place at which to rest and enjoy the blessings of a salubrious climate, and its position on the highway from the Atlantic states and Europe to Japan, China, East India and Australia, give rise to a want of larger hotel accommodation, the result of which has been the erection in the principal thoroughfare of the city of the largest hotel in the world!

This gigantic edifice is located at the corner of Market and New Montgomery streets, the former of which is the most important street in San Francisco and corresponds with Broadway, New York and Sackville Street, Dublin.

The Palace Hotel covers 96,250 square feet of land, or a little less than two and a half acres, has eight storeys, including the ground floor, the lower one of which is 25 feet high. The walls and petitions throughout are of stone and brick laid in cement and banded together with iron. The roof is covered with tin, while the entire basement floor and working apartments are wholly of concrete, rendering the building not only most substantial in all its points, but absolutely fire-proof.

Fronting the centre court from every story, there are verandahs 12 feet wide, illuminated by standard lights at each pillar and from the garden level to the verandah of the second floor is a grand staircase ornamented at its various landings with vases of flowers.

Midway up the staircase is the approach to the music pavilion for the use of an instrumental band of about 15 performers who will be exclusively employed at the hotel. From the centre court is also the entrance to the office, bar room, barbershop and billiard room. Here also we find our way to the breakfast room, the dining room, music room, ladies' reception room and reading room. On the second floors are the ladies' drawing room, children's dining hall and private dining rooms.

Every one of the bedrooms has a fireplace, closed closet and toilet room. And to every two rooms, there is a bathroom with hot and cold water ready at every moment of the day. The outer rooms, that is, those facing the street, have each a bay window. And there is not in the whole hotel a single dark or ill-ventilated room. There are five elevators and seven stairways leading from the garden floor to the upper story, the elevators being worked by hydraulic power, which, while the most desirable speed is attained, are secure and noiseless.

The chief cook of the hotel is a Parisian by birth, his name, Julius Harder. He has cooked banquets for Emperor William, the Czar of Russia, Queen Victoria, Louis Napoleon and Prince Bismarck. The confectionery department will be under the charge of an Italian named Raffa, while a Viennese is employed to superintend the making of bread.

The brain behind the machine has been Warren Leland, the future lessee of the hotel and one of a family which for three generations has been celebrated as caterers for the public.

Mr. Leland is a man in the prime of life with a fine constitution and gifted with those qualities which specially fit him for the arduous position he has assumed. A most energetic businessman, he is notwithstanding liberal and kindhearted to a fault, endearing himself to all who come into contact with him by his open-hearted generosity as well as by a genial manner, which leads every man to look upon him as a friend.

The construction of the Palace Hotel will work a complete revolution in the social life of San Francisco. Applications for apartments are daily reaching the proprietor, and half the house could even now be filled with regular boarders, while the number of travellers daily arriving from every quarter of the globe is such that it frequently happens that every bed in each of our present larger hotels is occupied and the latecomers have to search about the city for a place in which to rest their weary limbs.

CHAPTER 17
TEDDY

July 1880. San Francisco, California.

I have had to leave my dress to the dressmakers again. She says she doesn't know if it can be let out any further. I didn't expect to grow so large so quickly but this baby seems intent on blooming ahead of its time. George keeps insisting that I should purchase a gown from The White House department store, but he does not understand that I feel like a cow in calf! There are no gowns to fit, I explain. And besides, the ready-made gowns that I have seen are fussy and uncomfortable. I may be dragged to this damned masquerade ball but I refuse to truss myself up in lace like a fat bon-bon while I'm there!

Still, I suppose it is a good cause, Grace Church, for they do such charitable work, but who thinks of these things, Mystical Masquerade Night indeed! I don't know what those poor Irish, German and Italians all squashed up together in North Beach and Telegraph Hill would do without Grace Church. And Latins too!

We did well to get ourselves out of there, a fact which George is never shy in reminding me. Not that he likes to remind anyone *else* of where we used to live for George is quite precious about our house here on Jackson Street. He says if business continues as it is, we could look at moving to Nob Hill next year. He would like to spend time in Southern

California too. He waxes about Santa Barbara. Although I'm not too sure how I feel about that.

I suppose we could do with the space. Three children rattling round will be rather noisy I expect!

Despite our plans, I have a cloud hanging over me and a swirling pit of worry in my stomach, for George and I have not been getting along. He is quick to temper and most fretful.

I think he knows.

And I think, at the heart of his distemper, it is this baby and what he or she represents that bothers him the most.

Well, there's not a lot I can do about that now. I do try to pay him special attention. I make sure his slippers are warmed for when he comes in and I order our kitchen girl to have his soup heated just so (not too hot), the way he likes it. I try not to complain or natter on, although it is bothersome when my corset is clenching and the baby is sitting so high.

But, I fear, there has been a change. It is difficult to put my finger on, but something is on his mind. Never before has he been so quick to temper with me. He talks to me as though I am beneath him. And it irks me so. In all our travels together I was never beneath him. Not till … well, not till Grace of course.

I wait for news of Momo's boat. It was due to dock last week but so far there has been no sign. It is a long way to Cedros Island. I wish George did not send him so far away but I expect he will return with many fur seals and otter skins and George will claim he was right to send him away.

How I long to see him, to hold him, to place his hands on my stomach and show him. I think he will be glad. In his own way. Another bond between us, never to be broken.

Helki has been giving me a drink for heartburn. It is a repugnant white concoction but once I swallow it, I get a few hours' relief. I have had to sleep sitting up all this week for when I lie down, it feels as though a vial of acid has been tipped down my gullet! She says she is sure the baby is a boy for all this bother.

She also knows the truth, for Helki is a quiet observer of all that happens around her. Of course, I do not speak to her out loud, for I cannot put words on what it is that I, we, have. Our little square. Not a circle. For George has grown very close to Helki. He lays his hands on her, when he's speaking. I've seen him put his palm on her back to gently nudge her out of the way in the kitchen. He goes to the kitchen just to see her, for he has no real need to be there. He is always asking her for her advice on some ailment or (made-up!) worry.

I do not mind. I understand it. There is an attraction there. But I wish he did not take out his frustrations with it all on me. He has always blamed me for Grace. Always held it against me. And despite how hard I have tried, I have not met his expectations. Especially after saving me from ruin after the Virginia City predicament and starting us fresh here. I have not become the lady wife he longed for and thought if he spent enough money on, he would get.

Oh, I think this ball and my swollen state has got my dander up!

Social occasions are most tiring at the best of times, and now having to attend when I am so heavy with child seems cruel! I tried pleading with George again last night, stating that nobody would mind if I did not attend, for course they would not! Nobody would even miss me! But he says I must. He is hoping to meet Egbert Judson there and some bigwigs from the stock exchange. He wishes to appear established and trustworthy, a family man. A man on the up!

But I fear I may be a woman on the way down. I may fall out of my standing with tiredness at the Palace Hotel!

Ansel has been quite fussy this week. I suspect he knows that soon he will no longer be the baby of the family and the center of attention! Aren't children funny like that?

Grace has been an absolute dear, fetching me anything I need and rubbing my swollen ankles for me. Sometimes she asks to pat my tummy and kiss the baby good night. I love to stroke her dark little head. Her eyes are deep and mournful, as if they have seen a thousand sadnesses.

Like her father's.

She will be a great big sister. A true sister. Perhaps that is why Ansel is playing up so. He is grumpy. Like *his* father.

What an enigmatic square we make.

My dress has come back and just about fits. I relented to George's insistence on fussing over this ridiculous ball and sent Helki out for a garnet necklace and earrings yesterday that I'd seen in the window at Shreve & Co.

She came back quite upset; the jeweler gave her a time of it, wanting to know if she had enough money to pay and asking who her mistress was! He suspected the money was stolen and that Helki was up to no good! George was outraged when we told him and said he'd a good mind to bring the jewelry back and demand our money in return for such insults. But Helki calmed him down. She is used to such prejudice I suppose.

Her two friends Chetan and Saloso remain with us and sit around the fire in the evenings, sewing blankets. They are so quiet after all they have faced. They have sisters and brothers living on a reservation who they sometimes mention they would like to have come to San Francisco but they have nothing to offer, no jobs and no money, and I know they are loath to ask us for more help.

I might speak to George about it—especially if we got a larger house next year. We could always make room.

I have my masquerade mask ready now. I added some small black feathers to each side, and it does look quite enchanting, with tiny music notes adorning the edges. I hope between the garnets and the alluring mask, no one will pay any heed to my enormous girth!

I wish Helki could attend this ball with me. She would be a comforting companion, beside me all night, warding off those tiresome preening ladies who think so much of themselves and yet haven't one interesting thing to say. The gentlemen will pay no attention to me of course. George will be chasing them down like a greyhound on a rabbit!

She joked with me, saying, "Rather it is you, than me." She can be so funny without meaning to be.

Poor Grace has developed a cough. Helki has been administering a soothing syrup; hopefully, it will do the trick. I suppose tomorrow night will be an endurance.

But isn't that a woman's lot?

Our little Grace is quite ill. We heard her racking cough echoing through the house before we even got our hats and gloves off when we got home tonight. Helki is dreadfully worried I think and had been sitting up with her all night. How guilty I felt that we were at the ball, swanning around the Palace Hotel while my darling child needed me. She has settled down somewhat now, but her temperature remains high and I am sponging her down constantly. We are waiting to see how she gets through the next few hours and if she is still as bad, we will send for the doctor at first light.

I told Helki to go to bed. George collapsed as soon as we came in, worn out with all the buttering up of rich businessmen, helped to sleep by copious glugs of Irish whiskey. And so, here I write as I watch over Grace's fitful sleep, disturbed every few minutes by this awful, awful cough.

I am surprised I have the energy to write a word. Yet I am wide awake with both worry for little Grace and stimulation from the evening. And so, I must do something to pass the time. I cannot bear to embroider by lantern light.

The Palace Hotel was breathtaking. I've been there for afternoon tea many times but it was most magnificent this evening, the whole place decked out. They had added quaint little lanterns all strung up on bunting. I know there was much talk when the Palace opened five years ago about how on earth they were going to fill a hotel that took up an entire block, but I feel it was fairly filled tonight!

I must confess, I quite liked the masks when we got there. It gave rise to the intrigue—working out who was who, feeling hidden in plain sight and set free. You can behave differently when you are not yourself—disguised from the world. I think it riled George a little perhaps as it made it trickier for him to spot his targets. He very much left me to my own amusement in the grand atrium and I was forced to find a nice wide sofa to perch myself on and rest. Why he insisted on my being at the ball just to abandon me was vexing.

But fortune smiled upon me, for who came along and anchored right beside me, only Mrs. Lillie Hitchcock Coit! My, she's a character! I'd heard talk of her dressing in trousers and slipping into gambling halls with the men and even smoking cigars with them. Indeed, she took out a petite brown cigar and began puffing on it right there in the Palace atrium! I'd met her before at last year's Opera soiree but she didn't seem to remember me, for she asked me all manner of questions about myself.

I told her I felt like a whale and she said whales were very useful creatures. She told me that she and her husband had recently separated and she frequently took rooms at the Palace and if she had it her way, no woman would ever have to get married and we would be allowed to work and earn our livings just like men.

"Don't you see?" she said. "By keeping us in our skirts, they trap us like birds in a cage. Now if we were to be set free, how high we could soar!"

I very much enjoyed talking to her. She is most remarkable. When I told her George and I had witnessed the Chicago fire, she was most overcome and explained she herself is a mascot for the Knickerbocker Engine Company and helps raise money for volunteer firefighters. She visits them when they are sick and raises much money.

"Firebelle Lil they call me," she'd said with the deep brassy pride of a tuba—and that astonishing cigar perched at the corner of her mouth.

I wonder if she has a fear of fire, so great is her dedication.

After sitting for a time, Mrs. Hitchcock Coit grew restless and insisted I accompany her on a tour of the carnival tents, for they did look so whimsical.

The little tents were dainty affairs, red and white striped just like a real carnival.

There was a juggler in one and a bearded lady in another who sat in a throne-like chair stroking a cat! Mrs. Hitchcock Coit was most interested in her and asked many questions, such as how the lady went about her life day to day, did she receive much harassment and wouldn't it be so much easier for her simply to dress like a man?! She was so interested in her that I eventually had to tug on her sleeve to carry on, for I felt the poor bearded lady was beginning to feel she was under inquisition.

I rather liked the little monkey who ran up and down his master's arms and then sat on his head, eating peanuts. He could play a little tinkly piano, to match his master's accordion.

Oh, it was all delightful, I did enjoy that.

We had reached the tent of the fortune teller Madame Bowers. She is new to town but already has quite the reputation as a scryer, for the Adams attended her last week and were bowled over by her accurate insight. Just then, I spotted George walking by with a man who looked like Mr. Egbert Judson.

Now, Mr. Judson is a prominent man indeed. When I pointed them out to Mrs. Hitchcock Coit, she made a big scene, her voice launching like a lawn dart at George to come over so that she could "make acquaintance with my husband." He had to do as he was bid; otherwise, it would have seemed rude to ignore such a lady, but I could see he had a big scowl under that mask, having been pulled away from one of his main business bull's-eyes!

After a tepid introduction Mrs. Hitchcock Coit pushed George right into Madame Bowers's tent for a reading! He tried to escape out the door but Mrs. HC wouldn't hear of it and planted both her hands firmly on his shoulders and told him he must stay and have his fortune told!

Oh, I did find it all rather amusing, if I'm being quite honest.

Madame Bowers was not what you might expect from a fortune teller. She was in fact rather ordinary looking and wore no gold or bright colors. In fact, she seemed rather matronly and her soft Scottish brogue put us quite at ease.

George had to cross her palm with silver and then she read his fortune, first asking him his birth date and the hour he was born and consulting a chart while looking into a large crystal standing on the table.

"You have had some bad luck, but it is nothing to what you will have," was her first statement and then, placing her two forefingers apart and bringing them together, she said: "The planets that govern your life are coming together like this. And the nearer they approach each other, the worse luck you will have. You can't do anything successfully. You may enter into some business arrangement that you think will prosper, but at the last moment something will happen to disappoint you and defeat its accomplishment. The best thing for you to do would be to take a position and work for someone else."

George snorted and said, "Stuff and nonsense!" But Madame Bowers was stern and said he should pay heed.

"Your bad luck will continue for sixteen years, but four months from the seventh day of the seventeenth year the planets will pass each other, and as they go farther apart you will have luck fully as good as it has been bad; after that time you can't make a failure of anything. Everything you touch will turn to gold."

She then took out a set of tarot cards and ordered George to select three. She studied them very closely and warned that he would meet his death at sea unless he kept his feet on dry land and as she had already asked George what he did for a living, he laughed out loud and rudely exclaimed that as the owner of many a merchant hunting vessel this would be quite impossible!

"The cards do not lie," she whispered softly and firmly. "Deny them at your peril. For it is you and your family who will suffer."

George could stand it no longer and, as soon as his reading was over, marched out of the tent, anxious to find Mr. Judson again and get back to his whiskey. I know I will probably pay for all this later as George will likely be embarrassed by this episode, especially in front of Mrs. Hitchcock Coit, but what if the fortune teller is right? Shouldn't he pay heed?

Mrs. HC pushed me forward next and I crossed Madame Bowers's palm with silver and gave her my birth date as George had done. I could not give her my birth hour for I'd never been told that and my father was never very good at remembering such details and now that he himself is in heaven, I suppose that particular fact has been lost to all time.

Madame Bowers studied her crystal ball for minutes before pronouncing my "great unhappiness." Quite embarrassed now myself in front of Mrs. Hitchcock Coit, I shook my head and denied all knowledge of what she meant.

"Your heart it aches in longing, but it will be soothed," she said. "You must be brave and face up to what the heart wants."

I felt that aforementioned heart drop in my chest like a stone. She knew! The scryer knew!

I could feel Mrs. Hitchcock Coit staring at me, trying to catch my eye but I refused to grant her wish. How could I ever face up to being with Momo in the situation I found myself? Here I am, expecting my third child, to all outward appearances the good wholesome wife of a rising businessman?

How could I *face up to what the heart wants*?

"A love held in secret can dim in the darkness," intoned Madame Bowers. "You must bring it to the light and set your heart free, if it is true happiness you seek."

I shifted in my chair, feeling ever so uneasy and cursing that dressmaker for not letting the waist out further. I felt trapped in a mangle.

When Mrs. Bowers asked me to choose my three tarot cards, she spread them out in front of her. I could not see exactly what I'd chosen for the images, all beautifully colored, danced before my eyes and made no sense whatsoever to me.

But Madame Bowers froze. Then she looked up at me very intently.

"I am sorry," she said and she stood up, giving Mrs. HC and me quite a start. "I can read your fortune no further. Not today. You are with child and it would be remiss of me. You can come back another time if you like for another reading, I have rooms off Market Street."

With that she got up, pulled her shawl around her tightly, swept out of the tent and all but disappeared!

"What about me?" called Mrs. Hitchcock Coit after her.

It was most peculiar!

"She looked like she's seen a ghost," said Mrs. Coit. "How queer!"

We were both rather taken aback but all we could do was chuckle to ourselves and wonder, was it all part of the act?

The dinner bell gonged soon after and we were to take our seats in the banqueting room. I knew I could not handle much food, for the baby takes up so much real estate but I was feeling rather nauseous and full of bile and wondered if a few bites might soothe the fire. I hoped they'd have soup and they did, as one of our eight courses.

Mrs. HC joined us at our table and challenged the men to much stimulating conversation. I'm not sure George knew quite what to make of her!

There was an old bore at our table, a Mr. Merriweather, who had just taken a slumming tour of Chinatown and said it was most interesting and rather daring. He visited a brothel, a gambling saloon, an opium den and many dive bars and he witnessed a knife fight!

Mrs. Hitchcock Coit informed him that slumming tours were like theater shows—made up and put on for the paying punter and that what he witnessed was likely not real at all. She also admonished him for fueling a trade in the voyeurism of the poor. Well, that certainly set the cat among the pigeons!

There followed a lively debate on the issue of the Chinese then, for they are very numerous and there is a great worry that there simply isn't enough work and wealth to go around. Mr. Miller, another bore, said stowaways from places like Hong Kong and the Guangdong province are pouring into the city and need to be stopped, lest we be "overrun." Mr. Merriweather added that men from China come here to do laundry work and that "each man takes the bread from the mouths of our women. Small mercies their offspring aren't permitted in our schools to mix with our own."

But Mrs. HC would hear none of it and pointed out that the Chinese built the Transcontinental Railroad, faster even than the Irish. "They're far from lazy, and understand many a thing we don't," she said. "A China woman can cure ailments with herbs and powders that flummox our learned medical doctors who might throw up their hands and leave you to perish instead."

"Well I … just don't get me started on the Irish," said Mr. Merriweather and there was a great big guffaw around the table.

After dinner I was feeling rather fatigued but I returned to the atrium for some after-dinner drinks, longing for the carriage to bring me home.

We met two charming girls serving punch called Elizabeth Ashe and Alice Griffith, only twelve or thirteen, yet quite dignified. They were plainly dressed and took their work very seriously. They smiled and chatted with energy and maturity and did not spill a drop. Mrs. Hitchcock Coit knew them through her charity work and said despite their young age, she had her eye on them, for she could sense they would go far. There were quite a few volunteers helping out in aid of the church.

Mrs. HC said she reckoned I would go far too if I put my mind to it, but all I could do was laugh. "I won't go very far at the moment," I told her. "Not unless you turn me over and over like a roly-poly!"

She found this rather funny and said she would like to call on me once the baby was born. I agreed. It would be lovely to have a social call. She helped me track down George and we found him quite pickled at the bar and so it was a job to get him out of the Palace Hotel. But here we are, home now after a rather rousing—and indeed "mystical"—evening, home to our little ailing Grace.

I do hope she takes a turn in the morning and gets some rest. She is constantly coughing and waking herself up.

When I told Helki about the fortune teller she did not find the story amusing at all. She said, "When a scryer sees bad news they will not tell it, not to a woman with child."

This rather alarmed me, I must say. I do hope she is wrong! Goodness, whatever could that mean? Probably more business woes for us. That seems to have been quite the theme these days.

Adieu.

FUNERAL NOTICE

The funeral of Grace de Luca, 6 years of age, will take place tomorrow

23 July at Grace Church at 11 a.m., with burial afterward at Telegraph Hill.

The eldest daughter of George and Theodora de Luca, of 1450 Jackson Street, Grace died suddenly at home from whooping cough.

She will be sadly missed by her family. Family flowers only.

CHAPTER 18
ELLIE

September 6, 2019. San Francisco, California.

"¡*Mira*! Look what I can do!" Paulina cartwheeled across the small living room and tumbled against the wall. Fernanda gasped. "Paulina!"

But Paulina giggled and star jumped right up into the air.

"*Estoy bien*, Mama!"

She was such a happy little girl, her dark eyes flashing with her smile. Two equally dark plaits hung on either side of her face, wound by Fernanda's hands, although Ellie wondered how her injury had affected her technique.

The two-bed apartment was small, but it was clean and freshly painted—no roaches to worry about. Fernanda sat over her coffee cup at the island, smiling as her daughter performed another cartwheel.

"Eh!" said Fernanda. "Not in the house, *chica*." As a counterpoint, she pointed toward her middle child, Antonio, quietly reading the book Ellie had brought him.

Mira qué tranquilo está tu hermano!

Fernanda's youngest, another boy, Luis, was on the floor with crayons, ignoring the box of blocks Ellie had presented.

215

"He just love to draw," said Fernanda.

"An artist in the making," Ellie said, smiling.

They observed the children some more, while Ellie thought how relaxed Fernanda was now, so different from the frazzled woman she had come to know over the course of their case together. She'd taken a personal day off from her new job to attend parent-teacher conferences that day at her kids' school. With the social worker continuing to check and report on Fernanda's suitability to care for her children, she wouldn't dare miss school conferences.

"How are the kids finding school?" Ellie asked.

"Good," said Fernanda. "Paulina's English, so good now. She make lots of friends, and she smile all the time. Before, she always afraid, you know, of rats? She not sleep then, so worried at nighttime. We hear the roaches running on the walls, *tick-tick-tick*!"

Fernanda shuddered as she made the sound of the cockroaches scurrying.

"And what about work? It's all going okay?" asked Ellie.

Thanks to the vocational training voucher Ellie had negotiated as part of her settlement, Fernanda had found a job in another hotel. But instead of housekeeping, she was in charge of the accommodation team, helping recruit and manage the large number of Spanish-speaking workers, many of them migrants like her, while training in inventory management and supply.

"I like it," said Fernanda firmly. "The day—*poof*—gone, so fast, so busy. But you know, I need to better my English if I want a promotion."

"Have you considered night classes?" asked Ellie.

"Yes, but what I do with *los niños*?"

"I think there are lots of classes you can take at home, online."

"I have no computer."

It was so very difficult, thought Ellie. Everything for Fernanda had been a struggle. Had they waited to force more money out of the Assurance Underwriters of California, which Ellie knew they most certainly could have, buying a laptop would have been no problem. Then again, Fernanda finding an apartment and reuniting with her kids sent to foster homes were worth more to her than a computer.

Fernanda tucked her damaged finger under her other hand. Ellie noticed it was a habit, hiding her injury, as though shamed by it. Yet the finger had been salvaged by skin grafting.

"How's your hand feeling?" asked Ellie.

"Oh, better! My coworker tell me about Chinese doctor who use needles for … *como se dice* …?"

"Acupuncture?"

"Yes! This! It help so much for *recuperación*. Also the tea he give me."

The sound of a head knocking against drywall echoed through the apartment, followed by the crash of a small table and the shattering of glass.

A loud wail came from the crumbled heap that was Paulina on the floor.

"Ow!" she yelled. "Owwwwwwww!"

Fernanda leapt from her stool and rushed to her daughter. A steady stream of admonishment and comforting flew from her lips in Spanish as she picked her daughter up off the ground and held her to her ample chest.

"I tell her, no *gimnasia* inside!" She frowned.

The other two children barely looked up, well used to the clamor of living together in the small space.

"Is she okay?" asked Ellie, rushing to find a dustpan and broom.

"She is fine," said Fernanda, now examining her daughter's skull for bumps. "She will live. Please, leave that; I do it. Antonio! Luis! *¡No se muevan!*"

Ellie watched while Fernanda deftly deposited Paulina on the sofa and whizzed about the living room sweeping up the broken glass.

"I vacuum now," she said, raising her eyebrows at Ellie.

Ellie took it as her cue to leave.

"Well, I'd better move on. I have to pick up my son, and then we're meeting friends at the museum." She smiled.

"Oh, which museum?" asked Fernanda.

"OMCA."

"Oh, we love there. We get the BART to there on first Sunday of the month. It's free day!"

Ellie was meeting Anika, Leila, and Milo at the Oakland Museum of California, just off the Lake Merritt BART station. She'd collect Nathan early from day care, drive out to Luca's school, then make good use of her office parking space to hop on BART at Embarcadero. It was a rare half-day to celebrate Luca's fourth birthday. Joe was taking the kids that weekend, and she wanted to do something fun before she dropped them off the next morning. It was the first full weekend Joe was taking both kids, and while she appreciated the break, the anxiety still built. What if Luca had a meltdown? What if Joe couldn't cope?

When she realized Fernanda lived in the Richmond District, not too far from the Presidio, she had arranged to drop in to see how she was doing.

"It was so good to see you, Fernanda," Ellie said as she waved goodbye to her kids.

"Thank you so much for coming." Fernanda smiled. "Oh. *¡Espera!* Before you go!" Fernanda opened the fridge and took out a foil tray of chocolate cupcakes. "We make these for you."

"I did the frosting!" cried Paulina from the sofa, where she now sat rubbing her forehead.

Ellie eyed the slightly uneven frosting and grinned. "For me? You didn't have to—this is so sweet!" She could already picture Luca's and Nathan's wide-eyed delight at the sight of such a decadent treat. But more than that, the gesture hit her somewhere deep. She was so used to baking apology brownies—peace offerings for all the people she feared she'd inconvenienced, proof that she was trying, even when she felt like she wasn't enough. And now here was Fernanda, with everything on her plate, handing Ellie thank-you cupcakes. A small act yet a monumental one. Proof that resilience could bloom, that her work truly mattered.

Outside Nathan's day care, Ellie checked her phone to find two text messages from Sam. One told her he was thinking about the pictures she'd sent last night—body shots, where she just happened to be wearing her knee-high black patent boots and little else. The other was a follow-up with three red heart emojis. Heat bloomed across her skin as she smiled at his messages. How hard was she falling for him?

With her free weekend ahead, he was coming up to stay for the first time, and she felt nervous and jubilant all at once. She was looking forward to showing him around the city to her favorite spots: the meditation walking maze at Grace Cathedral after enjoying classic dim sum at Yank Sing; the buffalo at the Golden Gate Park Bison Paddock; the hang gliders at Fort Funston; ice cream at Polly Ann in the Outer Sunset district with its many eclectic flavors and colorful wheel to spin for choosing; and, of course, the Greenwich Steps and her beloved murals at Coit Tower (plus a tiny secret garden nearby). At the same time, it felt like quite the step, allowing him over the threshold of her life—her real life.

Sam's apartment was that of a bachelor—clean, modern, low-maintenance. Meanwhile, her apartment had mastered the art of controlled domestic entropy. Her superpower? Generating an endless supply of unfolded laundry, mysteriously multiplying toys, and a rotating display of art projects she was too sentimental to toss. Would he be able to accept it all? See the true her and still like it? More importantly ... would he accept her as a mother and still crave her?

She sighed, got out of the car, and ran, as was her habit, to the day care door, even though she wasn't late. Nathan was surprised to see her but ran toward her with his arms open wide. It wasn't long after lunch, and he wasn't expecting to go home for a few hours. She held him tight and squeezed him.

"He'll expect you early every day now." The day care worker smiled tightly as she held the door open for Ellie to leave.

Ellie knew she was supposed to feel guilty for disrupting the routine. But the guilt trend was starting to feel like last season's fashion. Instead, she checked her internal give-a-shit-ometer—nope, nothing. Amazing how her son being happy could be framed as yet another parenting shortfall. She pushed the thought from her mind as she reversed the car and headed toward Luca's school. He, too, might be a little unsettled by the schedule shift, but she wasn't about to spiral over that. They were going to play hooky, eat cupcakes in the car, and have a lovely afternoon, dammit—even if it cost her the Maternal Martyr of the Year award.

"Mama, look!"

While easing slowly through the traffic, Ellie turned her head to see Nathan holding up a piece of paper he'd just pulled from his little knapsack. The picture showed a stick figure: two uneven legs, one arm shorter than the other, and a giant bobblehead in orange crayon. Beside the large bobblehead were two small bobbleheads, one smaller than the other. A wobbly, uneven, and unconnected line drawing of what she thought was a heart, colored in red, connected all three of them. The stick figure was holding a circle with more colorful sticks on top dotted with yellow: a birthday cake.

Mom, Luca, and Nathan. Her heart swelled.

"That's beautiful, sweetie! You made that for Luca?" she said, glancing into the rearview mirror to catch Nathan's little smug smile—so satisfied with himself. "That's really beautiful."

He'd only drawn three figures in the family.

He'd left out Dad.

"Milo! Leila! Milo! Leila!!" Nathan cried out as he spotted Anika and her children, completely surprised and ecstatic to see them.

"You beat us!" said Ellie as she walked into the museum lobby and hugged Anika hello. "But look what we brought for a birthday snack!" She held out the foil tray of cupcakes she'd carried on BART—with a couple missing. Milo's and Leila's eyes lit up.

"Are we all set?" asked Ellie, smiling at Leila and Milo. She held Luca's hand tightly, though he was excited to be there as they regularly visited the museum; he particularly loved the sensory room.

"We sure are!" said Anika, grinning and answering for them. She seemed in a really bright mood, and Ellie was glad.

Ever since the Fuji Fun gala five months ago, she had seemingly returned to the old Anika—upbeat and bright—and had even increased her meditation and chanting schedule. It was something her grandfather had passed on to her: a quiet man who'd been imprisoned at Manzanar as a boy and had learned to survive by watching, breathing, listening. "Stillness kept him human," she'd said once, using toothpaste to patch a chip in her wall. "And sometimes that's all you've got." Ellie understood it was her friend's way of coping, but couldn't help feeling Anika was becoming a little too cocooned in her wellness routine and so much time alone.

She had tried speaking to her after the gala, once the hangover had subsided but, meeting with a wall of silence, Ellie had quickly changed the subject. She wouldn't risk upsetting Anika again and certainly didn't want another falling out. Anika did not want to talk about Ben, any affair, the other woman, or Hugo's death. She only wanted to talk about the banal. There was to be no looking back, no pondering, and no gazing too far into the future. Ellie realized that this was all Anika could do: one day at a time. So, she met her friend where she was.

They made their way into the California History Gallery, the kids babbling together; the museum was a familiar place—great for kids with interactive exhibits, and they each had their favorite activities. Nathan loved the huge red 1878 Amoskeag Steam Fire Engine toward the back of the exhibition and wouldn't be satisfied until he got to it and could make engine and splashing noises, pretending he was a fireman. He quite liked the giant four-seat California mud wagon too, likely because it had wheels. He was truck crazy. It had been built in the 1880s, with its cargo on display in the exhibit.

Today, Ellie was drawn to the exhibits on Native Americans, and while she had read the stories of the Californian tribes forcibly removed from their land before, she found herself unable to turn away from the images and firsthand accounts under the board featuring the title *What Is Genocide?*

"Mama!" called Nathan, anxious to get to the fire engine.

"I'm coming!"

But she felt glued to the spot. She couldn't take her eyes off the people in the photographs, their stricken faces as they tried to flee from slaughter.

So much blood had spilled on this land. The land they walked on, the land they, the white people, had stolen and built upon.

"Mama!"

"Coming, Glitter-Bug!" she cried, feeling a little exasperated now, feeling something deep and painful but a pain that was not hers. Angry at what had been done in the name of white people.

After the fire engine, they made their way to the sensory room, which was dotted with beanbags, lit with underwater images of jellyfish, and which felt womb-like. The children threw themselves into the beanbags, and as Ellie checked that Luca was okay, she felt her phone vibrate inside her bag.

She had told the office not to put any calls through to her under any circumstances. "Even if the building is burning down," she'd joked before she'd left. "I'm not a firefighter, so leave me out of it!"

She saw Ruby Martinez's number flashing.

Ruby!

A call from Ruby always sent a rush of adrenaline through her. She admired her so much, it was hard to believe sometimes that they'd now formed a trusting, professional relationship, which, over the course of preparing the case for the EEOC, had at times veered into the personal, as Ellie revealed parts of her domestic life and worries around her career and motherhood.

Ruby only ever called out of the blue with good reason.

"I need to take this," she mouthed to Anika.

Anika waved her on.

Ellie answered the phone while rushing past the exhibits for the Transcontinental Railroad and the California Gold Rush, heading for the exit.

"Ruby!"

"Ellie, can you talk?"

"Well, I'm at the Oakland Museum and just stepped away from a bunch of kids!"

"I wouldn't call unless it was important," said Ruby. "And let me tell you, this is important."

Ellie pushed her way into an outdoor patio area and sat on small bench. She felt her whole body stiffen. *Oh God, what now?*

"I've just gotten off a phone call with Leslie Stahl's producer at *60 Minutes*. Before that, I spoke to *The New York Times*. And before that, I took a call from NPR. I have three other missed calls on my phone, and I'm pretty sure they're media too, all looking for you!"

"What?" said Ellie. "Me? But why?"

"Are you sitting down?"

"I am, actually." She braced herself.

"So, you know how we presented your case along with a few others to the EEOC yesterday to urge them to publish formal guidelines on caregiver discrimination? Well, there was a journalist there covering; she's very well connected, and I know her from years back. Let's just say this is an issue she cares about. She published a piece this morning in *The Huffington Post*, and it's gotten a lot of traction. Now, others are picking it up, and they all want to speak to you. They've gone with the headline 'Who Cares? The Unprotected Workplace Bias Hidden in Plain Sight.' How do you feel about that?"

Ellie felt ... stunned. She knew there was a possibility that the media might pick up on the case. After all, Ruby was a powerhouse and often leveraged the media to help advance the causes she championed. But Ellie hadn't expected it so soon.

"I ... I don't know," said Ellie. "*60 Minutes*, you said?" The show was renowned for its in-depth investigations on global issues, politics, and culture.

"Now listen, I never force anyone into doing any media. You have to be sure before you go out there. But I will say, as I'm sure you realize, this is big. Really big. This is probably our chance. We get the right message to these channels, we're giving this legislation the absolute best chance it has of passing. This could make a huge difference for the advancement of not just law and public policy in this area but also for the caregivers of the future. This could change women's lives."

In other words, the bat signal was up. Would she answer the call? Or switch her phone to Do Not Disturb, break into a Costco carton of Goldfish, and binge *Big Little Lies?*

We'd need to talk strategy," said Ellie, her mind racing ahead to how Hutton & Fetterer would react if they saw her on *60 Minutes* or covered by *The New York Times* or NPR. How Dan the Man would recoil, grimacing as she appeared in her Theory Etiennette blazer—her guilt, her shame, *their* shenanigans—laid bare, uncloaked and unraveled for the nation to see. Did she really have the guts for that?

"Absolutely," said Ruby. "You'll have no problem, Ellie, with your court experience, but you're right, we'll get a media coach before you go out there, really hone our message. Can you meet this evening? We want to strike while the iron's hot."

"Um …" said Ellie, thinking of Luca's birthday movie night that included titles other than *Kung Fu Panda* and the packing she still had to do for the boys' weekend ahead.

"Tonight's no good. Tomorrow?" said Ellie, confident about prioritizing her family and mentally adjusting the sightseeing itinerary she had planned with Sam. Perhaps she could send him on an afternoon Alcatraz tour while she met with Ruby?

"Yes, good. And *The New York Times* wants a cover feature for their Sunday magazine. That'll be a sit-down, in-depth interview, probably next week."

"Sure," said Ellie, her voice portraying a confidence she wasn't sure she felt.

"Okay, great, let me take these calls, talk to our media guys, and I'll circle back. Keep your cell charged!"

Wow, thought Ellie, her head spinning and a wave of excitement tinged with nausea hitting her all at once. She'd been so afraid of this case, had waited so long to confront it. And now she was going to be completely exposed. In national media coverage!

"Once more unto the breach, dear friends," she muttered, focus sharpening, conviction settling in.

Back in the sensory room, she didn't mention anything to Anika but sank into a beanbag watching the jellyfish and krill ebb and flow, waiting for her heart rate to recede.

"I'm hungry," cried Leila not long after Ellie sat down.

"Me too!" said Milo.

"Me too!" said Nathan, who copied everything Milo and Leila did.

"You ready for the cafeteria?" asked Anika. She turned to Ellie. "Everything okay?"

"Yep," said Ellie triumphantly. "Yes, to both!"

They headed toward the cafeteria, where Ellie would order the boys a fried chicken sandwich, their absolute favorite, and then pass around Fernanda's cupcake tray. On the way, the children stopped by the migrating birds exhibit to say hello to their favorite feathered friends.

"Hello, Sandy," said Leila, petting a western sandpiper, a small shorebird that migrated along the Pacific Coast from Alaska to South America.

"Hello, Mr. Duck," said Milo, laughing and petting a northern pintail, a sleek waterfowl that passed through Northern California in large numbers.

Anika and Ellie looked on, amused by their kids' ritual of checking on these stuffed, motionless creatures every time they visited.

Luca, concentrating on the small grey dove that had always been an object of his affection, rubbed the downy head with his fingertips and grinned.

"*Birrr*," he said quietly, grinning to himself.

Ellie went still. Anika's mouth dropped, while Leila and Milo, old enough to understand, squealed.

"Did you hear that?" cried Leila, clapping her hands. "Say it again, Luca, say it again!"

They all concentrated on Luca, who continued petting his dove, quite oblivious to the utter silence he now commanded from his enraptured audience.

Was it a fluke? Had he really said it? Out loud?

"Birrr," repeated Luca, still smiling, a little louder this time.

"Oh!" cried Ellie, and unable to help herself, she scooped Luca up and squeezed him tight. He looked startled at the sudden aggressive embrace.

Her boy—just turning four—after hours upon hours at clinics; miles upon miles along the highway; endless days, weeks, months of reading

to him and teaching him sign language; traipsing to neurological music therapy, speech therapy, occupational therapy, physical therapy; communicating through hundreds of one-inch laminated and Velcroed picture cards covering the apartment walls; and visiting every and any place that might offer a breakthrough—had spoken his first word.
Birrr.
Bird.

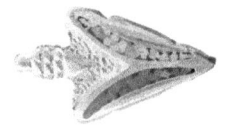

CHAPTER 19

TEDDY

November 1895.
San Francisco, California.

It is hard to believe the change in our fortunes. Had George told me even a short while ago that we would be living in such circumstances, I would never have believed him. We had gotten so used to our wealth. So used to our large house and our staff of helpers and the gardens and all our food and bills cared for. At least George does not take it lying down. At least he continues to seek work. I know many a man under such circumstances who would find such a fall too debilitating to get over. George does not see it that way. He says we will recover.

We must.

He has many regrets and one I must agree with is selling off all his otter boats. Had he kept at least one, he would have the option of hunting it himself or at least sending Momo, should he have mind to go.

Which I'm not sure he would, seeing as his and Helki's medicinal business has been flourishing. George and Momo have not exactly been seeing eye to eye. A distance has spread, perhaps from our time in Santa Barbara, when George continually sent Momo away and, in Momo's mind and mine, on purpose.

To be away from me.

When George is of a mind, there is no stopping him. Why, he simply NEEDED the sale of every single one of those old boats to fund his NEW otter boat!

It is hard to imagine our beautiful Santa Barbara house under the hands and housekeeping of another. I try not to dwell and think only to the future, when surely we once again will prosper.

I believe we will for fortunes come and go as any Californian will tell you!

It is hard on the children, as they have never really known lamentable circumstances, not like George and me. Still, we have managed to keep up their school fees and for that I am glad. Matilda is very facile with her French now which she avows will serve her well in esteemed society, and I can't help but smile recollecting that prosy Ms. Elmes and my self-sabotage of my own French skills just to spite her. As for Ansel, when he is of a mood, he will accompany Matilda's piano acumen on the violin. We are lucky to have hung onto the pianoforte at all here in San Francisco! For things really were getting dire!

I was ever so sorry to part with my gold necklaces, but needs must. What a fool George was to pour all of his assets into one new vessel. He pines about that boat every day and sometimes, especially when he has been on the whiskey, I have to tell him to put away his regrets because what good is crying over spilled milk? (Or spilled gasoline in this case—*the first vessel ever built in San Francisco with a gasoline engine*, he moans into his glass!)

I tell him he was lucky he wasn't on it and remind him of what that fortune teller told him, that he will die on the water! But of course, he is dismissive of me, as only George can be.

I suppose it *is* the worst luck to lose a vessel within a month of its launch and to not have insurance and every cent he has tied up in it! Very unlucky, or dare I say stupid! Why, oh why he left himself so short that he couldn't afford the insurance. Why is it that men feel so invincible against the meters of misfortune?

Our run of bad luck continues.

The job he secured to sail to lower California after a load of guano fell through after the man who hired him went and sold his half of the vessel three days before they were set to sail! The next job he secured, through a Mr. Cooper from Santa Barbara (who was always as slippery as an eel if you ask my opinion), went back on his word (as I'd wagered!) when George took him the contract to sign last Monday so the bottom fell out of that, too!

Nothing we touch works out at the moment. We are all quite despondent! Only seeing Helki and Momo doing well is keeping my spirits up.

Momo is on the road again, for wandering is in his blood and I suppose he will not change. He never seems to bring back enough plants for Helki's needs and so he must leave again soon after he comes home! He has not gone far though, mostly back out to the tribal lands along the coast so I expect to see him soon. I suppose he has got a break from the otter boats!

I like to help Helki as much as I can, for it takes my mind off things and keeps my hands busy, and she always heeds my advice, and I am certain it is through our conversations and discussions that she has done as well as she has.

Not that I am taking credit! Simply, I have learned from George and Helki has learned from me. I suppose we make a good team.

The four of us.

Of course, there is always plenty of work to be done at the Telegraph Hill Center, but since our fortunes have changed, I have found it hard to go there as much. Part of me feels it is <u>US</u> who will all be standing in queue there soon! George and I will have our hands out for the Boudin Bakery sourdough and Elizabeth's and Alice's eyes will be wide!

I should not jest. But how else should I try to live in such circumstances?

Ansel has been writing from school with all sorts of demands, and I have not the heart to describe to him the true straits we are experiencing and yet at the same time, he really does appear quite ungrateful.

He is so different to Matilda. She has been excelling at dressage and wrote last week that next summer she should like to go exploring on her horse with Momo! I wrote back to tell her she would be far too young at fifteen, which she will be by then, and she replied to say, she had thought about it and she will go dressed as a boy, in an Indian shawl, leave her hair down and nobody will be any the wiser!

Oh, how I laughed when I got that letter! She is her mother's daughter!

But I could not possibly let her go on the road. Dressed like that, she might face the perils of a native woman. She barely looks white and has passed thus far as an Italian. She has asked many questions. But so far, we have managed to avoid answering them. I do miss my little mute Theodore. I worry for him so. I long for Christmas to come when we will all be reunited.

This morning, George has gone to the Palace Hotel to see a man who is on a winter break from Alaska. He is in the employ of the Alaska Commercial Company and spends his winters here to defrost a little! He said Alaska is a country on the up and advised George to go there. His company does a very extensive business in fishing, mining, fur seal hunting and merchandising, all of which George could turn his hand to easily. It will be quite intriguing to hear what he has to say.

George joked that if he went to Alaska, he would bring Momo with him and leave us womenfolk to manage things here! I'm not sure whether he is jesting or really would take Momo with him. I think part of him could not stand that Momo was here with me, while he was separated from Helki, for you cannot go to Alaska for only a short while! It feels terribly far away and so dreadfully wild.

And how could Helki spare Momo all the same? He is the only one who understands the plants and foraging required, and she has to stay here to make up the medicines and bottles. He has such skill when it comes to finding what she needs and in such great quantities. How would she do that all by herself?

Although, I must say, Elizabeth and Alice are quite miraculous in the work they do at the Tel-Hi settlement house all day and helping Helki and me in the evenings and into the night. Firebelle Lil had been right about those two rosy-cheeked girls once serving punch! But Helki and Momo are key to its success and I fear it would fail should Momo have to bow out.

I do not wish for Momo to go north. I fear we will have a battle on our hands.

George can be cruel when he wants to be. He knows that Momo will forever be my soft spot.

That Momo forever will be mine.

Lady Luck, how we've missed you! How good to see you back! What an afternoon we had yesterday, my head is spinning!

When George came back from his meeting at the Palace he had the most exciting news. It is quite the extraordinary story and we are still reeling from the serendipity!

The man who George met, a Mr. Tinsley, originally from Ohio, had much to tell him about a company called the North American Transportation and Trading Company, for he said there were no openings at the Alaska Commercial Company where he was in employ, but there were at this other outfit. The company is newly established and headed up by a Chicago industrialist.

Well, George said, that was rather funny! For he knew of a Chicago industrialist.

And the man said, "Well, the man at the head of this company is called P. B. Weare!"

George nearly fell off his chair! Our old dear friend!

George came home and wrote to P. B. immediately, telling him he has three growing children here in San Francisco to support, of our extortionate education fees, about our run of bad luck in Santa Barbara, about the sinking of his gasoline engine boat and about the charitable Telegraph Hill Center to support immigrant families living in the area, for P. B. was always a philanthropist at heart.

He made sure not to leave out Helki and Momo too and their center and our involvement in setting up a safe house also for we know P. B. always had a soft spot for the Indians.

Surely P. B. will look upon us favorably. He has never let us down before.

The stars are aligning! Our fate surely is changing. And for the better!

Chicago, November 1895

My dear friend,

I received your letter and was both surprised and pleased to hear from you. Although you do not say so, it is possible that a few coin of the realm may be acceptable to jingle in your pocket and may change your luck. Enclosed you will find a draft for $50. Please accept as a souvenir of Auld Lang Syne.

In regard to Alaska, the best position now open with the company is that of a procurement manager at Circle City, but it only pays $60 a month with board and traveling expenses and the privilege of buying whatever you need personally from the company at cost. And you will have to agree to stay with the company for one year. If you want the position, you can have it and your salary begins as soon as you accept but will not be able to start until February.

It is warming to hear news of Teddy, I always took a shine to her and knew she would go far. I hope we will meet again in the near future, for I am very interested in your Indian enterprise that you support. I have heard some terrible tales. Stories that make my blood run cold. These American states can be a cruel and unwelcoming place and how we have treated the native peoples will no doubt be recorded as … well, dare I say, savagery.

Please write to say whether or not you are accepting the position.

We have built a warehouse at St. Michael's called Fort Get There. We have been working on it for two years. We had a river steamer built in Seattle, taken apart and loaded on a steamship and sent up in sections, where it was put together again on the beach.

I have called it the P. B. Weare. *A man must indulge his ego at this stage in life!*

We have been struggling to get a pilot to take it up the Yukon for the Alaska Commercial Company who also have a station at St. Michael's (and other companies too I might add), told the Indians that if they piloted our new boat up the river they would never be employed or sold supplies by the Alaska Commercial Company.

Eventually we found a Catholic priest stationed at one of the missions part way up the river who agreed to act as pilot as he knew the river to a point and after that we had to take our chances on finding an Indian further along the river who would pilot the steamer. I expect it will all work out now, but be prepared for adventure: Alaska, like all new territory, comes with its own unique set of challenges, generally, the most problematic of which will be caused by our fellow men!

With warm wishes and regards,
P. B.

December 1895. San Francisco.

We have had a new lease of life now that our plans are in place. With George on payroll now, the dark clouds have passed.

He would of course have preferred not to have had to commit to a year but so be it. We will see where we are in a year's time. $50 of his salary will be sent to me each month, while he will draw the other $10.

Helki can see the relief in my face, she says my shoulders have finally dipped, for they were as high as Mt. Tamalpais! There is a spring in my step!

I do have ambitions that in the future, once we got back on our feet properly, we could return to Santa Barbara, although of course, it wouldn't be to our own little house that we built, and we would have to rent or purchase a new one.

I can't imagine George leaving Helki, Momo and I to live out our lives contentedly here in San Francisco but so far, he has not brought the issue up.

I await in dreaded anticipation for the subject to be raised.

Momo has been traveling a lot and I miss him something awful, but we are expecting him back any day now.

Helki has a whole rack of bottles all lined up ready to go.

I long to see him, to touch him and stroke him and hold him. I pray that he arrives soon.

My Momo has returned!

Oh, how we clung to each other like limpets. He was the most passionate I've seen in a very long time. As though it was our last time on earth being together. I have been walking on air ever since.

I'm sure George noticed, for he does like to make comments, while I would never say a word about him and Helki. When he has a great big smile on his face, I always know why!

Momo says he won't have to go again for a while yet, probably not till January so we should all be together for our Christmas festivities. The children are coming home on the 21st and I intend to make an extra effort this year after this *annus horribilis*.

I have enjoyed having them back at school, as they have been shielded from the past difficult few months, but it is the greatest relief that we ourselves will not finish the year destitute!

Ansel has written to say he wishes for a cigarette case! A silver one! George scoffed but I did not find it so funny. What a brat. Matilda said she would be happy with a new riding crop. Theodore doesn't care about gifts, he just wishes to come home. Poor mite! I do think eight is far too young to be sent away, but the special school is our best hope for him. As for Ansel and Matilda, George reminds me, he certainly never had such an opportunity and our children are growing up in quite the different world than we did.

Momo does not say much for he has always left the issue of parenting to us. He says they will be growing up in a white world anyway.

Still, after all these years, we cannot talk about Grace. It is too sad. And I cannot bear to see him cry.

Well, after much pulling of teeth, I found out that George had words with Momo. I knew something was up, but of course he could barely admit to it. Poor Momo, always trying to keep the peace and not stir things up!

It is as I predicted.

George wishes for Momo to accompany him north for the following reasons:

1. He would be useful on the boats (true, Momo is terrifically skilled and can shoot an otter from a mile away!)
2. He is an expert hunter, trapper and forager on land (also true, although I always quite imagine Alaska is white with snow, with very little wildlife)
3. He would like his companionship

That's it, the three reasons he gave to take my beloved Momo from me.

Of course, he did not mention the fourth, which is that he does not want to leave Helki behind, while I and Momo would have free rein.

For all our peculiarities in our little squareship, we have always tried to retain an aura of mutual respect, but I suspect that George now wishes to throw that all away! At this precise moment I feel I should climb upon the rooftop and declare my undying love for my native man! I am so angry with George!

I have told Momo he must resist; he MUST come up with a reason why he cannot go!

Perhaps he will listen to Helki. She agrees that Alaska is too far. She argues that Momo is not built for such a climate. And surely, she is right.

They have never been separated for such a long time! Why it is only in recent years that she allows him to roam without her at all. When we met them first they were together, all across the prairies, for she could not bear to be apart from her beloved brother. Their tribe has already been scattered so. And now George wants to take Momo to Alaska, away from both of us!

I've told Momo he should not let George force him into anything and that things are not as they once were—for he and Helki have an income now from their medicinal business.

I'm surprised George is not insisting Helki go too! The tension is high. You might slice it in the air like one of Josephine's pies back in North Sandwich! What a situation for Christmas. I do hope George is for changing, but knowing what a stubborn oaf he can be, I very much doubt it.

Goodness are we having a spot of trouble.

I had hoped for peace and goodwill at yuletide, this Christmas Eve, but that is not what we got! Far from it!

George and Momo had a blazing row! In front of the Christmas fir tree! Can you imagine it, the candles burning bright and these two men choosing that of all times to turn on each other.

I am not the better of it. I sip a sherry as I write. It is not my first. Not even my second! I am hopping mad. At both of them!

It all came tumbling out, all the years of pent-up anguish. George said some very nasty things to Momo, accused him of stealing me from him! He said that I had never loved him then because of it and I had embarrassed myself and George over all these years. Helki tried to calm George down for she has seen him many times in a stupor of anger when he had over imbibed with the liquor, but he pushed her away quite roughly. It was all very dramatic and alarming and I am only glad that the children were in their rooms and did not witness it for it was all truly horrid!

The staff must have heard though. Thank goodness we had unwrapped our gifts earlier in the evening, although of course that is why George had indulged himself, for he likes to drink port on Christmas Eve when we are unwrapping our gifts.

I was quite taken aback by George's words and the venom with which they were delivered. It was all I could do to watch him and Momo go at it—my Momo, the quietest most gentle creature on earth! I was in such shock!

What a different side to him I saw this Christmas night; I would go so far as to say, it was a warrior side, a side that said he would not be treated like that and he would stand up for himself. For me! He squared right up to George and George took a big swing, but Momo easily sidestepped him and George fell forward into the fir tree, making quite the ruckus! The candles that hit the floor snuffed out, thank our Lord Almighty. I've had enough destructive fire for a lifetime!

I managed to pull Momo back, as he had his fists clenched and I felt that he might swing back at George for the insults coming his way.

"You are only a little white man!" Momo said. "You are nothing. You do not deserve my sister. You are nothing!"

Oh goodness, that had George seething like a rabid dog then. Helki held onto George while I managed to drag Momo from our drawing room but he fetched his blanket and went out the back door toward the stables.

I had to chase him, trying not to make a fuss and speak in a low voice, for they are a bunch of curtain twitchers around here and would surely be watching from those back bedroom windows, at such fracas.

"Please don't go," I begged him. "Please!"

But he would not listen. He held my arm, told me that he loved me, but said he was tired of being under George's command and tired of living this way and he could not stay. I asked him where he was going and all he said was that he would come back to see the children and me and Helki soon, but he would not be there tomorrow or the next day or the next.

Oh, how my heart shattered then. My sacred Christmas ruined. My true love scattering all because of the jealousies of my lawful husband!

I told him we would find a way. That we had always found a way, always worked through our many impasses. But I have been thinking lately that the lure of Helki, which once soothed George so, has been waning and perhaps does not have the hold over him that it once had. He has become quite the cantankerous old rooster of late, why, it is hard to put my finger on. The business failures perhaps. Or perhaps seeing that Momo and I truly love each other, passionately, devotedly, wholeheartedly!

Knowing that he may never have that, for even though Helki and he must love each other, it could not be a patch on what Momo and I have!

Perhaps the sherry is talking now. I must quit. But I do not want to wake to a Christmas morning without my Momo.

Helki said he will find cousins further south along the coast, for there will be New Year celebrations and they will welcome him.

I thought his home and heart might have been here. But clearly, I was mistaken.

New Year's Eve, 1895.

Still no word from Momo. I despair.

January 3, 1896. San Francisco.

I had the most vivid dream last night about Grace. She was not a child but grown, the age she might be now were she alive. I knew it was her, because of the raspberry birthmark on her neck and her aura. A mother knows her own child!

It was most strange! In one way lovely to see her and in another, quite chilling. How beautiful she would have grown.

How much I miss our beautiful firstborn.

January 5, 1896. San Francisco.

I think George is remorseful.

I have not been warm to him, but I am beginning to feel almost sorry for him now as he moves about the house like a wounded animal. We have not talked about anything, but I feel he may be sorry for driving Momo away.

As for his words: he seems to think that as they were the truth—you should never be sorry for speaking your heart!

Yet what a sorry mess we are now in. If only we could turn back time.

January 9, 1896. San Francisco.

Oh wretched, wretched heart. How I can barely write.

He is gone.
He is gone.
He is gone.

January 12, 1896. San Francisco.

The doctor had to sedate me. I have been living through a blur.

It cannot be true and yet with each waking moment, the cold realization that it IS true sweeps through me.

The cousin who came to Helki said it was a snake bite, a rattler they presume.

How? How could that happen to Momo when he lives off the land—he would never make a mistake like stepping on a snake! Unless he was angry and full of fury and not watching where he was going? I cannot help but blame George. Had they not had such a terrible row he would be here still!

My tears flow endlessly like our treacherous Missouri river crossing back on the frontier.

They have buried him along a waterway near their ancestral village in a scaffold in a tree. I will visit when I am strong enough. Helki is already there. She has been coping much better than me, keeping it all inside with her quiet dignity.

I wish to write to Matilda to tell her, but that would kick up its own hornet's nest. So now, all I have in this great house is George, who I cannot even bear to look at.

Momo, my poor Momo, my heart and my soul, my horseman, warrior, arrow carver, lover and friend. Never again will I know such passion. Never again will I feel at one with another man. My heart is shattered.

Now I know why Grace came to me in a dream. For now, they are together, forever and ever, reunited once again.

CHAPTER 20

ELLIE

October 7, 2019. San Francisco, California.

Ivy Glass embodied all the qualities Ellie imagined a good journalist should possess. Intelligence. Sincerity. Sharpness. And above all, searing, soul-boring eyes that made every part of you want to spill your innermost secrets. This was a woman who listened like you'd never been listened to before. More than that, Ellie felt an overwhelming urge to impress her. To have Ivy understand her. To *see* her.

Ivy's eyes were dangerous, though, because as much as Ellie had mustered the courage to share her story and be heard, she had to be careful. She couldn't shake the feeling that Hutton & Fetterer were right there in that hotel suite with her, the partners on her shoulder, staring over the fresh bowl of fruit with one slightly shriveled apple, over the premium sparkling and bottled waters, labels lined up like militant soldiers, eyeing the crumbly, untouched pastries that grew staler the longer she and Ivy spoke.

The room had been arranged by Ruby's PR team on behalf of the *New York Times Magazine*. Three digital recorders sat between them: for the journalist; for the PR director who sat in on the interview with them—a smart, sophisticated woman called Sabine who had been coaching Ellie since the green flag had dropped the previous Friday evening; and from Ellie's own attorney, Rebecca Swift, who also insisted on being present.

Was she really going public about Hutton & Fetterer? She imagined their faces: Dan the Man, ashen, staring at her, hating her, hearing the whispers and heightened sneering laughter as the assistants and junior lawyers and partners scuttled about the building after the cover piece released in the Sunday magazine.

Did you see how Ellie Benvenuto blabbed to the New York Times*?*
That bitch!
She couldn't do her job and wants to hang the blame on us? Pathetic.
We'll make sure she never gets hired anywhere again.
Ellie Benvenuto, Ellie Benvenuto, Ellie Benvenuto.

Her name, on everyone's lips. Not long ago, she could barely speak the law firm's name. Now, her name would be gospel.

Ellie's grandiose delusions were interrupted by Ivy's crisp voice. "And you liked your job?" she asked.

"I loved my job," said Ellie firmly. "And I was good at it. Truly. I was not phoning it in. My performance reviews? Stellar. I received so many commendations from my clients, from partners, even from judges. I made myself available for calls or consults at home, on the weekends, in the evenings. I was on the partnership track. That didn't happen at Hutton & Fetterer, especially for women, if you weren't good at your job, if you didn't show some hustle and produce results. I saw myself there forever. That was a lifelong career for me … and then …"

"And then?"

"Well, then I had two children, and that was that. I was damaged goods."

"But what exactly happened?" asked Ivy, leaning in closer. "Can you run me through the sequence of events?"

"Well, things were okay at first," said Ellie. "My first pregnancy was accepted. Like, 'Hey. It happens.' I took my leave. I came back to work, everything seemed fine. They gave me a slightly reduced schedule, which I appreciated, though it turned out to be the same amount of work just for less pay. But they were not impressed when I got pregnant a second time. I mean: Not. Impressed. The comments, the attitude, and then for my prenatal appointments, they demanded that I dock my timesheets for pregnancy-related medical appointments, which is against the wage and hour laws for an exempt employee like me. And I mean, this is a law office, right? We should be, you know, following the law?

"Anyway, when I protested, they still forced me to doctor my timesheets! I went along with it because I was heavily pregnant and was juggling so much at the time. Plus, my boss literally stood over me in my office one evening until I did it. There was so much going on at home. We hadn't gotten our diagnosis yet, but we knew. We knew that something wasn't quite …"

Ellie's words faltered again. The last few years, now that she was reliving them again had been so tough, she realized. She had buried much of the anguish she'd carried deep down. Worrying for Luca and his milestones. Watching them slip away one by one, while other children she knew surpassed theirs. Feeling the burden of a second quick pregnancy, dealing with swelling, vomiting to the point of dehydration, pain in her pelvis, heartburn, bone tiredness. And all the time, doing her best to soldier on at work. And then for them to …

"Yes?" urged Ivy.

"Well, then Nathan was born, and we got Luca's diagnosis. I mean, more than just one. It was like a curtain dropped. All in a matter of a few weeks. And I was due to go back to work. And I knew I was facing so many therapies. And we were trying to get Luca a good placement and services, and let me tell you, that's a whole other story, fighting for what your child needs! And I just needed some time, time to get settled. They turned me down for the leave I requested, even though I'd taken less leave time than other women—and I was the most senior person in our group other than the partners. I asked for a few more weeks, practically begged, just so I could arrange a second nanny to make up the gaps and that's when …"

She felt like a rushing river. She paused and took a deep breath.

"Yes? That's when …" Ivy was nodding her head, as though seeing how conflicted Ellie felt to relive it all.

"That's when I got the termination letter."

"It was a letter?"

"Yes. A registered letter. Sent to my home! They didn't even have the decency to have a conversation with me. I had asked for a meeting after a terse email from HR and … nothing."

Ellie remembered every word of that cold, clinical piece of paper. The normal-looking envelope. The firm's imprint. The moment she knew. Her coffee sat untouched, going cold. Nathan grizzled in his high chair. Luca stared blankly at the cuddly toys she'd arranged in a semicircle, as if a ritual could summon something—anything—from him.

Wish to inform you … due to your inability to return … employment has been terminated … clear out the office you occupied. The office she'd "occupied." Like she'd just been an inconvenient guest they were anxious to show the door.

And "inability to return" just wasn't true. She had two children under the age of two and had been making preparations to go back to work for weeks. She just needed a little more time. Then everything had been swept away, snatched from her grasp. Her income gone. Her validity, worthless.

"All that work. All those late nights, all those extra client meetings I did. I stayed late while I watched the boys' club go for drinks. I brought in new business for the firm—big name-brand clients! It meant nothing. It got me no goodwill. They had a preconceived idea that because I was now a mother, I couldn't do the job—especially when they found out about Luca's problems. And yet there were people there, other similarly situated attorneys in the office who did not have disabled children who'd been allowed 80 percent part-time schedules for years. They said my desk needed to be filled immediately. I know for a fact that my desk remained empty for at least another four months."

"And how did you feel, when you were terminated?" asked Ivy. "How did it affect you?"

"Well, I was just devastated," said Ellie. "Financially. Physically. Emotionally. I was embarrassed and humiliated. Like I wasn't worth anything and like I was totally disposable and my track record had been totally devalued. Like, 'What have you done for us lately, Ellie? Never mind you're the attorney we'd send our most cantankerous clients to handle because we knew you'd bring them around.' I realized that they'll promote women as long as they don't have children. Fathers are practically knighted and rise to the top. Mothers nosedive to the bottom. It's as simple as that."

Ivy scribbled a note on her page and underlined Ellie's last quote.

"And what would you like from your case?" asked Ivy. "What would be a victory to you?"

"Well, recognition for one thing," said Ellie. "Recognition for all the mothers out there and caregivers like me, who've been subject to such blatant discrimination. A regulatory change. Ruby Martinez, who set up the Center for WorkLife Law, has a whole raft of draft legislation that could be implemented if lawmakers really cared. Almost immediately. This isn't about financial gain for me. It's about fairness and equity in the workplace. Updating our outdated work practices, recognizing that a patriarchal-based corporate system just isn't fit for purpose anymore. And much of it is invisible."

Ellie laughed dryly. "For example—here's a fun fact, Ivy—did you realize that most office thermostats are still based on a 1960s model favoring the resting metabolic rate of the average 165-pound, forty-year-old man? And I always thought something was, like, *wrong* with me ... with my circulation or something, that I was always cold and needed a shawl!"

She paused, shaking her head as she took stock of a career spent playing against loaded dice—always betting on herself, taking too long to understand the house was designed to win. But the odds the house never accounted for? That women walking away would tank the whole damn casino.

"Look ... the bottom line is that women leaving the workplace is just bad for business! Ask Ruby Martinez herself."

"But you are seeking compensation?" said Ivy flatly. "You're suing for a payout."

"Well, that's how litigation works," said Ellie. "Monetary damages for a plaintiff are the law's way of trying to make a person whole. When you decide to open a business, there are rules. If you break them, there are consequences. I mean, my two-year-old understands that! Money is really all a court can provide. A judge or jury can't turn back time for a do-over."

You have to hit them where it hurts is what she really thought. But she stopped herself from saying it. Ivy was out for her story. The last thing she needed was to come across as a greedy, vengeful money-grubber.

"This is not about money for me," she stated firmly again. "It's about what's right. It's about justice. And fairness. You think with everything I have on my plate I'd put myself through this unless it could have wider benefits? We want our children to grow up as well-rounded, nurtured human beings. We want those who need care to receive it. And so, things have to change. We're not asking for anything crazy—these are small periods of time in people's lives, and yet, in my case or in other cases I see every day—with the discrimination faced—you're looking at devastating effects if the time is not given or needs are not met. Lifelong financial strain, serious debt, children being removed from homes because of callous, shortsighted employers who don't account for the caregiver economy in their business model!"

She was on a roll now, unable to stop the gush. Besides, if she crossed a line, Rebecca would step in—but Ellie pressed on.

"Don't forget that in these cases I'm talking about, myself included, people are at the most vulnerable point in their lives. They could be sick, injured, depressed because of it all and the inability to work, their self-worth totally trashed, which I've seen lots of cases of." Ellie was specifically thinking of Hansa and her subdued, voiceless demeanor in Ellie's office. "Or infertility treatments or postpartum. These employers are kicking people when they're at their most vulnerable, when they're unable to think straight, when they're barely able to survive. It's how they get away with it. It's despicable."

Had she said too much? Rebecca was a hawk and hadn't intervened, so she must have been okay.

A reverent silence impregnated the room as both Ivy and the PR woman, Sabine, held their breath. Ellie's words had been so heartfelt and dramatic, she had taken the two women completely aback. Rebecca gave her a little nod and a proud, subtle smile.

"That was great," said Ivy, switching off the recording, "You're a natural!"

Ellie smiled. She was relieved the interview was over, but the whole thing had felt a little like a therapy session. She'd had to bring up and relive painful memories. Still, she did feel a little better having spoken up. A little unburdened.

She had managed to keep her emotions about Hutton & Fetterer buried so deep that bringing her wounds to the surface now, exposing them to the air, holding them to the light was how she was going to heal, she realized.

"Off the record," said Ivy as she packed up, "I had to take eight months unpaid leave a few years back. Me. Not my brothers. My mother had terminal cancer. It was the worst time of my life. I ended up leaving the publication. Well, they practically fired me, too, now that I look back on it."

"Wow," said Ellie, thinking about what a formidable person Ivy Glass was. Another example of a caregiver, no matter their circumstance or personality, facing discrimination. "It's rampant," said Ellie. "There's just so many cases of people not being treated fairly or losing out when they're giving so much. I'm really sorry to hear that, Ivy, and I hope things change."

"Here's hoping this cover feature for the Sunday magazine will help," said Ivy as she shook Ellie's hand firmly.

Ellie realized that the article she would run would be fair. Impartial and discerning as she was, Ivy totally got it.

Ellie beamed as she made her way to the parking garage. It felt good to feel ... *good* again. To feel that flourish, that she was capable and she mattered. She had started to come to the conclusion that she hadn't been insane or hormonal or petulant or demanding when she'd been fired from Hutton & Fetterer. She was simply being discriminated against. And blatantly too.

In the car Ellie scrolled through her texts: messages from friends, one from her dad asking how the interview had gone, and three from Sam. Oh, Sam, how she badly wanted to see him—to ground some of the electric energy all this media attention was bringing, to plug into him.

She dialed his number and felt her whole body pulsing when he answered.

"I'm drinking coffee," he said on the other end of the phone.

"This late?" chided Ellie. She was trying to teach him better habits.

"How did it all go?" he asked.

"You know what, really well," said Ellie. "I'm happy. I think it'll be a good piece. She has a number of other interviewees lined up, but she was really interested in what I had to say, and I think she got it."

"That's great," said Sam, the clink of coffee cups in the background as she smiled, imagining him in the small café where they'd first met.

"I feel like I have to see you," she said suddenly. "I can't wait two weeks." With their commitments and plans, that was how long it would be till Ellie could visit Sam.

"Two weeks is an eternity," he said and then he paused. "I could drive to San Francisco? Tonight?"

"Seriously? What about work?"

"My appointments don't start tomorrow until eleven, and it's a reverse commute from your place, anyway. I'm supposed to be doing admin in the morning, but I guess I could skip it, drive back then?"

"You can do my admin!" teased Ellie, feeling a surge through her at the thought of seeing him that evening. Then it was her turn to pause. *What about the boys?*

"I'm not sure the boys' bedtime is something you're prepared for yet," she said. She had planned on making a bit of a fuss when officially introducing Sam to the boys; taking them for a picnic on Angel Island or the carousel at Yerba Buena Center—associating the trip with fun.

But she needed to see Sam today. The urge was an overpowering undertow, and resistance was futile. This was the life of a single mom—where romance had to be squeezed between *Peppa Pig* and existential exhaustion. Would she have time to shower and shave her legs before Dr. Sam arrived? Maybe, maybe not. Would he care? Maybe, maybe not. Would she care? At this point, questionable.

"Okay," she said resolutely. "I would love to see you, and the boys would love to officially meet you."

"Great," he said. "I'll drive straight down after work."

CHAPTER 21
TEDDY

March 1896. Alaska.

The mouth of the Yukon is 60 miles from St. Michael's. The Yukon has many mouths caused by one mouth getting stopped up with ice adrift and the vast volume of water having to back up and find a new outlet. I felt a relief when we finally entered the Yukon for I felt that at last, we were nearing our destination.

The scenery is much richer than I expected. I had in my mind that it would be snow, snow, snow, but the Yukon is a larger river even than the Mississippi and runs more water. The scenery is more varied and grander.

Some parts are through a level country before you run through another valley with timber covered mountains on both sides. Then the river will widen to a distance of 10 miles across in some places.

Our Boudin Bakery sourdough starter has been going down well. A real treat for the passengers who get it each morning. We are drawing up rations!

Helki very quiet.

George very bright.

I feel a little numb. Not sure if it's because of the cold, or I have lost the ability to feel any more discomfort.

Perhaps I am all full up.

The lumber wharf at St. Michael's is quite a way out for the water runs very shallow there and we had to anchor some three miles from the warehouse! All the goods were taken ashore on a large lighter which was run toward the beach and grounded. By the time we landed, it was too late to unload the lighter that night.

Somebody mentioned that there was an Indian camp not half a mile from us and I heard that sullen fellow from Sacramento ask the clerk of the boat how many men he would need to guard the lighter from the Indians.

"We don't need any," he replied.

"You are not going to leave the lighter loaded with goods without a guard and an Indian camp nearby!" cried the little indignant fellow.

The clerk said: "Those Indians will not touch a thing on that barge if it was left there for a month. There is not an Indian in that camp who would not walk twenty miles to save a white man's life."

He told the grumpy little oaf that last winter two prospectors had cached their provisions near an Indian camp further upriver and when the prospectors returned, they found a huge bundle of furs waiting for them. The Indians had taken some of the provisions to help them through the winter, for it was very bitter that year and they had more than replaced what they had taken.

The contrarian said under his breath that the Indians of his acquaintance would walk 200 miles just to get a shot at him when he wasn't looking.

I looked to Helki then thinking I could well understand why this loathsome little fellow would be the victim of a shooting, for I felt like taking a pot-shot myself!

I always wonder how she feels when these Indian affairs are discussed so, but her face was blank as a sheet.

I don't know how to bring her out of her shell. I wish she would cry like I have been crying. It washes down the soul, sluices out all the terrible feelings of loss.

But it seems she cannot.

When we saw the Indian camp in the daylight, it was clear those poor Alaskan Indians are living a miserable existence with very little proper food or clothing. The clerk of the ship said consumption has ravaged the camp.

We waited for the steamer to come down the river, and she arrived carrying gold dust and furs that had accumulated during the winter.

As I climbed aboard the steamer, I felt for the first time since Christmas, a tiny spark of something inside.

It has been so long since we have traveled. So long since we have gone on an adventure. I feel that I was perhaps built for adventure. Having a family can clip your wings. I feel perhaps I am growing my feathers again.

March 1896. Yukon River, Alaska.

The steamer carries about 300 tonnes of goods but a large space has to be left for firewood, because she burns wood about as fast as four men can throw it into the furnaces. There are plenty of trees floating in the river which the pilot has to be very careful to watch out for.

The Catholic priest who piloted us for the first leg of the journey seemed a quiet fellow. There are three Catholic and one Presbyterian missions along the river.

This morning, we stopped at an Indian encampment for more firewood. The Indians take the floating logs and trees to their beach and cut them into four-foot lengths, cord them up and sell them to the steamboats. It is quite a good enterprise, I suppose. They had salmon, it looked like, drying over fires.

When we stopped, the clerk of the boat went ashore to measure up what he wanted and the Indian women came aboard to buy cupfuls of flour and rice and beans. I watched the ship hand put his forefinger into the cup when he dipped, just to give them that little less. How badly they treat the Indians!

I probably should have said something and I regret that I did not. I have been quiet along this journey. Perhaps it is the tiredness.

No one has been as quiet as Helki, however. She is practically a stone statue!

March 1896. Fort Yukon, Alaska.

We have reached Fort Yukon!

Why they use the word "fort" for everything here in Alaska, I don't know, for there are no forts or anything resembling one!

We are for the first time inside the Arctic Circle, the furthest north we have ever been!

Not long till Circle City!

March 1896. Circle City, Alaska.

Well, we have arrived! Our home for the next year. Fifteen hundred miles we have traveled along the Yukon to get here.

As that steamer pushed further and further north, I really did have my doubts about our decision to come here, especially as Helki began to look less and less like herself, like a woman completely lost.

George tried to be cheery, for he is the champion of bringing us here, but even he has been a little bewildered as to how we can try to help our dear, bereft Helki.

Our square is no more. Forevermore, we will be a triangle.

When we got off the steamer we found a large store, a warehouse and an elaborate dwelling house built of logs in a very substantial manner that belonged to Captain John J. Healey, a man with an Irish lilt, although he was born in Vancouver. There were other buildings along the street, belonging to other commercial outlets, but none as big as those belonging to the North American Transportation and Trading Company.

Captain Healey is the general manager operating on the ground and was mightily pleased to see us arrive, for he knew we were bringing not one, but two women in our little group and his wife had been waiting anxiously.

They offered us a welcoming supper of fish pie, washed down with wine, which we most welcomed after our long journey.

I had to correct Mrs. Healey when she referred to Helki as my "servant."

"She is as we are," I said. "She is my companion and confidante."

"A lady's maid?" asked Mrs. Healey.

"No," I said. "I was married to her brother."

Well, the table went quieter than a graveyard at midnight just then as C. Healey and George and Helki listened on and I said out loud for all to hear that George was my first husband and Momo my second, that Momo had died suddenly at Christmas and we were all experiencing terrible grief over our dreadful loss.

I watched George's face then, looking at the many flickers across it, surprise, and anger, outrage even but as he stuttered at my words, I held my shoulders back and head high for I felt now a changed woman.

As we'd made our way all up along the Yukon, I could feel a tightness in my heart melting like the rushing snow water around me. Momo's death had done something to me and no longer do I want to live a lie or pretense. I don't care that we lose face. I care no more for society's rules and notions of respect!

All those times Momo and I could have spent together and didn't because we had to hide what we had. What we were.

"So … you are … a divorcee?" Mrs. Healey asked, like a cat on its hind legs in pointed fur fright. Her mouth had soured around the word "divorcee."

"No, George and I remain married," I told her, firmly. "Momo was my common-law husband."

Oh, you could very well hear a pin drop in that wooden establishment. You would have heard it bounce softly off the rug!

Mr. Healey's mouth was agape!

My words had brought Helki back to us for she looked around the table blinking.

"As a matter of fact, if you must know," I continued, pointing toward George. "My husband is Helki's common-law husband too, so we are all tied up with each other, and simply could not be separated. We might as well set things straight from our very first day. We don't appreciate rumors and we have nothing to hide."

Well, that got Helki's attention, I tell you. For the first time since Christmas, a smile appeared on her lips. George looked like he wanted to dive under the table and hide.

Mr. Healey shot up and asked George if he would join him for an after-dinner whiskey and George jumped up like a spring. They retired to the sideboard, away from us ladyfolk.

So much for Mrs. Healey expecting two women she would have something in common with. She could barely look at us after that and retired to bed early!

We have quite a roomy cabin featuring two bedrooms, and a fire had been lit to welcome us. Probably the last fire we'll have provided by Mrs. Healey!

We were so tired we fell into bed and I found that George's surprise and fury had mellowed into a benign exasperation thanks to the whiskey.

"What did you do that for, woman?" he asked, as he lay in the dark.

I told him that I was no longer prepared to live in secret.

"This is a new start for us, George," I told him, quite firmly. "And I want my conscience to be as fresh as that clean white snow out there."

He harrumphed.

"Ha! You'll have us arrested for polygamy!"

"It's not polygamy if you don't get married again under civil law," I told him.

"Scandal then!" he said.

"Momo is dead," I replied. "I only have one husband left."

He went quiet then.

"It is you who has two wives."

He shook his head, as ever quite bewildered by me, but when he turned around in bed, I reached out and put my arm around him and held him close for the first time in a very long time.

There was that love I felt for him, a love I'd always had. There was the warmth between us that ebbed and flowed and was sometimes out to sea. He has a lot of faults, George, and is by no means a perfect man. But he has never left me and I have never left him.

He is the only husband I have now.

And luckily for us, I don't believe they have rattlesnakes in Alaska.

April 1896, Circle City, Alaska.

On Friday we bought two wire mattresses, which were selling very fast at $45 each! One of the privileges of George's job is being able to buy things at cost. I could not believe it when he told me he only paid $2.50 each for the mattresses.

Helki was delighted to have a full new mattress to herself.

The way things are marked up here gave me an idea, for Helki has brought all her medicines with her in a big case—she could not bear to leave them behind in San Francisco—and only she knows the measurement and proportions.

I suggested to her that she should talk to C. Healey about offering them in the store, for there sure is nothing around like her cures. Healey agreed and we put a little sign up and showed some of the bottles and my goodness—weren't we out the door!

Helki was like a pharmacist and I her dispensing assistant. Some of the dried medicines have turned out to be worth more than gold dust! Yesterday she was asked to do a house call to a miner who was bedridden! If things keep going like this, the issue will be supply.

Things are very busy now here in the Birch Creek mining district. It is mostly men moving through (with many tenderfoots about!).

The usual saloon and gambling halls are open but the boom time for them will be in the fall, I'm told, when the miners come down out of the mountains. There is almost no money in circulation here. Everything is paid for in gold dust which is currently priced at $16 an ounce. Everyone carries a buckskin sack with his gold dust in it.

Captain Healey told me the gold scales are very sensitive.

He said you could take two pieces of paper that weighed exactly alike, write your name in lead pencil on one and the scales would weigh the amount of lead that had come off the pencil in writing your name! It is most fascinating.

George is still very busy organizing supplies. He is going up the mountains soon to look at plots on behalf of the company. I have asked to go with him and he has agreed.

I feel that he has changed in his attitude toward me somewhat. Sees me different somehow. I suppose I am not the naive little wife I once was.

I miss the children, even though they are still at school and would be away from me anyway. They will be in good hands with George's sister Victoria, but it's the knowledge that it will be so very long until I see them again. And that we are so very far away. At least we have only committed to the year here. I hope the children do not hold it against us later!

I have written many letters to Matilda re: Momo but burned them all. I feel it may be a burden. I would like to discuss the issue with Helki. But she remains as silent as the wind beneath a barn owl's wings.

May 1896, Circle City, Alaska.

Captain Healey has discovered that I was once a bookkeeper and informed me that there was nobody in Circle City who knows anything about bookkeeping and his books are in very bad shape.

I offered to start right in on the books and he agreed that if I could help, he would put me in his employ. Well, I brought out all of those books, forced a balance, transferred all the accounts to a new ledger, posted everything up to date and took off another trial balance (which consisted of ten sheets of journal paper), added it up and it all balanced to a cent first time!

Captain Healey was astounded and said he would put me on the payroll immediately. He said it was a pity I was a woman, for if I was a man, I would be earning more than George!

So now we have a double salary coming in, plus Helki is earning with her medicinal business. Only a few weeks in this place and already we feel rich!

Our fortunes certainly have changed.

There is no representative of the law here. Captain Healey told us they hold miners' meetings to represent the feelings, prejudices and passions of those who attend them.

They call one whenever they feel one is necessary and appoint a chairman who takes the ayes and nays. There is no way to enforce the decisions however and Captain Healey said the meetings are as useful as a chocolate teapot!

There seems little need for law enforcement though. This seems to be a quiet place. The men we've met are good people.

Tomorrow we're leaving to go and look at the company's claims with a view to having them opened up.

The company has hired a horse for George from a man in town who used to pack goods from the store to the mines but I had to pay for my own horse, as Healey said the company would never pay for a woman to go prospecting. He added that a woman could never have any experience or interest in mining. I had a good mind to tell him my history! I suppose he thinks I'm going up there to pick fruit!

Which reminds me, I may be able to gather something useful for Helki. She has been foraging here and finding plenty, although the plants are quite different to California and so she has had to experiment a little. I suggested she talk to a local medicine man for advice.

We met four men coming down this morning carrying a sick man to town on a stretcher. We stopped to talk with them, and the sick man told us he had been salivated with mercury.

Oh, he looked terribly ill, had a hacking cough, was finding it hard to breathe and complained of an unmerciful headache.

What had happened was most unfortunate, but a good lesson.

He had gathered the gold in his sluices with quicksilver, put the amalgam in a gold pan and placed it on the hot stove in his tent to evaporate the quicksilver. He knew that he ought not to stay in the tent while this was vaporizing, for fear of inhaling the vapor and getting salivated, so he went outside.

BUT—he had left some flour, a loaf of bread and the dishes he used on the table in the tent and when the quicksilver vapor condensed it fell into them and this is how he came to be poisoned.

I urged him to visit Helki in town for I was sure she would have something to help and gave him some of our sourdough to ease the journey down.

Birch Creek District is appropriately named. In all our travels over the years I've seen birch trees over a foot in diameter but some of these trees were three foot in diameter. The largest I ever saw.

We camp out tonight. I think I will rest easy, knowing we are safe from snakes!

The mines were already partly opened when we got to them. We prospected them all with a pan and were sure that two were undoubtedly very valuable claims. The third was not so good. We spent the rest of the day looking at other mines nearby, some of which George reckoned might be very valuable.

He talked non-stop about how he felt the other claims would be a good investment, that he knew the miner who had them and that if he offered him enough, he could surely secure them.

I had a bad feeling about the claims and thought this miner he spoke of may be all hat and no cattle. But George did not want to hear my opinions. He said I was a truculent old coot when I wanted to be! But I don't think my gut has steered me wrong yet.

I have taken many plants for Helki, although some I am not quite sure of what I have. I was surprised to see the hillside covered with blueberry bushes, eight or ten inches high. They will be laden come fall.

I couldn't help but think of the poor salivated man. What if all these bushes and fruit bushes are contaminated with all this mining nearby?

June 1896. Circle City, Alaska.

George did a deal with Tully, the miner who owns the claims next to the company's and has asked for a leave of a week to prospect on the claims he bought.

I don't think Captain Healey is too happy about it, but I can cover George's work when he is gone.

George returned yesterday.
He found nothing but a load of granite!

July 1896. Circle City, Alaska.

Helki has run out of many of her medicines and refuses to look for a local medicine man. I think she could really run a trade, but I do not want to push her. We have been doing a roaring trade in sourdough. She has finally been returning to somewhat of herself.

We had a conversation last week about her tribe and she told me the most interesting thing. In their society, the man and the woman have equal footing. Leaders are chosen on their characteristics, not birth right. The women have just as much authority as the men do when it comes to decision making.

I could not believe it! Imagine our world if women were allowed to have a say! I wonder how she has put up with George for so long if that is how she was raised!

It also sets me to thinking what else Helki has kept to herself all these years. Hers are surely still waters that run deep.

She has taken in laundry for there is so much of it here and there is good money to be made. I help her if I'm idle, for even though it is busy with the summer mining, I am quick with the books. She is looking at taking a cabin and turning it into a proper launderette.

We see lots of Indians passing through. Last week a man called George Carmack was in town with his Tagish wife who goes by the name of "Kate." Captain Healey said lots of miners didn't like him because of his wife.

"They don't believe in mixing," he said.

Almost as fast as he said it, I could see that he wished the words had not come of his mouth, for he was thinking of Helki and our unique situation. I'm sure people talk about us but I have not heard anything in earshot and besides, even if I did, I don't give one fig!

July 1896. Circle City, Alaska.

I got a letter from Victoria today, what a lovely surprise to hear from home, though she had posted it almost directly after we left, so there wasn't much news.

She said that all is well except that Ansel has been getting in trouble for impudence and he has had to be reprimanded severely. She took a riding crop to him herself. I don't like to think of him being whipped, although I do know how stubborn he can be and single-minded. There is a streak to his temperament that I really do not abide.

George wishes him to go to college, especially now that we will have the funds to pay for it, but Ansel has other ideas. He wishes to go to work immediately and has even suggested that he travel here to stay with us! I will not hear of it. He would be far better off staying where he is and getting an education neither George nor I could ever have dreamed of.

Speaking of mining, George has bought up more claims and has hired prospectors to work them. He leaves this Saturday to see that settle in. He is very enthusiastic! I pray it works out.

For him. And us!

August 1896. Circle City, Alaska.

George back.
    Nothing again.
    Very despondent.

I'm madder than a wet hen! I have just witnessed the most appalling thing!

I was walking to Helki's launderette when I came upon a man who was whipping his sled dog with an iron chain! I don't know what the poor mutt had done to displease him so, but I stopped and said, "If you strike that dog again, I'll punch your nose!"

Well, the man raised the chain and so I punched him right on the nose! He fell backwards onto the ground (possibly more with shock than the force of my right hook) and I managed a kick at him too, right in the side.

"I'll have you arrested!" he said.

I told him there wasn't a witness to prove it and I picked up the piece of the chain and walked away with it. That poor dog.

George said I *will* get arrested and I need to learn to keep my temper to myself. He's one to talk! I'm glad I did it. I can't abide cruelty like that.

And besides, who in a miner's meeting would throw me out, the only woman for miles who has control of all their accounts!

Rumors are reaching us of a new district in which gold has been discovered. It's about 300 miles up the river from Circle City and about 50 miles above Forty Mile post and Fort Cudahy in British territory. It's called Rabbit Creek but already they're calling it Bonanza Creek!

The story is that Joseph la Due, a fellow with a sawmill up there, let George Carmack (the fellow with the Tagish wife) prospect 14 miles above his mill.

Carmack got to work with his Tagish brothers-in-law but there was so much water in the bed of the creek that they couldn't get down to bedrock, so they went up one side of the gulch on the rim rock and got a shaft down to bedrock and that's where they found the gold.

Apparently la Due is all a fluster now and is looking to get a patent for a townsite so that he can sell lots. He is going around telling everyone in Fort Cudahy of the discovery for he sure would make a lot on his lumber if it took off.

There are a lot of tenderfeet about and I suppose they will all rush there now. I told George about the new discovery but he did not want to speak on it. I suppose he is still feeling a little sore after the last prospecting disaster(s).

September 1896. Circle City, Alaska.

George and I were talking to a fellow in the store today by the name of Langlow. He told us he's a claim in an area they're calling the "Klondyke." (The Indians call it "Thron-Diuck" meaning "fish waters" but of course, no one can pronounce it!)

He has No. 12 El Dorado Creek.

I asked him if he'd discovered any gold but he said no. He told me though that there is a report that Indians found gold two miles from his claims on another creek, so there is a chance. He said he would be interested in looking at a half share if we wanted in at $500.

I can't exactly explain it, but I have a fair notion about this claim. That we should do something about it.

George laughed about it with Langlow but when I brought it up after supper, he told me I'd no idea what I was talking about and he was not spending any more on useless empty Alaskan bedrock.

Many miners have been returning to town on account of the cold weather. The saloons and gambling houses have re-opened, and things are much more lively. The steamer will arrive on her last trip in October. All the goods will be stored in the warehouse then and the steamer will go into winter quarters. I suppose our log houses will be quite comfortable to live in over the winter.

George has been terribly busy as everyone is building up their cache. The supplies bought in October of course must last until spring. Shopping is quite different here, and nothing like at home. Nobody comes into the store, looks at the goods, money in hand, and says, "I want six cans of these tomatoes." Oh no! Here, in Circle City, people say, "How many cans of these tomatoes can I buy?"

What you'll hear in response from the clerk is: "Why, you bought two cans the day before yesterday. You can only have two more!"

Captain Healey has a particular method when it comes to estimating the supplies. He keeps everyone's shopping lists on file and is total master of the lists. It is he who decides what everyone will have. If one puts down six bags of flour, he will scratch it out and make it four. The miners of course trade among themselves but we are lucky to be able to buy at cost and, of course, Healey always looks favorably upon us.

I find it hard to imagine having no contact with home over the winter months. There will be barely any postal service whatsoever. I have written a whole bunch of letters to the children, a stockpile!

Sometimes I really do worry if we have done the right thing by coming here.

October 1896. Circle City, Alaska.

Frank Phiscator came to see Helki today looking for a paste she had provided to him when he was on his way up the mountains in spring.

He's run out and suffers terribly from ulcers. He'd come all the way down just to see her and she happened to have one small jar of it left. He gave her a pile of gold dust in return and I have never seen a man look so happy!

He told us he had a claim on 51 El Dorado Creek and that his pals Clarence J. Berry at No. 6 and Thomas Lippy at No. 16 were taking out a lot of gold before reaching bedrock.

"El Dorado Creek?" I asked.

He nodded.

If they were taking out gold on No. 6 and No. 16, then I knew for sure there had to be gold at No. 12, the claim Langlow offered us weeks back.

"Do you know a fellow by the name of John Langlow?" I asked.

"I know the fellow," Phiscator said.

"Would you take him a note from me?" I asked and he said he would be happy to do so.

George does not know but I sent Phiscator up the mountain with $1,000 in an envelope for Langlow and a note with a promise of another $1,500 on bedrock.

I am taking a risk. I know that George will be furious when he finds out but I am acting as a chieftess might in Helki's tribe. I am making a decision!

I pray that Momo is looking down upon me in agreeance.

November 1896. Circle City, Alaska.

Langlow has agreed to terms! He sent a deed down the mountain.

Now, he of course made the deed out to George with his name on the envelope. George found out by way of a stranger miner handing him over the paperwork today in the store! He was quite annoyed with me, but I fibbed and told him I'd sent $500 as I was sure it was a good bet. As long as he doesn't go counting our money, I might have got away with it!

When he reprimanded me later on when we were alone again I told him about Helki's tribe and how women can make their own decisions without needing permission. It struck him as so comical that he laughed and laughed and forgot all about being angry with me in the first place.

December 1896. Circle City, Alaska.

Miss Donaldson and Mister Carter, a young miner from New York, wish to be married. I suppose the winter boredom has set in. You can't blame the young whippersnappers and I suppose many women don't mind the idea of entrapment! Of course, there is no one within 500 miles authorized to perform the ceremony, not a priest or a magistrate of any kind to be had.

The matter was talked over and in the same way that a justice of the peace or a sea captain three miles from land can marry a couple, it was decided that the Collector of Customs, being the only man connected in any way with the law here, should have the same right to unite the loving hearts.

The wedding takes place on Friday. If only I'd packed a proper hat!

A wonderful, joyous day.

Mrs. Healey gave the happy couple a grand party and a turkey dinner to celebrate, though she put me and Helki at the far end of the table, the furthest away from her as possible.

Afraid we'll rub off on her, I guess!

I could not get out of bed today. I told George it was the start of a flu but he surely knows it is a flu of the mind.

This time last year he was still here.

Helki has gone very quiet. If she is lonely she does not admit it, but I know by how distant she gets. Like a still lake. Lots happening beneath the surface but her face a sheet of glass.

Christmas Day, 1896. Circle City, Alaska.

We dropped our frozen potatoes into boiling water and they cooked beautifully.

The general supposition is that freezing spoils a potato, but I have learned that it does not—only if you let it thaw out naturally.

Our frozen oranges were quite delicious.

December 25, 1896. Circle City, Alaska (evening).

I began crying after dinner and could not stop.

I miss the children. I am tired of the cold and snow. I am angry that George drove Momo away.

I blame God for making rattlesnakes.

What a cruel world we live in.

How has it already been a year? And my heartache still so raw.

January 1897. Circle City, Alaska.

C. Healey has agreed to release George from his contract early as things are quiet and there is much excitement about the Klondykes! The reports are very good.

We could only secure two dogs as they are scarce and had to pay $200 each.

Helki is not coming with us and will stay on with her laundry business. We have promised her we will return as soon as possible!

We got about twenty miles today. The sun could be seen for about an hour, though it is not dark.

The Aurora Borealis is breathtaking. The heavens look as though they are reaching to us, fingers of light, bending down to touch us here on earth.

I feel the hand of Momo near. Guiding me. Salving my heart.

We set up our little sheet iron stove in a corner of the tent by the entrance, with a pipe poking out the top. We start the fire with little strips of muslin soaked in coal oil that we keep in a bottle. We lie our robes on the snow and that is our bed.

The wind's got teeth and every inch of me is frozen, but I'll say this for Alaska: not a damn snake in sight. Small mercies.

How far we have come, George and I. Arid deserts to freezing tundra. The two of us, together. Never to be parted.

A wretched day today.

George's coat stops just above his mukluk boots (made of sealskin) and the cold has gotten into his knees. He can barely walk. I cut a heavy scarf in two and tied it around his legs.

There is no wind, except perhaps at the bend of a river, but it is very, very cold. A dry type of cold.

If we can get to Fort Cudahy then we will rest a while and have the dogs fed properly.

February 1897. El Dorado Claim No. 12, Alaska.

Well, we made it!

I'm not quite sure I will ever get the cold out of my bones!

How lovely it was to arrive and find that Langlow has built a log cabin in which we could shelter immediately.

The surface of the ground is covered everywhere with a growth of moss about a foot thick. Below that is a layer of very black soil from eight to twelve feet thick. We call it "muck" but it can be picked out like coal out of a coal seam.

Labor is scarce and the going rate is $15 a day.

George has been grumbling as his knees are very painful.

I keep telling him I am his lucky charm. That this time, things will work out. I do everything I can to keep him cheery. But he can be rather contrary and difficult to deal with.

Last night I dreamt of Momo and when I awoke, for quite a long time, I believed he still lived.

The frozen gravel cannot be pick-axed. Instead, we have been lighting fires at the bottom of the shafts, letting it burn and smolder all night to thaw out the frost, shovel that out and hoist it up with a bucket and start another fire.

Landlow keeps joking that he thought I was a "lady." He particularly likes to say it when I have a smear of black across my face. I tell him he knows nothing about my capacities, for I am a woman of experience, a woman of the frontier!

First shaft, 25 feet deep.
Nothing found.
A total dud.

La Due has sold lots fronting onto what will be a main street.
They are calling the town "Dawson."

March 1897. El Dorado Claim No. 12 Alaska.

Today, as we were working, I saw something white in a lump of muck about the size and shape of a small hen's egg. It lay curled up like boiled grey shrimp, its body made up of segments.

This is the first bug I ever saw in Alaska for there are no snakes, bugs, reptiles or insects of any kind that have to live through the winter here. Of course, there are flies and mosquitoes that hatch every year, but everything else has a layer of fur!

I have been reading about toads and turtles that have been found in solid rock that had, as one might say, come to life again after having lain dormant for perhaps thousands of years upon being exposed to the air and heat. I thought I would see if this little bug would come to life.

We sharpened a stick and prised it out very carefully. I placed it on a flat, warm rock in the sunshine. I went to look at it several times and about noon I noticed it had begun to change color, almost brownish.

By nighttime the little fellow could walk!

I've now placed it in a mustard bottle that has a large opening with a cork in it alongside some of the fine thawed out muck in the bottom.

What do unearthed ancient specimens eat, one wonders?!

Well, the little fellow, who I've named Pedro, spent rather a pleasant day in the spring sunshine on the window of our cabin.

This evening, I emptied him out onto newspaper and he walked all around the paper! I am not a scientist, of course, but when he walked, I noticed that he didn't seem to have quite as many legs as he needed for his little segmented body. I really do think we have unearthed something rather exciting, possibly even extinct.

My father would have loved to have seen him. I put a leaf into this jar, and two flies, but he didn't take to any of them. He has become very lively altogether. I am afraid if he does die (of hunger!) he will curl right up and shrivel and he won't appear as his magnificent self. I have come to the terrible conclusion that should I want to keep him as a specimen for perhaps the Smithsonian institute I will have to preserve him.

George has agreed and tomorrow I will go to Dawson to buy some alcohol.

Must we forever be cursed by ill winds?!

How cruel this world shows itself to be, again and again.

When I left for Dawson a miner came through and was speaking to George. George told him to go into the cabin to view our specimen and the man took a good look at it, opening the mustard bottle and left without replacing the stopper! When I got back, alcohol in hand, my poor Pedro had escaped!

Most likely through one of the large cracks in the floor.

Gone. No point in even searching for him.

I am heartsore. He might only have been a rare, extinct insect, but he was MY rare, extinct insect. I could throttle George, so I could!

George said not to worry, that he would drink the alcohol I'd brought!

April 1897. El Dorado Claim No. 12 Alaska.

Gold!

Gold!

We've struck gold! Our third shaft and it's all gold!

I was right all along. I was right all along about the claim!

This changes everything. There is no demise from this glory.

That claim is as much George's as it is mine. I could cry with happiness, but I like to save my tears for my child and true husband.

We will find new laborers and I will return to bring Helki here, for it looks like Dawson, for the foreseeable future, will be our new home.

THE EXAMINER
San Francisco, Sunday Morning, July 18, 1897
REPORTS FROM THE FAR-AWAY LAND WHERE THE EARTH SEEMS LINED WITH GOLD

HUNDREDS OF FORTUNE-HUNTERS ARE HURRYING NORTHWARD

STEAMSHIP COMPANIES REPORT A GREAT DEMAND FOR TRANSPORTATION

There is every prospect of a Yukon mining boom. "We would not be able to carry all who have spoken about going," said Lewis Sloane of the Alaska Commercial Company yesterday. "There has almost been a procession at times to ask about the Yukon country and to establish particulars as to transportation and rates. I think we had 200 inquirers in a day."

The North American Transportation Company has had a similar experience with applicants and it is evident that whatever the real value of the Clondyke mines may be, the stories brought by the passengers of the Excelsior have made a decided impression upon the public mind and there will be a greater rush than has been reported.

Only the dangers from cold and famine keep the exodus within reasonable bounds, the Alaskan shipping men think, and these dangers are admitted to be suffered by all, even the most reckless adventurer.

Joaquin Miller, the poet, will start for the gold fields tomorrow morning. He will go by steamer and cross into the country from there, following the river to the mining camps. The distance he will have to travel practically on foot is 600 miles and the mountainous country is difficult and dangerous.

Dispatches received from Seattle yesterday only confirmed the news that has already been published in the *Examiner* with particulars of mining successes that are fully as astonishing as the stories told by the passengers of the Excelsior.

At this time, the civilized world has its attention turned north: the attraction: Yukon Gold.

CHAPTER 22
ELLIE

November 28, 2019. Berkeley, California.

Ellie pulled the red-hot tray out of the narrow bottom oven and winced. She didn't curse out loud. She managed to hold her tongue, but the oven mitt she was using had gotten wet, catching a spray of milk that her father Stanley had knocked over when he'd opened a cupboard earlier and let an avalanche of seventies Tupperware boxes fall out. She hadn't realized the mitt was wet until her hand was firmly around the piping hot roasting pan containing the plump Thanksgiving turkey.

She let the glove drop into the sink and immediately ran her hand under the faucet. This was turning into more of a circus than she'd bargained for.

Enzo's kitchen was tiny. It had not been upgraded since it was installed in the 1950s; there weren't enough work surfaces and the breakfast nook seemed to invade rather than provide a welcoming spot to sit and sip a drink. Ellie never quite understood why homes of this era had such tiny kitchens to work in considering the homemakers of the time spent most of their time cooking, baking, and cleaning in them.

Oh, but wait. That tracked: putting women into workspaces structurally sabotaged to thwart success.

She'd managed to shoo most of the family into the living room. Simona understood the task at hand and had helped her prepare vegetables and potatoes earlier while holding the boys at bay. Stanley hadn't quite read the memo. He kept popping into the kitchen, looking for batteries or string or a set of marbles he was sure was tucked away in an old tin box in the overhead cupboard beside the refrigerator.

Ellie had already removed many of Enzo and Genevieve's belongings from the home. She'd had to declutter for any potential Realtor because she knew they would fetch a better price if the home looked more spacious and easier to remodel.

But what a job that was. Newspapers and magazines. Ornaments, knickknacks, records. Pottery and beautiful China sets covered in dust that she could never remember Genevieve using. "Too good," likely. Built only to sit on a shelf and be admired.

They still had a ways to go, and tomorrow, her parents would tackle the task of organizing and making decisions as to what to keep, what to sell, what to donate, and what to discard. It would be sad, no doubt frustrating at times, but it was unavoidable.

As a last hurrah, Ellie had suggested they gather for one final Thanksgiving at Enzo's house. It had been a last-minute decision and, at first, Simona had pooh-poohed the idea, saying it would be too much work for Ellie to take on at Enzo's. But Stanley had loved the idea and, considering they'd all had such fond memories there, Ellie thought how meaningful it would be to host a farewell family holiday to honor her grandparents. She wanted Thanksgiving to be perfect. It was more than just a dinner; it was a celebration of Enzo's and Genevieve's lives.

Plunging a thermometer into the turkey, Ellie watched the juices flow down the bronzed breast of the bird. Clear. The temperature was reading a little over. Time to come out. Taking two large forks, Ellie lifted the bird out of its tray with difficulty, when Stanley wandered in with her laptop.

"Does this thing have something called Zoom?" he said, holding it aloft like a futuristic obelisk. "I got a text from Leo; he said he'll 'Zoom' us later. He said it'll be on the laptop. I thought that was a kids' TV program."

Ellie's wrists felt like they might snap. She dropped the bird onto

Genevieve's blue Spode ceramic platter with a splash of grease.

"Dad! Yes, I have Zoom. It's a video conferencing app. Leo's NGO uses it. I will look at it later, okay? You have to let me cook in here!"

Stanley nodded and backed slowly out of the kitchen with the laptop shielding him from his daughter's temper. Immediately Ellie felt a wave of guilt: snapping at her father wasn't in the "perfect plan" for dinner today. Neither was missile Tupperware, milk-soaked oven mitts, or burnt, blistered hands. But she only had so much patience, and Stanley had a clueless way of tipping her over the edge.

Ellie missed her brother Leo today. As the eldest, he'd felt like the peacekeeping glue of the family. But such was the sacrifice of working abroad.

The truth was, Ellie realized as she lifted the turkey again to drain the juices into a pitcher for the gravy, that getting the house ready for the Realtor had churned up a Category 3 storm of memories. She was marinating in grief. Going through Enzo and Genevieve's things had taken a toll—even items that seemingly had no sentimental value could spark a whole wave of memories.

Thankfully, Anika had watched the boys while she'd done most of it in her evenings after work this past week. She thought she would complete the job much quicker if the boys were otherwise occupied (Enzo's house was decidedly not childproof), but instead of saving time, the task seemed endless as she kept getting mired in old letters, photographs, and memorabilia.

She'd found all sorts of odds and ends, from her father's bronzed baby shoes to old wooden tennis racquets, ancient Christmas cards and recipe books, and boxes of Genevieve's clothes representing multiple decades and fashion trends. She'd found a photograph of Enzo holding the grey-brown ridged stone she knew was in the big old wooden box in Enzo's living room captioned *Enzo with Mammoth Tooth.*

So, that's what it was! She'd thought it was some kind of fossil! Maybe Teddy had discovered it! Now that she had only two of Teddy's diaries left to read, she was deliberately savoring them, not wanting them to end. She had an idea of transcribing them for her father as a Christmas gift but just didn't have that kind of spare time.

As Ellie stacked out the appetizer plates, Simona appeared in the kitchen.

"Is he driving you crazy?" she asked.

Ellie rolled her eyes. "I'm sorry, Mom. You know what he's like."

"I do," said Simona, her voice deadpan.

Ellie couldn't help but laugh.

"Let me help you," said her mother kindly. "I'll do those. Throw a wet towel on the bird to keep it moist."

As Simona reached for the starter plates, the doorbell rang.

"Who in the world?" said Ellie.

"Maybe a neighbor?" said Simona, parting the venetian blinds and trying to see the doorstep.

"Could you get it?"

As Ellie patted the turkey, satisfied with the crispy skin, she listened to the sound of a man's voice in the hall, muffled and yet ... she turned, large turkey prong in hand, to find the one and only Dr. Sam Varma standing in Enzo's kitchen, holding a fruit basket.

"Sam!"

"I'm sorry!" he said. "I thought you would be finished with dinner. I just wanted to drop in on my way to the city. But I see you haven't even ..."

He raised the fruit basket sheepishly, reading the room.

"No," said Ellie, feeling the shock rush through her. *Sam. Here? At Enzo's. What?* "We got a bit behind schedule. Mom, this is Sam Varma; I mentioned him to you, remember?"

"I do," said Simona and she shook Sam's hand, searing him with her laser vision.

"How did you know where to find us?" Ellie asked, putting down the fork and wiping her hands on her apron to embrace Sam and kiss him on the cheek.

"You told me the address!" he said. "Remember? I helped you hunt for comps on Zillow."

"Oh right!" said Ellie.

"I have an interview tomorrow at UCSF Medical Center," said Sam. "I decided to come out today, stay the night so I was fresh tomorrow. I thought I'd surprise you."

Sam surveyed the chaos of the kitchen, almost in confusion.

Well, he had certainly done that.

"Now, who organizes an interview for the day after Thanksgiving?" asked Simona, frowning.

"The third-ranked Department of Neurology in the country, that's who," said Sam with a soft chuckle.

"Well, it's true that people need doctors every day of the year," said Simona.

"But we're not at home tonight," said Ellie, thinking Sam would want to stay at her place. She felt discombobulated now at this unexpected visit; she adored Sam and had enjoyed when he'd stayed over and met the boys. But this was different. This was Enzo's. This was family time.

"I'm booked at the Axiom Hotel," he said. "I'll be on my way; you're obviously crazy busy; I'm sorry to have disturbed—"

"You'll do no such thing!" said Simona. "You'll stay for Thanksgiving dinner. Plenty to go round! As for your seat ... well, you may be on a stool, I'm afraid."

Sam laughed, looking relieved.

Ellie called her father and the boys for dinner and watched her father shake Sam's hand and appraise him with more moderate scrutiny than Simona. His presence didn't seem to ruffle Stanley in the least. She waited for the shock of seeing him to subside. It was Simona they would need to win over at dinner, she realized; Simona held all her men to high standard. She had approved of Joe, at least at first, and wasn't about to let just anyone walk in and sweep away her daughter.

They sat for their starters, and Ellie barely tasted her butternut squash soup as she snuck quick glances at Sam, who was dressed in a pale pink dress shirt with contrasting thread at the buttonholes, a grey wool-blend jacket, and blue jeans and looked incredibly handsome. Of course, with all the panic, she felt flustered and red-cheeked and hadn't had time to change out of her slippers before dinner. She had always felt so comfortable at Enzo's—it was a place to relax and let loose. She hadn't expected to present herself as a sex kitten today.

When it came time to carve the turkey, Stanley stood and took his place—Enzo's old place—at the head of the table.

"I don't see why the man stands on ceremony for the carving, when the woman's done all the cooking," said Simona.

Stanley rolled his eyes before plunging the knife deep into the turkey breast in an exaggerated stabbing motion. Nathan giggled.

"Again!" called Nathan.

"Dad!" warned Ellie, reaching for her wine.

"Not thinking of anyone in particular," said Stanley and they all laughed.

Ellie felt her shoulders relax now that the cooking was done, but her stomach was still wound a little tight as she watched Sam laugh alongside her family. He fit right in, it seemed. But did she want him there? Today?

"So, Dr. Varma, you're at UC Davis? And thinking of moving?" asked Simona.

Here we go, thought Ellie. *The inquisition.*

"Please call me Sam. I like UC Davis; it has a great department," said Sam. "But UCSF has been the dream, and an opportunity came up."

Ellie suddenly realized what this interview meant for Sam; should he be successful in securing the position, he would be moving to San Francisco. Was he doing this for her? To be nearer to her? The thought seesawed in her head as she watched her mother rally back and forth with Sam.

"So, you like California then?"

"I can't complain," Sam said, "though the temperate weather takes some acclimation. Even after years in the States, I still brace for a monsoon when the skies turn grey."

They all chuckled. Ellie listened to the sound of her father chewing, willing him to ask Sam a question. She didn't want it to appear as if only Simona was interested.

"Ellie tells me you're in epidemiology at the public health department. That must be its own adventure," said Sam.

Simona smiled. "*Adventure* might be one word for it. Most people only find us when they need a vaccine or advice on something mysterious. Until then, public health is just a department no one can find."

Sam nodded. "It's the same everywhere, isn't it? India's no different—public health work happens in the background until it's urgent. People love a cure but rarely think about prevention."

"You know, that's exactly it," said Simona, pointing her soupspoon at him. "Prevention doesn't get the spotlight, but it's doing the heavy lifting."

Sam leaned in. "And what about when prevention isn't enough? Let's say something starts spreading faster than we can contain it. How do you think our health system would hold up if we had—I don't know—a massive outbreak of something contagious and fast-moving. Like a 'worst-case scenario'?"

Simona shook her head. "Honestly? I think we'd be scrambling. It's surprising how unprepared we still are, even with all the technology and advancements. The hardest part would be coordinating resources across states. And the public ... well, they don't always trust health agencies the way we hope."

"It's tough when you can't communicate quickly and clearly. People don't always realize the domino effect even a small outbreak can have on ... everything," Sam said.

"Exactly," said Simona. "We're not just talking about overrunning hospitals. It's how supply chains could be disrupted or misinformation could spread. I keep telling my colleagues, public health is as much about managing people as about managing pathogens."

"I couldn't agree more," said Sam. "I see it every day with my patients—people need clear, consistent information, or they'll fill in the blanks themselves."

Simona nodded and Ellie watched her mother regard Sam with a cool, approving smile. It looked like Dr. Sam Varma had passed muster.

"What are we playing after dinner?" piped up Stanley.

Finally, a contribution.

After-dinner games were legendary within the family, with board and card games lasting for hours and being ridiculously competitive.

"Charades?" Ellie said tentatively.

"What about Monopoly?" asked Simona.

"It would be nice to play something with the kids?" suggested Stanley.

"This is where you'll see our true family dynamic," joked Ellie to Sam. He smiled.

"It's very nice to be with family on Thanksgiving," he said.

Did he mean be with *a* family or with *their* family, meaning he thought he had already joined their pack? wondered Ellie. This encroachment into her sacred space rattled her. Why was that? On the one hand, his drop-by seemed presumptuous, but Ellie considered that maybe it was a cultural thing. She'd gathered from their conversations that if she just popped into his family home, she'd be folded in as found family—like "What took you so long to get here?"

After dessert, Ellie opened her laptop for the Zoom call with Leo. She had almost forgotten about it until Simona reminded her. She'd been watching the clock. A mother never forgot about her children, Ellie supposed, no matter how old they were.

Leo looked tanned but thin and waved at the family and smiled on the screen, which pixelated every so often with the poor internet connection.

Although they'd been close growing up, Leo was more of a lone wolf than a pack wolf. Unmarried and cautious about getting into any close relationship due to his itinerant work, Ellie was still the person with whom he shared the strongest bond.

Ellie introduced him to Sam, who waved quickly before disappearing out of frame. Leo raised his eyebrows at Ellie. She willed him to not say a word with a look in their shared secret language she knew he'd decipher. No doubt, she would receive a text later about finally laying eyes on the new "man friend" he'd heard about.

Leo was older than Ellie by fourteen months. They'd both been surprise babies. With Simona as an outlier working mom growing up in their small town outside Chicago, she and Leo had relied on each other as latchkey kids. Ellie remembered her elementary school principal calling up Simona on the phone, having noticed the house keys that she and Leo wore around their necks on a string, concerned that they weren't receiving adequate parental attention. Truth be told, Ellie and Leo sometimes wondered that themselves, though they also enjoyed their freedom. Once Ellie became a mom herself and realized the job was booby-trapped, she'd become a lot less judgmental of her own mother.

After the Zoom call ended, Simona made coffee and they sat around the living room in their post-turkey-and-stuffing daze, enjoying small slices of pumpkin pie, watching Nathan play with a set of old Matchbox cars Ellie had pulled from the attic earlier that week that had been Stanley's when he was a boy.

"I really should be on my way," said Sam as he drained his coffee. "Leave you all in peace."

"Oh, don't go yet!" said Simona. "We're about to start the games!"

"I wouldn't want to intrude," said Sam, standing up.

"Nonsense," said Simona. "In fact, you would even up the teams if we did Pictionary! Isn't that right, Ellie?"

Ellie nodded.

Last Thanksgiving, she'd been divorced from Joe for just three months and had felt numb. She never imagined things changing so much or feeling so different. It felt as though ten years had passed instead of just one. And it all felt a bit odd to her, today.

"I'll stay for a little bit," said Sam. "But I do have to get to the hotel, as I have some prep to do for tomorrow."

Ellie was relieved that Sam had made proper arrangements and had no expectation of staying over with her.

"What about Uno?" asked Simona. "Could Nathan play that?"

"He's a bit young," said Ellie.

"Ellie," said Stanley, "why don't you read us your *New York Times* article before our games. I'd like to hear it in your voice."

"Dad," said Ellie, groaning like a teenager.

"Oh yes," said Simona, clapping her hands in delight. "That's a great idea. I have a copy with me in my handbag. Let me get it."

Of course her parents had actual paper copies. Adorable.

"You carry it around with you?" she asked as her mother disappeared up the hallway in search of her bag. "Well, you never know," called her mother in singsong from the corridor. "It's an important article, Ellie!"

Ellie eyed Sam. He gave her a commiserating wink.

"She probably springs it on her colleagues when they're least expecting it," said Ellie sarcastically.

"It's in her job description as your mom," Sam said.

"We're proud of it," said Stanley. "And you. For speaking up."

Ellie felt herself blush. Her parents weren't normally this expressive. The past weeks of media attention had brought it out in them, as their neighbors and friends made comments about "Ellie being on the cover of the *New York Times Magazine*." They had bought many copies. She expected that on her next visit to Chicago, there'd be a framed copy of the cover on the wall.

Simona came back into the living room and handed a dog-eared copy of the magazine to Ellie.

"Strong, clear voice now," she instructed—the way her priggish moot court instructor had in law school, armed for each class with her red pen and unresolved childhood trauma.

"Yes, don't be shy," added Stanley.

Yep. Totally normal family moment.

"But it's not about me, guys. It's about a larger social construct," Ellie said, feeling tired. Still, the path of least resistance was to just play along.

Ellie took the magazine and cleared her throat. This all felt performative, like she should be wearing a tutu.

"*Until recently, lawsuits claiming workplace discrimination because of family caregiving obligations were rare—in part because employers could get away with it. But that's changing because of the ranks of people like Ellie Benvenuto. Ms. Benvenuto has recently gone public in a case against her former employer, Hutton & Fetterer, a global law firm based in San Francisco—*" began Ellie.

"Boooooo!" droned Simona at the mention of Hutton & Fetterer, as though she was in the audience at *The Rocky Horror Picture Show*.

"*Since the mid-1990s, the number of workers who have sued their employers for mistreatment on account of family responsibilities—becoming pregnant, needing to care for a sick child or relative—has increased by more than 300 percent. More than 1,150 such lawsuits have been filed in courts, a trend that has not gone unnoticed in the business world, not only because companies are aware of the negative publicity lawsuits can generate but also because plaintiffs can walk away with hefty damage awards.*

"*Some employers may be tolerant, even welcoming, of an employee who bears one child, only to balk when discovering she has become pregnant again. Attorneys who handle such cases refer to this as 'the second-baby syndrome.' Other times, tension arises when another factor—say, a disability—enters the picture. On both counts, this is what Ellie Benvenuto believes happened to her.*"

Thinking she might read only part of the article, Ellie drew breath but found herself continuing. Only when she'd finished the whole feature did she drop the magazine below her sightline to see her parents staring, mute, Stanley, his eyes gleaming and Sam, enraptured.

They all broke into a round of applause.

Ellie felt overwhelmed. All that terror about putting herself out there had paid off. She had been heard. And she had the support of her very nearest and dearest.

Simona rose from the saggy sofa and hugged her daughter.

"Well done, sweetie," she said and, for a moment, Ellie was back in her childhood, the scent of Enzo's pipe in her nose, her mother's bosom, warm, familiar, and comforting.

"Hey!" said Ellie, pushing herself away from her mother, worried that she might break down in unquenchable emotion, "you know what I brought that I thought you might enjoy? And seeing as it's the Family Reading Hour: Teddy's diaries!"

"You have?" said Simona.

"Yes!" said Ellie. "I'm in the middle of their Alaskan adventures! I could read you some of it! Some parts are really fascinating. I think it's cool, you know, to know what Enzo's grandmother was like. To see if we recognize any of her in him?"

"When I met Ellie, she was reading one of these diaries," Sam said. "She was totally absorbed with a schoolgirl's look of purpose on her face and oblivious to her surroundings."

"Yes, it took a code red to distract me," Ellie said and they all laughed again.

"Go get them, Els," said Simona.

As Ellie stepped outside to her car to fetch the diaries, she took a moment, breathing in the crisp fall night air, peering at the glowing windows of the houses all around, some with families, others with batches of university students, all in their own celebrations. In that moment, she thanked Enzo and Genevieve, feeling their presence and grateful she could continue to carry them within her.

"Oh, Dad," she said, as she went back inside and shut the door behind her, suddenly remembering the photo she'd found of Enzo holding the mammoth tooth and its inscription, which had led her to find out what the item was. "Did you know this was a mammoth tooth?"

Placing the diaries on the floor, she went to the large wooden box that Enzo had left on a bottom shelf and pulled it out. She opened the lid and unearthed the large ridged rock, the color of caramel ice cream.

"Sure," said Stanley. "I knew that. A molar, to be precise. My father would talk all about my legendary great-grandfather, George, the explorer. Just never really knew what became of it."

So, Enzo talked "all about" George but not Teddy. From what she'd learned in Teddy's diaries, Ellie was beginning to understand why. Women were routinely written out of history, and Teddy hadn't exactly followed the rules.

"Betcha it's Alaska! I bet Teddy and George discovered it!" said Ellie. "They discovered a prehistoric bug too. It came back alive and then escaped!"

"You're kidding," said Simona, pointing to the diaries. "Really? You read that in there?"

"Yes!" said Ellie with revived energy as she lifted out the diaries. "There's so much in here!"

She picked up one of the diaries in excitement and opened it. Out dropped a delicate folded piece of paper. Ellie bent down, carefully unfurled it, and began to read out loud.

"*October 15, 1899. Oakland, California*

"*Dear Mrs. DeLuca,*

"*I write to extend my deepest condolences for the loss of your remarkable husband, George DeLuca. The 'Monte Cristo of the Klondikes,' as I had the pleasure to dub him, was not only a man of unparalleled fortune but a force of nature—undaunted and driven, even by the wildest stretches of Alaska. His legacy will endure, immortalized in the great saga of the North.*"

Ellie stopped and looked up. Tears threatened her eyes.

"What?" she said. "George died!"

Stunned, she stared at the yellowed paper blankly.

"Sweetie, I hate to tell you, but all our ancestors died!" said Stanley.

"It's true," added Simona. "One minute you're young and fun; the next minute you're turning down the car radio to see better. Time claims us all, my dear."

"I know ..." said Ellie. "I know that, but I just didn't expect ... I ... I ..."

"Read the rest of it, sweetie," prompted Simona.

Ellie swallowed and read the rest of the letter out loud.

"*But it was not solely George who impressed me. Word of your own determination and spirit has reached me through those who marveled at your shared journey. You, Mrs. DeLuca, with your tireless resolve, have shown that behind every great man stands a woman of equal, if not greater, grit.*

"*Together, you weathered hardship and built a legacy not just of wealth but of unshakable fortitude.*

"*I imagine the frontier itself mourns George's passing, as I do. Yet the greatest tribute to his memory is not only in the gold or the tales of adventure but in the strength and courage you both displayed, which will be remembered for generations.*

Please accept my heartfelt respects and know that I carry George's memory—and yours—with me, as I continue to write of the untamed lands that shaped so many of us.
"*Yours most sincerely,*
Joaquin Miller"
"Joaquin Miller?" said Stanley. "Of Joaquin Miller Park? Eight miles from here? Where I played all the time as a kid in the waterfall?"
"Must be," said Simona. "Wasn't he a poet?"
"It was only 1899," said Ellie. "George only got to enjoy their wealth for two years." Had he even made it back to San Francisco? How had he died?
"Ellie's reading the diaries like an adventure story," said Sam. "That's why it's hitting her hard."
Ellie welcomed his thoughtfulness. He had witnessed her journey through them; her parents didn't seem to quite understand how these happenings, read alongside her daily life, were affecting her.
"They're more than just our ancestors. You know, they're real people right next to me. I feel so sad now."
"Oh, darling!" said Simona. "You always were a softy underneath!"
For the second time that evening, she embraced Ellie, giving her arm a squeeze.
Maybe reading aloud from Teddy's diaries before she'd finished them was a bad idea, thought Ellie.
"What's this?" asked Simona and she pulled out the large wooden contraption in the shape of a pie wedge from Enzo's wooden box.
"That's a sextant," said Stanley. "For navigation. George was a seaman."
"I know," said Ellie. She knew so much about Teddy and George—much more, she realized, than Stanley did at this point.
Simona reached into the box and withdrew the mother-of-pearl magnifying glass Ellie had found in January.
"This is so pretty," she said, looking through it and using it to examine the lines on her palm.
Ellie reached for the swath of fabric and unsheathed the thin, pointy, sharp stick topped with a metal carving.

"What do you think this is?" she asked the living room. "A letter opener maybe?"

"Looks like a skewer or ... oversized pushpin," said Sam. "Like one you might see on the virtual bulletin board we use to teach medical students."

"That's a hatpin," said Simona as she took it from Ellie's hands and examined it with the mother-of-pearl magnifier. "And it has a *T* on it, at the tip here, see?"

She held it up to the light.

"For Teddy!" said Ellie. "It must be Teddy's!" Ellie felt her skin prickle. Was the gauzy Native American patterned fabric it was wrapped in ... Momo's?

"Women wore them during the nineteenth century and especially during the Edwardian period, when they had those huge hats, you know. Sometimes they even had to use these for self-defense. I think hatpins were eventually outlawed for that reason."

"Oh, come on!" said Ellie. "You can't be serious."

Simona shrugged and stabbed the air, rather like Stanley had stabbed the turkey earlier.

"Hey, don't get any ideas!" said Stanley in feigned defense. He held out his palm, and Simona handed him the hatpin to look at. Suddenly he jumped and cried out.

"I've got it!" he said. "I know what we can play! The kids will love it!"

"Well?" asked Simona with measured patience, long suffering her husband's erratic mood changes and childish excitement.

"Pin the tail on the donkey!"

Stanley stabbed the air three times with the hatpin before rushing into the kitchen and yanking open an overhead cupboard.

Ellie winced at the sound of the Tupperware tower once more tumbling onto the countertop.

"I know we have a paper party donkey somewhere around here," he called joyfully from the kitchen. "It was a birthday party staple, and my parents saved everything."

"Tell me about it," said Ellie, her sarcasm on point now, the wine having loosened her.

Sam grinned at Ellie. "Families, huh?"

Ellie smiled back, but her mind wandered. Something tugged at her insides—an itch just under the surface, waiting to be scratched—as if it had been there all along but she'd managed to miss it.

What was it? What was in that room that she wasn't seeing?

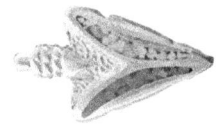

CHAPTER 23

TEDDY

March 16, 1907. San Francisco, California.

Today Elizabeth Ashe and I bicycled over to the office of Julius Martinelli in North Beach. Elizabeth is really not fond of the bicycle and was white as a sheet the whole way there! She kept asking me to slow down. She's been working tirelessly as a nurse helping city residents recover from the fiery aftermath, and I suppose she didn't care for me taking senseless risks. But I find it so exhilarating to whizz along, past the buildings at speed. I have no idea what velocity we travel at but it sure is fast. Why take a leisurely pace when such thrills are at the tips of your toes?! I suppose there is quite a lot of rubble about the place and you do need to be careful.

I wore the new breeches which were delivered yesterday by the seamstress. She is ever so afraid she will get in trouble for sewing them, so I will tip her handsomely when I settle the bill this month. Elizabeth got her breeches in a men's department store; she tells fibs and says they are for her husband—though she has no wedding ring, so how she gets away with that I have no idea. Of course, I cannot do that for it is well-known about the city that I am a widow. And of course, Elizabeth is so much slenderer than I, so it is an easier purchase for her, all things considered.

I also wore my new stockings secured with bicycle clips (wonderful invention) and a new little cap which I pinned to the side and managed to pile my hair up under. I have cut it quite short so I suppose I do look rather masculine when one thinks about it.

And what of it! The little cap is so much more comfortable than those gravity defying hats that are all the rage now. One must pierce their head with a mountain of hatpins, simply to keep the thing in place! You get quite the headache!

Elizabeth, who is really much more of a proper lady than me, refused to wear the little cap I offered and insisted on donning her large hat. I told her she was much more at risk, for if she came off her bike, she would likely be stabbed in the head! Perhaps that is why she kept asking me to slow down. Now if Lillie were here, I'd be the one struggling to keep up! I do thank her for introducing me to the bicycle. It has been ever so useful, since the earthquake, to get about the place.

Well, we were zooming down Union Street when out of the rubble sprang this big dusty chocolate-colored dog and with the shock, I braked and went right over the handlebars! What luck I didn't have those hatpins in my head! Poor Elizabeth thought I'd bought the farm, peering down at me with her ashen face as I lay there on the ground.

"Jesus, Mary, and Joseph, Teddy. Are you hurt? Can you hear me?"

The funny thing was, all I could think of, as I looked up at that grey sky, was the time I came off the pony in North Sandwich, when I was only learning to horse ride. I'd taken the pony without asking and my father found me in a crumbled heap in the meadow, and his face looming over me and he said, "Teddy, Teddy!" just like Elizabeth did and so I answered, "Father," and she thought I was hallucinating and concussed!

I don't know about concussed but I certainly tore my knee up bad and my lovely new trousers. Oh, I was in an awful state on that filthy ground. Elizabeth helped me up and there was the scruffy thing, sitting, all regal, not even barking just staring at the crumpled mess he'd caused.

The earthquake may have passed nearly a year, but the dirt and dust still resides everywhere; my hands were filthy as was my face. Elizabeth was rather worried about the cut on my knee, that it might get infected.

"He seems rather pleased with himself," I said, looking at the pooch.

I had to listen to Elizabeth give me a stern talking to then about the speed I always travel at and, while I don't generally pay much heed to those so much younger than I, I suppose she did have a point. Elizabeth has always been older than her years.

The big silly dog had big yellow amber eyes and there was something about him, the way he looked at me as if he knew me. He really did stare so. There are so many owner-less animals wandering the streets, half-starved, their owners all fled to Golden Gate Park or the beaches of Oakland and Berkeley. The reality is most will likely never come back. Or if they do, how would they find their old pets? I feel quite sorry for them.

When we looked at my bicycle we found the front wheel to be completely buckled. What a bang I'd given it. And myself!

It was all I could do to limp my way to the contractor offices. I suppose we must have looked a sight.

When we looked behind, we saw that the dog was following us!

"Looks like we made a new friend," I said to Elizabeth.

She called him an old mutt. I said he was probably ravenous.

"Like half the city," Elizabeth reminded me.

The dog followed us the whole way up Green Street. I felt sorry for the poor thing; he looked so very lost.

The contractors are situated on the corner of Green Street and Vallejo and like many of the buildings across the city, their offices have been scrambled together using corrugated iron sheets and heavy cardboard and whatever else they had to hand.

It is so difficult to see people, day in, day out, sheltering in those awful shanty buildings all about the place and miraculous at the same time to the industriousness of people as they open their little stores to sell supplies.

I imagine the builders have been busy tending to permanent buildings, as I know from my research that they have been working flat out for the past year, mostly on municipal buildings, to try and get the city up and running again. It's why Elizabeth asked to accompany me today—the original neighborhood center she and Alice Griffith started had been reduced to ruins in the fire, and they wished to approach a certain

Mr. Bernard Maybeck about designing a new one on Stockton Street. Elizabeth had said she wanted to "see me in action," which did amuse me.

We stood at the heart of North Beach, with all the hundreds of tents dotted about. How lucky we were not to have lost our home.

Outside the offices, we met an old Italian coming along with his walking stick and he stopped to chat. I think he was quite taken aback by my garb and wanted to test me out! He said many of the Italians have come back and some of the Irish and Polish too. They don't want to leave this neighborhood for it is their home. I was sure he wanted to ask me about my attire, for he did look at me quite confused, but he held his whist.

He asked if we'd heard about that rogue, Enrico Caruso, holed up at the Palace Hotel when the earthquake struck. I suppose he thought we would know of the singer because we looked like the type that would go to see *Carmen* and I told him we had not, simply to let him tell his story. (We did know, and of course *had* been to see *Carmen*, but it tickled me to see the man get so worked up, much to Elizabeth's consternation.)

"Fifty-four steamer trunks!" he cried, very animated indeed. "Fifty-four steamer trunks loaded onto a ferry boat to Oakland and, all around, people, Italians, gasping for food and water and a safe place to lay their heads! A rogue! Never will I go to see one of his shows. Never!"

It was still the juiciest morsel of gossip, Enrico Caruso and his trunks fleeing the Palace Hotel. I pity the poor hotel valet who had to organize all that among the chaos, but money talks, I suppose. Elizabeth giggled after he toddled on and said she guaranteed the old man had never been to a Caruso show in the first place, so it's not like the great opera singer lost a fan anyway!

We knocked on the door of the makeshift office (which did take us a little while to find, for it does look so small and decrepit from the street) and inside I found many clerks working diligently. When I asked the fellow at the front of the office whether Mr. Martinelli might be about, he said, with some cheek, "And who may I ask is calling?"

Elizabeth says I bring it all on myself for the manner in which I dress but I really did not care for that young man's tone. He looked me up and down like a mannequin and practically scowled at me!

"Mrs. DeLuca. Mrs. Theodora DeLuca," I told him quite assertively. Well, he changed his tune then; it seemed he had indeed heard of me and he told us that Mr. Martinelli was not too far away at all and he would go and fetch him, immediately.

Elizabeth and I waited outside, our bicycles leaning against the broken footpaths. They really are a trip hazard. So many trip hazards all around. My fall today is not my first accident, as you know dear diary, nor do I expect it to be my last. Helki is almost certain I broke my elbow that time I came off my bike on Telegraph Hill, but I try not to dwell on it. I'd rather not know if it's broken or not, as what difference will that make to the healing process anyway?

North Beach seems to have been hit terribly by the earthquake. I suppose the buildings were so jammed together and of such poor quality. When they rebuild I certainly hope they make them strong and fireproof.

Hard to believe it's been nearly a year since that fateful morning. I never thought I would see such a sight again, not after the Great Fire of Chicago. All those people fleeing in their nightclothes, children screaming in terror, the acrid smell of burning lingering for weeks and weeks.

Of course, in Chicago, I had George to rely on. I didn't have him this time. Didn't have his practicality and forthright decision-making. I don't know what I would have done without Helki and Alice and Elizabeth. I wish Lillie had been about too, though she of course feels lucky to have been living away. And the Paris papers were full of it. I understand she had to get away after that unpleasantness that unfurled in her rooms at The Palace Hotel.

While Helki has always been a support to me, I can't help but feel that the earthquake changed her, rather completely. She had been holding everything together for so long, keeping going, when all around her, everything has changed. The loss of the Indian Center was just too much I suppose. Especially when it escaped the earthquake and then the fires, only to be blown up by the firemen to save the street! It really was too much. And that is why I am so determined I suppose. To put things right. To try and do what I can for Helki. To try and bring her back to some of what she was before.

Herself.

If these builders are half as good as their reputation, then we will be doing just fine. (Not like those Irish delinquents fresh off the boat that I had to part ways with unceremoniously last year, the blackguards. Always those out to make a quick buck out of other's misfortunes!)

When the clerk appeared around the corner with Mr. Martinelli (looking rather sheepish, I may add), Mr. Martinelli looked frazzled but he had a smile in welcome for Elizabeth and me, as so often happens, as my reputation does precede me. A walking wealthy widow can be quite useful to a builder I suppose. Especially one as philanthropic as I have the reputation to be.

"Where's best to talk, my good man?" I asked him.

Mr. Martinelli said he no longer had a fine office to hold meetings in but we were welcome to "walk and talk" down the street and then he asked, rather politely, if I'd had an accident.

"Flew off my bike on the way here," I told him. "The sooner we get these streets back up and running the better!"

He said he was surprised I haven't got myself a motor car. Said they invested in one at the start of this year and it's been a wonder. I could see Elizabeth wincing, for if she thought I got up to high speeds on a bicycle imagine what I could do had I an engine behind me!

"You ought to visit the auto show at the Old Coliseum later this year," Mr. Martinelli suggested. "Pick yourself out a fine little number."

I told him I might just do that.

After that, we got down to business. I told Mr. Martinelli I had seen his work and that I was quite impressed by it. He said he was quite impressed by my work too, by which he meant the schools and museum I funded in 1905. He says he thinks the park I've had built is very smart, especially the little fountain where the dogs can take a drink. I suppose they'd have been lost without it this past year and I told him I was quite glad it had been restored after the earthquake. I told him my projects have been a distraction. That I had turned to them after the loss of George and that while some say time is a healer, I say for me, it has not been.

I didn't talk of Momo. I find people simply do not want to discuss this part of my life.

Martinelli said he'd read about George's accident in the newspaper—funny that he remembered, seeing as it's eight years ago now.

"Yes," I told him. "A tragedy."

I wanted to add, as I do whenever anyone brings up George's demise, but in most particular, funnily enough, strangers, that it was a preventable tragedy for if George had listened to me when I begged him not to go and paid heed to Madame Bowers's prediction that he would die at sea right at that very point in time, he might just have saved himself. We didn't need any more gold dust.

The past few years since his death have been the loneliest I could have imagined. George was greedy. And because of that greed and the knowledge that other miners were furthering their fortunes, I was left behind, to parent the family quite alone, calling on Helki more than any friend ever should.

I don't know what I would have done if it weren't for my building projects and joining the suffragists, although it does amuse me so, that I refused to do so for so long. Then again, George wouldn't have approved. "Rabble-rousers," he called suffragists during the campaign of '96 when we'd caught wind of it in Circle City.

Good old dust-kicking Lillie again, pushing me out of my stubborn comfort, into something she knows will do me good.

I suppose it was my comrades there who led me to do these good will projects, when I think about it. I put all the anger I had over George's death into fighting the real cause—ensuring women have some say over our own lives.

Wealth for the sake of wealth does not interest me. I will do good with what I have. I will make a difference. And so, I took from my pocket the large, folded sheet of paper I'd brought with me (that's another terrifically handy thing about breeches—pockets!) and handed it to Mr. Martinelli.

He unfurled it, observed my meticulous floor plan and exclaimed: "What's this?"

I could see he is a very good builder as his eyes took in the full dimensions of the building in seconds.

"It's my new Indian Center," I declared.

I told him that our center that had been dynamited had been small and so the new one I wish to build will move sites, be much bigger, have a hospital and it will care for not just Indians but all manner of people who need care and can't get it. I pointed out the crafting rooms, the little warehouse for storing the goods we make and the stables at the back. I also showed him an area I'd allowed for the shelter I was thinking of, where we could house stray animals.

(Even though Elizabeth thinks it's a terrible idea—as she says no well-to-do lady is ever going to adopt a mangy mutt, but I say pooh to that, for many women simply cannot help who they fall in love with, be it a man *or* a mutt.)

Mr. Martinelli did seem rather impressed but was quick to tell me how tied up they are with housing projects, particularly with the building going on in North Beach and that he simply wouldn't have time to take on something as non-urgent as an Indian Center. He also told me he's making it a mission of his to build far superior buildings than what came before in that run down area.

I told him I understood that he was building for the Italian people and that his work was not solely about profit. I told him, that I too, similarly, was passionate about providing for my Indian brothers and sisters and if he could see to start my center, I would fund, in full, two blocks of housing on a street of his choosing.

Well, that stopped him in his tracks, I can tell you. He laughed, shook his head and asked me, in earnest, who had done my drawings.

"I don't see a name here. I know every architect in this city and work principally with Mr. Paul DeMartini. They're all backed up with work these days."

"I did them," I said.

"You?" he cried.

"You know women really are capable of so much more than you menfolk think," chimed Elizabeth, just at the right moment. She really is a dear.

I told him I'd been taking the ferry to classes at the University of California across the Bay at Berkeley, somewhat to the vexation of my fellow male students.

"I trust we have a deal then?" I asked.

"I believe we do," he replied.

And so, as I have watched many a man seal a deal before me (and to Elizabeth's horror), I spat into my palm and offered it to Mr. Martinelli. Reluctantly, he obliged the gesture in return.

"A pleasure doing business with you, Mr. Martinelli," I said.

"Likewise, Mrs. DeLuca. Likewise," he replied.

I can't suppose he reckoned upon coming across a filthy, disheveled architect widow today!

And then, do you know what we heard?

Two sharp barks from behind us and there was that chocolate dog, sitting wagging his tail, quite agreeing with my plans and approving our new Indian Center.

"Oh Lord," groaned Elizabeth. "That thing's been tailing us all afternoon."

Well, I walked over to him, patted his head and do you know, a small puff of ash puffed up into the air with each pat.

"Cinders," I said. "He can be the first registered dog into my animal shelter! And if no one wants him, I'll keep him."

"You'll be keeping him then," Elizabeth muttered, for she really is no fan of animals, despite her myriad admirable qualities.

A fine, intelligent creature. I do hope I get to keep him—once he's had a proper wash.

CHAPTER 24
ELLIE

November 29, 2019. Berkeley, California.

That night at Enzo's house, Ellie slept fitfully. A combination of the wine at dinner, the champagne she'd sipped while cooking the turkey, the sweets and coffee after dinner and the surprise visit from Sam did nothing to help her mind rest. She'd tossed and turned in her old bedroom, Nathan and Luca, having joined her in the middle of the night, a tangle of limbs beside her in the bed.

When the sun rose on Friday morning, causing an early morning fog that wrenched Ellie's mood, she remembered her dream that had seemed to repeat itself all night, a dream of Teddy. She had never seen a picture of her great-great-grandmother, had found nothing in all the keepsakes and family archives she'd been pulling out over the past week, and yet she knew that the woman in her dream was certainly Teddy. She was youthful and dark-haired and she held out the hatpin in her palms. Her mouth didn't move, but Ellie found herself waking with Sam's words on repeat in her mind.

Push. Pin. Push. Pin.

How strange! For a while, she had forced herself back into a restless sleep where another dream saw Sam's face loom large. He was dressed in traditional dress, smiling almost maniacally, like a clown. It disturbed her. She awoke to Nathan kicking her in the kidneys, and a headache. A long day stretched ahead. She'd planned to use the vacation day off work to help her parents with the packing and sorting.

"Morning, Glitter-Bug!" she croaked to Nathan, who blinked groggily. The only way to get on with things was to pretend she felt fine. Fake it till you make it, right?

Checking her phone to find messages from Joe, who had missed the boys last night, and Sam, telling her he was thinking of her and that he was feeling nervous before his interview, Ellie didn't respond to either. Not yet. Not before coffee.

She allowed herself to sit in silence in Enzo's messy living room, the aftermath of family game night, board games boxed up and pushed aside, stray Jenga blocks peeping out from behind cushions, and small squares of Pictionary paper now keeping Nathan occupied with doodling.

When Simona and Stanley got up, they fizzed with an energy that Ellie simply couldn't match. They began punching out a set of flattened cardboard boxes before they'd even had their own coffee, ready for the *keep*, *donate*, and *trash* piles. Ellie sighed and surfed up the energy to join the effort. After two hours of frenzied sorting, bagging and containing her frustrations—Stanley had an innocent gift for scratching at her nerves—Ellie felt spent.

"You know what?" she said. "I'm going to take the boys on home. You guys keep at it. I need a little break."

"Not like you, Els," said Simona, frowning. It was true. Ellie usually had energy bordering on mania. But something was bothering her, making her testy. Something itching under her skin. She had to get home. She couldn't explain it, but the pull was undeniable.

"I can come back later maybe," she said, rubbing her tired eyes, longing for the eye drops that lived in her cabinet back at her apartment.

"Absolutely not," said Simona. "We got this. You've done enough. Now go on home with the boys; maybe take them to the park. Get some fresh air."

"Stop by Joaquin Miller Park!" Stanley suggested cheerfully.

But on the drive home, Ellie did not go to Joaquin Miller Park. The thought did cross her mind—she knew the boys would enjoy the run-around—but the feeling of urgency propelled her straight into her apartment, her mind ticking like a metronome. She could bring the boys to a park later. For now, she needed to cocoon.

While whipping up the boys a couple of grilled cheese sandwiches with sliced cantaloupe spears, Ellie found her eyes drawn to her laptop sitting on the breakfast bar. She tried to look away—she knew if she opened the screen, she'd get sucked into the black hole of emails, legal memos, and existential dread, never to be seen or heard from again.

Well, maybe just a few emails, she told herself, after she had given the boys their grilled cheese. Might as well get ahead of the weekend.

And—poof, just like that, she was right back in the job. Thirty minutes passed before she'd even looked up, rushing to check on the boys, who were ominously quiet. But tummies full, Nathan was playing with his trains and Luca was plopped in a giant beanbag squishing molding clay in his hands.

Back at her laptop, she reached into her briefcase for a file on the Hansa Nambootiri case. The case was scheduled for an upcoming hearing; the defense still seemed eager for a global settlement, but the collection of documents and records Ellie needed to better assess the case had been painfully slow. Out of nowhere, she heard a voice.

Push.

Pin.

A shiver crawled up Ellie's spine. What the actual …? She jerked her head up, scanning the room. Empty. The boys were playing, oblivious. She pressed her palms to her temples, willing away the sudden chill.

It was just exhaustion. A caffeine crash. *Snap out of it, Ellie!*

And yet … hadn't Teddy been holding the hatpin box in her dream?

Deciding there and then to put her work away and take the boys to Washington Square Park in the hope that it might clear some cobwebs, Ellie lifted a document to file it and found her fingers lingering over a picture printed on white copy paper.

The picture was grainy, from the set of photos that Hansa's sister Rashila had printed and brought for their first intake meeting. It showed the whiteboard in the back room of the discount dollar store where the roster for the week was sketched out in dry-erase marker. Hansa had wanted to show Ellie the long, late shifts she'd been assigned and the treacherous conditions of the room, ripe for injury.

Ellie had seen the photo various times before while working the case, but today it wasn't the schedule that caught Ellie's attention. Instead, her eyes were drawn to a corkboard next to the whiteboard. What was that on the corkboard? Ellie grabbed the small mother-of-pearl magnifying glass she'd claimed from the artifact box and brought home with her.

It was Hansa. It was a single Polaroid headshot of Hansa—with a red pushpin inserted in the center of her forehead, and then some words in what looked like a black Sharpie marker scrawled on the whiteboard with an arrow pointing to the photo: "Hindi with a Bindy" punctuated with a smiley face.

"Oh my God," said Ellie out loud. "Oh, my freaking God!"

She lifted her cell and dialed Hansa's number. It went to voicemail. But twenty seconds later, the call was returned, Hansa's voice timid at the other end of the line.

"Ms. Benvenuto?"

"Hansa! Hi! I'm going through your case documents, and I've found a photograph of you in the back room?"

"Yes?" said Hansa.

"Your photo is pinned to a corkboard ... Have you seen this?"

Ellie waited a moment. Hansa made no reply.

"They have a red pushpin in your forehead! And it says, 'Hindi with a bindy,' spelled wrong of course."

"Oh," said Hansa. "That. I think Chad did that."

Chad. The vapid, twentysomething, chubby-cheeked, community college dropout bully of a store manager—nephew of one of the puffy-chested executives.

Hansa continued, devoid of emotion. "It's so silly. I don't even wear the bindi. Where I'm from only the married woman wears the bindi.

I'm not married. I don't think he even knows that I have no bindi. He probably never even noticed."

"Weren't you bothered by it?" asked Ellie.

"Not really," said Hansa, and Ellie heard her client relax a little now that she knew what the call was about. Her self-esteem was already tanked, and Ellie usually only called by appointment. It was perhaps a little unsettling to call out of the blue like this.

"He is ignorant," said Hansa. "Just a silly man, you know."

"He's a very silly man," said Ellie. "A very silly man, indeed."

Ellie felt all her senses prickling. Hansa was a woman, like so many of her clients, who simply accepted the racism and discrimination heaped upon her and had no other choice but to internalize it because humiliation and subjugation was the norm. How could an illogically racist picture possibly be legally significant in Hansa's eyes?

Ellie drew a breath.

"What we have here, Hansa, is smoking gun evidence," she said, her sense of indignation raising her voice a notch. "Because not only do we have an administrative injury case, which has limited forms of relief as I've explained to you, but a full-blown wrongful termination lawsuit based upon gender and national origin discrimination. This opens up significant liability for the company."

"Oh," said Hansa quietly. Her voice belied a "whatever you say, Mrs. Benvenuto."

Ellie gave her a second and then gently laughed.

"Hansa, this is big, okay? I can't believe you never mentioned this to me before, but I guess it shows how you normalized this sort of behavior in that place."

Hansa paused, as though waiting to hear more. Eventually, she said, "Thank you, Mrs. Benvenuto."

"Don't thank me yet; we still have a quite a way to go, but it is an incredible find. Great work on taking and keeping these photos."

Ellie had barely hung up with Hansa when her cell phone rang. She answered the phone without even checking the number because Nathan had wandered over, grabbed her hand, and pulled her back toward the living room, pointing at the TV.

Absentmindedly, she looked for the remote while listening to the sound of her attorney Rebecca's voice, which was unusually animated.

"Are you sitting down?"

"No," said Ellie. "Should I?" It was difficult to sit down around children who were hankering for *Paw Patrol*.

"I've just got off the phone with Hutton & Fetterer's lawyers. Evidently, Curtis Hutton feels 'things have gotten out of hand.' They want to go to mediation!"

Ellie felt the noise of the room get sucked out. She grabbed for the sofa and backed into it.

"Can you … say that again?" she asked quietly.

Rebecca laughed.

"They want to mediate. Congratulations, Ellie! This is huge. They really need your case to go away. It's not a good look for them."

"Really?" asked Ellie, thinking of all the times she had delivered news like this to her own clients. Now, she knew how it felt to be on the receiving end. Overwhelming. Totally overwhelming.

"We're almost there, Ellie," said Rebecca. "You've pushed them to the precipice, and they've flinched."

"I'm so happy," said Ellie, and she felt the quiver in her voice.

"I think it was all the press coverage that did it," said Rebecca. "They're wounded. They need it to end."

"We hit them where it hurts," said Ellie. "Their reputation and their pockets."

"Well, they do have deep pockets!" said Rebecca.

"Yes. And we gotta remember that," said Ellie. "Thank you for all your work."

"Thank you for being a great client."

Ellie stared out the window at Coit Tower after she hung up, at the afternoon light settling. She wasn't sure how long she stared, but when she looked down, Luca was tugging on her jeans and handing her a one-inch laminated card with a picture of a sippy cup, his little fingers gripping the material.

"Joo," he mumbled, staring directly at Ellie.

He wanted some juice.

Ellie smiled at the sound of his voice, his very own words emanating from his voice box. She knelt down and smelled his hair as she handed him the juice; a scent of Enzo's home nestled there. When Hutton & Fetterer had fired her six months after Nathan was born, the awful thought had regularly crossed her mind that maybe it had been a mistake to have children at all. It had all been too much: Luca's diagnosis, recovery from birth, sleepless nights, and a hopelessly pressurized relationship with Joe; it seemed having children was the key factor behind all her distress.

Now, she could see how utterly precious her beautiful boys were, and it was Hutton & Fetterer who had been at fault for forcing her into such a dire situation. What an insidious scam—convincing a mother that her own children were the problem instead of the system rigged against her.

"Who wants to go to the park?" Ellie called, to which Nathan cried, "Me!"

She fetched their winter jackets from the hook in the hallway. She helped Luca put his on.

"You want to go to the park?"

Luca looked at her with intensity. He loved Washington Square Park and all the activity there. Loved Saints Peter and Paul Church, watching the number 8, 30, 39, and 45 bus lines that stopped there, the saucer swing at the playground, the dogs playing, the busy post office, and sometimes getting a hot cocoa at Mario's. She put on his jacket and ushered them out the door.

Ellie thought that she should call next door to Anika, to deliver her good news, but decided to savor it for herself a little longer. She would hold it and hug it, for it was almost too delicious to be shared. She would spend the next few hours, just her and the boys. As they made their way down the building stairs, Ellie's phone chimed again. What was with today? Who would have expected the day after Thanksgiving to be so busy? Wasn't everyone supposed to be out shopping Black Friday deals?

It was Sam.

Taking the stairs as carefully as she could, Ellie listened as Sam told her his interview had gone well. He asked where they were, and she told him she was taking the boys to the park.

"I'll meet you there," he said. "I can be there in twenty minutes; traffic's light."

"Um ... okay," said Ellie, her mind whirring.

Things had been so busy today that she'd totally forgotten about Sam and his interview. Talk about "not a good look." What's more, she'd been hoping for a carefree hour or two in the fresh air with the boys, just the three of them. If Sam came along, she'd have to be engaged. Yet things were going so well with Sam and he'd made such an effort with Thanksgiving, so why would she say no?

"Sure," she said, hoping the chirp in her voice surpassed her true energy levels.

They had just reached the bottom of the hill and were making their way to an available bench when Sam pulled up in his car and turned on his hazard lights to double park. They greeted each other warmly, with Sam planting a kiss on her lips. Despite her fatigue, Ellie felt a thrill rush through her body. He electrified her.

"So, it went well! What happens next?"

"Hard to tell with these things," he said. "But yeah, it went pretty well. I'll know soon enough about the panel." Sam beamed at Ellie. He always seemed to gaze at her like it was his first time.

If Sam was accepted, he would be put on an employment panel, and as soon as the right job in neurology arose, he would be next in line. Ellie wondered what it would be like if he did get the job and moved to San Francisco. Would they see each other every day? Would that ruin what they had—their exciting meetups in hotels, at his bachelor pad, the time apart, counting down the days till they could be together again? Or would it be a marvel, having this man that she so desired at her beck and call?

"Let me find parking, and I'll tell you more," said Sam as cars honked on Stockton Street for him to move.

Ellie couldn't help herself.

"Where would you stay if you came to San Francisco?"

"Not sure yet." He shrugged. "Maybe I'll marry you, and we can all live together in a little house in the Marina."

He laughed.

Ellie didn't.

Marriage! Was he insane? Ellie had absolutely no intention of ever marrying again. She wasn't long through divorce. There was no way she was locking herself up again. And marriage to Sam, who came from a culture where family expectations around marriage could be intense, would bring its own challenges too.

"Well, the entire Marina is built on landfill, so that's a hard 'No.' And I hate to burst your bubble, Dr., but I don't believe in marriage any longer."

Sam froze. He looked crestfallen.

For half a second, Ellie wondered if she should soften—if maybe she wanted to believe in marriage again. But no. She'd played that game before. And she'd learned better. *Fool me once, shame on you; fool me twice, shame on me*, she thought.

The horn honking persisted. Ignoring the cacophony, Sam furrowed his brow and frowned. "Really? You don't believe in the sacrament of marriage, or you don't believe you could be happy in any marriage again?"

"Both," said Ellie adamantly.

"Huh," said Sam. He stroked his chin as he remained unfazed by the traffic jam he was causing.

Ellis signed. "Look, Sam. It seems to me marriage is sold to us as a product from a very young age. A product of security and legitimacy. In my experience, though, it's a vice to control and subjugate women and a means for men to look good to other men. I'm just not falling for the con a second time. I refuse to be the dumb girl in the B-horror movie who goes down to the creepy basement when the audience is shouting at her to get out of the house. The vows people take on their wedding day are a lie—they just don't know they're lying at the time. I question lifelong monogamy as a healthy or durable structure at all. It's a naive grasp at certainty in an inherently uncertain world that just sets people up for disappointment and failure."

Ellie couldn't help thinking of Teddy just then and how far ahead of her time she'd really been—how well she'd understood herself from an early age—with her triangle or square or whatever geometry Ellie's great-great-grandmother had assigned her nontraditional relationship that caused her descendants to never mention her.

Sam seemed stricken.

"Horror movie? I'm sorry you feel that way. I see marriage as a beautiful union. A shared love, a happy home, a commitment that you know you can't just walk away from."

"I get that. You've bought into a prepackaged product backed by guerrilla marketing tactics. And is that what you think I did? Just walked away from my marriage?" said Ellie, her hackles raised now.

"No!" said Sam. "I simply mean that ... it's a commitment, you know. You work hard to stay together. You don't throw in the towel at the first disagreement."

Ellie felt the blood rush to her head. What did Sam really think of her? That she had abandoned Joe at the first quarrel?

"You know, I'm going to head back home," Ellie said, putting her hand to her head, feeling the onslaught of that headache that she'd woken up with but that had been held at bay by the two adrenaline rushes she'd experienced already.

"Are you all right?" Sam asked, concerned.

"I'm fine," said Ellie tersely. "It's just been a long few days. C'mon, boys, we can come back another day."

"No!" called Nathan, who had been chasing around a frisky little pug named Billy.

"C'mon," said Ellie firmly. She really wasn't in the mood for a tantrum now. "Let's make hot cocoa at home. I even have mini marshmallows."

"I feel I have upset you," said Sam, looking upon her gently, lovingly.

Ellie shook her head and braved a smile.

"Honestly, I'm fine. I just want to get these guys back. I'd offer for you to stay, but we've had a lot of excitement over the past few days."

Sam held his hands up.

"No problem," he said. "No problem at all. Let me drive you back up the hill and—"

"No. Really," said Ellie and she tugged on Nathan and Luca's hands, nudging them gently toward the corner of Filbert and Stockton streets. "It's fine. We'll walk. I'll call you tomorrow, okay?"

"Sure," he said, holding his palms up in détente.

As Ellie made her way back down the path toward home, she felt her confusion swirl. The case win had sent her soaring. Now, in the span of an hour, she felt drained, brittle, like a match burned too fast. Why had she been so prickly with Sam? Why was she pushing him away? The idea of him folding into her life should have been comforting. Her temple throbbed. Was it just the headache? Or something deeper? She wasn't sure. All she knew was that she felt like she might drop from exhaustion and the golden glow of her news from Rebecca earlier had dimmed a little.

Matters of the heart were confusing. Matters of the law were much more straightforward once she got a handle on them.

Usually. Mostly.

At least, when she could hold onto the illusion of control.

The New York Times
March 22, 1910

HATPIN ORDINANCE PASSED: Chicago Women Cry "Shame!" at Measure Which Regulates Their Dress.

It is now a misdemeanor for any woman to wear a long hatpin in public places in Chicago. Any woman caught wearing one is liable to arrest and a fine of $50. A crowd of women gathered to protest against the measure on the ground that the city had no right to attempt to regulate women's wearing apparel, and that long hatpins often at night formed women's only weapon of defense.

The ordinance decrees that "no person while in the public streets … shall wear any hatpin, the exposed point whereof shall protrude more than one-half inch beyond the crown of the hat …"

The argument for the measure was that long hatpins worn in crowded places endangered the eyes, noses, and faces of people. When the vote was announced cries of "Shame! Shame!" came from women in the galleries.

CHAPTER 25

TEDDY

December 15, 1909.
San Francisco, California.

My, what an evening this has been. I think the hair is still standing on the back of my neck.

We have had many exciting evenings at the Suffragists Association but tonight took the cake. There wasn't an empty seat in the Golden Gate Hall. We knew it would be busy, but nothing like a controversial guest to bring out every pair of boots.

There was great anticipation when we heard she'd arrived—not early, but just on time. It was as if she had planned it perfectly—for there was no time for greeting or idle chat that I could see.

She swept in like a tornado and straight to the podium, barely a minute for her introduction and I think our chair, Mrs. Jennings, was quite taken aback. But Mrs. Wells is a busy woman and the entourage she had with her were there to check their watches and keep things moving. She had another engagement straight after us apparently.

Her opening line was: "For too long we have stood by and let these men rule us with an iron fist! But I say no longer!"

Oh, that's when my hackles rose. The energy she ignited was palpable—her voice, diminutive, but her words, powerful. Her speech was delivered with fortitude and an intelligence and grit simply impossible not to admire. There was much stomping of boots and cheers as she whipped us right up into a frenzy.

"We have shown time and time again, what we are capable of. When we stand together, we stand strong. Our voice as one, for we are many in number. Hard of spirit. And we shall not be defeated!"

That line hit hard!

Lillie Coit and I leapt to our feet, we simply couldn't help ourselves, and then others followed and the room was a roar.

"Isn't she a marvel?" Lillie said, that stinking cigar tucked between her teeth. (I wouldn't be surprised if the committee soon passes a motion to ban smoking within the hall, although, I suppose, they are simply delighted to have Old Firebelle Lil back in their midst again after those years of exile in Paris.)

"I don't know how I'm going to follow her!" I said.

"You'll be smashing, darling," she told me.

I do love her for that, that resolute belief that she has always declared in me.

But we simply couldn't take our eyes off Ida. How a woman, given the worst possible start in this country, born a slave, has managed to rise up and become such a renowned activist, a colossal campaigning voice on anti-lynching and segregation and make such a mark. And she is a young woman yet!

"Together means together! It does not mean a vote for white, but not for black. It does not mean segregation, of our children, of our education systems, a building up of us and them. Us and you. You, the white women in this room."

We could hear that old bat Margaret McKinley jabbering the whole way through. No respect for Ida B. Wells whatsoever. Honestly, the higher born these women, the worse their manners.

"She's a good speaker," she said out loud toward the end of Ida's speech (to that insufferable Joan Benetton, her lapdog companion, who never raises her voice above the level of a mouse. How Margaret McKinley ever hears her is beyond me as the woman is as deaf as a post and everything she says comes out in a roar.) "But when the black suffragists march with white, it damages our campaign. Have a white march or a negro march, but not both!"

Lillie said both of them should have been thrown out by the scruff of their necks. (She calls them "Lily-white purists"!)

But of course, Mrs. McKinley remained oblivious. She is an old woman set in her ways and despite our numerous debates at the Golden Gate Hall, still maintains the belief that it will be impossible to secure the vote for women if the campaign includes colored women too.

"Ssssshhhhh," Lillie reprimanded her then, simply unable to contain herself. She took the cigar out of her mouth and did it again. "Ssssshhhhh!"

Still, Mrs. McKinley chattered.

If Ida had heard the remarks she did not let on, but I suppose the young woman is probably used to such prejudice. And then her wonderful speech was over and we all stood (well, none of the Lily-whites stood, but they at least clapped) and she got a rapturous reception.

The suffragists of San Francisco are certainly a fan of Ida B. Wells! I longed for a word with her afterwards, but she was swept away by her entourage and there went my chance for a tête-a-tête.

It was my turn then to take to the podium, even though I felt the butterflies bouncing inside. While I know I have grown into the art of speech-making, I am not sure it's something that comes naturally to one, and I often feel like quite the underdog when it comes to these things for my knowledge comes from the books I have read over the years and the studies I have undertaken myself, whereas many of the suffragists of course were born into a rigorous private education. I do so often feel on the back foot. Or rather unworthy.

In any matter, I cleared my throat and got to it. I stood up, put my hand up into the air and held up my precious brightly colored cloth.

"This was woven by a Great Coast Miwok woman," I announced. "Her name: Helki. She was working on it in the days before she died.

The pattern is unique to her tribe, a coastal tribe who survived on shellfish and seal. She knew a particular way of life. A coastal life that we as conquerors have sought to destroy."

I told them that Helki, as many of them know anyway, was a very special person in my life, a wonderful medicine woman, who spent all her time working to treat every ailment known to man.

"And woman! For we suffer so much more!"

They liked that indeed, for a peal of laughter and applause broke out!

"It is utterly cruel then that a woman who spent all her time treating the sick, who knew so much about the body and complicated illnesses and maladies and how to treat them, should succumb to the common cold. These sicknesses brought by whites have wiped out so many of our fellow Indian sisters and brothers in the same way that we have wiped out the buffalo across our great plains, and we must acknowledge that! We need to acknowledge the great damage that we, the white settlers, our ancestors have brought."

And of course, what did I hear from that old curmudgeon Mrs. McKinley: "I didn't realize we were in for an anti-white evening. I thought she was supposed to talk about hatpins, but she's got a bee in her bonnet about Indian rights, too?"

And so, duly, from the cloth still held high in my palm in the air, I unsheathed my sword from its scabbard.

"This, my dear friends, as you all well know, is a hatpin. A hatpin I had specially made, for although you usually see me in this garb ..." I pointed to my bloomers then and again there was much laughter "... I do occasionally behave like a woman and wear a respectable hat!"

"Will you be wearing one tomorrow evening?!" heckled Lillie.

"Indeed, I will," I retorted. "It will match my tuxedo perfectly!"

I had to wait for the laugher to die down in the room then!

"This hatpin, believe it or not, was once an arrow, one of three arrows I bought from an Indian man along with a bow he had crafted. The most dashing, intelligent Indian you could ever imagine! I fell deeply in love with him and he with me. I suppose you could say it was Cupid's very own arrows I bought from him that day."

"Oh, for the love of Pete," groused Old McKinley.

I did not let her put me off.

"Momo, the man who made the arrows, the man who I loved deeply, was Helki's brother. The arrows will be left to my sons. The hatpin arrow I will leave to my daughter, Matilda. A few years ago, I would have not declaimed my friend Momo so readily, and certainly not in public."

Then I looked right at Mrs. McKinley and directed my next words at her.

"For too long, I've hidden my desires and my thoughts as a woman. For too long, I've been kept quiet. But, as I've had time to reflect over my life, I've realized that even though I've only been campaigning in recent years, I have been a suffragist all my life. I have rebelled in so many ways. Fought my own corner like a tiger. Followed my heart, worn what I felt like!"

"Hear, hear!" said Lillie.

I could see Mrs. McKinley shifting uncomfortably in her seat. That got her.

"I never knew my mother. So, I cannot say where I got this spirit from. What I do know is what I would like to see happen now, for my own autonomy and for that of my daughter Matilda and for her daughters. Here we are again, facing another dreadful piece of legislation, this proposed hatpin law, drafted by our good men in government, aimed solely to keep us women down at heel. Another law of oppression!"

And do you know, a spontaneous round of applause broke out.

"Why *should* we women not protect ourselves? Are they really so scared of us, the weaker sex? God may not have given us muscles. But he gave us wit. He gave us our wits which we can use as both shield and sword. Should a man approach or attack and we defend ourselves with one of these, then so be it! Hands off our hatpins!"

Then I stabbed the air triumphantly with the hatpin, to the rhythm of stamping boots.

What a moment it was. Electrifying. I could feel the hairs on the back of my neck again, and this time it was my own words that did it!

"It cannot be the woman who has done wrong but the man who accosted her! The government must be made to see this. We *must* stand up for ourselves. And so, I urge you to join me, on our hatpin march in January. Bring your placards. Paint your slogans. Wear your hatpins. Wear all your hatpins! Because this proposed ban is not really about fashion or men's safety. It is about man's desire to dominate woman and keep her helpless! I will forever fight for the right for us to be free in our thoughts, in our dress, in our minds, in our marriages, in our lives!"

"Teddy DeLuca for President," cried Lillie, jumping from her chair and clapping wildly.

The whole room applauded then, even the conservatives who, I suppose, I did win over.

"Thank you," I said and I think I was blushing as I re-sheathed my beautiful arrow hatpin. My cheeks were burning. I always get embarrassed at the end of my speeches, but I am completely absorbed while in the moment. Often, I can barely remember what I've actually said.

When I got back to my seat, Lillie grabbed my arm and said, "I mean it, Teddy. You truly could be president."

"That'll be the day," I scoffed. "When America votes for a female president."

"It'll happen," said Lillie. "We may not live to see it, but some day."

December 16, 1909. San Francisco.

"Too ill to go. Very sorry. Knock 'em dead."

That's the telegram I got from poor Lil this afternoon, just a short while before I was due to pick her up.

Oh, blast it, I thought. She must be feeling quite poorly, as she really would never miss anything as big as this and then of course, she would now have to leave me on my lonesome!

I got in the motor car, though I find that wretched car seat to be quite uncomfortable. I really must get the mechanic to look at it. It seems my girth has been expanding and there is not enough room behind that steering wheel. I suppose I rarely cycle these days, for the car is so convenient for San Francisco's vertical hills. Four wheels really are better than two.

I cannot stop nibbling on Emile's pies of late either. That's the problem with hiring a French chef and pâtissier. Which reminds me, when we have the café open at the Indian Center, we really must send his pastries in along with the Boudin sourdough.

As I drove along Taylor Street, I thought about how for all the motor car's benefits, the one thing I do miss about the horse and carriage is how sheltered it was. You feel that damp grey fog rolling in from the bay; it penetrates the bones.

Lillie's maid told me that her mistress was ailing and I did think when the maid opened the door that she had a gaunt look about her, as if she'd been run ragged nursing her. (Though it's hard to tell with the Irish girls, most I've met look gaunt anyway. The girls from England are much more rosy-cheeked, I find.) I went up to Lillie's bedroom and could practically feel the fever from the door!

"Don't come close!" she rasped at me. "I don't want you catching whatever this is. Why did you come? I sent a telegram."

I told her I had brought her Emile's pastries to keep her strength up. She was quite miserable and said she was too out of sorts to eat them. Then she asked me what on earth I was wearing. She peered over the blankets, her eyes watery and puffy, her face swollen.

"I'm dressed for the occasion," I told her.

"You weren't joshing when you said tuxedo!" she said.

Even I can still surprise.

"Quite!" I said.

I am rather proud of my tuxedo, if I may say myself, with its shiny lapel and matching black trousers, which to my shame had to be let out this week, but so be it.

Blame Emile, not me.

My frilly white blouse matched splendidly with my voluminous hat and of course the whole thing was stuck all over with hatpins. Every single one I owned, plus a few more I'd borrowed.

"So that's what you wanted with the hatpins," said Lil.

"Well, I wasn't making an art painting!" I told her.

"I don't know," she said. "Your head looks like a Medusa sculpture!"

"I'm making a statement," I said.

"You're a walking statement, all right," Lillie said.

"You're one to tease, parading about in your Knickerbocker No. 5 helmet at events."

I told her I dearly wished she was coming and she was quite apologetic and said, next time, Ted.

"There won't be a next time!" I told her. "The Palace Hotel will not be reopening again for … well, as long as we don't have any more earthquakes and fires, I suppose."

She said she was feeling so unwell she wasn't sure she'd make it through the week. I warned her not to talk like that, for I have so few friends left.

She promised she'd try not to pop her clogs while I was gone. I told her the firemen would miss her too much anyway.

"They couldn't be without their queen!"

She said she's been thinking of doing something for them. Some tribute on a grand scale. But she doesn't know what yet. I told her she'd think of something, and that I'd revert to her soon to organize a game of whist and deliver a detailed report of the evening.

I drove then to New Montgomery Street and, do you know, it was difficult to find a spot in which to park, there were so many motor cars all stacked up. I've never seen that before!

Well, here is all the wealth, I thought. On show. I traipsed along then into the hotel, for I knew the place would be filled to the brim with not just the richest men in San Francisco, but the whole of California. How utterly dreary.

From the outside, I must say, the new hotel has a much plainer front than the ornate Victorian façade that had been there before the fire. I did wonder whether the inside would also be rather plain, but when I walked through those doors, my, I think my breath left my body.

The atmosphere felt otherworldly! The interior is the opposite of plain! I suppose there was a reason the hotel has taken three years to re-open. It was truly magnificent. I stood, simply drinking in the atrium, taking in the greenery and the Christmas trees and decorations and it took me a moment to recover, so beautiful was the whole thing. When I composed myself, I blinked and looked about and realized, not for the first time in my life, that I was being gawked at, with long, disapproving gazes. All around, men in shiny tuxedos glared at me.

Then the whispers behind palms. Well, that was the plan. Get them talking. Here I am, fellows!

I looked all about but couldn't find one person I recognized. Oh, how I wished dear old Lil was by my side then. There were so many men. Hundreds of men!

I made my way through the crowd and ambled through the atrium, peering past the grey and dark pomaded heads and moustaches and saw that, quite obviously, I was the only woman in the room. Even the staff were male. How queer.

"Mrs. DeLuca," called a voice and I turned around to find Mr. Amadeo Pietro Giannini, good old A. P. coming toward me.

"Ah, a friendly face!" I said.

I do care for A. P. It's the measure of a man who salvages funds from his Bank of Italy vault—smuggled out under a wagonload of oranges to avoid looters, no less—to set up a makeshift "bank" on a wooden plank resting on barrels in the streets of San Francisco after the fire. Indeed, he's a man of my own heart, offering loans on nothing more than a handshake to the working-class citizens of a city, seeing to those less fortunate, immigrants turned away by everyone else.

"You look magnificent!" he said.

He seemed to have his eyes turned upwards, looking practically at the ceiling and I realized that my hat probably does add at least a foot to my height. He told me he had never seen a woman in a tuxedo. I said, "Well you have now!"

We toured the hotel ground floor, taking in the new stained-glass ceiling, which A. P., ever the money man, told me cost $7 million alone to create! It is breath-taking but I wondered how many houses could have been built with that money. A. P. said terraced houses could never be as spectacular as a $7 million glass ceiling.

"We've done our part to rebuild the city for its families, Teddy. And we'll keep doing so. We can also give people some grandeur."

In the Pied Piper Bar, we marveled at Maxfield Parrish's mural: a scene of Hamelin, leading a flurry of young children across a mountainous scene. A. P. pointed at two of the women in the mural and said rumor has it that Parrish has painted both his wife and his mistress into the painting.

Quite the scallywag!

When it came time to sit for dinner, it was clear how large a crowd had been invited to the grand opening, for hundreds upon hundreds of dining places were lined up banquet style, the red-runnered linen tables peppered with tall green table arrangements and four-armed silver candelabras topped with tiny lampshades. Colored menus sat awaiting our hungry hands.

"How many do you think they have?" I asked A. P.

He said he'd heard a thousand!

"A thousand men! And one woman!" I said.

And just as I uttered that I heard a man with a great big handle-bar moustache behind us say, "I didn't know women were invited to this, a gentleman's occasion!"

One of his companions said: "Yes, she seems quite confused for she is half-dressed as a man!" Then they chortled, sounding like harbor seals.

"She's quite the attention seeker," said another.

"A very rich attention seeker," chimed his companion.

"The only reason she's here, I suppose! The benefactors obviously need her money!"

Well, that got me. I got up and marched right over. I stuck out my hand.

"Teddy DeLuca!" I introduced myself and I forced every one of them to look me in the eye and shake my hand. The handshakes in return were limp—as you'd imagine a seal's flipper!

"So wonderful to see you here," I said. "Such interesting fellows, no doubt. I'm so looking forward to hearing all about your viewpoints throughout dinner. If you could just speak up, so I can hear over the din. Thank you ever so much."

They blustered and turned away, embarrassed, but I had laid bare their old-fashioned opinions. How dare they.

"You're a riot," A. P. said when I returned to my seat.

Oh, how I wished Lil had been there to see me in action. She would have enjoyed that altercation and more than likely joined in, offering them a cigar! I must tell her about Maxfield Parrish's mural, how it was such a talking point and conveyed such emotion. She does so love art, our Lillie.

Just before the first course was served, Julius Martinelli appeared with Paul DeMartini, shaking my hand warmly and clapping A. P. on the back.

"Quite the spectacle!" DeMartini said.

I said they must be quite inspired, as a master architect and builder.

"How do you fancy an atrium ceiling on the Indian Center?" joked Martinelli.

"Only $7 million," said A. P.

I asked them how the build has been going as I haven't been to the site in two weeks. The weeks leading up to Christmas had been busy as Matilda had given birth to her second child and I'd been traveling up and down the coast to campaign for women and the vote. No doubt my George, rest his soul, would spin in his grave if he knew I'd taken up donning masculine garb again as "Mr. Theodore Ellis" to slip into men's clubs for the cause. Though I still don't abide cigars, Lillie taught me well enough how to pull off a stogie without giving myself away. So I listen and puff slowly, sipping a bit of cognac. I learn their countermeasures against us suffragists and, though rare, now and then spot a friend to the cause. These men are so smitten with the sound of their own voices and the sight of their cigar rings, they pay no mind to the quiet one in the room observing all—especially if that figure has funds enough to pay dues and keep the liquor flowing.

Martinelli said things have been going well and A. P. wanted to know if we would be ready by the spring.

"We will be open March 1910," I told him.

"Quite the slave driver," joked Giannini.

"There will be no slaves working on any of my projects, I can assure you of that," I told him sharply. Of course, the men raised their eyebrows at me and smiled, but they are all well used to me and made no retort.

Glasses were clinked then as they tried to get everyone's attention from the top table for the speeches were about to start.

"There's a photographer," said Martinelli. "Huddle up, look smart!"

We took our seats and smiled. I could hear the men behind me tutting then.

"I can't see beyond that giant thing!"

I did not move. No siree.

And just now, as I took my afternoon tea, the *San Francisco Examiner* lay before me. With much anticipation, I unfolded the paper and found the headline: "New Palace Hotel Reopens, 750 Businessmen Attend Opening Dinner."

There was that very photograph on the front page. I traced my finger along the rows and rows of men, trying to find exactly where we were seated. There was Martinelli. And DeMartini. And A. P. All smiling in their tuxedos. And, as I had been seated directly beside A. P. I expected to see myself and my lovely hat, but alas, I was nowhere to be found. The photograph had been cut to remove me completely. It seems the newspaper editor felt the sight of a woman in her own tuxedo and large hat-pinned hat was too much for his reading public!

I had to be wiped away. Extinguished like the flames of a fire. There was no mention of me on the attendee list or in the article. It was as though I was never even there.

Well, I will never forget that paper's attempt to pretend I did not even exist. They can crop their photos all they like. I shall not be erased. Up and down this country us women go unrecognized, cut out, day after day after day.

If this isn't proof, I don't know what is.

I have canceled my subscription to *The Examiner*. And I will urge all my suffragist friends to do so too.

We shall not be snuffed out.

We shall not be erased.

CHAPTER 26

ELLIE

December 2, 2019. San Francisco, California.

The knock came sharp and loud on Ellie's door, and before she could even answer, Mercedes Ortiz, the communications director of the San Francisco Immigrant Legal Defense Collaborative, strode in. She was a stylish, striking woman who had started out as a local television reporter in the Central Valley of California. Having moved to the city and advocacy PR, she kept her hair in a sashaying bob, always poised to step on-screen at a moment's notice. The latest update evidently involved Ellie.

Ellie exhaled, bracing herself. Mercedes Ortiz bursting through your office door usually meant drama.

"Have you seen this?" Mercedes asked in her news anchor voice.

Ellie looked up from the assault case file on her fast-food-worker client. A gang of youths had surrounded the young man during his graveyard shift while his two coworkers were out back smoking. They pulled him across the counter onto the floor, kicking him in the stomach and back as they emptied the till. While he was still recovering in the hospital, the restaurant had him served with fake deportation papers in a blatant attempt to intimidate him into dropping his injury claim.

"Seen what?" Ellie asked as brightly as she could manage, for her brain was deep in the case at hand and preferred not to be distracted.

The cases came fast and furious at the ILDC. Too many clients in dire straits, too little time.

"Twitter," said Mercedes.

Ellie just stared at Mercedes. She avoided the sinkhole of social media during the day as much as possible. She barely looked at it at night either but realized it was the way to stay relevant. LinkedIn was as far as she could stomach, though she did have other social media accounts. It came in useful for her cases, especially because defense counsel routinely ran social media investigations of her clients.

Mercedes held up her phone to face the screen to Ellie, then placed it firmly on top of the paperwork so she could fully take it in. On the screen was the photo of the notice board from the discount dollar store where Hansa Nambootiri worked. The image had been zoomed in on to enhance the red pushpin inserted into Hansa's forehead.

This is what my sister had to deal with. "Hindi with the Bindy"—except *she doesn't even wear a bindi. Since coming to America, all we've gotten is ignorance and racism. All we've done is work hard. But this country still treats us like we don't belong. #Racism #ImmigrantStories*

"Perfect. Just what we needed. Tell me this isn't blowing up," said Ellie, peering closer at the screen. "Wait. *My sister?* Who wrote this?"

Using her fingers to zoom in on the screen, Ellie saw the profile picture attached to the account more clearly. It was Hansa's sister, Rashila.

"I only found out who she was when it kept getting tweeted at our account. They've tracked down that we're representing Hansa. By *they*, I mean multiple news agencies and off-the-wall actual racist dumb-bots. My feed has blown up. It's been retweeted 50,382 times. And that was before I came to find you. It'll be more now."

"Wow, almost fifty-four thousand," said Ellie, reading the counter under the tweet. "Why would Rashila put this out there? This is part of our case. This is our smoking gun!"

"You're using this in the case?"

"Well, I was!" said Ellie. "I contacted Hansa over the weekend about it."

"It's kicking up some dust," said Mercedes. "Lots of people replying saying Americans aren't racist. Lots of talk about immigrants. That they're taking American jobs and increasing crime. Then others saying she's only looking for a handout. It's brewed a helluva storm. And all the usual suspects coming on fire, you know the type; I mean they come at us all the time to the ILDC account, but this is ugly."

Ellie was aware, from the regular meetings they had with Mercedes and the ILDC directors, that there were lobbyists who followed their work and liked to put out counterarguments in both broadcast and online media to further their own interests. And then there were the keyboard warriors.

Rubbing the furrowed flesh between her eyebrows, Ellie sighed again.

"Okay, what does your playbook say to do now?" she asked, happy to turn the decision over to her communications director. If crises management were an Olympic event, Mercedes would have not only won all the medals, but she'd also have rewritten the rulebook, optimized the training regimen, and negotiated a better sponsorship deal.

"It's out there now," Mercedes said. "We can't ask her to take it down, and besides, she's not actually our client; her sister is. It might look weak if she deleted it."

"I don't think she would anyway," said Ellie, thinking of the forthright Rashila, who had made such an impression when she and her sister first visited the office.

"It'll damage our case, though, right?" said Ellie. "Even if we do use it now, they'll be prepared. I mean, I think they knew the store manager was a knob and a bigot in general, and that's why they've been pushing a settlement, but I don't know that they knew about this."

"Yes, she's blown our cover now, I guess," said Mercedes. "It's a pity. Main thing is to check they're both doing okay and advise them to not respond to the comments they get. I'm not sure they realize the power of Twitter; there are some nasty accounts out there. They're already vulnerable."

"Well, Hansa certainly is, for sure," said Ellie, stroking her chin now while she thought through the possibilities for the action now. "Rashila could probably take some of them on."

She groaned. Social media—the curse of the modern age. A vortex of scrolling, tweeting, and pointless chatter she had neither time nor patience for. Worse, it was out of her control, and *that* she hated most of all.

"I'll call Hansa," she said, reaching for the phone.

"I'll prepare a few statements in any case," said Mercedes. "Good to have official lines. I have a feeling this one could grow legs with track shoes."

"All right," said Ellie, dialing Hansa's number. Mercedes was a newshound, which meant her instincts were usually right.

Ellie sighed as Hansa's quiet voice answered. She was already exhausted. And it was only Monday.

"Hansa?" said Ellie. "We need to talk."

That afternoon, Ellie began going over Hansa's case notes again (she was too distracted now, so the fast-food-assault case would have to wait until tomorrow) and found the dollar store had zero electrical and plumbing permits loaded onto the official property records online database.

She had noted the hazardous wiring pictured in some of the photographs Hansa had given her and wanted evidence to prove that the owners were negligent in the maintenance of the property. She had a hunch she could nail down the Serious & Willful charge on their botched maintenance jobs, showing a top-down lack of care for the people who worked under its disastrous roof.

To fully prove her theory, however, they would need to double-check online at OSHA and at the City Building and Planning office in person to make sure there was nothing there in paper that wasn't online. It was something she usually got an intern to do, but this case had gotten under her skin. And besides, an hour or two out of the office would do her no harm.

She still hadn't told anyone about Hutton & Fetterer. No need to jinx it. She'd had a fretful weekend, tossing and turning after she'd been short with Sam on Friday. Joe had taken the boys Saturday and Sunday, and she had cleaned her own apartment before joining her parents again at Enzo's to help with more purging and organizing.

They had done a good job, she had to admit, and had gotten through a massive amount of stuff. The house was looking pretty empty now. She had loaded her trunk to take boxes of clothes and small items to the thrift store at some stage that week, but they'd needed a van to collect the larger pieces of furniture.

Anika had invited her over for a glass of wine on Sunday night; they had barely seen each other over Thanksgiving. But Ellie had told her she was too tired and would see her during the week. It wasn't an untruth, but it was really unlike her not to want to catch up with her best friend—and tell her the big news!

It was strange to feel in such a slump after scoring such a win. Her emotions refused to cooperate. The long week of preparing Enzo's house for sale had done something to her, hung a cloud over her normally bright sky. She felt like she was breaking away, letting something go, and she wasn't quite ready to do that yet.

Sam had texted after Washington Square Park, saying he hoped he hadn't overstepped. It was a kind, thoughtful message—and one she wasn't ready to answer. Ellie knew she had been short with him. She wished she could stop pushing him away. They hadn't been in contact since then, and she wasn't quite sure how she felt about that. She kept filing it to the back of her mind to deal with "later."

As the historic F-line streetcar noisily made its way along Market Street, she watched the tourists, commuters, and families around her. She enjoyed being out in the hubbub of the city, people-watching. She wondered if she'd ever caught the same trams Teddy had. Surely, they'd traveled along the same streets at times, though Ellie had never been brave enough (so far) to go by bicycle.

The Indian Center fascinated her, and she had Googled the street, trying to see where exactly the building was. But all that she could see on Google Earth were modern-looking buildings. She was starting the last diary now, and she realized that was probably adding to her blue mood. She would eke it out for as long as possible. So many things, it seemed, were coming to an end.

As she felt her senses relax a little now that she was away from the office, she thought that Anika had the right idea with all her woo-woo habits: focusing on her breath in the morning, chanting her moments of calm, lighting her incense and candles, and wafting all her troubles away. But some problems simply wouldn't waft. Some things you had to face. Hugo's death had complicated matters so much for Anika and her family. Ellie had come to understand that her friend's need to hang on to her dying marriage was tied up with holding on to the memories of her little boy. If she let Ben go, Ellie supposed, Anika might feel that she was letting go of her little boy forever too.

Shaken from her ruminations by the streetcar bell, Ellie jumped off at her stop.

In the Building and Planning department at City Hall, Ellie asked for the files she needed at the desk. The archivist checked and double-checked for her.

"Nothing here on file," said the archivist, coming back from an overcrowded-looking room housing long shelves filled with paper files.

"Absolutely nothing?" asked Ellie.

"Not a thing," replied the archivist. She wore thick glasses and was abrupt in her manner.

"All right, thank you so much," said Ellie and she turned to leave.

But then she paused. The office was so calm, imitating the main library just across the plaza, inviting people in with its dull carpet and soft echo. It made her want to stick around a bit longer.

"Actually," said Ellie, turning back. "Would you mind checking something else for me? I'm looking for the property records of a building in North Beach. I think the original building has since been demolished, but I'm interested in its history."

The archivist raised her eyebrows, sighed, and went back into the shelved room.

Ellie tapped her foot and looked around. Young interns with stacks of folders were busily taking notes at the long bench tables. She remembered spending hours in records offices like these during her own internship.

She had always been a bit of an archaeologist—except instead of digging up fossils, she unearthed corporate screwups and bureaucratic negligence.

It didn't take long for the archivist to come back with a brown paper folder, thick with papers. "Thank you so much," said Ellie and she took the bundle over to a bench and sat down. Opening up the folder felt a bit like peeling back the door to Narnia. What would she find in there?

On top were documents relating to the new buildings—a set of three modern-looking apartment blocks that had been built in the 1970s. They took up almost three-quarters of the folder. Ellie quickly riffled through the paperwork, sifting to find what was underneath. Turning over a document, Ellie's fingers happened upon a very old folded document. She took it out, unfolded it carefully, and opened it out flat.

It was a set of plans. An architect's plans. Her eyes scanned the scale of the building, noting a warren of rooms and what looked like dormitory accommodations. At the bottom of the plans was a name, handwritten.

Theodora DeLuca.

"Oh my God!" Ellie said out loud.

A few interns turned their heads to stare. Ellie looked over to see the archivist glaring at her, and she shrugged in apology.

Wow!

Underneath the plans were more documents relating to the construction of the building, permits, and change of uses over the years. The building had been used as a hospital, and she read that the stables and "animal welfare sheds" had been converted into accommodation in the 1940s. Teddy must have gotten her animal shelter, for a time at least.

When she was done with the file, Ellie asked the archivist if she could check if she had any more records under the name Theodora DeLuca. While the archivist grumpily typed into her computer, Ellie felt her phone vibrate.

It was Stanley.

"I have to take this, but I'll be right back," Ellie told the archivist, already striding toward the corridor.

"Dad?"

"Ellie," said her father, and she felt that pang of panic she always did when she got an unexpected call from her parents.

"Honey, I think we have an offer. On the house."

"What?" said Ellie. "Who? How?" The house hadn't even gone on the market yet.

"Well, it's a strange one, but your mom and I got talking to a guy today, outside. He was walking past; he's a housing officer at Cal."

"Okay …" said Ellie. She knew many of the houses in the area were rented to university students, some housing up to thirty at a time.

"He saw us moving boxes and asked us if we had recently sold. We told him we were getting ready to sell. He said the university is always looking at good properties close to campus. Anyway, we got to talking, and I told him about your job at the ILDC and that evening clinic you do at the Cal law school. He said they're interested in setting up a center, a type of—not a shelter—but, you know, a support place specifically aimed at immigrants attending Cal, people who have children and need a little extra help. He thought this house would make a great housing and resource center!"

"No way, Dad! Really?"

"Yep," said Stanley. "They pay fair market value, you know; we'd get a good price."

"And you wouldn't have to go through the bother of listing it for sale and a bunch of strangers traipsing through, not to mention the agent fee you'd pay," said Ellie practically.

"And your mom says Enzo and Genevieve would have loved it."

"They would, Dad!"

"So, you think it's a good idea?"

"I'd like more details, but I think it's a great idea!"

"Well, there you go; never know who you'll bump into, huh?"

Ellie couldn't help but think of Teddy's Indian Center and Elizabeth and Alice's neighborhood center. A drop-in support building, a place where people in need could come and go. The cycle, albeit on a smaller scale, was repeating.

"Hey, Dad," said Ellie. "I found architectural plans today from Teddy. I mean, it was a fluke. I'm in the property records archive for a case of mine."

"You're kidding!" said Stanley.

"The building I'm looking at was torn down in the seventies, though, it seems. Do you know what year Teddy died?"

"Not sure," said her father.

"Well, I mean she wouldn't have lived till then, but still, I was just wondering. She achieved so much."

"I know that now because of you, dear," said Stanley and she could feel him smiling at the other end of the phone.

"That's great news about the house, Dad. Great news! I gotta go, okay; check in with you later."

Her parents were returning to Chicago the following day. They'd insisted on taking BART to the airport in the morning, so tonight, she would drive out to Enzo's house to say goodbye to them before they left. Ellie would arrange for a van to remove the last of the furniture during the week. And now, likely, there would be more urgency, if a sale was imminent.

Back at the desk, the archivist handed over a tall stack of folders. Her eyebrows raised as if to say, "That's it for today, right?"

Ellie smiled.

"All these?"

"All filed under Theodora DeLuca," said the archivist, matter-of-factly.

Ellie took the stack of files back to the table, their weight solid in her arms. *Teddy*, she thought. *You secret agent, you. You were really quite the real estate mogul!*

The first three files related to properties in North Beach. Ellie studied the plans, which had the name of the P. DeMartini architectural office at the bottom, and, within the file, the contractor was J. Martinelli. She had read about them in Teddy's diaries. She noted some Art Deco touches to the drawings of the buildings and even recognized two as still standing. The buildings had been funded, according to further paperwork she read, by Theodora DeLuca. It filled her with pride to see such a legacy.

From the fourth folder, Ellie took out a set of plans and saw that the drawings here were by Teddy. She recognized the building, though it took her a few seconds—it was strange to see the windows and doorway etched out in pencil on yellow paper.

"Holy hell!" she said, and for the second time that day, several heads swiveled in her direction.

The archivist issued a sharp, "Shhhh!"

Ellie did not look over or apologize. Instead, she stared dumbstruck at the drawings in front of her, scrutinizing every inch of the stone and woodwork. Lifting the drawing she pulled out a document from underneath and there was her absolute proof.

The proprietor of the building built in 1911 was Theodora DeLuca.

Ellie's apartment block. Anika's apartment block. Their children's apartment block. They were all living in a building designed, funded, and built by Ellie's great-great-grandmother.

"Teddy, you brilliant badass!" whispered Ellie, a huge grin lighting up her face. "No wonder I've always felt at home there. No wonder I've never wanted to leave."

CHAPTER 27
TEDDY

April 20, 1919. San Francisco, California.

Lil called over today. I knew by her face that she was stricken by my appearance. I've lost a lot of weight. She said I looked like a little bird. I told her I looked like that crusty old crow at the suffrage/hatpin meeting. She did guffaw at that.

Lil has certainly not lost any weight. If anything, she's gained a fair few pounds! I didn't say that to her, of course. She is my dear friend and I'd hate to upset her, but I do worry about her health.

She's still fundraising tirelessly for her firemen. Sometimes I think if Lillie were born a man, she would have been the fire chief in the city. Certainly, that's what she would have been.

Too tired to write. My eyes are giving me trouble. My hands ache.

April 25, 1919. San Francisco.

Matilda called over today and stayed most of the afternoon. I seem to be getting quite a lot of visitors these days. It does exhaust me, but it is nice to see people, I suppose. Alice seems most in charge of the comings and goings.

I don't get up early. In fact, if I'm being truly honest, I don't get up at all. All last week, I simply got out of the bed when the sheets were changed and got straight back in. I'm so tired. I miss my energy, my vitality. Where has it gone?

Matilda says it has all gone on others. On Indians. And suffrage. On buildings. On animals. On protesting against government men.

Perhaps she is right. Perhaps I have used up all my energy on others. And has it made a whit of difference? Was it all a waste? Were all my plans and efforts the folly of a dreamy girl?

I do not know.

It is hard to feel bright when you cannot leave the bed. I think about the Great War. Of all those young men lost. All those mothers and wives without their men. I think of Elizabeth as a nurse in Northern France, so close to the front lines enduring air raids and such. She wrote to me of her return to San Francisco this July (won't dear Alice be pleased at the reunion!). I wager she's forged nerves of iron by now and wouldn't bat an eye at a speedy bicycling jaunt.

I think about the great flu pandemic just last year that still looms. All the souls it claimed, and all the people Helki saved. What a thing to happen! A hundred years from now, medicine will be so advanced that such a calamity will be unthinkable.

I try not to feel weary. I try to be jolly for my visitors. But it is difficult.

Too tired to write more now.

April 30, 1919. San Francisco.

What will become of my Theodore? I fear I'm the only one who understands him and how to truly care for him. No one understands his foibles like I do. Matilda assures me that all will be well. And I can't see Ansel ever returning from New York. He likes the East Coast too much. He is quite the adventurer, like his father. Matilda says I mustn't get downhearted and I must keep my spirits up. But I don't want him to be a burden for her. She has her own life. When you have children, you don't expect that in your very latter years, you will still be worrying about them as adults in this way.

It was God's choice, I suppose, in the children he gave to me.

And took away.

May 2, 1919. San Francisco.

I've been having most vivid dreams. Momo comes to me over and over, holding out his palms. He doesn't say anything, just looks at me. Sometimes he's on his horse. Other times he's at that wall in Denver where we … oh, it seems so long ago now. Yet I still ache for him.

The aches of memory, the frailty of an old woman.

And George has appeared too! But it is a young Chicago George, not the George of his later years that would irk me so and cause quarrels. It's George when he thought I was a most fascinating creature. Always George was fascinated by me, I suppose. Or perhaps perplexed.

I am afraid to tell my visitors that I'm dreaming of the deceased. They say it is a sign. That they are visions, not dreams.

I will not tell Matilda. It would dreadfully upset her, I imagine.

May 12, 1919. San Francisco.

A contingent of suffragists visited me today! They're all atwitter, for the 19th Amendment will come before the house of representatives on the 21st. This is the greatest chance we've had since 1878.

All our work, all the decades of campaigning. It is within our grasp!

I have not been able to put my mind to rest since the ladies left.

Could we really win the vote? Could it finally be ours?

May 16, 1919. San Francisco.

A stampede of buffalo came through last night, trampling me, I thought, in my bed. It was terrible.
　More delusions.
　I feel so very weak. My body not my own any longer.

May 18, 1919. San Francisco.

Terrible fever.
　Doctor has confirmed the flu, Spanish.
　My hours are spent more sleeping than waking. A kit of carrier pigeons soars above me.
　Matilda dreadfully concerned about … me.
　The vote … three days' time.
　Too weak to write more.
　Vive les femmes. May we rise.

CHAPTER 28
ELLIE

February 2, 2020. San Francisco, California.

"Oh no! No, no, no!"

Ellie flicked past the last page of Teddy's inky scrawl, her fingers fluttering past blank page after blank page. Nothing.

In a panic, she ran to the closet, searching for the box of Teddy's items that had originally come from Enzo and Genevieve's attic and rifled through it in the vain hope that she had somehow missed a diary. Perhaps one had slipped from the stack, got caught under something else, been hidden all this time? But there was only the neat stack of the diaries she had already read, tied up with ribbon. That was it. Nothing more.

Vive les femmes. Those were the last words Teddy had written, a few days before the vote on the Nineteenth Amendment. Had she lived to see it pass? Could another diary have been lost? How much longer had Teddy lived?

She grabbed her phone and dialed Stanley.

"Dad," she said frantically when he answered. "I've just finished Teddy's diaries!"

"Oh, really?" he said. He sounded like he was in the garage. She heard Dogzilla barking, probably at a squirrel.

"Yes, just a few minutes ago. Have you any idea when she might have died? I don't know if this really is the last diary. I mean, she had the Spanish flu. Maybe she ... recovered?"

"Sorry, love dove. As I said before, I've no clue. We weren't exactly the best recordkeepers in our family. I mean I'd barely even heard of her till you started reading those diaries. Now, George? I knew all about George. He was a legend. But not Teddy."

"I feel so deflated," Ellie said, voice thick. "Like she just died in front of me."

Stanley chuckled. "I don't know why you let yourself get so worked up over this. I mean, you knew she was going to die, right?"

Ellie didn't find it amusing. She really did feel bereft.

"I know, Dad. But this feels so real. Like she was a friend. Like I knew her."

"Maybe you were very similar," said her father, who had been quite taken aback when Ellie had told him about her discovery on the origins of the apartment block. "By all accounts you two do seem to have a lot in common."

"I have to find out more," said Ellie. "I can't let it rest."

"Well, no better investigator to find out," he said kindly. "Hey," he added, before Ellie ended the call, "the housing officer for the university wants to do the exchange of keys this Friday. Could you handle that?"

"Eh, sure, Dad," said Ellie, wracking her brain through her appointment diary. Friday was usually a hectic day ahead of the weekend, but hopefully, she could squeeze it in and rush back to her desk, if BART was running smoothly and the officer could meet around lunchtime.

"I don't think there's any need for us to fly out again. We've said our goodbyes," said Stanley stoically. Enzo's house had now been fully cleared. All the paperwork had been completed and the funds transferred in what was a painless transaction with the university.

Feeling somewhat despondent, Ellie gathered up the boys and went across the hall, walked right into Anika's, and plopped onto her usual counter stool.

"Can we hang, or are you busy manifesting abundance or whatever?" asked Ellie.

"Well, hello, Sunshine. What's got your panties in a twist?"

"I finished Teddy's diaries. There are no more."

"Ah. Well, I get it. I felt like that when I finished Anne Frank's diary," said Anika. "It was terrible, turning the pages to … nothing. Wine?"

"May as well," said Ellie.

Anika filled Ellie in on the past few days' happenings; Ben was preparing for another trip to London, this time for ten days, while Milo had a terrible chesty cough. Ellie gave a tight-lipped smile and forced herself not to react to news of Ben's globe-trotting. Then, feeling her tension mounting, Ellie burst out that she had something important to tell Anika.

Anika spun round, her eyebrows raised.

"I haven't told anyone. I've been keeping it in for weeks now until I knew for sure," said Ellie quietly.

"Oh my God, you're pregnant. Is that why you're so unhinged? Hormones?"

"What?" said Ellie. "Christ in a casserole dish, Anika, why would you say that?"

"I dunno." Anika smiled. "I mean, who would blame you? Sam is a total hunk. If I had a man like that, I wouldn't let him out of the bedroom!"

Ellie snorted. "I'm not pregnant," she said.

Nowhere near it. Sam had found out in January that he had indeed been added to the panel for the new job in San Francisco, and this news had Ellie pulling away even further. They had only managed to see each other once since Thanksgiving weekend, for a quick coffee at UC Davis when Ellie had brought Luca for his appointment.

Ellie knew Sam was feeling disappointed and couldn't help but keep up the contact between them—it was he pursuing her—but she was still confused, her head and heart in conflict. She really, really liked Sam, but because of that, she didn't feel like she could really let herself fall for him. She had her family to think of, and her career. For the moment, her head had the lead over her heart. She didn't want to hurt him, and at the same time, she needed to protect herself.

"You're not sick, are you?" asked Anika now, seriously, her face dropping.

"No!" said Ellie. "It's Hutton & Fetterer."

"Ew."

And it all came gushing out of Ellie. "We're going to mediation. They want to settle. It could be all over, done and dusted, maybe as early as next week. And ... I think I love Sam, but I don't want to get married again, and I told him that 'cause I'm not gonna get trapped, but I don't want to lose him. And also, after reading Teddy's diaries, I'm not sure I'm even Italian, and I'm kind of freaking out!"

Anika chuckled lightly and placed her hand on Ellie's.

"Okay, my little hummingbird. You have permission to breathe. First of all: H&F! Wow! You are kidding!"

"Not even a little bit."

"Ding-dong!" Anika whooped, channeling her best Munchkin energy. She slammed their empty glasses down and rushed over to Ellie, giving her a massive bear hug. "I'm so, so happy for you. That is just the best news. I knew you could do it. You bested the evil empire, Elle Belle!"

"Well, I held them accountable," said Ellie. "I'm really happy and really relieved. And you know what? They may have done me a favor. The work I'm doing now is way more important."

"I'm so proud of you," said Anika. "Really. Now, as for sexy Sam. No duh you love him. Anyone with 20/400 vision and a cracked phone screen can see that. Talk to him, Elle. Let him in. That wonderful man has depth and breadth—not to mention the fact that he puts up with the likes of you! I bet you two can work something out that doesn't have to include marriage and you feeling caged."

Ellie nodded, wordless, her eyes shining.

"As for your heritage? Well, you can find out easily enough. They have easy home kits for that, you know."

"But do I even want to?" asked Ellie.

"Only you can decide that, supernova."

"Thank you," said Ellie. "And thank you for all your support. I couldn't have gotten through it without you. You really are my rock." Ellie felt tears glisten in her eyes. She would be totally and utterly lost without her friend.

"What are friends for?" Anika smiled. "Speaking of which, why didn't you tell me before I opened the cheap Chianti? I could have at least popped cheap prosecco!"

"Oh, I think it's the perfect occasion for a raffia-wrapped victory lap and questionable tannins," said Ellie, and they dissolved into laughter.

As Anika dished out food—ancient grains all around and chicken tenders for the kids—Ellie felt herself relax into the peaceful harmony of simply being together. She had finally revealed her happy secret, and with it went the tension oozing from her shoulders.

"Why don't you try the library?" asked Anika, nudging aside her now-empty bowl.

"What do you mean?" asked Ellie.

"Why don't you see if the main library has any records on Teddy? Don't they do those old newspapers, on microfilm or something? I bet she made the papers at some stage."

"Why didn't I think of that?" said Ellie, looking completely intrigued.

"Always glad to help," said Anika to which Ellie held out her glass.

"Could you help with more wine?"

The two women fell into a fit of youthful giggles that startled not just the kids but Bravo the Labrador too, and he waddled over to them, wagging his tail.

What was all the fuss about? And could he play too?

Ellie stood for the longest time in her old bedroom at Enzo's house, staring at the tartan wallpaper. So many hours over so many years, just staring at that pattern as she lay in her single bed night after night.

The bed was gone. The armoire was gone. The shelves remained mounted to the wall but were now completely empty. This had been a sanctuary. It was here in this place, that she'd really gotten to know herself. Here, she'd spent hours reading, writing in her own diary, dreaming of her future, listening to the soft movements of Enzo and Genevieve as they puttered about the house, and the sound of a football game on the television. Feeling at home.

It was hard to believe that they were gone now and that she was no longer a teenage girl and a Cal student starting out in life. Back then, life had seemed slow. Back then, she couldn't wait to get going. She couldn't wait to graduate, start earning her nest egg, achieving her goals. Yet in hindsight, it had all flickered by so fast. How was she a grown woman now, with her own family? She still felt like that little girl inside—vulnerable and unsure. Unsure if she was good enough. Unsure if she could actually get through life.

Walking over to the bedside wall, she touched the wallpaper one last time, feeling its slight bareness under her fingertips. The room looked much smaller now, with all Enzo's belongings taken away. She couldn't bear to close the door as she left, so she left it wide open as if to say, *Hey, you can come back anytime.*

In the kitchen, she ran her hands along the cupboards and the work surfaces. She thought of Genevieve's hands as they'd wiped and worked, as she'd smoothed her apron and ran her fingers behind her ear, pushing away nonexistent strands of hair, in a hangover from her youth. Genevieve's hair had been cut short many decades before, like all women of her era.

Enzo's slow, shuffling movements seemed to follow her about the house now, as if he were right there with her. As if he was wondering where all his things—his great black leather easy chair—had gone.

She'd been so busy preparing for this day, giving up her free time after work and at weekends to undertake the gargantuan task of clearing a house fully from three generations of active living. The whole process had been exhausting, but now that it was completed and she was spending her very last moments in this beloved place, she realized the clear-out had been cathartic.

It was all over now, the only remnants remaining of these lived lives the many sentimental items she'd kept, some in memory boxes, others finding new homes in spots around her apartment. The mammoth tooth had gone into the boys' room. The mirror hung by a ribbon in her kitchen. She had come to understand the importance of family heirlooms but also of letting go.

The knock came to the door, and the university's housing procurement officer seemed a little frazzled and under pressure. He looked far too young to Ellie to be handling something as complex as a property sale. Her *grandparents'* house sale.

"I'm just required to do a quick final visual inspection," he said, stepping into the house, while Ellie waited in the empty living room, staring at the fireplace, which looked cold and lonely.

Genevieve had hung up Ellie's stocking each Christmas there—one embroidered with *Santa, I can explain!*—even after she'd moved out. Ellie turned and looked out the living room window for the last time. Then she closed her eyes in a silent goodbye.

Bye, Enzo. Genevieve. Thank you—for everything.

"All set," said the housing officer, rejoining her in the living room. "Good to go?"

"Yep," said Ellie brightly, her voice belying the emotion clogging her throat.

For the last time, Ellie walked out the front door of her grandparents' house and turned the key in the lock. With ceremony, she dropped the keys into the housing officer's palm.

"Thank you so much," she said.

"We have great plans for this place," he said. "You should come back and visit when it's finished."

"I could do that," she said, nodding, although she wasn't sure if she really could. She wanted to remember the house as it was now. She wasn't quite ready to see any torn-down walls and the familiar tartan wallpaper stripped away.

Ellie felt her phone buzzing in her bag. It was time to go. She walked away, down the flagstone path, then took a moment to turn and gaze upon her grandparents' house once more. Taking the phone from her bag while simultaneously waving goodbye to the housing officer, Ellie noticed the New York phone number before answering quickly, keeping the call from rolling to voicemail.

"Ellie Benvenuto?"

She listened as a richly accented and elegant voice introduced herself as Jasmine Nouri, president of UN Women.

"Oh," said Ellie, totally taken aback. "Hi!"

Jasmine said she'd been impressed by her *New York Times Magazine* piece, and she'd seen the viral tweet about Hansa's case and discovered Ellie was the lawyer on the case.

"Eh, yes, well, it was her sister who took to social media, but yes, we're actively — *I'm* actively — handling that case."

"Well, your name keeps coming up for me. You're making a real difference," said Jasmine. "We have our sixty-fourth annual session of the UN Commission on the Status of Women coming up, March 9. Now, there's some sort of virus circulating in China, and a few of our overseas speakers are a bit edgy and have canceled their travel plans. It's opened up a few speaker spots. How would you be fixed to be added to a panel? The topic is women and girls as caregivers and the caregiver economy, or we have another panel on refugees and workplace discrimination. Actually, I think you'd be really well placed for either—or both. If you were interested in that, Ellie?"

Ellie felt her heart miss a beat. UN Women wanted her to speak? At the actual United Nations?

"Um, yes, yes, I'd love to!" she replied, trying to keep her cool.

"Great," said Jasmine. "You'll be a wonderful addition. My office will be in touch about the logistics. Great to have you on board!"

And with that, the deal was done. In just over a month, Ellie would be flying to New York—to speak at the sixty-fourth UN Commission on the Status of Women!

Wow, she thought. Teddy would have grinned like she'd won a bet no one knew she'd placed. And then, her thoughts fell to the boys, and reality set in. How could she just skip off to New York City? The session would be during the working week. The ILDC would support her doing this, but what about the boys? Could Anika take them? Could Joe? Unlike Ben, she didn't have the freedom to jet off to the next shiny new robot toy.

Taking a last long look at Enzo's house, Ellie went to sit in her car, gathering her thoughts. So much was racing through her mind. Her phone beeped and she saw a message from her assistant.

"In case you don't get to check emails, your 2:45 p.m. has had to cancel. Next appt is 4 p.m."

Suddenly she had the grace of an extra hour.

Feeling adrenaline coarse through her, she pulled out and quickly drove through the narrow streets of North Berkeley, parking her car in her favorite secret unmonitored spot right on campus behind Sproul Hall.

She hopped out, passing by the campanile, also known as Sather Tower, the ivory bell tower that watched over the campus. It now seemed like yesterday she'd run around these buildings as a young student on her own way to lectures. She slowed as she neared the building, one of her favorite spots on campus. There it was, the dignified halls of the otherwise unassuming-looking Bancroft Library.

She'd meant to check the San Francisco History Center next week at the main library, across the street from the law school, where she was due to supervise clinic students. But why wait?

C'mon, Teddy, she thought as she opened the heavy doors into the library, her emotions electric after saying goodbye to the house, getting the call from Jasmine, and now having an unexpected, glorious research hour all to herself in this magnificent treasure chest of a library.

"Show me what you got, Great-Great-Grandmama. Bid me a proper farewell."

SAN FRANCISCO SUN
May 29, 1919

The city mourns the loss of Theodora Ellis DeLuca, a well-known figure in the city of San Francisco, famed for her philanthropy and generosity to the inhabitants of the city. Her family confirmed her death of Spanish flu.

Born originally in North Sandwich, Boston, Theodora "Teddy" Ellis lived in Chicago and pioneered to San Francisco across the plains in the 1870s. She married George DeLuca, "Monte Cristo of the Klondikes," an entrepreneur and miner who made his fortune in the Yukon gold rush and perished at sea in 1899.

Mrs. DeLuca, well known for her forthright opinions, cut quite the figure in San Francisco society throughout the decades and was an early adopter of both the bicycle and the motorcar. She was a keen horsewoman and a lover of animals and built an animal shelter to house pets in need, one of the first of its kind in the United States, as part of her Indian Center on Vallejo Street.

Mrs. DeLuca braved a keen interest in Indian affairs and campaigned against their mistreatment. She was a suffragist and an agitator on hatpin laws, defeating a proposed ban of such in San Francisco. A large contingent of masked San Francisco Suffragists Association were present at her funeral and read a eulogy at her graveside, making much of the fact that she died on May 22, the day after the 19th Amendment was passed in the U.S. House of Representatives.

A keen artist and reader from a young age, according to her surviving family, Mrs. De Luca studied architecture at U.C. Berkeley and drew many of the plans for the buildings she funded and had built after the great earthquake of 1906. Her legacy lives on in a number of beautifully designed buildings throughout the city.

She is survived by her daughter Matilda, who is married to journalist Mr. Edmund Beauchamp; her son Ansel, who traveled from New York for her funeral; her lamented son Theodore; and three grandchildren.

May she rest in peace.

CHAPTER 29
ELLIE

March 6, 2020. San Francisco, California.

"Oh wow, did you hear?" said Anika, scrolling her phone while seated cross-legged on a floor cushion. Her spine stayed effortlessly straight, the stillness of her morning meditation still clinging to her like a second skin. Oddly, Anika was hooked on social media, particularly her Instagram account, where she liked to post motivational quotes. Ellie suspected she maybe even had a secret account or two to spy on Ben, going against her claims that the conglomerate-led tech bros were mining not just her data but her chakras too.

"No. Can I buy a vowel?" said Ellie, wondering what she should have heard about when Anika didn't give her any clues.

"They stopped a Princess cruise ship coming ashore. It's docked in the bay. Twenty-one people on board have tested positive for COVID-19!"

"Yikes," said Ellie. "That's terrifying. Trapped on a ship with a virus spreading? And I thought 'Snakes on a Plane' was a creepy thriller movie pitch."

"Well, we certainly don't want it coming ashore here," said Anika.

"It probably already is here, according to my mom," said Ellie.

"What?" said Anika, her eyes now torn away from her screen. "In the city?"

"Yep, she said with the airport being international and direct flights, you know, coming straight from Asia, it's probably been here a while. She says being in an airport and flying at all is the last thing I should be doing. She really doesn't want me to go. And clearly, she's not going to take the risk either."

"Well, that's … wildly unsettling," said Anika, her eyebrows lifting. "If your mom is right, we're all screwed."

"I know, right? She said this virus is going to be bigger than anything she's experienced in her lifetime," said Ellie.

"Bigger than bird flu?" Anika asked.

"She says we have no idea."

"Isn't your mom a bit … you know, doomsday when it comes to these things?"

"She can be," said Ellie. But that was the job, she supposed. Planning for worst-case scenarios.

"But you're still going? Maybe you should listen to your mom."

"Well …" Ellie paused.

Ellie didn't feel like she could back out of the convention now. Jasmine had told her when she'd confirmed her spot a few days ago, that they'd already had a lot of speakers pull out. And besides, Ellie didn't want to. She couldn't remember feeling so excited about anything else in her career—except, perhaps, the day she got into UC Berkeley, the day she graduated, or her first day at Hutton & Fetterer. Maybe it was selfish, but speaking at the sixty-fourth annual session of the UN Commission on the Status of Women was quite the satin sash of distinction—as Teddy might put it.

"Well, yeah. It's too late to back out now. Everything is in place. Besides, I mean, this is kinda my *Katniss volunteers as tribute* moment, right?"

"Damn straight it is."

They both giggled, Ellie desperately hoping her overly cautious epidemiologist mother was being … overly cautious.

Originally, Simona had agreed to fly out from Chicago to care for the boys from Sunday until Tuesday, with Anika as her trusty sidekick. Joe would have them Friday and Saturday evening and would pick Simona up on Sunday and bring her back to the apartment to take over with the boys. It was a ninja-level stealth mission of coordination—minus the cool soundtrack. But just yesterday, with more rumors of the virus swirling even among laypeople, Simona had called and, with regret, told Ellie she couldn't travel to San Francisco on Sunday. She didn't feel it was safe, and she was in demand at work. It had left Ellie scrambling to put new plans in place. Seeing Ellie's distress over the whole thing, Anika had stepped in and told her that of course, she'd take the boys and ordered Ellie not to worry. "I know you'll pay me back in contraband Nutella brownies!"

Ellie really owed her a lot more than brownies.

"Are you sure?" she'd repeated. "Really? You don't mind?"

"Ellie, stop. They're practically mine at this point. Besides, Leila and Milo dressing Nathan up like a pint-sized *Chorus Line* extra with feather boas and jazz hands actually gives me a break. And Luca's happy staring at my ceiling fan until the planet entropies. Beyond that, it's just a bit of transportation and extra pasta. Next time come to me with, like, a *real* problem!"

When she put it like that, Ellie couldn't argue. Her dreams of a maternal commune had somewhat come to pass; they were simply separated by the front doors of their respective apartments that they hardly kept locked anyway.

Now, adding the various meals she had prepared to cover the time she'd be away to Anika's refrigerator, Ellie felt the thrill of anticipation of what the next few days would bring. She could never have imagined this time last year that she'd be in such a position.

Taking on Hutton & Fetterer had changed her life, given her a profile, and brought her back, if not even further along, on the career trajectory she had imagined for herself. More than that, the caregiver protection Ruby had presented to the EEOC had been turned into official agency guidelines, and Ruby was working toward formal legislation now.

She was reminded of what Martha had said during their card reading. *Your actions in the coming year will generate big results. It is now much easier to manifest your dreams. Wonders are blossoming in your life, including great love.*

Was Sam her great love?

Oh, Sam. She had pushed him away again and again, turning down his requests to meet with one excuse or another. Just last week, giving in to her own desire, she'd met him at the Claremont Hotel in Berkeley, where they'd spent glorious hours reconnecting. But in the days that followed, the old hesitation returned. She still couldn't bring herself to agree to his wish for exclusivity. Once again, she'd left him dangling—unwilling to commit.

"Try and get some rest," urged Anika as Ellie made for the door.

"I will," she said.

Later, after Ellie had hugged the boys to within an inch of them needing CPR when Joe picked them up, she tended to some last-minute packing. Her suitcase was already stocked with the latest fashion shipment from Martha, who'd sent Ellie the pitch-perfect ensemble for her UN debut. A sharp knock came to the door, and thinking it would be Anika, Ellie threw it open wide, dressed in her plush robe, her hair disheveled and her makeup long wiped free.

There stood Dr. Sam Varma, looking as dashing as ever.

"Sam!" she cried. "What are you doing here?"

They embraced, Ellie unable to stop herself from dissolving into him just a little, wrapping her arms tightly around his neck. His warmth and scent filled her, stirring both desire and comfort as they held on for a long moment.

"I had to see you before you go," he said. "I drove here straight after work."

"But why?"

"Sit," he commanded, and Ellie laughed.

"Okay, bossy!" She sat down in Enzo's majestic black leather recliner, salvaged from the grand purge of her grandparents' home.

Sam began rooting in the backpack he had brought.

"The airport is probably the worst place you can be going," he muttered as he searched in his bag.

"That's what my mom said," said Ellie.

"And she would know! I know you're set on going to go to New York. And I would never tell you what to do …"

"You just told me to sit!" teased Ellie.

"But …" he said, and he produced a plastic envelope containing what looked like a flattened mask, the type you'd wear for hazardous material removal, the word *Medical* emblazoned on the packaging, out of the bottom of his bag.

"As a doctor, I advise you to wear this at the airport, on the plane, and at the conference as much as possible."

"I'm not planning on demolishing asbestos!" Ellie joked, turning the mask he'd handed her over in her hand.

"Funny you mention asbestos," said Sam. "This virus attacks the lungs. That's what they're seeing, in Asia and now in Europe. Terrible respiratory problems. I think we're really unprepared here, when this thing gets out of hand."

It was a bit of a downer, Ellie thought, her last night before she went away to be listening to this end-of-the-world stuff. But the fact that Sam had driven all the way down here meant he was really worried—and wanted to protect her.

"Okay, okay. I'll be a good patient." She held up the mask. "Do I at least get a lollipop for compliance?"

Sam sat on the sofa opposite and gazed at her. He looked so beautiful, she thought, his soft eyes boring into her.

"Could I fix you a seltzer or something?" she said, starting to rise from the recliner.

"No," he said. "No, I want to … Well, I'd like to talk, Ellie. Properly."

"Oh, jeez," said Ellie. Really? A deep and meaningful? Now?

"I know you've been pushing me away," Sam said. "And I get it. You've built a life on your terms, and you don't want to lose that. But I don't want to change you, Ellie. I don't need marriage. I just need you."

Ellie let out a small, embarrassed snort. Wow. Straight to the point, huh?

"Well, that's a relief," she said.

"I want to be with you. I need to be with you. I'm tired of this in-between—never knowing when we'll see each other, or if you even want to."

"I do want to," Ellie said softly. "I do. An awful lot. Too much."

"I feel that. But then you disappear on me."

"I know," she said. "And I hate that I do."

"Can't we figure something out? Once I move up here, I'll be around. But I don't want you to feel awkward, like you have to keep your distance. Let's be honest about what we want and just … make a plan. If once a month is all you can give, fine. I'll count the days. Whatever works."

"Oh, Sam." Ellie shook her head gently. "Of course I want to see you. Quite a lot, actually. It's just—it's not that simple."

"But it is," he said. "You're making it complicated."

"No," she said. "I'm being realistic. You're going to want to get married someday. Have children. I know you will."

"You don't know what I want," Sam said. "What I want is you. And you keep pushing me away."

He pinched the bridge of his nose, and Ellie saw it—he was trying not to cry.

Her heart cracked open just then. She scooted beside him and took his hand.

"I'm so sorry," she whispered, folding into his arms again. He ran his fingers through her hair, messy and unwashed, and she felt more wanted than she had in years.

"Please," he said. "Stop pushing me away. I'm not trying to trap you. I want you to be free—and I want you. I want us. Whatever that looks like. Something that works for both of us. You're the one who said relationships don't have to follow the old script. And honestly? That's not even fringe anymore."

"I don't want to stop seeing you," she murmured.

"Then we won't." His voice brightened. "We'll make it work?"

"I guess we can," she said, a quiet smile blooming. "I'd like that."

And then his mouth found hers, and he pulled her so close she thought he might consume her completely.

"Did you just come here because you guessed the boys would be away?" she asked coyly, standing up and leading him toward the bedroom.

"No. I came to bring you that mask," he said. "But if the house is free, then what a bonus, huh?"

March 9, 2020. New York City.

"Look at you," said Leo, embracing her tightly, Ellie feeling the sinews on his back. He looked even more gaunt in person than he had on the laptop screen at Thanksgiving. "You look great! Even though it's hard to recognize you under that mask!"

Ellie wanted to return the compliment, but she didn't want to sound insincere. She felt a little silly wearing the mask Sam had given her. Hardly anyone was wearing one.

"Brother, what are they feeding you over there because it doesn't look like much! It's so great to see you!"

Leo shrugged. He'd never been a foodie.

They sat for their coffee, Ellie's second that day, but she needed the extra spring in her step—today was the big day. She took the mask off to drink and to speak to Leo, but she would put it back on when walking through crowds in the conference center.

"I'm pretty lucky to be here," he said. "My NGO got me back but may not have if they'd waited even another day."

"I'll bet," said Ellie, picking at a glazed doughnut. "Mom wouldn't even take the chance. When is your flight booked for Chicago?"

"Well, I was going to take a few days here in New York, meet up with some friends, but I changed my itinerary over the weekend and I fly out tonight."

"I think that's a good idea," said Ellie, fearing that he might not get out to see their parents at all if he didn't move soon. "Though Mom will probably quarantine you in the doghouse for a week."

"She's careful like that," joked Leo. "Besides, I don't mind bunking with Dogzilla."

"Hopefully, they'll get it contained fast and you'll be back out to Malawi in no time," said Ellie.

"Hopefully," said Leo. "I've seen firsthand how quickly these things can spread. But you know, we have good resources in the West. The problem is we're constantly on the move."

"Yup," said Ellie.

"All set for your speech?" asked Leo. "How are the nerves?"

"Pretty good, considering."

"It's a big deal," said Leo. "We're all proud of you, sis."

"I know," she said.

"Mom snail-mailed me a copy of the *New York Times Magazine*."

"You and all her friends," said Ellie, with a mock face-plant.

Ellie lifted the coffee cup to her lips and, from the corner of her eye, caught the entrance of a woman radiating peak Girl Boss energy—Jasmine Nouri, sweeping in with an entourage of clipboard-wielding staffers, and the kind of presence that made people instinctively straighten their posture and curse their coffee breath. The conference was kicking off in just over half an hour, and the atmosphere buzzed with last-minute tension. Jasmine spotted Ellie and strode right toward her.

"Ellie Benvenuto!" she said, holding out her hand for Ellie to shake.

"Um ..." said Ellie, desperately not wanting to appear rude. "My epidemiologist mother says I'm not allowed ... because ... science." She nodded at Jasmine's hand while keeping her own firmly by her side.

God, this was torturous.

"Oh," said Jasmine, blinking and withdrawing her palm. "Of course."

"This is my brother, Leo," said Ellie, changing the subject. "He's just flown in from Malawi. He's a procurement specialist with an NGO."

"Oh, good guy to know," said Jasmine.

Ellie expected Jasmine had been up against it over the weekend as more and more participants had decided not to travel due to restrictions being put in place and fear over the spread of the virus. The program had been truncated, and Ellie was due to speak just before lunch. Still, the woman was the epitome of professionalism and managed to look completely unflappable.

"Listen, Ellie, while I have you, I'd like to talk to you about something

"... A colleague of mine at the Friends of Islam Society in San Francisco, funnily enough, got in touch with me about a case of a woman called Bita Massoudi from Iran."

"Oh," said Ellie, bending her head slightly to listen over the drone of the espresso machine.

"She was a professor over there at a university but fled due to the violence she experienced at the hands of the morality police on the hijab laws. Here, she's been working teaching Spanish at an after-school elementary program in San Francisco, and a group of parents approached her and accused her of imposing her religion on their children just for wearing her hijab. They said that her hijab was confusing for the children and a 'symbol of female oppression.'"

"I see," said Ellie, nodding.

"Bita became fearful of returning to the school, reported the matter, and after a week they 'investigated' and found 'no evidence of harassment.'" Jasmine mimed air quotes with both hands.

"They then required her to remove her hijab as a condition of continuing to teach in the after-school program. When Bita refused, they fired her. Seeing your work on Hansa Nambootiri's case, I think you'd be ideally placed to help. Would you be interested?"

Ellie was taken aback. Hansa's case had been settled the week before, the insurers paying out a hefty sum after the case continued to go viral and sales at the chain of discount dollar stores declined. The settlement would get Hansa the surgery she needed and enable her to move on with a more comfortable life.

"Sure," said Ellie. "I'm interested. That's what I do!"

"That's what you do best!" Jasmine said. "I'll have my assistant send you the details?"

"Okay," said Ellie. "Great!"

"Best of luck later; see you in there," said Jasmine and she moved on. Ellie sat back down at the table.

"Well, look at you. In demand. Corporate lawyer turned social justice avenger," said Leo.

"Okay, smart-ass. But yeah. It's busier than ever," said Ellie. "There are so many cases. So many people egregiously mistreated and just left to … suffer. Like they don't even matter."

They sat in comfortable silence finishing their drinks, two siblings at one in each other's company listening to the hubbub around them. After their coffees, they left the café and made their way toward the auditorium for the opening address.

"What's that in your hair?" asked Leo, pointing to Ellie's head as she walked ahead of him across the lobby.

She touched the back of her head and felt the elastic of Sam's mask pulled tight. She had pinned her hair in a neat chignon, in a style that would have looked rather chic on Teddy herself.

"This," said Leo and she felt him touch the letter T at the end of the metal arrow.

Ellie moved her hand around and felt the tip of the hatpin—the very arrow that had brought Teddy and Momo together—and its skewer pushed through her hair. She shivered.

"Just a little good luck heirloom. It once belonged to a great, great woman. And now it's mine."

"Huh," said Leo. "It's cool. C'mon, there's two good seats over there."

They moved toward them, Ellie listening to the sounds of the delegates filing in. Soon she would be on that stage. Soon, she would have the room in her command, talking about unmet needs and how they could make progress to meet them.

It had been one hundred years since the death of her great-great-grandmother. And when she made her way to that podium and felt the nerves rattle and her breath quicken, all she had to do was pat the hatpin in her hair for courage, close her eyes, and place her hand on her heart.

For there beat the spirit of Teddy. And Helki. And Lillie. And Genevieve. And Simona. And all the great women who had gone before her and she had come to know. There was the legacy. There was a woman's soul.

54828 JOURNAL—CITY COUNCIL—CHICAGO 10/28/97
COMMITTEE ON POLICE AND FIRE.
EXONERATION OF MRS. O'LEARY AND HER COW FROM ALL BLAME IN REGARD TO GREAT CHICAGO FIRE OF 1871

The Committee on Police and Fire submits the following report:

CHICAGO, October 6, 1997.

To the President and Members of the City Council:

Your Committee on Police and Fire held a meeting on Monday, October 6, 1997, and having had under consideration a resolution introduced by Alderman Edward M. Burke (14th Ward) to forever exonerate Mrs. O'Leary and her cow from all blame in regard to the Great Chicago Fire of 1871, begs leave to report and recommend that Your Honorable Body Adopt the proposed substitute resolution transmitted herewith.

This recommendation was concurred in by all members of the committee present, with no dissenting votes.

Respectfully submitted,

(Signed) WILLIAM M. BEAVERS,

Chairman.

Author's Note

(Yep. Ellie got COVID. She was dreadfully sick, recovered, and rolled up her sleeves again.)

I did end up in a role with UN Women, though the sixty-fourth annual session of the UN Commission on the Status of Women in New York City was canceled due to COVID-19. Instead, it convened for a procedural meeting on March 9, 2020.

Speaking of what "really happened" versus what didn't, let's get the most pressing question out of the way: **How much of this story is true?**

TL;DR answer: most of it. Either specifically or generally.

While remastering the 1919 unpublished manuscript of my great-great-grandfather George Francis Ellis, I was struck by a couple of things.

First, his remarkable feats and near-mythic adventures—surviving against mind-boggling odds, moving through a world teeming with risk, opportunity, and reinvention. He really was on a train with General Custer. He really saw Buffalo Bill on the frontier. And in 1896, he really went to Alaska on business for the North American Transportation and Trading Company—before the gold rush frenzy had fully ignited.

He was ahead of his time, securing claims No. 12 and 13 on El Dorado Creek, which, for a period, yielded $10,000 every twenty-four hours, making him an immense fortune—before he lost it in spectacular fashion, as these Old West legends often go. Joaquin Miller, in his *Letters from Alaska*, dubbed him "the Monte Cristo of the Klondike."

Second, I noticed the paucity of women in his account. His story is thrilling—but it is also a white man's story, recorded in a white man's world. The women and Indigenous people he encountered are mere footnotes in his manuscript, mentioned in passing and quickly discarded.

His own wife, my pioneering great-great-grandmother Mary Rogers Ellis (aka "Teddy"), is not even named (though known through other sources).

This is how women's and other nonwhite male histories have been sublimated. But history—real history—is not so singular.

Using the breadcrumbs George left behind, I tracked down these forgotten figures and their extraordinary, turbulent lives.

Some women did disguise themselves as men to work claims in the gold mines. Cities did pass laws banning people from dressing outside their gender. In San Francisco, an 1863 ordinance made it illegal to appear in public in "a dress not belonging to his or her sex." "Teddy" lived within these shifting constraints—leveraging them, outmaneuvering them, defying them when necessary.

Madame Bowers, the San Francisco fortune teller? Real. As is Ellie's reading at The Palmer House in Chicago, reflecting my own. Madame Bowers's prediction in this novel is word for word from my great-great-grandfather's papers. The difference in real life? George heeded her warning—he skipped the voyage she predicted would lead to his death. That ship vanished at sea, and all aboard were lost.

The Chicago counterfeiter Mrs. Joubert, P. B. Weare, Elizabeth Ashe, Alice Griffith, Lillie Hitchcock Coit—all real.

Elizabeth Ashe and Alice Griffith (born 1869 and 1868, respectively) founded San Francisco's first settlement house in 1890, providing health care, day care, and education for immigrant families living in overcrowded, unsanitary conditions. Their work remains foundational to this day, and "Tel-Hi," the community center they founded, is just a few blocks from my home in San Francisco.

Lillie Hitchcock Coit (born 1843) was an eccentric and fearless figure, smoking cigars and wearing trousers before it was socially acceptable and dressing as a man to gamble in North Beach's male-only establishments. She fled San Francisco after a scandal at The Palace Hotel in 1903, resurfacing years later after cooling her jets in Paris for a while—in time for the hotel's 1909 post-fire reopening, where she took up rooms again. She was a well-known supporter of firefighters in the city, having been made an honorary member of Knickerbocker Engine Company No. 5 as a teenager. Her legacy and the design of Coit Tower (built in 1933) have become intertwined with the city's firefighting history, with the Art Deco–style tower resembling a firehose nozzle (though not the design intention of its architects).

Amadeo Pietro Giannini, who founded the Bank of Italy (later Bank of America), was instrumental in rebuilding San Francisco after the 1906 earthquake and fire. His radical idea? Lending money to working-class immigrants when no other banks would. (Fun fact: my boys attended A. P. Giannini Middle School in San Francisco.)

Given that George wrote his manuscript the same year the US Congress passed the Nineteenth Amendment (of which George was not a fan) and that his exploits unfolded during the industrial revolution—the single greatest driver of women's economic and social mobility in history—I felt an imperative to surface the untold stories of women and Indigenous people who shaped the American frontier. In fact, the timing felt rather urgent, as women's evanescent rights correlate with climate crises and the depletion of the very resources that made them possible.

Ellie's Clients: fictional names, real cases drawn directly from my own career

Fernanda Salinas represents the many undocumented women I assisted who fled unlivable conditions in Mexico and were separated from their children after a series of unfortunate events.

Hansa's case: I really did discover the red pushpin photo and caption on my own. Like the real "Hansa," many women fear pursuing justice, even when the evidence is irrefutable—and often avoid mentioning key details, even to their own attorneys, when they are embarrassing. Also, like "Hansa," my client didn't wear a bindi and, therefore, dismissed the photo as too stupid to be significant.

Bita Massoudi's case? Also real. Aggression toward women often manifests subtly. While in her home country, Bita may have faced a brutal beating for an improperly donned hijab; in the US, her oppressor was a bit less menacing.

Ellie's Own Struggles

Her wrongful termination.

Her battle as a special needs mother (including all those MIND Institute trips, the ping-ponging feelings, passion for her children, and emergency dried bean extraction with tweezers);

Her fight against a former employer who underestimated her;

All my own.

The Timesheet-Gate scandal? Real.

The crack about "this is the last of the pregnant women, right?" and the email stating I couldn't "toe the line" with a special needs child? Real. (I remember vividly because *toe* was misspelled as *T-O-W*. Lawyers. If it's not in Latin, we can't spell it. And if it is Latin, it probably means something bad.

In fact, every word and deed attributed to the fictionally named Hutton & Fetterer law firm and its characters is directly sourced from my career.

My case leading to EEOC guidelines and legislation on caregiver discrimination and landing the cover feature of *The New York Times Magazine*? Also real. At the time—about a dozen years before the timeline represented here—caregiver discrimination was not yet a protected category. My battle, alongside others, helped push for change. The real "Ruby Martinez" at UC College of the Law, San Francisco (formerly UC Hastings), was the one who convinced me to stand up and fight—at a time when I'd been knocked down and thought I'd better stay down.

And yes, I taught at both the UC law schools where Ellie supervises law clinic students, and was a student in the Workers' Rights Clinic myself during law school before becoming a volunteer supervising attorney for years.

A Personal Connection to North Beach & the Coast Miwok

My Italian roots trace back to early San Francisco and North Beach. Ellie's flat in North Beach? Based on a real five-unit building on Greenwich Street, designed by Paul DeMartini, built by Julius Martinelli, and commissioned by Albert Pezzi in 1913. As of the completion of this manuscript, it's still owned by the Pezzi family.

In 1994, I volunteered at Olompali State Park in Marin County, California, braiding tule reed for the construction of new huts (called *kotchas*) for a replica Miwok village. The park's neglect and erasure of Miwok history when I returned (in 2024 for this novel)? Also real.

The myth of Indigenous extinction is dangerous. The Coast Miwok still exist.

As Coast Miwok and UC Berkeley professor Peter Nelson puts it:

> "Portraying us as broken, divorced, and relocated from our history and knowledge is harmful. Our allies, co-conspirators, and accomplices must join us in celebrating the empowerment, health, and well-being of our communities."

A Whisper from the Past

One day, while sorting through my family's artifacts, I found a carefully swaddled monogrammed hatpin.

It belonged to my great-great-grandmother.

Holding it, I felt as though she were whispering to me across a century—her voice a flickering campfire, keeping a story ablaze.

This novel is my answer to her.

And Finally, about Mrs. O'Leary's Cow

No, it did not start the Great Chicago Fire—but anti-Irish immigrant sentiment made sure Catherine O'Leary took the blame (not her husband, Patrick, despite how uncommon it was at the time for a woman to own her own property or chattel).

Besides, as Teddy aptly noted: Who milks a cow at 9:00 p.m., which is when the fire broke out?

The fire started near their barn, but meteorological data suggests a meteor shower and wind patterns carrying embers across Lake Michigan to the dry conditions in Chicago were the true cause. Growing up in a small town outside of Chicago, "Mrs. O'Leary's cow" was what we were taught in school. Not until 1997 was the O'Leary name cleared (though the cow was exonerated eleven years earlier in 1986—no joke).

At any rate, the fire left George Ellis "broke and in debt to P. B. about three thousand dollars," so we women were nothing but trouble when all was said and done. And since the story wouldn't be complete without blaming a woman for the downfall of civilization, that tracks.

As Jane Goodall put it:

> "It actually doesn't take much to be considered a difficult woman. That's why there are so many of us."

The real "Teddy," Mary Rogers Ellis; and George F. Ellis, my great-great-grandparents

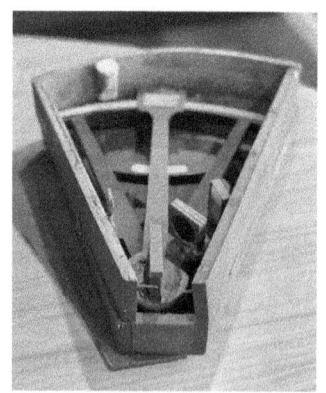 

George's sextant from his 1896 Klondike voyage and the mammoth molar

Ellie's apartment building on Telegraph Hill in 1913 (pre–Coit Tower)

1909 Reopening of The Palace Hotel

Ellie's Puttanesca Sauce
(Chapter 1—prepared by Anika)

Puttanesca pairs well with a long thick (or flat) pasta shape such as spaghetti, bucatini (my personal choice), tagliatelle, or fettuccine.

- ¼ cup olive oil
- 1 cup finely chopped onion
- 6 cloves minced garlic
- 2 tablespoons minced anchovy fillets (about 8 fillets)*
- 2 (28-ounce) cans crushed tomatoes, with juice
- (optional) 1 glass of dry white wine (after you've taken 2 sips, which is all Ellie got)
- 1 cup tightly packed Kalamata olives, pitted and halved
- 2 tablespoons tomato paste
- 2 tablespoons drained capers
- 1 tablespoon minced fresh basil (or 1 teaspoon dried crushed basil)
- ½ teaspoon dried crushed red pepper flakes

In a large pot, heat the olive oil over medium-high heat. Add the onion and sauté until soft and lightly caramelized, about 6 minutes. Add the garlic and anchovies and cook an additional 2 minutes. Add the tomatoes and the remaining ingredients and simmer until the sauce is thickened and slightly reduced, about 40 minutes.

Adjust seasoning to taste. Don't be hasty to add salt because this sauce is already salty with the anchovies and olives.

Finally, as always, add your perfectly al dente pasta to the sauce—not the other way around!

*Can't stand anchovies? Ditto. But I read on the page of John Thompson's—the Canadian food blogger—that there isn't really an alternative, unless you use anchovy paste a little at a time, instead of anchovy fillets. Some people substitute tuna, but Thompson doesn't buy it. The point is to add umami depth to the finished sauce rather than the taste of anchovies. So, I went with it and can vouch for it!

Ellie's Salted Nutella ("Apology") Brownies

- 1 (26-ounce) jar Nutella
- 5 eggs
- 1 cup all-purpose flour
- Coarse sea salt (for sprinkling)

Preheat oven to 350°F.

Line a 9x13-inch baking dish with parchment paper and spray with baking spray. (Helpful hint: Spraying the dish before lining it with parchment helps keep the parchment in place.) If this pan size feels big for brownies—trust the process!

In a large mixing bowl, whisk 5 eggs together.

Microwave the Nutella (be sure to completely remove the foil seal first!) for 30 seconds to 1 minute, just enough to soften it. Add the warm Nutella to the eggs, scraping out the jar with a spatula, and mix until fully incorporated. (Electric beaters work great here!)

Add 1 cup flour and mix lightly until no streaks remain.

Pour the batter into the prepared baking dish. Sprinkle coarse sea salt evenly over the top.

Bake for 22–24 minutes. Test for doneness by inserting a toothpick into the center—it should come out with a few moist crumbs but not wet batter.

Enjoy—they actually taste amazing frozen too!

Book club discussion prompts for *The Covert Buccaneer*

1. **Ellie's discovery of the diary sparks a journey of self-discovery** and connection with her great-great-grandmother, Teddy. How does this multigenerational link—and its timing in Ellie's life—shape her understanding of herself and her role in the world? Can you relate to this sense of genealogical connection with your own family history?

2. **Theodora (Teddy) Ellis was a trailblazer, yet her contributions remained invisible to history.** How does this reflect broader themes of women and minorities being overlooked across generations? Why do these untold stories matter now? Do you think uncovering hidden histories can reshape our understanding of both the past and present?

3. **Both Ellie and Teddy face challenges tied to gender and societal expectations.** In what ways do their struggles mirror one another across time? How do they navigate these limitations to carve out their own paths?

4. **Teddy often wished she were a man** to gain the freedom and opportunities denied to women in her time. How does her use of disguise to access male-dominated spaces reflect broader themes of gender nonconformity? How does the

novel explore the fluidity of gender roles and the constraints placed on women—both historically and today? How do Teddy's strategies for navigating a patriarchal world compare to those available to women now?

5. **The novel intertwines themes of immigration, climate justice, women's rights, and Indigenous communities,** showing how these struggles are interconnected across history. Ellie's work as an attorney for climate migrants and undocumented workers echoes these broader social and political themes. How do you see these issues playing out across the novel? How does Ellie's journey reflect the unfinished work at the intersection of climate justice, gender equity, and human rights?

6. **Teddy dedicated much of her life to assisting immigrant families and marginalized communities,** yet she still harbored biases—such as her dismissive remark about the Irish in Chapter 23. How do you think Teddy viewed herself in relation to the people she helped? Did she see herself as separate from them, or did she believe she was one of them? Do you think she had white savior complex, or was she simply a woman of her time? How should we evaluate historical figures who were progressive in some ways yet flawed in others?

7. **The diary's discovery ultimately helps Ellie solve Hansa's legal case.** How does this symbolize the past shaping the present? What significance do Indigenous rights hold in both Ellie's and Teddy's worlds? Can understanding history help provide answers to contemporary issues?

8. **Both Ellie and Teddy rely on deep, complex friendships.** How do these relationships help them navigate challenges—from societal expectations to personal

struggles? In what ways do these friendships serve as sources of strength, solidarity, and understanding across generations and cultural backgrounds?

9. **Teddy and Ellie resist monogamy, viewing it as a trap for women.** Teddy's relationship with George, Helki, and Momo suggests a polyamorous arrangement, while Ellie, even after finding new love, remains determined to maintain her independence. How does the novel explore the challenges and benefits of nontraditional relationships for women? How do these characters' views on love and freedom challenge societal norms, both in the past and present?

10. **Ellie's proud Italian identity is questioned** by the discovery of Teddy's relationship with Momo—and the possibility that Ellie may descend from him rather than George. Why had Ellie never heard about Teddy, despite living with Enzo and Genevieve? How does this uncertainty about her ancestry affect her sense of belonging? The novel ends with Ellie undecided about finding out for sure. Should she? Would you? How reliable are the family stories passed down to us?

Acknowledgments

My husband, *mio caro* Francesco, should be knighted for living with me throughout this odyssey (hey, it's not just a car—*wink, wink*). I don't know how people manage as partners of writers. He cooked meals with love and good cheer, was awoken in the night by me whispering voice notes into my phone, and was interrupted mid-sentence by me abruptly walking away to type some urgent and inspired thought. He listened to me work through characters' interactions as though they were right there in our family room. He read drafts and checked my logic when I was too mired to trust my own mind. In short, he not only put up with me—he understood that this project was a personal imperative.

And then there's my father, Steve, the family historian. He protected George Ellis's manuscript all these years; constructed a family tree; painstakingly organized, labeled, and scanned historic family photos and letters; and listened when I pointed out the missing data points in George's story. He supported me in filling those gaps, regularly asking how it was going, reading drafts, and sitting with me at my dining room table with a map of Alaska to show me the route my great-great-grandfather had taken (the "easy" way) in 1896 to eventually claim his massive fortune.

None of this would have come to fruition (no, seriously) without the patience and skill of my keen development editor, Nicola Cassidy. How she struck that just-so balance of support and rigorous scrutiny of the work is an unsung art. She's a Jedi master in her own right.

To four high school English teachers at Adlai E. Stevenson High School who called it early: "You're destined to be an author," predicted Mr. Cramer, Ms. Francis, Dr. Walschmidt, and Mr. Granner. It took me a minute. I was a little busy with other things.

Speaking of teachers, let's give it up for librarians and docents. I can't believe I can just walk right into incredible places (for free!) like the UC Berkeley Bancroft Library, the Chicago Public Library (Archives & Periodicals), the Oakland Museum of California, and the History Center of the San Francisco Public Library and talk to librarians and docents who helped me—with delight and enthusiasm. They rounded up goodies like microfiche reels for me to play with. What an embarrassment of riches and a human experience that AI simply cannot emulate.

As for my own Anika—you know who you are. You wouldn't appreciate me outing you here. Many years have passed since those early motherhood days. That damn robotic dinosaur. Your broken cupboards and unruly garden-scape. The way you would bother to transfer the mac and cheese to a lovely ceramic serving dish (just creating more dishes to wash). The middle-of-the-night visits to one another. Our heartache (and laughter) was too big for our bodies, and we remained standing (some days, not so much) by clinging so tightly to each other. I hold you in my heart, my dear friend.

About the Author

S. LUCIA KANTER ST. AMOUR is an attorney, VP emerita for UN Women USA, and author of titles spanning historical fiction, children's literature, poetry, non-fiction, and feminist theory. Faculty at two University of California law schools, she has spent her career advocating for equity in law and policy. *The Covert Buccaneer* draws from these themes, weaving real historical events and characters with contemporary resonance. She lives in San Francisco, right next to Coit Tower.

www.ingramcontent.com/pod-product-compliance
Ingram Content Group UK Ltd.
Pitfield, Milton Keynes, MK11 3LW, UK
UKHW040452151025
8378UKWH00066B/416